Robert Bryndza is the author of the international #1 bestseller *The Girl in the Ice*, which is the first in his Detective Erika Foster series. Robert's books have sold over 3 million copies and have been translated into 28 languages. In addition to writing crime fiction, Robert has published a bestselling series of romantic comedy novels. He is British and lives in Slovakia.

NINE ELMS

ROBERT BRYNDZA

sphere

SPHERE

First published in Great Britain in 2019 by Sphere

1 3 5 7 9 10 8 6 4 2

Copyright © Raven Street Ltd 2019

The moral right of the author has been asserted.

A CIP catalogue record for this book
is available from the British Library.

Hardback ISBN 978-0-7515-7272-8
Trade Paperback ISBN 978-0-7515-7271-1

Typeset in Garamond by M Rules
Printed and bound in Great Britain by
Clays Ltd, Elcograf S.p.A.

Papers used by Sphere are from well-managed forests
and other responsible sources.

Sphere
An imprint of
Little, Brown Book Group
Carmelite House
50 Victoria Embankment
London EC4Y 0DZ

An Hachette UK Company
www.hachette.co.uk

www.littlebrown.co.uk

For Lola and Riky

AUTUMN
1995

CHAPTER 1

Detective Constable Kate Marshall was on the train home when her phone rang. It took a moment of searching the folds of her long winter coat before she found it in the inside pocket. She heaved out the huge brick-like handset, pulled up the antenna and answered. It was her boss, Detective Chief Inspector Peter Conway.

'Sir. Hello.'

'Finally. She picks up!' he snapped, without preamble. 'I've been calling you. What's the bloody point in having one of these new mobile phones if you don't answer?'

'Sorry. I've been in court all day for the Travis Jones sentencing. He got three years, which is more than I—'

'A dog walker found the body of a young girl dumped in Crystal Palace Park,' he said, cutting her off. 'Naked. Bite marks on her body, a plastic bag tied over her head.'

'The Nine Elms Cannibal . . .'

'Operation Hemlock. You know I don't like that name.'

Kate wanted to reply that the name had now stuck and was bedded in for life, but he wasn't the kind of boss who encouraged banter. The press had coined the epithet two years earlier, when seventeen-year-old Shelley Norris had been found in a wrecker's yard in the Nine Elms area of south-west London,

1

close to the Thames. Technically, the killer only bit his victims, but the press didn't let this get in the way of a good serial killer moniker. Over the past two years, another two teenage girls had been abducted, each in the early evening, on their way home from school. Their bodies had shown up several days after their disappearances, dumped in parks around London. Nothing sold newspapers more than a cannibal on the loose.

'Kate. Where are you?'

It was dark outside the train window. She looked up at the electronic display in the carriage.

'On the DLR. Almost home, sir.'

'I'll pick you up outside the station, our usual spot.' He hung up without waiting for a response.

Twenty minutes later, Kate was waiting on a small stretch of pavement between the station underpass and the busy South Circular where a line of cars ground slowly past. Much of the area around the station was under development, and Kate's route home to her small flat took her through a long road of empty building sites. It wasn't somewhere to linger after dark. The passengers she'd left the train with had crossed the road and dispersed into the dark streets. She glanced back over her shoulder at the dank empty underpass bathed in shadows and shifted on her heels. A small bag of groceries she'd bought for dinner sat between her feet.

A spot of water hit her neck, and another, and then it started to rain. She turned up the collar of her coat and hunched down, moving closer to the bright headlights in the line of traffic.

Kate had been assigned to Operation Hemlock sixteen months previously, when the Nine Elms Cannibal body count stood at three. It had been a coup to join a high-profile case, along with promotion to the rank of plain-clothes detective.

In the eight months since the third victim's body was

found – a seventeen-year-old schoolgirl called Carla Martin – the case had gone cold. Operation Hemlock had been scaled back, and Kate had been reassigned to the drug squad, along with several other junior officers.

Kate squinted through the rain, down the long line of traffic. Bright headlights appeared around a sharp bend in the road, but there were no police sirens in the distance. She checked her watch and stepped back out of the glare.

She hadn't seen Peter for two months. Shortly before she was reassigned, she had slept with him. He rarely socialised with his team, and during a rare night of after-work drinks they'd wound up talking, and she'd found his company and his intelligence stimulating. They had stayed late in the pub, after the rest of the team went home, and ended up back at her flat. And then the next night he had invited her over to his place. Kate's dalliance with her boss, on not one but two occasions, was something that burned inside her with regret. It was a moment of madness – two moments – before they both came to their senses. She had a strong moral compass. She was a good police officer.

I'll pick you up at our usual spot.

It bothered her that Peter had said this on the phone. He'd given her a lift to work twice, and both times he had also picked up her colleague, Detective Cameron Rose, who lived close by. Would he have said *our usual spot* to Cam?

The cold was starting to creep up the back of her long coat, and the rain had seeped in through the holes in the bottom of the 'good shoes' she wore for court. Kate adjusted her collar and huddled into her coat, turning her attention to the line of traffic. Almost all the drivers were men, white, in their mid- to late thirties. The perfect serial killer demographic.

A grimy white van slid past, the driver's face distorted by the rainwater on the windscreen. The police believed the Nine Elms Cannibal was using a van to abduct his victims. Carpet fibres matching a 1994 Citroën Dispatch white van, of which there were over a hundred thousand registered in and around London, had been found on two of the victims. Kate wondered if the officers who'd been retained for Operation Hemlock were still working through that list of Citroën Dispatch white van owners. And who was this new victim? There had been nothing in the newspapers about a missing person.

The lights up ahead turned red, and a small blue Ford stopped in the line of traffic a few feet away. The man inside was a City type: overweight, in his mid-fifties and wearing a pinstriped suit and glasses. He saw Kate, raised his eyebrows suggestively and flashed his headlights. Kate looked away. The blue Ford inched closer, closing the gap in the line of cars until his passenger window was almost level with her. It slid down, and the man leaned across.

'Hello. You look cold. I can make you warm . . .' He patted the seat beside him and stuck out his tongue, which was thin and pointed. Kate froze. Panic rose in her chest. She forgot she had her warrant card, and that she was a police officer. It all went out of the window and fear took over. '*Come on*. Hop inside. Let's warm you up,' he said. He patted the seat again, impatient.

Kate stepped away from the kerb. The underpass behind her was dark and empty. The other vehicles in the line had male drivers, and they seemed oblivious, cocooned in their cars. The lights ahead remained red. The rain thrummed lazily on the car roofs. The man leaned farther over and the passenger door popped open a few inches. Kate took another step back, but felt trapped. What if he got out of his car and pushed her into the underpass?

'Don't fuck me around. How much?' he said. His smile was gone, and she could see his trousers were undone. His underpants were faded and dingy. He hooked his finger under the waistband and exposed his penis and a thatch of greying pubic hair.

Kate was still rooted to the spot, willing the lights to change.

A police siren blared out suddenly, cutting through the silence, and the cars and the arch of the underpass were lit up with blue flashing lights. The man hurriedly rearranged himself, fastened his trousers and pulled the door shut, activating the central locking. His face returned to an impassive stare. Kate fumbled in her bag and pulled out her warrant card. She went to the blue Ford and slapped it against the passenger window, annoyed that she hadn't done it earlier.

Peter's unmarked police car, with its revolving blue light on the roof, came shooting down the outside of the row of traffic, half up on the grass verge. The traffic light changed to green. The car in front drove away, and Peter pulled into the gap. The man inside the Ford was now panicking, smoothing down his hair and tie. Kate fixed him with a stare, put her warrant card back in her bag and went to the passenger door of Peter's car.

CHAPTER 2

'Sorry to keep you waiting. Traffic,' said Peter, giving her a brisk smile. He picked up a pile of paperwork from the passenger seat and put it behind his seat. He was a good-looking man in his late thirties, broad-shouldered with thick dark wavy hair, high cheekbones and soft brown eyes. He wore an expensive tailored black suit.

'Of course,' she said, feeling relief as she stashed her handbag and groceries in the footwell and dropped into the seat. As soon as she closed the door, Peter accelerated and flicked on the sirens.

The sunshade was down on the passenger side, and she caught her reflection in the mirror as she folded it back up. She wasn't wearing any make-up, or dressed provocatively, and Kate always thought herself a little plain. She wasn't delicate. She had strong features. Her shoulder-length hair was tied back off her face, tucked away under the neck of her long winter coat, almost as an afterthought. The only distinguishing features were her unusual eyes, which were a startling cornflower blue with a burst of burnt orange flooding out from the pupils. It was caused by sectoral heterochromia, a rare condition where the eyes have two colours. The other, less permanent mark on her face was a split lip, just starting to scab over, which had been caused by an irate drunk resisting arrest a few days before. She'd felt no fear when dealing with the drunk, and didn't feel ashamed that he'd hit her. It was part of the job. Why did she feel shame after being hit on by the sleazy businessman? He was the one with the sad, saggy grey underwear and the stubby little manhood.

'What was that? With the car behind?' asked Peter.

'Oh, one of his brake lights was out,' she said. It was easier to lie. She felt embarrassed. She pushed the man and his blue Ford to the back of her mind. 'Have you called the whole team to the crime scene?'

'Of course,' said Peter, glancing over. 'After we spoke, I got a call from the assistant commissioner, Anthony Asher. He says if this murder is linked to Operation Hemlock, I only have to ask and I'll have all the resources I need at my disposal.'

He sped around a roundabout in fourth gear, and took the exit to Crystal Palace Park. Peter Conway was a career police officer, and Kate had no doubt that solving this case would result in a promotion to superintendent or even chief superintendent. Peter had been the youngest officer in the history of the Met Police to be promoted to detective chief inspector.

The windows were starting to fog up, and he turned up the heater. The arc of condensation on the windscreen rippled and receded. Between a group of terraced houses Kate caught a glimpse of the London skyline lit up. There were millions of lights, pinpricks in the black fabric of the sky, symbolising the homes and offices of millions. Kate wondered which light belonged to the Nine Elms Cannibal. *What if we never find him?* she thought. *The police never found Jack the Ripper, and back then London was tiny in comparison.*

'Have you had any more leads from the white van database?' she asked.

'We brought in another six men for questioning, but their DNA didn't match our man.'

'The fact he leaves his DNA on the victims, it's not just carelessness or lack of control. It's as if he's marking his territory. Like a dog.'

'You think he wants us to catch him?'

'Yes ... No ... Possibly.'

'He's behaving like he's invincible.'

'He *thinks* he's invincible. But he'll slip up. They always do,' said Kate.

They turned off into the north entrance to Crystal Palace Park. A police car was waiting, and the officer waved them through. They drove down a long straight avenue of gravel, usually reserved for people on foot. It was lined with large oak trees shedding leaves, and they hit the windscreen with a wet flapping sound, clogging up the wipers. In the far distance the huge Crystal Palace radio transmitter poked up above the trees like a slender Eiffel Tower. The road banked down and ended in a small car park beside a long flat field of grass, which backed onto a wooded area. A police tape cordon ringed the entire expanse of grass. In the centre was a second, smaller cordon around a white forensics tent, glowing in the darkness. Next to the second cordon sat the pathologist's van, four squad cars and a large white police support vehicle.

Where the tarmac met the grass, the tape of the first police cordon flapped in the breeze. Kate and Peter were met by two uniformed police officers – a middle-aged man whose belly hung over his belt and a tall, thin young man who still looked like a teenager. Kate and Peter showed their identification to the older officer. His eyes were hooded with loose skin, and as he glanced between their warrant cards, he reminded Kate of a chameleon. He handed them back and went to lift the police tape, but hesitated, looking over at the glowing tent.

'In all my years, I ain't never seen nothing like it,' he said.

'You were the first on the scene?' asked Peter, impatient for him to lift the tape, but not willing to do it himself.

'Yes. PC Stanley Gresham, sir. This is PC Will Stokes,' he said, gesturing to the young officer, who suddenly grimaced, turned away from them and threw up over the police tape. 'It's his first day on the job,' he added, shaking his head. Kate gave the young officer a look of pity as he heaved and threw up again, thin strings of spittle dangling from his mouth. Peter took a clean white handkerchief from his inside pocket, and Kate thought he was going to offer it up to the young officer, but he pressed it to his nose and mouth.

'I want this crime scene locked down. Not a word to anyone,' said Peter.

'Of course, sir.'

Peter fluttered his fingers at the police tape. Stanley lifted it and they ducked under. The grass sloped down to the second police cordon where Detective Cameron Rose and Detective Inspector Marsha Lewis were waiting. Cameron, like Kate, was in his mid-twenties, and Marsha was older than all of them, a thickset woman in her fifties, wearing a smart black trouser suit and long black coat. Her silver hair was cropped short and she had a gravelly smoker's voice.

'Sir,' they said in unison.

'What's going on, Marsha?' asked Peter.

'All exits in and out of the park are sealed, and I've got local plod being bussed in for a fingertip search and house to house. Forensic pathologist is in there already, and she's ready to talk to us.'

Cameron was tall and gangly, towering above them all. He hadn't had time to change, and looked more like a louche teenager than a detective in his jeans, trainers and a green winter jacket. Kate wondered fleetingly what he had been doing when he got the call to come to the crime scene. She presumed he'd arrived with Marsha.

'Who's our forensic pathologist?' asked Peter.

'Leodora Graves,' said Marsha.

It was hot inside the glowing tent, where the lights were almost painfully bright. Forensic pathologist Leodora Graves, a small dark-skinned woman with penetrating green eyes, worked with two assistants. A naked young girl lay face down in a muddy depression in the grass. Her head was covered by a clear plastic bag, tied tightly around her neck. Her pale skin was streaked with dirt and blood and numerous cuts and scratches. The backs of her thighs and buttocks had several deep bite marks.

Kate stood beside the body, already sweating underneath the hood and face mask of her thick white forensics suit. The rain hammered down on the tight skin of the tent, forcing Leodora to raise her voice.

'The victim is posed, lying on her right side, her right arm under her head. The left arm lies flat and reaching out. There are six bites on her lower back, buttocks and thighs.' She indicated the deepest bites where the flesh had been removed, deep enough to expose the girl's spine. She moved to the victim's head and gently lifted it. The length of thin rope was tied tight around the neck, biting into the now bloated flesh. 'You'll note the specific knot.'

'The monkey's fist knot,' said Cameron, speaking for the first time. He sounded shaken. Everyone's face was obscured by the masks of their forensic suits, but Kate could read the looks of alarm in their eyes.

'Yes,' said Leodora, holding the knot in her gloved hand. What made it unusual was the series of intersecting turns, like a tiny ball of wool, almost impossible to replicate with a machine.

'It's him. The Nine Elms Cannibal,' said Kate. The words came out of her mouth before she could stop them.

'I'll need to conclude more from my post-mortem, but ... yes,' said Leodora. The rain fell harder, intensifying the thundering thrum on the roof of the tent. She let go of the young girl's head, placing it gently back where it lay on her arm. 'There is evidence that she was raped. There are bodily fluids present, and she's been tortured, cut with a sharp object and burned. You see the burn marks on her arms and outer thighs? They look to be caused by the cigarette lighter from a car.'

'Or a white van,' said Kate. Peter gave her a hard stare. He didn't like being corrected.

'Cause of death?' he asked.

'I need to do the post-mortem, but off the record, at this stage I would say asphyxiation with the plastic bag. There are signs of petechial haemorrhaging on her face and neck.'

'Thank you, Leodora. I look forward to the results of your post-mortem. I hope that we can quickly identify this poor young woman.'

Leodora nodded to her assistants, who brought in a pop-up stretcher with a shiny new black body bag. They placed it beside the body and gently turned the young woman over onto the stretcher. The front of her naked body was marked with small circular burns and scratches. It was impossible to tell what she looked like – her face was grotesque and distorted under the plastic. She had large pale-blue eyes, milky in death and frozen in a stare. The look in her eyes made Kate shiver. It was devoid of hope, as if frozen in her eyes was that last thought. She knew she was going to die.

CHAPTER 3

Viewing the young woman's battered body left Kate disturbed and exhausted after what had already been a long day, but an investigation of this scale had to move fast. As soon as they left the forensics tent, Kate was assigned to head door-to-door enquiries on Thicket Road, a long avenue of smart, detached houses on the west side of the park.

Despite there being a team of eight officers, it took almost five hours to work their way down the street, and the rain didn't let up. Their lead question, *Have you seen a 1994 Citroën Dispatch white van and/or anyone acting suspiciously?* sparked fear and curiosity in the residents of Thicket Road. The search for the white van had been widely reported in the press, but the police weren't allowed to comment on the details of the case. Even so, most people Kate spoke to knew she was investigating the Nine Elms Cannibal, and had their opinions, questions and suspicions. All of which generated endless leads, which would have to be followed up.

Just after midnight, Kate and her team were called back to the rendezvous point at the station. The young woman's body was now at the morgue for the post-mortem, and the fingertip search of Crystal Palace park was being hampered by poor visibility and pouring rain, so they were told to stand down for the night and that things would resume the next morning.

The officer Kate had been working with went to get a bus back to north London, leaving Kate alone in the car park. She was about to call a cab when lights flashed on a car in the far corner, and she saw Peter walking towards his car. He saw her and stopped, waiting for her to catch up.

'Need a lift home?' he asked. He was soaked through and looked tired, and Kate gave him points for rolling up his sleeves and not sitting it out in one of the support vans with a cup of coffee. She looked around the car park. There were three squad cars left, but she presumed they belonged to the officers who had drawn the short straw to stay up at the park.

He saw her hesitate.

'It's no problem, and you left your bags in my car,' he said. His lack of enthusiasm at the prospect of driving her home made her more willing to accept the lift.

'Thank you. That would be great,' she said, suddenly craving a hot shower, tea and toast slathered in butter and honey, and then her warm bed. He opened the boot of the car and took out a stack of towels from a laundry bag.

'Thank you,' she said, taking one and wrapping it around her shoulders and wringing out her wet ponytail. She opened the passenger door and saw that her shopping bag was still on the floor. Peter opened the driver's door and, leaning across, pulled open the glove compartment. He rummaged around, pulling out a car manual and a bunch of keys, until he found a box of baby wipes. He quickly cleaned off his hands and chucked the dirty wipes under the car.

'Anything from the fingertip search?' she asked.

'Some fibres, cigarette ends, a shoe ... but it's a park – who knows who they belong to?'

He arranged a towel on the passenger seat, then took a Thermos flask from the central console and handed it to her before draping another towel over the driver's seat. Kate watched in amusement. He seemed so domesticated, bustling and tucking the towels into the corners of the seat cushions with an unconsciously camp manner, making sure the improvised seat covers were neat and would stay in place.

'I think you're the first person who I've seen attempt hospital corners on a car seat,' she said.

'We're soaked, and it's a new car. You don't know how hard I had to fight to get it,' he said, frowning.

It was the first time that evening he'd displayed any emotion. His dirty car seats gave him real anxiety. Kate wondered if that's what happened after a long time in the police. You shut yourself off from the horrific stuff, and you sweated the small things.

They were silent on the journey back to Deptford. She stared out of the window. Torn between trying to get the image of the young girl out of her head and trying to keep it there. To make sure she didn't forget her face, to file every detail away.

Kate lived in a ground-floor flat behind a long, low row of shops just off Deptford High Street. The front door was accessed through a potholed gravel car park, and Peter's car bounced and bumped its way through the waterlogged holes. They came to a stop at her front door under a sagging awning, next to the delivery entrance of the local Chinese restaurant where there was a pile of crates filled with empty soft drink bottles. The car headlights reflected off the pale back wall of her building, illuminating the interior of the car.

'Thanks for the lift,' she said, opening the door and stepping out widely to avoid a puddle. He leaned over and handed her the shopping bag.

'Don't forget this, and it's ten o'clock tomorrow morning at the station.'

'See you then.'

She took the bag and closed the car door. His headlights lit up the car park as she rooted around in her pocket for her key and opened the front door, and then it was dark. She turned to see his tail lights vanish. She'd made an idiotic mistake in sleeping with her boss, but after seeing the dead young woman, and knowing there was still a killer on the loose, it seemed to pale to nothing.

CHAPTER 4

It was cold inside the flat. A small kitchen looked out over the car park, and she quickly closed the blinds before switching on the lights. She took a long shower, staying under the water until the warmth came back into her bones, then pulled on a dressing gown and came back into the kitchen. The central heating was doing its work, pumping hot water with a gurgle through the radiators, and the room was warming up. Suddenly starving, she went to take a microwave lasagne from the shopping bag, and saw nestled on top of her groceries the bunch of keys and the Thermos flask from Peter's car. She put the Thermos on the counter and went to the phone on the kitchen wall to call his pager, so he wouldn't get all the way home before he discovered he didn't have his keys. She was about to dial, when she noted the keys in her hand. There were four, all substantial and old.

Peter lived in a new build flat near Peckham. The front door had a Yale lock. She remembered this clearly from that second night when he'd invited her over for dinner. She'd hesitated outside the door, staring at the Yale lock, thinking, *What the hell am I doing? The first time I was drunk. Now I'm sober and I'm back for more.*

The keys in her hand were mortise keys for heavy locks, and a small length of rope was tied around the key ring. The rope was thin, with a red and blue woven pattern – heavy-duty rope, or cord, tough and well made. She turned the loop of rope over in her hand. Tied at the end was a monkey's fist knot. She replaced the phone on its cradle and stared at the keys.

Kate felt as though the room was tilting under her feet, and the hair on the back of her neck stood on end. She closed her eyes and the crime scene photos of the dead girls flashed behind them – bags tied tightly round their necks, vacuum-formed, distorting their features. Tied off with the knot. She opened her eyes and looked at the keys and the monkey's fist.

No. She was exhausted and letting her imagination run away.

She pulled out a chair and sat down at the kitchen table. What did she know about Peter outside work? His father was dead. She'd heard odd bits of rumour about his mother being mentally ill and in hospital. He'd had quite a difficult upbringing that he'd struggled to extricate himself from, that he was proud to extricate himself from. He was highly thought of by top brass. He didn't have a girlfriend or wife. He was married to the job.

Perhaps the keys belonged to a friend, or his mother? They were the type that fitted a large door, or a heavy padlock. There had been speculation that the killer would need a place to keep the van and his victims – a lock-up or a garage. If Peter had a lock-up he wouldn't have mentioned it, but she remembered him complaining about the building where he lived. He said he paid a fortune for a space in the underground car park, and that didn't include a garage.

No. It had been a long, stressful day and she needed sleep.

She put the keys on the counter and retrieved the lasagne from the bag. She peeled off the outer packaging and placed the small plastic box in the microwave and keyed in two minutes. Her hand hovered over the timer.

She thought back to when they had brought in an expert, a retired scout master who explained the monkey's fist knot to the incident room. What made the knot stand out was that it could only be tied by someone with a level of expertise. The monkey's fist was tied at the end of a length of rope as an ornamental knot, and a weight, making it easier to throw. It got its name because it looked similar to a small bunched fist or paw.

The lasagne spun slowly in the microwave.

The retired scout master had told them that most young boys learned to tie knots in the scouts. The monkey's fist knot had little practical use, but it was a knot tied by enthusiasts. Everyone in the incident room had attempted to tie the knot under the expert's watchful instruction, and only Marsha had managed it. Peter had failed miserably, and he had made a joke out of how bad he was.

'I couldn't tie my own shoes until I was eight!' he'd cried. All the officers in the incident room had laughed, and he'd put his hands over his face in mock embarrassment.

The keys were old, with a little rust. They'd been oiled to keep them in good use. The rope was shiny in places, and the monkey's fist knot looked old, with oil and grime worn into it.

Kate chewed on her nails, not noticing that the microwave had given three loud pips to say it was finished.

She sat down at the kitchen table. The first three victims had been schoolgirls between fifteen and seventeen years old. They had all been abducted on a Thursday or a Friday, and their bodies had shown up at the beginning of the following week. The victims had all been sporty, and in all three cases had been grabbed on their way home from after-school training. The abductions had been so well executed that the killer must have known where they would be, and lain in wait.

They had questioned PE teachers across the boroughs, and brought several in for questioning, and done the same with a couple of male teachers who had 1994 Citroën Dispatch white vans registered to their names. None of their DNA had matched. They then looked at the parents of the victims, and friends of the parents. The net kept getting wider, the theories wilder as to how the victims could be linked to the killer. Kate remembered a question that had been written up on the white board of the incident room.

Who had access to the victims at school?

A thought went through Kate, like a jolt of electricity. There had been a list of teachers, classroom assistants, caretakers, lollipop ladies, dinner ladies — but what about the police? Police officers often go into schools to talk to kids about drugs and anti-social behaviour.

On two occasions Peter had roped her in to join him on a school visit, to talk to some inner-city schoolkids about road safety. He had also worked on an anti-drugs presentation given around London schools. How many schools had he visited? Twenty? Thirty? Was it staring her in the face, or was she just tired and overwhelmed? No ... Peter had commented that he had visited the school of the third victim, Carla Martin, a month before she went missing.

Kate got up and looked in her cupboards. All she could find was a bottle of dry sherry she'd bought to offer her mother on her last visit. She poured herself a large measure and took a gulp.

What if they had no leads because the Nine Elms Cannibal was also Peter Conway? The nights they spent together moved to the front of her mind, and she pushed it back, not wanting to go there. She sat, shaking. Did she really have the balls to accuse her boss of being a serial killer? Then she spied Peter's Thermos flask sitting beside the microwave. He'd drunk from it in the car. He would have left his DNA on it.

Kate got up, her legs trembling. Her bag was on the floor by the back door, and it took some effort to get the clasp open. In one of the inside pockets she found a new plastic evidence bag,

The flask has Peter's DNA on it. We have the Nine Elms Cannibal's DNA. I could quietly put in a request.

She pulled on a clean pair of latex gloves and approached the Thermos like she would a wild animal needing capture. She took a deep breath, plucked it off the counter and dropped it into the evidence bag, sealing the bag. She placed it on the tiny kitchen table. It felt like a betrayal of everything she believed in. She stood in the silence for a few minutes, listening to the rain hammering on the roof, and took another swig of the sherry, feeling it warming her insides and taking the edge off her panic.

No one needs to know about it. Who could she ask who was discreet? Akbar in forensics. She'd bumped into him once coming out of a gay bar in Soho. It had been an awkward moment. She had been with a guy and so had he. He'd invited her for a drink the next night after work and she had assured him that his secret, if it was a secret, was safe with her.

She would call him first thing in the morning, drive it over early and get the flask swabbed. Or maybe, if she got some sleep, this would all seem like a crazy theory in the morning.

There was a knock at the door and she dropped the glass. It shattered, spraying glass and brown liquid across the linoleum. There was a pause and then a voice said: 'Kate. It's Peter, are you okay?' She looked up at the clock. Almost 2 a.m. The knock came again. 'Kate? I heard breaking glass. Are you okay?' He hammered on the door harder.

'Yes! I'm fine!' she trilled, looking at the mess on the floor.

'You don't sound it. Can you open up?'

'I've just dropped a glass on the floor, by the door. What are you doing here?'

20

'Have you got my keys?' he said. 'I think I might have dropped them in one of your bags.'

There was a long silence. She stepped over the shattered glass and quietly put the chain on and opened the door. Through the gap, Peter stood, soaking wet, the collar of his coat pulled up. He smiled a broad white smile. His teeth were so straight and white, she thought.

'Good, I thought you might have gone to bed. I think you have my keys?'

CHAPTER 5

Kate peered up at Peter. The car park was dark behind him, and she couldn't see his car.

'Kate. It's pouring down. Can I come in for a sec?'

'It's late. Hang on,' she said, leaning over the broken glass to grab the keys off the counter. 'Here.' Their eyes met as she held them out to him in her palm. He looked down at the little loop curled round in her shaking hand with the monkey's fist knot, then back up at her with a smirk.

Later on, Kate would think what she could have done differently. If she'd made a joke about it being the same knot the killer used, would he have taken the keys and gone home?

'It's my car. I got a flat tyre up the road. Then I saw my keys weren't in the glove compartment,' he said, finally breaking the silence, wiping the rainwater from his face. He didn't take the keys, though, and she stood there with her hand outstretched.

'Kate. I'm getting wet here. Can I come in?'

She hesitated, and swallowed, but her throat was dry.

He shouldered the door, and the chain snapped easily. He stepped over the threshold, forcing her to move back into the kitchen. He pushed the door closed behind him and stood there dripping wet.

'What?'

She shook her head. 'Nothing. Sorry,' she said. Her voice was a thin rasp.

'I need a towel . . . I'm soaking wet.'

Everything about the situation was surreal. Kate left the kitchen and went to the small airing cupboard and took out a towel. Her mind was racing. She had to act normally. She looked around for something to defend herself with. She grabbed a small smooth glass paperweight, the only thing she could find remotely close to a weapon.

Her breath caught in her throat when she went back into the kitchen. Peter stood in the middle of the room, staring at the Thermos flask sitting in its plastic evidence bag on the kitchen table. When he turned to her his features were the same, but anger had changed him. He was like an animal about to attack. His eyes were wide, pupils dilated and his lips were curled back, baring his teeth.

Do something! shrieked a voice inside her head. But she couldn't move. There was a thud as the paperweight fell from her hand onto the floor.

'Oh dear, Kate. Kate, Kate, Kate,' he said softly. The broken glass crunched under his feet as he went to the back door and locked it.

'Peter. Sir. I don't think for a second that you . . . it's my job to investigate . . .'

He was shaking, but his movements were calm as he went to the phone. In one swift motion he wrenched it clean off the wall, still attached to its metal bracket. Kate flinched as the tiny nails holding the wire to the wall popped out and skittered across the linoleum. He yanked the cable from the socket and placed the phone on the counter by the fridge.

'It's funny. You said the killer would slip up . . . The keys . . . the fucking keys.' He took a step towards her.

'No. No. They're just keys,' said Kate. If he took another step forward he would block her path out of the kitchen.

'The flask . . .' He shook his head and laughed. It was a cold, metallic sound, devoid of humour.

Kate made a dash for the living room, where her mobile phone was charging, but he was quicker. He grabbed the back of her hair, swung her around and slammed her into the tall fridge door. Pain exploded in the side of her face, but he was on her, twisting her shoulders around to face him and gripping her neck with one hand.

'Rough area, where you live,' he said calmly, pinning her against the fridge door with his shoulder and left leg. He gripped her throat with his right hand. She kicked out, hitting him in the side of his leg, and she tried to claw at his face and neck but he used his elbows to keep her arms down. 'There was a break-in. You scared the intruder. He panicked and he killed you.'

His fingers gripped her throat harder. She couldn't breathe and his face, looming over hers, began to blur. She scrabbled around, her fingers feeling the edge of the counter. Peter leaned into her chest and she felt his strength pushing the remaining air from her lungs. She cried out as she felt one of her ribs crack.

'I'll make sure to be the one who leads your murder case. The tragic death of a rising star in the police force.'

Kate writhed and pushed back, managing to free up her left arm a little. Her hand felt along the edge of the counter and found the phone, where Peter had left it. She didn't have much strength as she swung it, but the sharp edge of the metal bracket glanced off his forehead, slicing through the skin above his eye.

His grip loosened for a moment and she was able to push him away. He staggered back in shock, blood pouring from the gash in his forehead.

Kate held up the phone on its bracket and advanced on him, not feeling the broken glass under her bare feet. Peter staggered back, spitting blood. He lunged for the block of knives by the sink and pulled one out.

The knives! Why didn't I go for the knives? she thought. She turned and ran into the living room but tripped, landing on the phone, knocking the air from her lungs. She rolled back and tried to get up, but he was on her. He punched her hard in the face, dragged her kicking and writhing through to the bedroom and threw her on the bed. Her head hit the headboard and she saw stars. Her robe was open and she was naked underneath. He climbed on top of her, his face slick with blood, reddening the whites of his eyes and giving his smile a pink mania. He knelt on her hip bones and pulled her wrists down, pinning them under his knees.

He held up the knife and grazed the tip of the blade over her nipples, down to her belly button, and pushed the blade into her skin. The sharp steel sliced through her flesh easily and through the muscles of her abdomen. She screamed out in agony, unable to move. It was terrifying how fast the blood pooled on her belly. He calmly twisted the knife and dragged it up through the flesh of her stomach, towards her heart. It snagged on one of her ribs.

Peter leaned close, lips curled back over pink-stained teeth. The pain was unbearable, but she summoned up the last of her strength and fought and writhed, freeing her knee and bringing it sharply up into his groin. He groaned and fell backwards off the bed, landing on the floor.

Kate looked down at the knife sticking out of her abdomen. Blood was saturating the white robe and bedclothes. *Leave the knife in*, said a voice in her head. *If it comes out, you'll bleed to death.* Peter started to get up, his eyes crazed with rage. She thought of all the victims, all those young girls who had been tortured. The anger gave her a surge of adrenalin and energy. She grabbed the lava lamp from beside her bed, and brought down the heavy glass bottle of paraffin and wax on the top of his head, once, twice, and then he was still, slumped weirdly, his legs splayed outwards.

Kate dropped the lamp. The pain in her abdomen almost made her black out, and it took all her will not to pull the knife out as she limped through to the living room, the knife shifting as she moved. She found her mobile phone and dialled 999. She gave her name and address, and said that the Nine Elms Cannibal was Detective Chief Inspector Peter Conway, and he had just tried to kill her in her apartment.

It was then that she dropped the phone and lost consciousness.

FIFTEEN YEARS LATER

September 2010

CHAPTER 1

It was a grey morning in late September as Kate picked her way through the sand dunes. She wore a black swimsuit and had her goggles hooked in the crook of her right arm. The sand was dry as she weaved her way through the undulating dunes where pale yellow marram grass grew. Her bare feet cracked the thin crust made by the sea spray.

The beach was deserted and this morning the tide was far out, exposing a few strips of black rocks before the waves broke. The sky was a pearly grey, but towards the horizon it twisted into a knot of black. Kate had discovered sea swimming six years previously, when she'd moved to Thurlow Bay on the south coast of England, five miles from the university town of Ashdean, where she now lectured in Criminology.

Every morning, whatever the weather, she would swim in the sea. It made her feel alive. It lifted her mood and was an antidote to the darkness she carried in her heart. Unmasking Peter Conway as the Nine Elms Cannibal had almost killed her, but the after-effects had been more devastating. Her sexual relationship with Peter Conway had been discovered by the press, and it played a big part in his subsequent trial. Fifteen years later, she still felt like she was picking up the pieces.

Kate emerged from the dunes, feeling the sand grow wet

and solid as she made her way to the water's edge. The first wave crashed down a few metres from where she stopped to pull on her goggles, and the surf surged up around her knees. On the coldest days, the water plunged into her skin like a knife, but she pushed through. A healthy body really was a healthy mind. It was just water. She knew how a knife felt. The six-inch scar on her abdomen was always the first place to feel the cold.

She put her hands down into the surf and felt the pull as it dropped away, leaving her on the wet sand with a few strands of green seaweed between her fingers. She shook them off and tied back her hair, which was showing a little grey, and pulled the elastic strap of her goggles over her head. Another wave crashed in, jostling her on her feet and surging up and around her hips. The sky was growing darker, and she felt spots of warm rain on her face. She dived headfirst into a breaking wave. The water enveloped her and she swam off, kicking out strongly. She felt sleek and fast, like an arrow cutting through the surf under the breaking waves. She could see down to where the sand rapidly fell away to a rocky gloom.

The roar of the water came and went as she broke the surface every four strokes to breathe, surging towards the storm. She was now far out, moving as one with the swells of water as they rolled towards the shore. She slowed and allowed herself to float on her back, rising and falling with the waves. Thunder rumbled again, louder. Kate looked back at her home sitting on top of the rocky cliff. It was comfortable and ramshackle and sat on the end of a row of widely spaced houses, next to a surf shop and snack bar which was closed up for the winter.

The air was fizzing with static; the storm was close, but the water was still. Kate held her breath and sank down under the water, the currents close to the surface diminishing as her body slowly descended towards the sandy bottom. Cold currents moved on either side of her. The pressure increased.

Peter Conway was never far from her mind. On some mornings, when getting out of bed seemed a Herculean task, she wondered if he found it hard to face each day. Peter would be locked up for the rest of his life. He was a high-profile prisoner, a monster, fed and cared for by the state, but he'd never denied what he'd done. Kate, in comparison, was the good guy, but in catching him she'd lost her career and her reputation, and was still trying to salvage a normal life from the aftermath. She wondered which one of them was really serving the life sentence. Today she felt even closer to him. Today he would be the subject of her first lecture.

With her lungs about to burst, Kate gave two strong kicks, broke the surface and started to swim back. The thunder rumbled and as the shore came closer, she rode the growing swells, feeling her heart pumping and the zing on her skin from the salt water. A wave rose up behind her and she caught it as it broke, her feet wheeling under her, pulled along the sandy bottom, feeling the exhilaration of riding a wave until the sand was under her feet and she was safe again on dry land.

The lecture theatre at the university was large, dusty and drab, with rows and rows of raked seating stretching up to the ceiling. Kate liked to watch her students as they filed into the lecture from her vantage point on the small circular stage. She was shocked by how little they noticed about their surroundings, all engrossed in their phones, barely looking up as they took their seats.

Kate was joined on stage by her assistant, Tristan Harper, a tall, well-built man in his early twenties. He had dark hair, closely cropped to his head, and elaborate tattoos on his muscular forearms. He wore the uniform of male academia – beige chinos and a checked shirt rolled up at the sleeves. The only difference was that he shunned the usual pale loafers or dark brogues and today wore a pair of bright red Adidas high-tops.

He leaned down and checked the slide carousel, which he had pre-loaded beside the lectern.

'I've been looking forward to this lecture,' he said, handing Kate the remote. He smiled, and left the stage. Seconds later the lights went out, plunging the lecture theatre into darkness. There was a murmur of excited chatter, and Kate could see the students' faces, lit up by their mobile phones. She waited until they fell silent, then clicked the button on the projector remote.

THE NINE ELMS CANNIBAL flashed up on the huge screen.

There was a collective gasp as a crime scene photo filled the screen. It was taken in a car scrapyard. A young girl's naked body lay on its side in the churned-up mud, next to a pile of rusting and half-crushed cars. The piles of scrap cars stretched away into the distance, with the misty London skyline and the four chimneys of Battersea Power Station in the background. A lone crow perched on top of a pile of cars, looking down at the young girl's body. The mud and exposure to the elements gave her flesh a rust colour, like metal, some small grotesque object that had been dumped by its owner.

'The course you've signed up for is called "Criminal Icons". And it reflects how we, as a society, are obsessed with murder and serial killers. It's fitting that I start with a serial killer I knew. Peter Conway, the former Met Police detective chief inspector who is now known as the Nine Elms Cannibal. The young woman in the photo was his first victim, Shelley Norris ...' Kate stepped out of the glare of the projected image and stood to one side. 'If you find this image distressing, good. That's a normal reaction. If you want to study Criminology you'll need to get down and dirty with the worst of humankind. The photo was taken at the Nine Elms Lane wrecker's yard in March 1993,' said Kate. She shuttered the slide carousel around. The next photo showed a wide-angle shot of a young woman's body from behind, lying in long grass. A low mist hung above the surrounding trees.

'The second victim was fifteen-year-old Dawn Brockhurst. Her body was dumped in Beckenham Place Park in Kent.'

The next slide was a close-up of the body from the front. Her face was missing, leaving just a bloody pulp, and only part of the bottom jaw and a row of teeth remained.

'Kent, on the London borders, has one of the largest populations of wild foxes in the UK. Dawn's body wasn't discovered for several days and the plastic bag tied over her head was torn off by scavenging foxes, and part of her face was eaten.' Kate moved to the next slide, a close-up of bite marks. 'The Nine Elms Cannibal liked to bite his victims, but because Dawn's body was decayed by the elements, the bites were wrongly attributed to the foxes. This prevented the first two murders from being immediately linked.'

There was a thudding sound as one of the wooden chairs flipped up, and a student, a young woman in the centre of the auditorium, dashed out with her hand over her mouth.

Kate moved through slides of Conway's next victim, ending with the crime-scene photo of the fourth victim, Catherine Cahill. Kate was taken back to that cold rainy night in Crystal Palace: the hot lights in the forensic tent which intensified the scent of decaying flesh, but also made the grass smell like it does on a summer's day; Catherine's eyes staring through the plastic wrapped tight over her head. And after all this, Peter tucking the towels over his car seats, concerned they'd get dirty.

Kate pressed the button and the slide image clicked to a picture of Peter Conway, taken in 1993 for his warrant card. He smiled into the lens wearing his Met Police uniform and peaked cap. Handsome and charismatic.

'Peter Conway. Respected police officer by day, serial killer by night.'

Kate told the story of how she was a police officer working alongside Peter Conway, how she came to suspect he was the Nine Elms Cannibal, confronted him and barely escaped alive.

The next slide showed Kate's flat in the aftermath of Peter's attack: the Thermos flask and bunch of keys sitting on the kitchen table, each with a numbered evidence marker; the living room furniture, old and shabby: her bedroom, with its damp, peeling wallpaper, curling at the edges with a pattern of yellow, orange and green flowers, the double bed with a knot of blood-soaked sheets, clumps of hardened orange wax and glass from the broken lava lamp she'd hit him with.

'I came very close to being the Nine Elms Cannibal's fifth victim, but I fought back. Quick-thinking doctors saved my life after I was stabbed in the stomach. They also pumped Peter's stomach, where they found partially digested pieces of flesh from Catherine Cahill's back.'

The lecture theatre was silent. Every student was transfixed, and Tristan was with them.

Kate went on: 'In September 1996, Peter Conway was tried and in January 1997 he was jailed at Her Majesty's pleasure in Blundeston Prison in Suffolk. After deterioration in his mental state, and an attack by another prisoner, he is now being indefinitely detained under the Mental Health Act at Great Barwell Psychiatric Hospital in Sussex. It's a case that still haunts the public imagination, and a case I will always be inextricably linked to. That's why I chose to present it first.'

There was a long pause after the lights went up. The students in the auditorium blinked at the brightness.

'Now. Who has any questions?'

There was a long pause, then a young woman with closely cropped pink hair and a pierced lip put up her hand.

34

'You effectively solved the case, yet you were used as a scapegoat by the police and left out to dry. Do you think this is because you are a woman?'

'The Met Police were embarrassed that their star officer was the killer in their most high-profile case. The case dominated the headlines for many years. You may have read that I made the mistake of having a sexual relationship with Peter Conway. When this became public knowledge, the press assumed I was somehow in possession of the facts, when I wasn't.'

There was a short silence.

'Would you ever go back to the police?' asked a young guy sitting on his own in one of the corner seats.

'Not now. I always wanted to be a police officer and I feel my career was cut short. Catching the Nine Elms Cannibal was my greatest triumph. It also made it impossible for me to continue my career in the force.'

He nodded and gave her a nervous smile.

'What about your colleagues? Do you think it's unfair that many of them were able to stay anonymous and carry on with their careers?' asked another girl.

Kate paused. She wanted to answer, *Of course it was fucking unfair! I loved my job, and I had so much to give!* But she took a deep breath and went on: 'I worked with a great team of police officers. I'm glad that they still have the opportunity to be out there, keeping us safe.'

There was a moment of hushed chatter, and then the student with the pink hair raised her hand again.

'Erm ... This might be too personal, but I'm intrigued ... You have a son with Peter Conway, is that correct?'

'Yes,' said Kate. There was a shocked murmuring from the students. It seemed that not everyone knew her business. Most of them had been three or four years old when the case was playing out in the press.

'Wow. Okay. So, he's now fourteen?'

Kate was reluctant to talk about him.

'He was fourteen a few months ago,' she said.

'Does he know about his past? Who his father is? What's that like for him?'

'This lecture isn't about my son.'

The pink-haired student looked at her two companions on either side, a young guy with long mousy dreadlocks and a girl with a short black bowl cut and black lipstick. She chewed her lip, embarrassed, but determined to find out more.

'Well, do you worry that he will be, like, a serial killer, like his father?'

Kate closed her eyes, and a rush of memories came at her.

The hospital room felt like a hotel suite. Thick carpet. Flock wallpaper. Flowers. Fresh fruit fanned out on a plate. A gold embossed menu on the bedside table. It was so quiet. Kate longed to be on a normal maternity ward, like any other normal mother, cheek to jowl, screaming in pain, seeing the joy and sorrow of others. Her waters had broken in the early hours of the morning at her parents' house, where she had been staying. She'd welcomed the contractions, the short sharp pains cutting through the dull feeling of dread that had nibbled insidiously at her over the past five months.

Her mother, Glenda, was at her bedside. Gripping her hand. More out of duty, tense and fearful, showing no joy at the prospect of her first grandchild. One of the tabloid newspapers was paying for the private room. It had been a last resort, ironically, to try and gain some privacy. In return for footing the bill, the newspaper would have an exclusive photo of mother and baby, taken at a time of Kate's choosing, through the window of the hospital room. For now, the blind had been pulled down, but Kate noticed how her mother kept eyeing it, knowing that a photographer was waiting on the other side, in the office building across the street.

Kate hadn't known she was four and a half months pregnant on the night she cracked the case. Her internal organs had been sliced up badly, and the attack left her in intensive care with complications and a serious infection for several weeks. By the time she could make the choice to have a termination, the pregnancy had gone beyond the legal limit.

It was a long and painful birth, and when the baby finally fought his way out, his first scream was chilling to Kate. She sat back, exhausted, and closed her eyes.

'It's a boy, and he's healthy,' said the midwife. 'Do you want to hold him?'

Kate kept her eyes closed and shook her head. She didn't want to look at him or hold him, and Kate was grateful when they took him away and the crying ceased. Glenda left her bedside for a few hours to get some rest in the nearby hotel, and Kate lay in the dark. She felt she was in an alternative reality. The baby had been forced upon her by fate. She resented it, and she resented everyone. And it was a boy. Boys become serial killers, not girls.

She fell into a restless sleep, and when she woke up the room was dark. A cot had been placed by the bed. A soft gurgling sound drew her towards it. In her mind the baby had been born with horns and red eyes, but she found herself looking down at the most beautiful baby boy. He opened his eyes. They were a startling clear blue, and one had an orange burst of colour, just like hers. A tiny hand reached up. She put out her finger and he grabbed it, giving her a gummy smile.

Kate had heard how the maternal instinct kicked in, and it was like a jolt to her body, a switch being flicked. An overwhelming wave of love crashed over her. How could she think this tiny, beautiful baby was bad? Yes, he shared Peter Conway's

DNA, but he shared hers too. They both shared the same rare eye colouring, and that had to count for something. Surely it meant that he was more like his mother than his father? She reached down and gently picked him up, feeling how his warm little body fitted perfectly in the curve of her arm, how his head smelt, that heavenly smell of tiny baby . . . her baby.

Kate came back to the present. The students were staring at her with concern. The silence in the lecture theatre was thick and heavy.

She clicked the projector round to the final slide, and a news clipping flashed up of Peter Conway being led in handcuffs into the Old Bailey court in London. Above it was written:

KILLER CANNIBAL JAILED FOR LIFE

'This is something we'll debate during the course. Nature versus nurture. Are serial killers born, or made? And to answer your question . . . I want to . . . no, *I have to* believe it's the latter.'

CHAPTER 2

After the lecture, Kate went up to her office. Her desk was beside a large bay window looking out over the sea. The campus building sat right on the edge of the beach, separated by a road and the sea wall.

The tide was far in, and waves rolled and smashed against the wall, shooting up a stream of spray into the sky. It was a cosy office, with two cluttered desks next to a battered sofa, and a large bookshelf covering the back wall.

'You okay?' asked Tristan, sitting at his desk in the corner and sifting through a pile of post. 'It must be tough, to keep reliving it.'

'Yes, sometimes it's like *Groundhog Day*,' said Kate, pulling out her chair and sinking into it, relieved. They'd grabbed coffee on their way up, and as she took the plastic lid off her cup she wished she had a miniature whiskey to add to her Americano. Just one little Jack Daniel's, warm and soothing, to round off the hot bitterness of the coffee and take all the feelings away. She took a deep breath and pushed the thought of alcohol away. *It's never just one drink.*

Everyone on the faculty knew the story of Kate and Peter Conway – including Tristan – but this was the first time she had talked about it in detail in front of him. She refused to be a victim of her past, but once you were a victim in the eyes of others, it stuck.

'I can't think that many students who take Criminology have a lecturer who actually *caught* a serial killer,' he said, blowing on his coffee and taking a sip. 'Pretty cool.' He turned and booted up his computer and started to type.

Tristan hadn't looked at her differently, nor did he want to delve deeper and ask her questions. He wanted to carry on as normal, and for this she was grateful. One of the reasons she liked having a male assistant was that guys were much more straightforward. Tristan worked hard, but he was laid back and easy to be around. They could work in comfortable silence without having to make conversation. She turned to her computer and switched it on.

'Have you heard anything back from Alan Hexham?'

'I emailed him on Friday,' said Tristan, scrolling through his emails. 'He hasn't replied.'

Alan Hexham was a forensic pathologist Kate had been working with for the past three years. He came in once or twice a semester as a guest lecturer on her cold case classes.

'Try him again. I need him to confirm for next week's lecture on forensic protocols at a crime scene.'

'Do you want me to call him?'

'Yes, please. His number is in the contacts folder on the desktop.'

'I'm on it.'

Kate opened her inbox. She didn't recognise the address of the first email, and she clicked on it.

Clearview Cottage
Chew Magna
Bristol
BS40 1PY

25th September 2010

Dear Ms Marshall,

I'm sorry for writing to you like this, out of the blue. My name is Malcolm Murray, and I'm writing to you on behalf of myself and my wife, Sheila.

Our daughter, Caitlyn Murray, went missing on Sunday the 9th September 1990. She was only sixteen years old. She went out to meet a friend, and never came home. For reasons I'll explain, we are convinced that Caitlyn was abducted and murdered by Peter Conway.

Over the years we have become more desperate, first, working with the police, and then when the case went cold, we hired a private investigator. All to no avail, and it seems that our darling girl just vanished off the face of the earth. Last year we felt we had reached rock bottom when we went to visit a psychic, who told us that Caitlyn had died and she is now is peace, but that her life ended shortly after she went missing in 1990.

Earlier in the year, I bumped into Megan Hibbert, an old schoolfriend of Caitlyn's, who emigrated with her family to Melbourne a few weeks before Caitlyn went missing. This was back in 1990, before the Internet, so Megan hadn't been as exposed to the Peter Conway case (and Caitlyn went missing five years before the Nine Elms case made headlines).

I got talking with Megan, and she remembered Caitlyn saying she had been out on a few sly dates with a policeman. Megan says she saw Caitlyn with this man, and described him as similar to Peter Conway. As you know, Peter Conway served as a detective inspector for Greater Manchester Police from 1989 to 1991, before his move to the London Met.

I recently wrote to the police with this information, and they

41

duly reviewed the case file and updated Caitlyn's details on their missing persons website, but they say it's not enough information for them to re-open the case.

I write to you and ask if you would consider looking into this?

We both now believe that Caitlyn is dead. We just want to find our little girl. I hate to think that her remains lie forgotten somewhere in a ditch or a drain. Our wish now is to give her a proper Christian burial.

We would, of course, pay you. My mobile number is written below. You can also email me back.

With best wishes, in hope,

Malcolm Murray

Kate sat back in her chair. Her heart was thumping loudly in her chest, and she looked over at Tristan, certain he must hear it too, but he was on the phone leaving a message for Alan, asking him to call back to confirm his lecture appearance.

She drained the last of her coffee, wishing more than ever for a dash of Jack. There had been rumours, and stories in the press, that Peter Conway might have killed other women. And over the years the police had pursued lines of investigation, but come up with nothing. This was the first she had heard of the name Caitlyn Murray.

She looked out of the window and across the sea. Would it ever be over? Would she ever be able to escape from the shadow of Peter Conway and the terrible things he did? She read the email again, and she knew she couldn't ignore it. There was a part of her that would always be a police officer. Kate pulled her chair closer to her desk and started to write a reply.

CHAPTER 3

Thirty miles away from Kate's office, the rain was lashing down as forensic pathologist Alan Hexham hurtled along a winding country road in his car, the hills and vast craggy landscape appearing in flashes through the dense trees. His mobile rang as it slid around on the passenger seat, next to a Sausage & Egg McMuffin. He grabbed the phone with his free hand, but seeing it was an Ashdean number he cancelled the call and threw the phone back on the seat. He picked up the McMuffin, unwrapped it with his free hand and took a bite.

Alan hadn't expected to be on duty today, and his mind was still foggy after a late night at the morgue. Now that he was in his late fifties, he couldn't burn the midnight oil like he used to.

The rain fell harder, reducing his view to a blur, and he switched the wipers to full power. His phone rang again, and seeing it was one of his team he picked up, speaking through another mouthful,

'I'm there in five minutes ... Where are you? ... Jesus, put your fucking foot down. This rain is pissing away forensic evidence.' He ended the call and chucked the phone down as the road narrowed to a single lane and wove between two high rock faces where the hills converged. He switched on his headlights in the gloom, praying that he wouldn't meet another car coming in the other direction. He sped up as the rocky face on either side dropped away and the road widened out to two lanes.

Alan saw a squad car parked next to an opened gate in a low drystone wall. He parked behind it and a buffeting gust of air slammed the car door into him as he got out, whipping his shoulder-length grey hair across his face. For a brief second, he heard his mother's scolding voice: *You won't get far with that hair, you need a haircut, Alan, a short back and sides!* He took one of the elastic bands he kept around his wrist and tied it back, still feeling defiant even though she was long dead.

He could see two police officers waiting inside the squad car. They got out and joined him at the gate. They both looked to be in shock. The woman, PC Tanya Barton, he had worked with before, but the young man with pale, almost translucent skin was new to him.

Alan towered over the two young officers. He had always been tall, but he had filled out over the years and was now a broad, imposing bear of a man, with a weather-beaten face and thick beard showing as much grey as his hair.

'Morning, sir. This is PC Tom Barclay,' said Tanya, having to yell to be heard over the wind and rain. Tom held out his hand.

'I need to see the scene,' shouted Alan. 'Rain and forensic evidence don't mix!'

Tanya led the way through the gate into a field. They hurried across a mix of thick gorse and grass, in places littered with the bones of sheep, keeping their heads down as the wind roared around their ears and the grey cloud seemed to press down on them. The land banked sharply towards a river which had been swelled by the storm. Brown water surged over rocks, taking with it large branches and floating rubbish.

The body lay amongst rocks and gorse on the riverbank, and Alan could see it was already in an advanced state of decay. There was severe bloating and the skin was marbled with patches of yellow and black. The body lay on its front with a long mane of filthy, straggly hair. There were six open wounds over the back and thighs, and in two places, flesh had been bitten away, exposing the spine.

Something about the way the body was lying set off alarm bells for Alan. He moved around to the head to see if it was male or female, and he felt the food in his stomach shift. The face was missing. He was used to blood and guts, but sometimes the violence of an act seemed to linger in the air. It looked as if it had been torn away, leaving just a part of the bottom jaw and the jawbone with a row of teeth.

He moved closer, pulling on latex gloves.

'Did you touch the body?' he shouted. The wind changed direction, blowing the smell of putrid flesh at their faces. The two young officers winced and took a step back.

'No, sir,' said Tom with his hand over his mouth.

Alan gently lifted the torso and saw that the body was female. She lay on her left side with her head on her shoulder, one arm reaching out. He could see something bunched around the bloated neck. With his free hand he lifted the head, resting the heel of his other hand on her hip so that she wouldn't roll down the riverbank into the murky torrent. A piece of thin rope was tied tightly around her neck, encased in the remains of what had been a plastic drawstring bag. As he lifted her head higher, the rest of the rope was pulled up out of the mud, and he saw the knot at the end. A small ball of intersecting turns.

'Oh, fuck,' he said, but it was carried away by the wind. He turned back to Tanya. She looked the less likely of the two to puke her guts up. 'I need my phone. It's in my left coat pocket!' he shouted, keeping hold of the young woman's head and indicating the pocket. Tanya hesitated and then reached over and rummaged gingerly in the folds of Alan's long coat. 'Quickly!' She found the phone and held it out to him. 'No. I need you to

45

take a photo of this rope round her neck and the knot,' he said, keeping hold of the head. 'PIN number is two, one, three, two, four, three.' With trembling hands, she unlocked the phone, stepped back and held it up. 'Closer, this isn't a holiday photo. I need a close-up of the rope around her neck and then the knot!'

As Tanya took photos, Alan noticed that there was also a Chinese symbol tattoo on the victim's lower back. A corner of it had been bitten away. The remainder of the tattoo had bloomed out and distorted with the bloating of the skin. Alan gently let go of the young woman's head, and got up. He was relieved to see the forensics van pulling into the field at the top by the gate. He removed the gloves and took his phone from Tanya. He scrolled through the photos, finishing on a close-up shot of the rope and the muddy knot. He pinched the screen and zoomed in on the knot. He wouldn't have recognised it as a monkey's fist if all the other pieces of the crime hadn't been in place – the bites, how she was posed, the torn-off face.

He looked up at the two young officers. They were watching him intently.

Alan put his phone away, and pushed thoughts of the Nine Elms Cannibal to the back of his mind. He concentrated on preserving as much evidence as possible from the crime scene.

CHAPTER 4

After lunch, Kate was left alone in her office. There was a stack of papers to mark, but she couldn't concentrate, and she kept checking her email to see if Malcolm Murray had written back.

We just want to find our little girl ... Our wish now is to give her a proper Christian burial.

In her reply to him she had avoided making any promises. What could she do? She was no longer a police officer. She had no access to any kind of investigative tools. She'd offered to speak to him, and to put him in touch with one of the police officers from the original case, but she wished she hadn't been so hasty with this. She wasn't in contact with any of the officers. Cameron was now a DCI and married with kids. He lived up north. Marsha had died of lung cancer four years after Peter was convicted, and the rest of her colleagues had scattered to the wind.

Kate put the marking to one side, pulled up the Google homepage and did a search online for information about Caitlyn Murray's disappearance. There was very little local online newspaper archive material going back to 1990, and all she found was a tiny follow-up article from 1997, when the missing persons case had been officially closed by the police. Kate then logged on to the UK Missing Persons Unit website. It was heartbreaking to see the thousands of people being sought out by family members and loved ones.

It took some digging, but she finally found Caitlyn in the database. Her name had been misspelled as 'Caitlin'. There was one photo, where Caitlyn wore a school uniform of black brogues, a short green skirt and black tights with a cream shirt and green blazer. It looked like it was cropped from a larger class photo. Caitlyn sat on a plastic chair, and behind her was a corner of a grey suit jacket belonging to a male pupil or teacher. She had been a beautiful girl, with a heart-shaped face and wide blue eyes. Caitlyn's hands were clasped on her lap and her shoulders a little hunched over. Her light brown hair was tied back, and long wisps were carried off to one side, which made Kate think the photo had been taken outside on a cold windy day. It struck Kate how she engaged with the camera, staring straight on with confidence and a wry smile.

The tiny newspaper article she'd found from 1997 was taken from the *Altrincham Echo*. It said that Caitlyn had been a pupil at Altrincham Old Scholars Grammar School. Kate pulled up the school website, but their archive of photos only went back to 2000. As the afternoon wore on and the sun sank down over the sea, she felt she'd reached a dead end. Just before six, Kate checked her email for the last time and, seeing there was still no reply, she left the office.

The house was lovely and warm when Kate stepped into the hallway. The central heating was ancient, and now the weather was turning bad, she worried it wouldn't last another winter. She hung up her coat, and it was comforting to hear the click and clank of the boiler in the roof, followed by a gurgle as hot water surged through the pipes.

The ground floor of the house was open plan, and the hallway led into a huge living room and kitchen. A picture window ran all along the back wall looking out to sea, and next to it sat a comfy armchair. This was where Kate spent most of her free time. There was something hypnotic and deeply soothing about watching the sea. It was always changing. Tonight it was clear, and the day's storm had blown itself out. The moon was almost full, and cast a silver slick on the water.

The rest of the furniture in the living room was old and heavy – a battered sofa and coffee table, and an upright piano that she didn't play against one wall. The house came with the job and the contents had belonged to her predecessor. The other walls were covered in bookshelves stacked untidily with novels and academic papers. Kate went to the kitchen, dropped her bag on the small breakfast bar and opened the fridge. It shone a bright yellow triangle over the dark room. She took out a jug of iced tea and a plate of sliced lemon. The impulse to have an after-work drink had never left her. She took out a tumbler and half filled it with ice, adding a slice of the lemon and the iced tea. She kept the lights off and went to sit in the armchair by the window, looking out at the dark rolling sea glittering in the moonlight. She took a sip, savouring the cold sweet-and-sharp of the tea, sugar and lemon.

Kate was in Alcoholics Anonymous, and in AA this was frowned upon. There was no alcohol in the iced tea, but it had all the ritual of an after-work drink. But screw it, she thought. It worked for her. She went to meetings, she kept in contact with her sponsor and she had six years of sobriety under her belt. She'd always been a drinker. It was part of police work culture to go down the pub after work and get smashed. Both good days and bad days on the force warranted a drink, but after her world was turned on its head by the Nine Elms case, her drinking became a problem, and this affected her ability to be a responsible mother.

Jake had never come to any harm, but often Kate had drunk

so much that she was unable to function. Her parents, Glenda and Michael, would have him at weekends. They stepped in many times to look after him, and he spent several extended spells staying with them so Kate could get her act together.

Things came to a head one Friday afternoon when Jake was six. He had just started primary school in south London, and Glenda and Michael had gone away for a long weekend. Kate had been drinking during the week, nothing that she thought excessive, but on the Friday afternoon she'd collapsed in the supermarket and was rushed to hospital with alcohol poisoning. She didn't turn up to collect Jake from school, and when they tried to contact Kate and then her parents, no one picked up. It got late, and the school called social services. Jake only spent a few hours with a kind foster family until Glenda and Michael were finally tracked down, but the incident blew the lid off the problem of Kate's drinking. She agreed to go to rehab and Glenda and Michael were given temporary custody.

Looking back, Kate realised that she had been in a bad place mentally. She didn't take rehab seriously. In her mind, she thought that Jake was just staying with her parents, like always, and they would be reunited once she'd paid her dues and got clean. She'd thought there must be other parents who fell ill and didn't make the school run. It could happen to anyone. But when she was discharged from rehab, three months later, Kate discovered Glenda and Michael had applied for permanent legal custody of Jake – and won.

In the years that followed, Kate struggled to get back on track. She found herself fighting against her parents to see her son, and she launched several legal appeals to be reinstated in the police. Peter Conway's legal team appealed his conviction, which kept the case in the news headlines, and the whole media circus kept on rolling.

Kate finally made sobriety stick six years ago, when she was offered a lifeline – the job at Ashdean University. It came with a house and a complete change of scenery, and she found the life of an academic fulfilling and non-judgemental. For so long her goal had been to be reunited with Jake, but by then he was eight years old. He was in a great school, he had friends and he was very happy. Kate saw that Glenda and Michael had been there for him when she couldn't, and it was in her son's best interests to stay with them. As the years passed, she mended their relationship and she saw Jake at every school holiday and some weekends, and they Skyped every Wednesday and Sunday. They had a good relationship. It was to her eternal guilt and shame that her son had been taken away from her, but she held onto her sobriety and the good things for dear life.

As he got older, she saw that it was better for Jake to have Glenda drop him at school and at play dates with his friends. That way he wasn't the kid with the notorious mother, the kid fathered by a serial murderer. With that distance from Kate, he was able to live a relatively normal life. He was able to be the kid who lived with his grandparents in the big house with the huge garden and a cute dog.

Jake knew that his father was a bad man who was locked away, but Peter Conway didn't play any part in his life. Peter was forbidden to have any contact with Jake until he was sixteen, but Kate could sense trouble looming in the future. In two years, Jake would be sixteen. He had already pestered Glenda to let him join Facebook, and he was hitting those teenage years of self-awareness and questioning.

It always felt wrong that Kate came home alone while her son lived somewhere else, but she had to keep looking forward; she had to keep believing that the best was yet to come. Jake was going to have a wonderful life. She was determined to make it happen, even if it meant distancing herself from his formative years.

A small table next to the armchair held framed photos of Jake. There was his latest class photo, and another photo of Jake in her parents' large leafy garden with Milo, his beloved Labrador. Kate's favourite photo was the newest, taken in late August on the beach below the house. The tide was far out in the background, and they were standing next to a huge sandcastle they'd spent all afternoon building. Jake had both his arms around her waist and they were smiling. The sun was shining in their faces, highlighting the burst of orange they both had in the blue of their eyes.

She picked up the photo and stroked his face through the glass. Jake now came up to her shoulder. He had kind eyes and dark hair, cut in the floppy boyband style worn by the boys in One Direction. He was a handsome kid, but he had Peter Conway's nose, strong and slightly pointed at the end.

'Of course he's going to look like his father, that's nature,' said Kate out loud. 'The nurture, that's my . . . that's my parents' job. He's happy. There's no reason for him to turn bad.'

She felt her eyes fill with tears. She put the photo back and looked down at her glass of iced tea. *It would be so easy to have a drink. Just one drink.* She shook the thought away, and it went. She drained her iced tea and looked at Jake's school photo. The kids in his class were posing on two rows of benches with Miss Prentice, a pretty blonde in her early twenties. Jake was surrounded by his four close friends, like a little boyband in the making, and smiling, squinting at the sun.

Kate's mind went back to the school photo of Caitlyn Murray. She didn't look happy like Jake.

Kate got up to switch on her laptop and check if Caitlyn's father had replied to her email, when her mobile phone rang. She went to her bag in the kitchen and saw it was Alan Hexham.

'Hello, working late?' she said. She liked Alan. He came and lectured to her students every term, and as well as being a brilliant forensic pathologist, he had become a friend.

'Kate, are you busy?' he asked.

'No. Everything okay?'

'I want you to come down to the morgue ... I need a second opinion.'

'A second opinion?' she asked. He was normally so upbeat, but tonight he sounded rattled. Almost scared.

'Yes. Please, Kate. I could really use your help and insight.'

CHAPTER 5

The morgue was on the outskirts of Exmouth, only a few miles from Kate's house. It was in the basement of a large Victorian-era hospital, and the car park was quiet and empty. A tall chimney rose out the back of the building and thick black smoke was pouring out into the clear sky.

The morgue was accessed through a side door, and then Kate was in a damp tunnel, banking down into the basement. It smelled of mould and disinfectant, and dim yellow lights dotted at intervals flickered and fizzed.

The tunnel opened out into a bright reception area with a high ceiling and ornate Victorian plasterwork. The pattern made Kate think of tightly curled intestines, or brain tissue. She signed in and was shown through to a lecture theatre. Raked wooden seats rose up around it, and vanished into the shadows.

A large naked corpse lay in the centre of the theatre, on a stainless-steel post-mortem table. Alan worked with two assistants. They all wore blue scrubs with clear Perspex masks. The bloated, blackening corpse was slit open from just above the groin up to the sternum, where the cut diverged out across each shoulder to the neck. The rib cage was split down the middle and bent out, like open butterfly wings. The hole where her face should have been gaped obscenely, a row of bottom teeth poking up through the flesh, which was like a cluster of poisonous mushrooms. Kate hesitated in the entrance, taking in the stench, mingled with the dusty wooden smell of the old auditorium.

'Lungs are good and healthy, though close to liquefaction,' Alan was saying, lifting them up in his bloodied hands. They hung wetly above the dismembered torso, reminding Kate of a dead octopus. 'Quickly, they'll disintegrate.'

He saw Kate, and nodded in acknowledgement as one of his assistants rushed to him with a stainless-steel organ dish. He placed the lungs carefully inside.

'Kate. Thank you for coming,' he said, his voice echoing off the high ceiling. 'Fresh scrubs are on the back of the door, and do remember shoe covers.'

She quickly pulled on a set of scrubs and came back, stopping a few feet from the body. The room was cold, and she folded her arms over her chest. She was close enough to see the remainder of the teenager's organs, all packed neatly into the open torso. She wondered what the body of the young woman had to do with her. It had been so long since she'd attended a post-mortem, and she hoped her stomach was still up to it. Alan towered over his two assistants as he brought Kate up to speed, explaining where and when they had found the body.

'Despite having no face to identify, her body wielded a wealth of samples: semen, saliva, three separate strands of hair, pubic hair in the vagina, an eyelash from one of the bites on the back of her legs . . .'

'Bites?' said Kate.

'Yes. Six,' said Alan, looking up at her.

One of his assistants carefully lifted out the heart and carried it reverently in two hands, taking it over to a set of weighting scales.

'Liam. Bring the dish to the organ. Don't go walking around the room with it! Samira . . .'

Liam froze in the middle of the room, holding the heart while Samira fetched a small steel bowl for him to place the organ in. Kate ignored this little double act and moved closer to the body, smelling decaying flesh. A surgical saw, congealed with blood, lay on the adjacent table. A post-mortem was always conducted with such an intense calm. 'Ripping apart someone with care' is how she had once heard it described.

'Was she asphyxiated?'

'Yes,' said Alan. 'See the ligature marks on the neck and throat, small red pinpricks, like a rash?' He indicated with his finger. 'Indicates rapid loss of oxygen, then the blood being rapidly re-oxygenated. She was deprived of oxygen to the point of death, and then revived . . .'

'Was she posed? Lying on her side, with one arm outstretched?'

'Yes.'

'Her body left in parkland?'

'Moorland. Dartmoor National Park, but yes, out in the elements.'

'Have you identified her?'

'Not yet. Looking at her remaining teeth, she's only just out of teenage years.' He went to a trolley and picked up an evidence bag containing the torn neck of the drawstring plastic bag and the rope with the knot. He handed it to Kate. 'And this was found tied around her neck.'

For the second time that day a piece of the past was suddenly thrust into Kate's present. A chill ran through her body as she fingered the knot through the thick plastic, feeling the tight ridges on the small ball. She looked up at Alan.

'Fucking hell. A monkey's fist knot?' she said. Kate looked back at the body, which was so badly decayed and bloated that it was difficult to tell what she would have looked like alive. 'What do the police say?'

'About you attending my post-mortem? They don't know,' said Alan.

Kate looked up and raised an eyebrow. 'That's not what I meant.'

'A young female DCI is heading this case. I think she was still playing with her Barbie dolls when Peter Conway was on the rampage. I haven't told her. I wanted you to look at this before I start linking this murder to a historical case.'

Kate looked at the knot again. 'There's no doubt in my mind. Look at it all. It's the Nine Elms Cannibal.'

'Peter Conway hasn't escaped, in case you're worried. He's still tucked up nicely in his cell at Her Majesty's pleasure.'

Kate nodded. 'I know. If he escapes I'm one of the first to be told. There are measures in place to protect me and my son . . .' Kate could see a tinge of pity in Alan's eyes. They had never discussed her situation, but he obviously knew. 'Whoever did this, it looks like a copycat. Am I making a leap here? There is too much here for it just to be a coincidence.'

'Yes. I agree,' said Alan.

'Do you know when she died? Time of death?' asked Kate, returning her attention to the body.

'She's been out in the elements – wind and rain, creepy crawlies. We have maggots in the flesh behind the left ear and in the shoulder, and the body is bloated. I'd put time of death five or six days ago.'

'That would make it last Tuesday or Wednesday. Conway grabbed his victims on a Thursday or Friday. He'd have the weekend to torture them, kill them, then he'd dump their bodies on a Monday or Tuesday,' said Kate. She looked up at Alan. 'Did you get dental impressions from the bites?'

'No. The skin has decayed too much.'

'What about her face? Do you know how it was removed?'

Alan took a small plastic bag from the pocket of his scrubs. It contained a long tooth.

'A canine left incisor,' he said, holding it up. It was smooth and white.

'A dog?'

Alan nodded. 'From a Doberman or Alsatian. It would need to be pretty riled up to do this. I dread to think what was done to it. We found the tooth embedded in the remnants of her upper right-hand jawbone, but I don't believe that the dog alone got the face off. There are also incision marks from a serrated blade.'

'As if the dog attacked and the face was removed, or finished off with a knife?'

'Yes,' said Alan.

'Have you come across any other murders that have the hall-marks of Conway?'

'No.'

'Can you check?'

'Kate, I asked you for your professional opinion on this body, which I am grateful for . . .'

'Alan. You have access to police databases. If someone out there is copycatting Peter Conway's murders, then this woman is the *second* victim. Conway's second victim was Dawn Brockhurst. She was dumped next to a river . . . Foxes tore off the plastic bag covering her head and ate part of her face. Shelley Norris was his first victim and she was found dumped in the wrecker's yard on Nine Elms Lane . . .'

Alan put up his hands. 'Yes, I'm aware . . . My job is to give the facts, the cause of death.'

'Can you at least look? Or direct the police to look into it?'

Alan nodded wearily. His assistants were now gently closing up the ribcage in preparation to sew up the long Y-shaped incision on her sternum.

Kate looked down, and saw she was still holding the plastic evidence bag containing the soiled length of rope with the

58

monkey's fist knot. Her hand shook and she thrust it back at Alan, feeling if she held it any longer it might contaminate her and drag her back into the turbulent hell of the Nine Elms Cannibal case.

CHAPTER 6

Kate didn't remember leaving the morgue, or saying goodbye to Alan. She found herself emerging from the long dank tunnel into the car park.

Her legs moved, and the blood pumped so hard and fast in her veins that it felt painful. The sound of the cars was muffled as she crossed the busy road, and a thin mist was starting to manifest around the dull yellow of the streetlights. The fear she felt was irrational. It wasn't one image, or one thought, but it consumed her. *Is this fear going to finish me this time, once and for all?* she wondered. Her neck and back were running with sweat, but the cold air made her shiver.

She found herself in an off-licence across the road from the morgue, and she looked down. There was a bottle of Jack Daniel's in her hand.

She dropped the bottle and it smashed, splattering the grey-ing linoleum floor and her shoes. A small Indian man sitting behind the till watching a film on his laptop looked up at the noise of the bottle dropping. He pulled out his earphones and picked up a big blue roll of tissue.

'You pay for it,' he said.

'Of course, let me help,' she said, kneeling down and picking up a piece of the broken bottle. It glistened with the amber liquid. It was so close to her tongue and she could smell it.

'Don't touch anything,' he said. He looked at her with distaste – another drunk. Reality clicked back into place for Kate.

She rummaged in her bag and pulled out a twenty-pound note. He took it and she picked her way through the broken glass and out of the door.

She didn't look back as she hurried across the road, narrowly missing a van which honked its horn. When she reached her car, she got inside, locking the doors. Her hands were shaking and she could smell the whisky on her shoes and feel the wetness on her legs. A part of her wanted to suck it out of the material. She took a deep breath and opened the window, feeling the cold air circulate in the car, dampening the whisky smell. She took out her mobile phone and sent a text message to Myra, her sponsor at Alcoholics Anonymous.

Are you up? Almost drank.

She was relieved to receive a reply immediately.

You're in luck kiddo. I'm up and I have cake. I'll put the kettle on.

Myra lived next door to Kate, in a small flat above the surf shop, which she owned and ran. The surf shop was closed up for the winter, and the small car park at the front was empty apart from a cash machine strapped to the wall, and a two-sided roto-sign with ridged edges. It was spinning fast in the wind, flicking between cold drinks and ice cream. Kate went to the side door and knocked. She looked over at the cash machine, which was glowing in the corner. In the summer months it was used by the surfers, but off-season Kate was one of the only people who used it, and only then because she was too lazy to go into town.

Myra answered the door carrying two steaming mugs of tea.

'Hold these,' she said, handing them to Kate. 'Let's go down and get some air.'

She pulled on a long, dark winter coat and stepped into a pair of Wellington boots. Her face was heavily lined, but she had clear skin and a head of white hair, which glowed luminously under the light in her hallway. Kate had never asked Myra her age, nor had it been offered up. Myra was a private person, but Kate figured she must be in her late fifties or sixties. She must have been born before 1965, which was the year Myra Hindley and Ian Brady were captured for the Moors Murders – not many people had wanted to name their daughter Myra after that.

They came out of the door and past the terrace overlooking the sea, where three rows of empty picnic tables sat in the shadows. A crumbling set of concrete steps led down to the beach, and Kate followed slowly after Myra, concentrating on not spilling the tea.

The sound of the wind and the waves grew louder as they reached the bottom of the steps where a couple of rusting deck chairs nestled in the dunes. The chairs creaked in unison as they sat. Kate sipped gratefully at the hot sweet tea. Myra took a box of Mr Kipling's mini Battenberg cakes from her coat pocket.

'Why did you want to drink?' she asked, her face serious. There was no judgement coming from her, but she was stern, and rightly so; six years of sobriety were not to be taken lightly. Over cake, Kate told her about the day's triple whammy: the Peter Conway lecture, the email she'd received, and then the post-mortem.

'I feel responsible, Myra. The father of this girl, Caitlyn. He's got no one else to turn to.'

'You don't know if she was abducted by Peter Conway. What if it's a coincidence?' said Myra.

'And then this young woman tonight. Jesus, the way she was lying there, like a beaten-up piece of meat ... And the thought that it's all starting again.'

'What do you want to do?'

'I want to help. I want to stop it from happening again.'

'You can help by talking and sharing what you know, but remember that recovery never ends, Kate. You have a son who needs his mother. You have yourself to think of. Nothing is more important than your sobriety. What happens if you go back to an off-licence and you don't drop that bottle of whisky? And you go to the counter, and you buy it, and then you relapse?'

Kate wiped a tear from her eye. Myra reached out and took her hand.

'Peter Conway is locked away. You put him there. Think of how many lives you saved, Kate. He would have kept on going. Let the police deal with this. Let Alan do his job. And as for this missing girl – what do you think you can do to find her? And how can her parents be sure she was killed by Conway?'

Kate looked down at the sand and smoothed it under her feet with the edges of her boots. Speaking to Myra had calmed her. The adrenalin was no longer surging through her body, and she felt exhausted. She checked her watch. It was almost 11 p.m. She turned and looked out to sea, at the row of lights from Ashdean twinkling in the darkness.

'I need to get some rest, and get myself out of these jeans. They stink of booze.' Kate could see Myra's concern, but she didn't want to have to promise she would leave the cases alone.

'I'll come with you, and help you put them in the washing machine,' said Myra. Kate was about to protest, but nodded. She'd done some crazy things when she was drinking, and the smell of stale booze had tipped her over the edge in the past. 'And we're going to the early meeting tomorrow,' Myra added sternly.

'Yes,' said Kate. 'And thank you.'

CHAPTER 7

Peter Conway walked down the long hospital corridor at Great Barwell Psychiatric Hospital, flanked by two orderlies, Winston and Terrell.

The long years of incarceration and limited activity had given Peter a paunch and skinny, under-developed legs, which poked out of his slightly too short bathrobe. His hands were cuffed behind him, and he wore a spit hood. It was made of a thin metal mesh, and covered his whole head. A thick reinforced panel of plastic at the front moved in and out as he breathed. His grey hair was wet from the shower, and it snaked out from under the hood, hanging over his shoulders.

It had been a year since Peter's last violent episode. He'd bitten another patient during group therapy, a manic depressive called Larry. The disagreement had been over the subject of Kate Marshall. Peter carried a huge number of emotions towards her – rage, hatred, lust and loss. Before this particular group session, Larry had found an article in the paper about Kate. Nothing huge or significant, but he had taunted Peter. Larry threw the first punch, but Peter had finished it by biting off the tip of Larry's fat little nose. He'd refused to consent to his stomach being pumped to retrieve the missing piece, and he now had to wear cuffs and the spit hood when he was outside his cell, or 'room' as the more progressive doctors liked to call it.

There had been several incidents over the years where Peter had bitten an orderly, a doctor and two patients, and various bite guards and even a hockey mask à la Hannibal Lecter had been used on him. Biting for pleasure and self-defence were two different things in Peter's mind. Tender female flesh had a delicate, almost perfumed quality to be savoured like a fine wine. Male flesh was hairy and gamey, and he only ever bit a man in self-defence.

Peter's solicitor had successfully appealed against the use of such restraints, citing the Human Rights Act. The spit hood was used by the police during arrests to protect them from bodily fluid exposure, but it was the only acceptable solution for Peter which was agreed by the hospital, courts and his solicitor.

Peter's room was at the end of the long corridor. The doors were made of thick metal, with a small hatch which could only be opened from the outside. Yelling, banging and the occasional scream seeped out, but to Peter and the orderlies on the usual morning walk to and from the shower it was background noise, like the tweeting of birds in a field. Winston and Terrell were both huge, imposing men, over six feet tall, and built like brick shithouses, as Peter's mother liked to say. Despite it seeming like a leisurely stroll back from the bathroom, they both wore heavy-duty leather belts and carried mace.

Patients on the high-security wards were kept separate from each other, in single occupancy rooms, and they rarely had contact outside. The hospital corridors were monitored by an extensive network of CCTV cameras, both for security and to choreograph the daily movements. Peter knew he needed to be back in his room in the next few minutes to allow the next patient access to the shower.

He had occupied the same room for the past six years. When

they reached the door, Peter stood against the wall opposite the door, watched by Terrell, as Winston unlocked it. When the door was opened, Terrell undid the straps on the back of the spit hood and Peter went inside. The door was closed and locked.

'I'm going to open the hatch, Peter. I need you to back up and put your hands through,' said Winston.

Peter felt the draught as it opened and he pushed his hands through. The cuffs came off, and he pulled his arms back through and started to work on the spit hood. He pulled it off and handed it through the hatch.

'Thanks, Peter,' said Winston, and the hatch closed.

Peter shrugged off his robe and dressed in jeans and a blue linen shirt and sweater. A small amount of luxury had been permitted to creep into his room over the six years. He had a digital radio, and while many of the local libraries in the UK had been closed due to funding cuts, Great Barwell's was well stocked, and a stack of books sat on the small bedside table next to the bed. Peter's only regret at having attacked Larry was the loss of his kettle. Hot drinks privileges were hard earned, and he missed not being able to make his own cup of tea or coffee.

The longing to be free never left Peter. His latest read was a book about chaos theory, and he was captivated by this and the butterfly effect. There were numerous doors and razor-wire fences between him and freedom, but he knew that sometime soon a pair of wings somewhere would flap, signifying a small shift or opportunity, and he might get the chance to escape.

He heard the squeak of shoes in the corridor outside and the low rumble of a trolley. Long ago he had learned the hospital divided time into blocks of five minutes. Once, when he went to see the hospital doctor, there was an incident with another patient, and he was taken back to his room on an elaborate detour, along unfamiliar corridors. Through an open door he had glimpsed the inside of the CCTV control room, a vast bank of television screens showing an image of every gate and corridor in Great Barwell. Despite the length of his stay, the complete layout of the hospital eluded him. It was vast.

There was a knock at his door, and the small hatch opened. A long nose, almost comically long, poked through, with red wet lips surrounded with acne.

'Peter?' croaked a voice. 'I've got your post.'

'Morning, Ned,' said Peter, moving to the hatch. Ned Dukes was the longest-serving patient. He had been inside for forty years for imprisoning and raping fourteen young boys. He was tiny and wizened, and his long nose and fleshy acne-ridden mouth sat in the middle of a large round face. His blind milky eyes rolled from side to side as his hands groped around on a trolley stacked with letters and packages. Ned was accompanied by an older woman, an orderly, whose lipless mouth was set in a grim line.

'On the shelf below,' she said impatiently. Ned wasn't the most efficient mailman, but he had been doing the job since before he'd lost his sight, and he became extremely agitated and distressed if he didn't have the structure of his mail round. The last time the hospital tried to take him off the post round, Ned had protested by pouring boiling hot water over his genitals. He'd lost his hot drinks privileges, but got to keep his job as the unofficial mailman.

Ned's breath was loud and nasal as he reached down and fumbled along the neatly stacked letters, dislodging one of the piles.

'On the bottom! There!' snapped the woman, grabbing his wrist and placing his hand on Peter's pile of letters. Ned picked them up and handed them through the hatch.

'Thanks, Ned.'

'Bye, bye,' said Ned, grinning with a truly gruesome set of broken brown teeth.

'Bye, bye, bye,' muttered Peter as the hatch slammed shut.

He went back to his bed and sifted through the post. As usual it had been opened by the hospital, checked and badly stuffed back into the envelopes.

There was a letter from Sister Assumpta, a nun who had been writing to him from her convent in Scotland for several years. She wanted to know if he liked the bathrobe she'd sent him, and was asking for his shoe size because she'd found a set of matching slippers on Amazon. She finished the letter by offering up prayers for his soul. The rest of the correspondence was tedious to Peter: a request from a writer to supply a quote for his true crime book; a man and a woman, writing separately, to say they were in love with him; and a copy of the *Reader's Digest* – somehow his name had found its way onto their mailing list.

He had written to Kate only once – a long letter during a weak moment when he was on remand awaiting sentencing. He had heard she was carrying his child, and he asked her to keep it. He also asked to be part of its life.

He never heard back from her. The only information he gleaned was from his mother, Enid, and the press. He had never written to Kate again. Her rejection of what he felt was his genuine heartfelt letter was a worse betrayal than discovering his crimes. A court injunction was in place which prevented Peter and Enid from contacting Jake or knowing his address. Of course, Enid knew people and she had Jake's address, not because she had any interest in Jake, but because she wanted the upper hand with the authorities.

In two years' time Jake would be sixteen, and the court injunctions would expire. He knew Kate was a lost cause, but one day he would meet his son, and it would give him so much pleasure to turn him against her.

Peter went to the door and listened. The corridor was silent. He moved to the radiator in the corner, which was welded to the wall. The radiator had a large plastic dial fixed to it to regulate the temperature, and a few weeks ago, when he turned the dial, it had come away from its housing, the moulded plastic shearing neatly off. It was a gift, having a place to hide things. Rooms were searched meticulously every day.

Peter slowly turned the radiator dial to the left, jiggled the plastic, and it came away. He picked up his reading glasses and, using a stem, fished around inside the housing. He turned the dial over in his hand and a small capsule fell out. It was the dissolvable capsule from a vitamin tablet. He teased the two halves of the casing apart and, using his fingernails, took out a small roll of very thin paper, tightly bound. He put the vitamin casing back together and placed it on his pile of books. He sat on the bed, scooting up so he lay flat against the wall and couldn't be seen if the hatch was opened. Carefully, he unrolled the paper. It was a thin, white, waxy paper. It came from one of those little machines that print off till rolls.

The small strip of paper was filled with neat black writing.

WHEN I WROTE TO YOU BEFORE, AND TOLD YOU I HAD KILLED A GIRL IN YOUR HONOUR, YOU MUST HAVE THOUGHT I WAS ONE OF THE SAD, LONELY FANTASISTS WHO WRITE TO YOU.

I WRITE AGAIN TO TELL YOU I AM GENUINE. I AM REAL.

I ABDUCTED AND KILLED A SECOND GIRL. HER NAME WAS KAISHA SMITH, AND I LEFT HER BODY CLOSE TO THE RIVER NEAR HUNTER'S TOR ON DARTMOOR.

VERY SOON THIS WILL BE REPORTED IN THE PRESS.

I CONTINUE IN YOUR FOOTSTEPS, AND HOPE TO BE WORTHY OF YOU. PLEASE KEEP OUR LINES OF

70

COMMUNICATION OPEN. YOU WON'T REGRET IT.
I HAVE PLANS TO CONTINUE YOUR WORK, BUT I
ALSO WANT TO MAKE YOU HAPPY. I WILL HELP YOU
SETTLE OLD SCORES, AND ULTIMATELY, I WILL GIVE
YOU FREEDOM.
    A FAN

Peter had read this letter many times in the past few days. His mother assured him that this 'fan' was genuine, and she had met with him. It frustrated Peter that people outside the hospital gates could communicate in the blink of an eye while he had to rely on letters, and agonisingly slow response times.

He reached over, switched on his digital radio and scrolled through the list of stations, just in time to hear the 8 a.m. news headlines for BBC Radio Devon. He switched between Radio Four and local radio every morning in the hope that something would be reported, and what had been written in the letter from this 'fan' would be confirmed. He listened to the full news reports, but there was nothing.

He switched off the radio, and was rolling the letter back up tightly when he heard a trolley in the corridor. He couldn't find the empty capsule on his pile of books, and he spent a frantic moment searching until he found it under the bed. It almost disintegrated in his sweaty hands as he pushed the note back inside. He'd only just got the radiator knob fitted back on when there was a crash and the hatch in the door opened.

'Coffee,' cried the voice of the woman who delivered refreshments and meals.

Peter went to the hatch and saw the lurid red plastic sippy cup. He was permitted one hot drink every morning, served in the sippy cup for safety. To Peter it seemed to be designed as a way to humiliate him. 'Milk and no sugar?' he asked.

'*Yes . . .*'

'You don't sound sure.'

'You can't open it in front of me,' the woman snapped. 'Either you want to drink it, or I have to take it away.'

He picked it up. 'Thank you,' he said, then muttered '*Cunt.*'

'What did you just say?'

'I said, any chance of a biscuit?' He flashed her a brown-toothed smile. She shook her head, a look of disgust on her hard face.

'I'll be back in an hour. The cup comes back—'

'Empty, upturned, with the lid off . . . Yes, I know,' Peter said.

She slammed the hatch closed. He tipped it back and took a sip. It was cold, milky and sweet.

He went to his desk, took out a piece of writing paper and, using a ruler, tore it neatly into a thin strip. Then he started to write a reply to his fan.

CHAPTER 8

Kate went to an AA meeting the next morning with Myra. It was their regular meeting in a church hall just outside Ashdean. Kate spoke about nearly losing her sobriety and, as always, gained strength from the people in the meeting, sharing their stories of recovery. When she and Myra parted on the steps of the church, Kate was glad that Myra didn't press her further on what she was going to do.

Tristan was already in and working at his desk when Kate arrived at the office.

'Morning,' he said. 'Alan Hexham got back to me. He can make the lecture next week. He also wanted to know if you are okay. He was concerned the post-mortem last night upset you.'

'Thanks. I'll call him,' said Kate, sitting at her desk and switching on her computer. She could see Tristan out of the corner of her eye, wanting to know more. Why would Alan leave such an indiscreet message? He didn't know if Kate shared everything with her assistant. She opened her email and saw there was a reply from Malcolm Murray, asking to meet.

Kate looked up at Tristan. He was working on the cold case exercise for the upcoming lecture, which had involved taking the police file and reports and collating the information for the students to read. She made a decision.

'Do you want to grab a coffee?' she asked.

'Sure, what would you like?' Tristan pushed back his chair.

'No, I mean let's go and have a coffee. There's something I want to talk to you about.'

'Okay,' he said, his thick dark brows furrowing. 'Is there a problem with my work?'

'God, no. Come on, I'm dying for some caffeine, and let's talk.'

They went down to the shiny new Starbucks on the ground floor of the faculty building. It was warm and cosy, and when they had their coffee, they managed to bag a table by the window, looking out over the seafront. Kate glanced around at the busy tables where students worked on their shiny new laptops, guzzling muffins and three-quid lattes, and thought back to her own poverty-stricken student days – her freezing cold bedsit, and living on a diet of lentils and fruit. A Starbucks latte and muffin cost more than her weekly food budget had been back then.

'So many of these students must be minted,' said Tristan, echoing her thoughts. 'See that guy over there?' He indicated a handsome, dark-haired guy lounging in one of the arm-chairs and talking on his mobile. 'He's wearing Adidas Samba Luzhniki World Cup trainers, limited edition.'

Kate looked over at the white-and-red-striped trainers.

'Really? They just look like trainers.'

'There were only a few thousand pairs made, and they have bison leather and suede. He can't have got much change out of five hundred quid . . . Sorry, what did you want to talk about?'

'No worries,' she said, smiling. The more she got to know Tristan, the more she liked him. She told Tristan about the email from Malcolm Murray, and her meeting with Alan Hexham last night. She edited out the part about nearly falling off the wagon. She also showed Tristan the email.

'Do you think they're linked? The dead girl from the post-mortem and then this email about Caitlyn?'

'No. Although the way in which this young woman was murdered is horrific, and it has all the hallmarks of Peter Conway, but he's locked up, and the police are dealing with that case. I want you to help me look into Caitlyn's disappearance.'

'How?' he said, looking at the email.

'You've been preparing all the stuff for my cold case lectures. You've dealt with the historical case files. I'd like you to come with me when I meet Malcolm and his wife, so I can have a second opinion. I'm very close to the case, obviously, and I'd welcome your thoughts.'

Tristan looked surprised, and excited. 'Absolutely. I've loved doing the cold case stuff, reading through the old police files. It's such interesting stuff.'

'How much work do you have on for tomorrow?' Kate asked. Wednesday was a non-lecture day, but it was still used for preparation and paperwork.

'I can juggle some stuff around, stay a bit later today. You want to go tomorrow?'

'Yes. We'd need to leave early in the morning, and of course it's classed as a work day and I'll pay your expenses.'

'Sounds good,' said Tristan, downing the last of his coffee. He looked at the email again, and at the photo Kate had found of Caitlyn online.

'This must feel like unfinished business for you. Peter Conway was your case, and now there could be more victims.'

'We don't know that yet. There's no body, but unfortunately for me, the Peter Conway case will always feel like unfinished business . . .'

Tristan nodded. 'What was he like? Peter. I know what he is now, but he must have seemed like a normal person. No one suspected him for years.'

'He was my boss, and even though we had an affair, I wasn't on joking terms with him. He seemed like a decent bloke, popular with his team. Always bought a round of drinks after a long hard day. There was a female detective whose husband left her, and Peter gave her a lot of slack and let her do her job, pick up her son from school, that kind of thing. Back in 1995, if a female police officer had children or any childcare issues she was bunged on a desk job quicker than you can say Equal Rights for Women.'

'You think there was a normal person lurking inside him?'

'Yes, and with most multiple murderers the two sides of their character are often in conflict. Good and evil.'

'And evil often wins.'

'I would hope that good triumphs as much as evil …' Her voice trailed off. She wasn't so sure any more.

Tristan nodded. 'Thanks. I promise I won't bug you with any more questions about him … This is very cool, that I get to see you being a policewoman again and investigating crime.'

'Hold your horses, I just want us to visit Malcolm and his wife, nothing more. I'm not making them any promises.'

CHAPTER 9

Kate and Tristan set off early the next morning. It took two hours on the motorway to drive to Chew Magna, a pretty village about ten miles outside Bristol.

The cottage belonging to Malcolm and Sheila was on the outskirts of the village, down a short track which was muddy from the recent rain. They parked close to the front gate, and Tristan had to leap from the passenger seat to the grassy verge by the front gate to avoid a huge muddy puddle.

The cottage was quaint, and not how Kate had imagined Malcolm and Sheila's home. She'd envisioned a dingy little Victorian terrace, or a council flat, similar to the other victims' houses. The cottage was whitewashed, and a thick wisteria wound its way up the drainpipe and under the eaves. Its branches were bare and a few yellowing leaves hung on, dancing in the wind. As they walked up to the front door, the grass in the front garden was at knee height and tall weeds grew through the cracks in the concrete.

Malcolm answered the door. He was short and plump with rounded shoulders. His hair was very thin, a baby-fine fluff that clung onto his veiny scalp. He wore blue jeans with an ironed crease down the front and a red-and-blue diamond-pattered jumper.

'Hello, hello, so pleased to meet you,' he said in a raspy voice, smiling and shaking both their hands. Kate noticed he had dark patches on the backs of both hands, and she guessed he must be in his late eighties.

'We made it here quicker than we thought. I hope we're not too early?' asked Kate. It was just after nine in the morning.

'We're much better before lunchtime. The earlier the better, before we go a bit gaga.' Malcolm grinned.

He stepped back to let them inside. There was a thick carpet of faded mauve, and the dimly lit hallway had a low ceiling. It smelled faintly of disinfectant and furniture polish. Kate slipped off her shoes and hung up her coat. Malcolm watched Tristan as he undid the laces on his trainers and carefully pulled them off to reveal immaculate snow-white sports socks.

'My, they're snazzy,' said Malcolm, adjusting his thick spectacles with a shaking hand.

'Thank you,' said Tristan, holding up the trainers. 'Vintage Dunlop Green Flash.'

'No. I meant your socks. They're so white! Sheila would never let me wear such white socks. They must show the dirt.'

Tristan laughed. 'They do a bit, but I'm the one who does the washing in our house,' he said, hanging up his coat.

'Are you married?'

'No, I live with my sister. She's the cook. I'm the bottle washer and sock washer.'

Kate smiled. She didn't know this about Tristan, and made a mental note to ask more.

'Malcolm! There's a draught! Shut that door!' came a reedy woman's voice from the living room. 'And find them some slippers.'

'Yes, we can't have you getting colds,' said Malcolm, reaching round to close the door. 'Now, where are those slippers?'

Kate and Tristan both declined the slippers, but Malcolm

insisted, rummaging around in a large trunk under the coat rack until he found them each a yellowing pair of hotel slippers with HAVE FUN, HAVE SUN, HAVE SHERATON! written on the front. He dropped them down on the carpet in front of their feet.

'There we go. We went to Madeira for the millennium. It was the last holiday we had before Sheila's agoraphobia took over . . . and then, well, anyway. Pop them on and you'll be toasty, and they'll keep those white socks clean.'

Malcolm went off as Tristan pulled a face at Kate. The tiny slippers looked ridiculous crammed onto the end of his huge feet. They passed a large grandfather clock in the dim hallway, ticking loudly, and went through to the living room which was much brighter. It was a mess: two armchairs were pushed up under the front window with a nest of tables between them, and a dining table and chairs were stacked up at the other end under the window looking out into the overgrown back garden. When Kate saw Sheila, she understood why. The middle of the room had been cleared to fit a large, high-backed chair where Sheila sat, tucked up under a fluffy blue blanket. She had long grey hair, escaping in wisps from a ponytail, and her skin was a deep yellow. Next to her was a huge dialysis machine, humming and whirring with a row of small lights flashing, and on the other side was a high table covered with bottles and packets of medication, with a yellow sharps bin next to it for disposal of needles and dressings. There were indentations in the carpet where the furniture had been. Thick blood-filled tubes emerged from under the blanket and into the machine where a cannula turned, pumping it around and back into Sheila's veins.

'Malcolm! You should have warned them. Look at him, poor lad,' she called, looking at Tristan, who was now a little pale. 'Hello, I'm Sheila,' she said.

Kate and Tristan went over to her, and they all shook hands.

'Isn't he handsome!' said Sheila, keeping hold of Tristan's hand. 'Is he your son?'

'No, he's my research assistant at the university.'

'That must be an interesting job. Have you got a girlfriend?'

'Yes, it is and, no, I haven't,' said Tristan, averting his eyes from the blood.

'A boyfriend? One of my nurses, Kevin, is gay. He's just come back from a Disney cruise.'

'No. I'm single,' said Tristan. Sheila finally let go of his hand and indicated that they should sit on the sofa. Kate had the impression that Sheila didn't get many visitors; she talked constantly until Malcolm came back with a tray of tea things. She explained that she was on the waiting list for a new kidney. 'I'm lucky that our local authority brings this machine in three times a week.'

Kate looked around the room and saw that the mantelpiece above the fireplace was the only part of the room that hadn't been rearranged. There were five photos of Caitlyn. One was of her as a wide-eyed baby, looking up from a blue blanket in a crib. In another, a much younger version of Malcolm and Sheila were on a beach, kneeling next to Caitlyn who was five or six. It looked to be a gloriously sunny day, and they all held ice creams and were smiling at the camera. There was another, which must have been taken at a professional studio a few years later. It was a close-up of the three of them sitting in a row against a blue-and-white dappled background, and they were all staring wistfully into the middle distance. There were two others of Caitlyn as a young teenager, one with a beaming smile standing next to a tall sunflower, and another where she held a tabby cat. The school photo that had been used in the newspaper wasn't there. The way the row of photos abruptly finished was chilling. Caitlyn never got to grow up and have a wedding photo, or a picture with her first-born baby.

*

80

A while later they were settled with their second cups of tea, and Sheila was still chatting away about the three nurses who came to visit. Malcolm was perched on a dining chair, which he'd brought in and placed next to her. He finally put up a hand.

'Darling, they've come a long way. We've got to talk to them about Caitlyn,' he said gently.

Sheila stopped abruptly and her face crumpled, and she began to cry. 'Yes. Yes, I know . . .'

Malcolm found her a tissue and she blotted her eyes and blew her nose.

'I know this is going to be hard,' said Kate. 'Can I ask some questions?'

They both nodded. Kate took out a notebook and flicked through the pages.

'You said in your email that Caitlyn went missing on ninth September 1990? What day was that?'

'It was a Sunday,' said Sheila. 'She went out with her friend – this was back when we lived in Altrincham, near Manchester. They were just going to go and have lunch and see a film at the cinema. I remember what she was wearing the morning she left. Her blue dress had a pattern of white flowers on the hem, which matched her blue leather sandals and handbag. She always looked beautiful. She always knew how to dress.'

'The friend she met. Is it the friend who emigrated to Australia?'

'No, this was another schoolfriend, her best friend, Wendy Sampson,' said Malcolm. 'Wendy told the police that they went to an Italian cafe where they had lunch on the Sunday and then they went and saw *Back to the Future III* at the cinema. They left the cinema just after three p.m. and they parted ways at the end of the high street. It was a bright sunny day, and Caitlyn always walked home from town if it was nice. It was just a twenty-minute walk . . .'

'She never arrived home,' finished Sheila. 'One woman remembers seeing her at the newsagent's which was midway between town and our house in Altrincham. She said Caitlyn popped in and bought a tube of polo mints.'

'Can you remember her name?'

'No.'

'How soon was this after she'd left Wendy in town?' asked Kate.

'Half an hour or so. The woman didn't know the exact time,' said Malcolm.

'It was as if Caitlyn vanished, without a trace. I didn't want to move, even ten years after she went missing. I thought she might come back and knock on the door. I couldn't bear the thought of us not being there if she did,' said Sheila.

They were silent for a moment and there was just the beep and hum of the dialysis machine.

'Do you have Wendy's details? Phone number or address?' asked Kate.

'She died two years ago of breast cancer. She did marry. Her husband invited us to the funeral,' said Sheila.

'I can look up his address,' said Malcolm.

'What did Caitlyn like to do outside school?' asked Kate.

'She went to the youth club, which was just around the corner from our house, on Tuesday and Thursday evenings,' said Malcolm. 'And she had a part-time job at a video shop on Monday evenings, and all day on a Saturday. The video shop was called Hollywood Nights and the youth club was called Carter's. I never knew the official name, but the caretaker was a miserable old git called Mr Carter, and the nickname stuck.'

'Do you know his address?'

'Oh, he's long dead. He was knocking seventy back in 1990,' said Sheila.

'Did Caitlyn play sport at school, or was she in any after-school clubs?' asked Kate. Sheila shook her head and dabbed at the end of her nose with a tissue.

'What about this schoolfriend from Melbourne?'

'Megan Hibbert,' said Malcolm. 'It was strange. We go back up to Altrincham every year to put flowers on Sheila's mother's grave. Sheila couldn't go this year, so I went on me own, and when I was at the cemetery this woman came up to me and asked if I was Caitlyn's dad. It proper shook me up to hear a stranger say her name. It turned out it was Megan and she had come back to the UK after all those years to visit family and she was there to pay respects to her granddad. We went and had a coffee. She hadn't heard about Caitlyn until a few years later, what with being so cut off back then on the other side of the world. She mentioned that Caitlyn had talked about being in a relationship with a policeman . . . It knocked me for six, because, well, we thought we knew everything about her.'

'Did Megan ever see Caitlyn with this policeman?'

'She said that one evening, when they were at the youth club, they were playing table tennis, and Caitlyn left, saying she was going to the loo. She didn't come back for a while, so Megan went looking for her, and found Caitlyn outside. She was standing by a car parked up at the front and talking to a man through the window . . . ' Kate and Tristan saw how Sheila was reacting to this – her face was crumpled up and she was wiping her eyes with a soggy clump of tissue.

'Come on love, it's okay,' said Malcolm, getting her a fresh tissue.

'What did the man look like?' asked Kate.

'Megan said she didn't really see him, as it was dark. He looked very handsome, in his twenties. He had dark hair slicked back, straight white teeth. The car was new – a dark blue Rover, H registration. She said Caitlyn was laughing and flirting with him. He put a hand out of the window and around her waist, then she got in the car and they drove away. Caitlyn didn't tell Megan what his name was, but she did say he was a copper. This wasn't the day Caitlyn went missing. Megan said that Caitlyn came to school the next day, and she was fine. Happy.'

'Did Megan ever see them together again?'

'No.'

'Did Caitlyn say anything else?'

'No. They were friends, but not best friends.'

'When was this?'

'Megan said it was in the summer, towards the end of July. It was just getting dark at around 9 p.m. It would have been either a Tuesday or Thursday.'

'What about the police investigation into Caitlyn's disappearance? Do you have the names of the police officers who worked on it?' asked Kate.

'We only ever met two. A woman and a man. The woman was young. PC Francis Cohen, and her boss, a Detective Chief Inspector Kevin Pearson. We don't know where they are now,' said Malcolm.

'They were very nice with us, but there was nothing for them to go on,' said Sheila. 'By the time Caitlyn went missing, Megan had moved with her family. They emigrated at the end of August. She never said anything to anyone, and it seems that Caitlyn never told Wendy about this policeman.'

'Peter Conway was a police officer in Greater Manchester Police from early 1989 to March 1991, after which he moved to London. Do you know if he worked on the case?' asked Kate.

'We did a freedom of information request a few weeks ago to ask if he was working on the case, but nothing has come back yet,' said Malcolm. 'We heard that he was working in narcotics, and Greater Manchester Police is a big organisation. He did live just a few miles away from our house in Altrincham. He rented a room in a house in Avondale Road in Stretford. It's written in one of those books about him. We saw the pictures of him too, when he was younger. He does look like Megan's description – handsome with dark hair slicked back, and he had very straight white teeth. Of course, we know what he did with those teeth.' Sheila broke down completely and buried her head in Malcolm's shoulder. 'Love, mind the tubes, careful,' he said, untangling one of the blood-filled tubes from his wrist. He got up and went to a sideboard next to the fireplace. He took out a large box file and handed it to Kate. 'This is everything I've kept over the years.' Kate opened the file and saw stacks of photos and paperwork. 'There are press cuttings, photos of Caitlyn. There are details of where she went on the day she went missing . . . We don't think she's still alive but, as I said, we just want to find her so we can put her to rest.'

'I know this is a difficult question,' said Kate, 'but do you have any reason to think that Caitlyn ran away? Was she unhappy about anything, or did you have an argument about something?'

'What? No!' cried Sheila. 'No, no, no, she was happy. Of course, she was a teenager, but no! No. Malcolm?'

'I didn't know of anything. We'd had a lovely Saturday night the day before she went missing. We got fish and chips and watched *The Generation Game*, and then a James Bond film. All together in here, happy as larks.'

'I'm sorry, but I had to ask,' said Kate.

Malcolm nodded.

Sheila regained her composure. 'I feel like you're our only hope, Kate,' she said. 'You were the only officer who saw through Peter Conway's facade. You caught him, and you put him away.' She reached out to Kate, and Kate got up and went to her, taking her outstretched hand. It felt like dry paper, and her yellow skin was so shiny. 'Please, say you'll help us.'

Kate looked into her eyes, and saw so much pain.

'Yes, I'll help you,' she said.

CHAPTER 10

Ninety miles from London, Enid Conway arrived in a taxi outside Great Barwell Psychiatric Hospital. She gave the taxi driver the exact money – she didn't believe in tipping – and slammed the door. She was a small, thin, beady-eyed woman with a helmet of jet-black hair and a hard face accentuated by heavy make-up. She wore a long houndstooth coat and had a pink Chanel handbag hooked over her shoulder. She took a moment to admire her reflection in the taxi window before it pulled away.

The hospital grounds backed onto a line of smart residential houses, and on the other side of the road there was a twenty-foot-high fence topped with razor wire. At the front gate was a small visitors' check-in building. Enid went to the window, where a hard-faced older woman sat behind a bank of television monitors.

'Morning, Shirley,' said Enid. 'How are you?'

'This weather ain't good for my joints,' said Shirley, holding out her hand.

'It's the damp. You need to get yourself some thermals . . . I'm here to see Peter.'

'I need your visiting order,' said Shirley, her hand still outstretched.

Enid put her new bag on the counter between them, making

sure the metal-embossed Chanel logo was facing Shirley, and made a show of rummaging around inside. Shirley didn't look impressed.

'Here you go,' she said, handing over the order.

Shirley checked it then pushed a visitor's pass through the hatch. Enid slipped it into her coat pocket.

'You know the rules. All visitors must clip their visitor's pass to their person.'

'This coat is brand new, from Jaeger. You might not have heard of Jaeger, Shirley, it's a very expensive brand,' said Enid.

'Clip it on your belt then.'

Enid gave her a nasty smile and walked away.

'Someone's come into some money,' Shirley muttered, as Enid stalked up the driveway. 'You can't polish a turd, though.'

The hospital was a vast sprawl of Victorian red-brick buildings, with a new futuristic-looking visitors' wing tacked onto the front. Enid came to the first security checkpoint and unbuttoned her coat.

'You one of the new ones?' she said to a small skinny lad who waited by the airport-style scanner. He had a turn in his left eye, and a shock of very thin black hair barely clinging onto his oversized head.

'Yeah. My first day,' he said nervously. He watched as Enid took off her coat, revealing smart slacks and a crisp white blouse. He held up a tray for her and she took off her high heels, a gold bracelet and earrings and placed them inside. She placed the Chanel bag and a carrier bag full of sweets in another tray. She went through the scanner, only for it to beep.

'Bloody hell. I've taken everything off. Surely you don't need me to take out my bloody hearing aid?' she said, tilting her head to show it in her left ear.

'No, that's fine. Have you got a metal plate in your head, or any bones pinned? Sorry, we have to ask.'

87

Enid glanced over at her things as they moved along the conveyor belt towards the X-ray machine. Through a hatch in the wall she could see the control room where two officers sat behind a bank of screens.

'No. It's probably the underwire in my bra that set it off,' she said.

The conveyor belt had stopped, and the tray containing her Chanel bag and the carrier bag was going back through the scanner. The two officers in the control room were peering at the X-ray image, one pointing out something. Enid reached out and grabbed the young lad's hand, pressing it to her breasts.

'Here! Check it, have a feel,' she said, raising her voice. He tried to pull away. She then moved his hand down and pushed his fingers between her legs.

'Madam! Please!' he cried.

'Can you feel that? That's me, nothing but me,' she said, leaning her face close to his. She looked over at the control room and saw she had the officers' attention. They were now staring with wry amusement. The tray with her bags continued through the scanner and she released the young lad's hand. The scanner beeped again as she went through.

'See. My underwire,' she said.

'Yes. That's fine,' said the lad, his voice shaking. Enid collected her coat and bags and went to a thick glass door, giving the two older men in the control room a wink as she passed. After a moment, she was buzzed through the door and into a small square room with mirrored glass, where a sign read:

STAND WITH FEET APART
AND LOOK UP AT CAMERA

There was a yellow square painted on the floor containing faded footprints. She stood in the square and looked up at the camera. There was a faint whirring as the lens twitched and focused in on her. The door opposite beeped and popped open a few inches. This led through to another checkpoint, where her bag was searched again by a tall black officer, who Enid didn't like. He then looked in the plastic bag and pulled out packets of sweets and chocolate.

'You know I always bring in sweets for Peter,' she said as he looked at each packet of sweets. She was nervous that he might open one of the bags. 'You think you've got X-ray eyes? They've been through the bloody scanner!' He gave her a look and nodded, waiting as she repacked the sweets into the carrier bag.

He then shone a small flashlight into her mouth, and she lifted her tongue. He checked her ears and her hearing aid. Finally, he waved her through.

Peter Conway was still classed as a Category A violent patient, and was dealt with as such, but Enid had successfully lobbied to have face-to-face visits with her son without a glass partition between them.

They met twice a week in a small room. Their meetings were recorded on CCTV and hospital orderlies were always present, watching them through a large observation window. The room was starkly lit, with just a square plastic table and two chairs bolted to the floor. Enid was always placed in the room first, and then Peter was brought in. She'd had to sign numerous legal documents to say that she met Peter at her own risk, and she had no legal recourse if he attacked her.

She waited in the room for ten minutes before Peter was led through by Winston and Terrell, cuffed and wearing the spit hood.

'Good afternoon, Mrs Conway,' said Winston. He guided Peter to the chair opposite Enid, then undid the straps at the back of the spit hood and removed the handcuffs. Peter rolled up his sleeves, ignoring both of the orderlies as they backed away to the door, one with a baton, the other with his Taser drawn. As soon as they were through, there was a buzzing and the sound of a lock being activated.

'All right, love?' asked Enid. Peter reached around to the back of his head, pulling the hood off. He folded it neatly and placed it on the table, as if he had just shrugged off a sweater.

'Yeah.'

'Another new guard,' she said, indicating the orderly watching them through the glass. 'Do they specify fucking ugly on the application form for this place?'

She knew their conversation was being broadcast outside the room, and she got a kick out of the fact that they had no idea what was *really* going on during their visits. The orderly outside didn't react and watched them impassively. They stood and Peter leaned over and kissed Enid on the cheek, and they embraced. He stroked his mother's back, tracing down her spine to the curve of her buttocks. Enid pushed herself against him and gave a little sigh of pleasure. They held the embrace for a long moment, until the orderly knocked on the glass. They reluctantly broke apart and sat down.

'I brought your sweeties,' she said, picking up the carrier bag and pushing it across the table.

'Lovely. Thanks, Mum.'

Peter took out three bags of boiled sweets, three bags of jelly babies and three bags of chocolate eclair toffees.

'Ah, my *favourite*, the chocolate eclairs.'

'Something to enjoy later with a nice cup of tea,' she said with a knowing smile. 'Any luck getting your kettle back?'

'No.'

'Bastards. I'll contact Terrence Lane again, get him to write another letter.'

'Mum. They won't give it back to me, and it'll be another few hundred quid in solicitors' fees.'

'It's a basic human right to be able to make yourself a cup of tea!'

'Seriously, Mum, leave it.'

Enid sat back and pursed her lips. *Just you wait*, she thought, looking at the guard staring at them through the glass. *You lot won't know what's hit you.* She picked up the pink Chanel bag and placed it reverently between them on the table.

Peter whistled. 'Jesus, Mum. Is that real?'

'Course it's bloody real!'

'How much did that cost you?'

'Never you mind. But it's as real as the money what bought it ...' She sat back, smiling, and bit her lip. She had to stop herself from saying more, and wished for the thousandth time that they could speak freely.

'Seriously, Mum?'

There was a knock on the glass and they turned to see the orderly signalling to put the bag back down on the floor.

'What difference does it make if my fucking bag is on the table or the floor? They've already searched me!'

'Mum, Mum, please,' said Peter. Enid pulled a face and put the bag on the floor.

'I wouldn't put it past them to stick a camera up my arse to see what I had for breakfast,' she said.

'That's what they do to me,' he said.

She reached out and took his hand. She went to say something but stopped herself.

'Peter. The chocolate eclairs. When you get back to your room, open them, yes?'

She patted his hand, and a look passed between them.

'Of course, Mum,' he said, nodding. 'I'll do that.'

CHAPTER 11

Kate and Tristan stopped at a motorway service station on their way back from meeting Malcolm and Sheila in Chew Magna. It was still early, and they both ordered fish and chips and found a quiet corner in the dining room before the lunch rush. They ate in silence for a few minutes. Tristan shovelled his food in, but Kate pushed hers around her plate. The greasy battered fish was making her feel queasy.

'I just felt so sorry for them both,' said Tristan. 'They looked broken.'

'When you went up to the bathroom, I was asking them about the psychic they went to see. The one who told them Caitlyn was dead. She charged them three hundred quid.'

Tristan swallowed and put his fork down. 'And they believed her?'

'She was the first person who gave them a conclusion. I've seen it before in cases I've worked on. When a loved one vanishes it's not only devastating but it plays with the mind. If there's a body, it's closure. You heard Sheila say she didn't want them to move house, in case Caitlyn came home,' said Kate.

'Do you think you've got enough information to make a start?'

'This man Caitlyn was seeing. There has to be a reason why

she kept it a secret. It could have just been that he was older, but she hid it from her best friend.'

'It's a shame the best friend isn't here to answer our questions,' said Tristan.

'Her husband is,' said Kate, looking over at the box file sitting on the edge of the table. Even though it was just paperwork, she didn't feel comfortable leaving it in the car, knowing how valuable it was to Malcolm and Sheila. She wiped her hands on a napkin and opened it.

On the top was Caitlyn's last school photo, the one that had been cropped for the newspaper. All the girls in the class were in two rows. The girls on the front row were sitting, knees together, hands clasped in their laps. The picture was taken on a grassy field, and behind the class was a white Portakabin where sports equipment was stacked outside: hurdles, a bag of netballs and a pile of crash mats. There were twenty-four girls in the class. Kate turned the picture over. A small sticker on the bottom listed the names of the pupils, the teacher and the photographer.

'I want to start by tracking down her classmates. Are you on Facebook?'

'Of course. Are you?' asked Tristan, chasing a pea around his plate with the tip of his fork.

'No.'

He stopped, his pea-laden fork halfway to his mouth. 'Seriously?'

Despite the sombre mood, Kate laughed at his shock. 'I don't want people knowing my business, especially with my past. Can you help me with looking them up?'

'Sure,' he said, shoving the last of his chips in his mouth.

'I also want to talk to the friend in Melbourne. Sheila gave me her email address.'

Tristan wiped his hands on a napkin, took the school photo

from Kate, and studied it closely. 'She doesn't look happy, does she, Caitlyn?'

'I thought that. But she was at school. She could have just been pissed off they were stuck out in the cold with no coats.'

He handed the photo back. 'Do you think she could still be alive?'

'She could be. I've seen a lot of strange cases in my time, people showing up after years missing, but Sheila and Malcolm didn't allude to anything being a problem with Caitlyn. I suppose she could have run away and then something happened to her.'

'Or Peter Conway killed her?'

'That's possible too. He was living close by. It could have been him in the car, but tall, dark and handsome isn't much to go on. It doesn't fit his style. He didn't date his victims. He abducted them during the week so he could have the weekend to torture and kill them, but then again, serial killers develop their signature style over time.' Kate put the photo down and rubbed at her tired eyes. 'There are a ton of questions and leads we can look into.'

Her mobile rang, and she fumbled in her jacket, which was hanging over the back of her chair, and pulled it out. It was Alan Hexham.

'Hi Kate, have you got a minute?' he said.

'Sure.'

'The police have identified the young woman from the post-mortem, a schoolgirl local to the area, sixteen-year-old Kaisha Smith. The family have been informed, so it's been released it to the press. I also looked into any cases involving young women dumped in wreckers' yards in the past six months. And you were right. On Wednesday twenty-eighth July, the body of a young woman called Emma Newman was found dumped naked amongst the scrap metal cars at the Nine Elms wrecker's yard near Tiverton. She was seventeen years old. She'd recently left the children's home where she'd lived since she was small. No one reported her missing. She'd been bitten, Kate, just like Kaisha.'

'This first girl was found at a wrecker's yard called Nine Elms?' asked Kate, suddenly feeling very cold.

'Yeah, creepy, I know.'

'You're sure?'

'Yes. I pulled the file.'

'How close is this wrecker's yard to the second crime scene?'

'It's just outside Tiverton, around twenty miles away.'

Kate looked up and saw Tristan had moved closer to a TV mounted on the wall above some tables opposite. The lunchtime news was showing an aerial view of the river and surrounding landscape from the second crime scene. Underneath was written BODY OF MISSING SIXTEEN-YEAR-OLD DISCOVERED.

'Alan, it's just coming on the news now. I'll call you back.' Kate hung up and went to Tristan. 'This is the girl from the post-mortem,' said Kate.

'They must have put up a drone,' said Tristan, watching the images on screen taken from high above, sweeping over the whole desolate crime scene, the rocky, gorse-covered landscape with the white forensics tent pitched next to the surging filthy river. The drone banked down a little and caught the moment from two days previously when the black body bag was carried across the field from the forensics tent to the pathologist's van. It then cut to a reporter standing at the top of the field, next to a drystone wall. Her blonde hair was being blown about by the strong wind.

'The victim has been identified as sixteen-year-old Kaisha Smith from Crediton. She was a pupil at Hartford School, a local independent school.' A photo flashed up of a teenager wearing her school uniform and grinning at the camera. Her hair was fair and permed with a straight fringe, and she wore a shirt and tie tucked under a brown blazer. Kate shuddered. The bright young girl looked nothing like the bloated battered corpse at the morgue. 'Kaisha was reported missing twelve days ago, after vanishing on her way home from school. Local police are appealing for witnesses.'

The news report moved on to the next story. The restaurant was starting to get busy, and Kate and Tristan returned to their seats, where Kate filled Tristan in on her conversation with Alan.

'Nine Elms wrecker's yard?' said Tristan. 'That's a creepy coincidence.'

Kate nodded. It wasn't just creepy, it terrified her. Two young women killed in exactly the same style. She looked down at her half-eaten fish, the grease pooling around the yellowing batter, and she thought of Kaisha's decaying yellow flesh. She moved the plate to the next table. Tristan pulled out his phone and tapped at the screen, then he turned it towards her.

'What?' she asked.

'The Nine Elms wrecker's yard is just off junction six of the M5. We're going to drive right past it on our way home.'

CHAPTER 12

When Peter got back to his cell, he switched on his radio and lined up the three packets of chocolate eclair toffees next to each other on his bed. He was looking for the pack that was slightly shorter.

Enid had a plastic heat sealer at home, but opening and then resealing a bag of sweets meant a small amount of the bag's lip had to be cut off. He found the shorter bag, opened it and tipped the paper-wrapped toffees across the blanket. There were thirty-two in total. He started to open them, examining each and rewrapping it. When he opened the sixth, he found the faint white line in the toffee he was looking for. Cadbury's chocolate eclairs are made of hard toffee, with a soft chocolate centre. He pressed his fingernail into the faint white line and the two halves of toffee eased apart. The chocolate centre had been scraped out, leaving a small cavity which had been filled with a clear pill capsule. He took it out and popped the two halves of the toffee in his mouth. Carefully he wiped the capsule on a piece of tissue. He could see the paper inside, tightly wrapped up. He went to the cell door and listened. The post trolley rumbled down the corridor. It slowed, and then moved past.

He sat back on the bed with his back to the door, eased open the pill capsule, took out the strip of paper and unrolled it. It was filled with his mother's neat writing in black ink.

Peter, this man who calls himself 'a fan', he's the real deal. I asked for ten grand to show he was genuine - and he paid! It arrived in my bank account two days ago. The money came from a limited company account. He's calling it a 'sweetener' - a payment to establish trust.

Enclosed is another letter from him. I haven't read it. I don't want to know about what he does to young girls. And I don't want you talking about it with me either. What I'm interested in is his plans for me and you. He says he can break you out of there. He says he has a plan. He will arrange for me and you to start a new life somewhere far away.

I'll find out more

Enid

Peter had communicated privately with his mother like this on and off for the past eight years, always being careful how and when they did it. This man had approached Enid a few months back, when she was walking in a park, and he let it be known that he was 'a fan' and wanted to communicate with Peter. This had happened before. People would often approach her to pass on gifts to Peter, or to get things signed by him, and Enid always made sure it was worth her while. The Fan had bigger, bolder plans and he had the money to make them happen.

The radio had been playing in the background in Peter's cell, but when the news headlines came on, the top story made him sit up.

'The body of sixteen-year-old Kaisha Smith has been found dumped and mutilated on a stretch of riverbank near Hunter's Tor in Devon. Kaisha was a pupil at Hartford School, a local independent school, and she'd been missing for twelve days. Police are treating her death as suspicious.'

Peter got up and went to the radiator dial and retrieved the last letter from The Fan, the one he should have thrown away. With trembling fingers he unrolled the paper. He already knew what it said, but he just had to be sure. Yes, Kaisha Smith was the name of the girl, and the location was the same. Peter searched through the rest of the chocolate eclairs on the bed and found the second note inside. He read it with mounting excitement.

He lay back on his thin bed and imagined feeling the sun on his face, sitting with Enid by the sea, making his own tea and drinking it from a proper cup. They would have new identities, and money. Peter liked to see her enjoying new clothes, but hoped she wouldn't change her perfume. His mother had used the same perfume ever since he could remember, Ma Griffe.

He thought back to when he was little, and how he used to perch on the end of her bed and watch her get ready to entertain one of the many uncles who used to call at the house. She'd take out the square bottle from her nightstand and, using a cotton bud, she'd dab it on her throat, and between her bare breasts. If he was good she let him dab it on for her, as long as he was careful and didn't spill any. She'd hold out the bottle as he dipped the end of the cotton bud, and then tip back her head. The skin on her neck so smooth back then, and her breasts were small and firm with large, dark nipples. When he was four she was only twenty. *So young.*

Peter lay back on his bad and pulled up his T-shirt, patting the white flesh of his belly. He had swallowed all of the letters from his mother, and now the ones from The Fan. Once digested, a little part of them became part of him. Ink and paper into new flesh. He looked around the small cell and he was excited, but cautious. Who was this person? Could he really break him out of the hospital and take him away somewhere and give him and Enid a new life?

Peter closed his eyes and conjured up that image of his mother as a young woman, perched in front of the mirror at her nightstand, head tipped back as he daubed her with perfume. He reached down and placed a hand under the waistband of his trousers.

Together again. Me and Mum. Together. A new life.

CHAPTER 13

Kate came off the motorway junction and felt her heart beat faster. She glanced across at Tristan who was navigating on his mobile phone. Very soon they were driving through moorland and the road was surrounded by thick trees on both sides.

'Take this next right,' he said as Kate slowed and they passed an old-fashioned red phone box next to a field of sheep which scattered at the sight of the car. After a few minutes there was a sign on the right for NINE ELMS WRECKER'S YARD. They took the turn and bounced down a muddy potholed track surrounded by trees and fields and some derelict houses.

Kate suddenly felt anticipation and excitement. She'd spent so long in the comfortable world of academia, and now she was back out in the real world. The track curved to the left before coming out into a huge muddy yard, which seemed to stretch out into the distance with piles and piles of wrecked cars. Puddles sprayed up mud on the windscreen.

'This place is huge,' said Kate. She heard a fire bell ringing on and off and stopped, winding down her window. 'I bet that's their office.'

It carried on ringing, and she followed the sound, and at the next crossroads between piles of old cars she took a left. It led down past a long row of rickety shipping containers. A skeletal

Christmas tree sat at an angle on one of the roofs, next to a blow-up doll dressed in a Santa outfit, a cigar poking out of its obscenely open mouth. When they reached the end of the row of shipping containers it opened out to a rough-looking parking area, next to a Portakabin. A faded red sign on the front read: CASH ONLY. NO CARDS!!!!

The windows were spattered with mud, and Kate could hear a radio inside playing 'Love is All Around' by Wet Wet Wet.

She stopped the car. 'What should we say?' she asked.

'I'm your son. I'm a bit of a boy racer, I wrote off my car and forgot to take my St Christopher necklace out of the glove compartment. It's probably gone, but we want to take a look,' he said.

'Did you just come up with that?' asked Kate, impressed.

'I was cooking it up as you drove.' He grinned.

'That's good. Do you want to take the lead then?'

'Okay.'

Kate parked the car next to a dirty truck. Straw had been laid on the ground to soak up the mud, and they picked their way across it to the office and knocked.

The door was opened by an older man wearing faded blue tracksuit bottoms spattered with mud and paint, and an equally grubby thick fleece and body warmer. He had scraps of long wild hair clinging to his scalp and a bushy grey beard. He squinted at Kate, giving her the once-over, and then at Tristan.

'Can I help you?' He had a strong Scottish accent.

Tristan gave him the spiel about the crashed car.

'You'll not find something like that,' the man said, gesturing to the piles of cars stretching away. 'The gypsies pick these cars over like locusts. My lads are under pain of death to take anything, but you can't police them.'

'Would it help if we had a number plate to put in your

102

system?' asked Kate. She was prepared to give a fake one to bolster their story.

The man took a packet of cigarettes from his pocket and lit one. 'That's ma filing system!' he snorted, expelling smoke from his mouth and nostrils and tipping his head back to indicate an old grubby landline phone on a desk and a thick yellow ledger with its pages curling up.

Kate turned to Tristan. 'It's your bloody fault for crashing your car! That necklace was from your grandma!' she shouted, hoping Tristan would take her cue.

'It was an accident! I didn't see the lorry stop at the traffic lights.'

'Because you were eyeing up that girl coming out of Tesco!' cried Kate, enjoying their bit of role play.

The old man watched them, picking a piece of tobacco off his tongue.

'I thought it was Sarah, Mum, and she said she was too ill to come out that day.'

'It was probably because of Sarah you took it off. I told you not to let her wear it!'

The old man put up a grubby hand. 'All right, all right. When was it, yer wee bump in the car?'

'It was a crash, and about five weeks ago,' said Kate. 'He rear-ended a lorry at a traffic light. The whole front was crumpled. It was a red Fiat.'

'You see the yard. We've got sections,' said the old man, demonstrating with the flat of his hand. 'See back there, they're all from the last two months. Your car might be here. Although you shouldn't be going inside a car what's piled up. It's more than my job's worth to let you . . .'

He licked his lips and looked at Kate beadily. The cheeky old goat wanted money. She rummaged in her bag and took out a twenty-pound note. The old man took it, rubbing it between his fingers gleefully.

'You've got an hour until my boss comes. If anything happens, you're on your own. Get your mother to call fer an ambulance . . . I don't want the police here again.'

'What do you mean again? Is it 'cause of those gypsies?' asked Tristan.

'No. Back in late July a young girl, a prostitute, was found dumped over there in the top corner. Poor wee lass. If she was hooking I don't know how she got this far out.'

'Did you get anything on CCTV?' asked Kate.

The man sputtered a spume of smoke. 'This ain't fucking Harrods. We're a wrecker's yard.'

'A dead body? Here?' said Kate.

'I found her,' he said, nodding sagely. 'Up by the graffiti of a huge picture of Bob Marley.'

'Who was she?'

'We don't know. The police questioned everyone, and then it went quiet. She was pretty battered up. Covered in mud, she was.'

'Was she dumped at night?'

'She must have been,' he said. 'There's no one here at night. It's pretty isolated. Gives me the creeps sometimes when the wind howls through the metal work . . . Good luck finding yer necklace.' The old man wheezed and flicked the butt of his cigarette into the mud. 'And watch yourself on the metal. If you cut yourself, get a tetanus injection sharpish.'

They promised they would, and went back to the car.

'Good job,' said Kate, watching until the old man was back in the office before turning to Tristan. 'Have you got a data signal on your phone?'

He took it out of his pocket and held it up. 'Yeah.'

'Google the crime scene from the first victim of the Nine Elms Cannibal.'

She started the engine and headed towards the back where the man had indicated.

'Okay, the photo is on Google,' said Tristan.

'If someone's copycatting Peter Conway, they would have chosen a part of the yard which resembles the original crime scene.'

'But this is miles away from Nine Elms Lane in London,' said Tristan.

'It's all being redeveloped in London. The Nine Elms Lane wrecker's yard is gone, as is my old nick, Falcon Road, which was close by. It's all going to be posh offices and executive housing.'

They drove past piles of wrecked cars, which were crushed and smashed. On several windscreens and on the upholstery inside there was blood spatter. In some cars it was almost brown; in others it looked fresher.

'We're looking for two piles of cars with a sort of path between them,' said Tristan, zooming in to the image on his phone screen. 'The cars are piled four high.'

They came out into a small clearing and Kate craned her head to look around. Then she saw it, a huge mural of Bob Marley spray-painted across the side of a caravan with its wheels sunk into the mud. With three other piles of cars, it made up one corner of a crossroad junction. Kate turned off the engine and opened the door. There was thick deep mud.

'I've got wellies in the back,' she said. She got out and picked her way to the car boot, returning with two pairs of Wellingtons. 'This is the bigger size,' she said, handing them to Tristan. 'They belong to my spons . . . to my friend, Myra. We go walking together sometimes.' Kate bit her tongue, realising she sounded like an alcoholic dating her sponsor.

Tristan took the boots without comment and they both changed. They got out of the car and stared up at the piles of cars. It was quiet, but there was a slight wind which made pieces of twisted metal from the surrounding cars move and groan. Tristan held up his phone.

'What do you think? Her body could have been around here?' said Kate, comparing where they stood to the picture on the screen.

'The cars are different. There's no London skyline, but I suppose a wrecker's yard is a wrecker's yard,' said Tristan.

'That's the problem,' agreed Kate. 'Maybe I should just pony up another twenty and ask that old man to show us exactly where ... No, he said by the Bob Marley.' She looked behind them. Bob Marley's eyes stared mournfully out at them. She turned back and peered more closely at Tristan's phone. 'Shit. Look.' She took his phone and zoomed in on the photo to the top of the pile of cars on the right. Then she looked up at the pile of cars to the right of where they stood. 'Bloody hell.'

'What?' asked Tristan.

'In the photo there's a crow perching on top of the right-hand pile of cars. See? I remember reading in the original police report that forensics had a real problem with it. They would shoo it away, but it kept landing back on the top car. They were worried it would try and peck at the body ... Anyway, look – there's a crow on the top of that car, in the photo, and there in front of us.' She pointed up at the topmost car on the right-hand side.

There was a crow perched on the roof of an old yellow Mini, attached to the front bar of a roof rack.

'Jeez,' said Tristan, peering with her. Kate whistled but it didn't move. They clapped their hands and the sound echoed around the yard.

'Obviously, it's fake,' said Kate. 'But who put it there? Bit of a coincidence.'

CHAPTER 14

They stood in the wrecker's yard for a few minutes, staring at the bird on top of the pile of cars. Its feathers moved in the wind, but it was still.

'Should we call the police?' asked Tristan.

'And say what? Come quickly, there's a stuffed bird stuck on top of a car in a scrapyard?'

'Yeah. We would sound crazy.'

He took a photo with his phone and they studied the image, zooming in on the crow.

'It looks like it's tied on with something,' said Kate. 'There could be DNA on it. If it's been out in the elements it's a very slim chance, but still. An opportunity. Are you good at climbing?'

'No. I'm really scared of heights.' He looked at her and gave a feeble smile. 'Like, shit-my-pants scared.'

Kate paced around the tower of four cars. They had their doors and windows missing. She could use them like steps. She thought back to her years in the police, and to the number of times she had scaled scaffolding, trees and high walls. It had been a while since she had been physically fit. Sure, she swam, but it was a different kind of fitness, and she never did great distances, just a ten-to-fifteen-minute dip each morning.

'Should we call the old man?' asked Tristan.

'Did he look nimble enough to scale a tower of cars?'

'No. Shit, I'm sorry,' he said. He appeared agitated just at the thought of climbing.

'It's okay. Have you got any plastic? An old plastic bag?'

Tristan rummaged in his pocket and pulled out a carrier bag, handing it to her.

Kate and Tristan moved to the pile of cars, and she grabbed the first, a large green Rover. She shook it. It felt solid and the glass in the windows was missing.

'Here,' said Tristan, grabbing a couple of old tyres from the mud. He heaved them over and stacked them by the car door. 'A step.'

Kate stood on the tyres – they boosted her up a few feet – and she was able to hook one foot up on the sill of the open window.

'Careful in those wellies,' said Tristan, wincing.

'Don't pull that face. I'm only on the first car.'

'Sorry.'

Kate saw the second car was a people carrier, and the gap between its passenger window and the Rover's window below was large.

'Tristan. Can you give me a boost?'

'Sure, um . . .'

With a lot of inelegant heaving, where Tristan had to put both hands on her butt and push her up, she made it so she was standing on the window opening of the second car. It seemed a hell of a long way down to the mud and twisted metal below, and there were still two cars to go. Kate was glad of her thick leather gloves as she gingerly held onto the window frame of the second car, which still had shards of glass from where the window had broken.

'You okay?' Tristan said, wincing again.

'Yeah, just getting my breath back.'

The third car was a low sports car, whose bonnet had been crushed and obliterated on impact. As she pulled herself up, she avoided looking at its interior. The white leather was grubby with dirt, bird droppings and a spatter of blood across the headrest.

'Okay?' Tristan called up. He now had his eyes closed.

'Yes!' she lied. He looked so small down below. It reminded her of when she'd climbed a high diving board on holiday once. Her brother Steve had jumped off it with no problem, but she had taken one look at the treacherous drop and the tiny square of blue water below, and gone back down the ladder. 'Come on, you can do this,' she muttered to herself. She gripped the sill of the passenger door in the fourth car, a Mini which had suffered a rear impact, crushing the back up like a concertina. As her feet left the sports car and she pulled herself up, the door of the Mini creaked and swung open. Kate was caught unaware, and she swung out with it, her feet suddenly dangling in the air.

'Shit!' she cried. 'Shit!'

'Oh my God!' shouted Tristan. He rushed to the bottom car, jumped up on the tyres and started to climb. Kate's gloves slipped a little on her sweaty hands and she felt her grip loosen.

'Tristan, get out of the way! I could fall on you!' The Mini didn't have another car on top to keep it steady – it started to rock, and the door began to bend on its hinges. Kate managed to get both arms hooked through the window, and she swung her legs to try and get them hooked too. 'Oh fuck,' she squealed, feeling drool in the corner of her mouth and her arms starting to shake. It had happened so fast, and here she was, dangling in mid-air with a ten-metre drop between her feet and the thick mud. After all that had happened in her life, was she going to die in a scrapyard?

'Are there any blankets in your car? To break your fall?' Tristan was saying, his voice shaking. He was rummaging in the boot of her car.

Kate swung her legs, feeling her underused stomach muscles burning, and managed to get her left foot into the window of the Mini.

'I'm okay!' she said. She pulled herself up the inside of the car before scooting around so that she was sitting on the passenger seat. She peered out.

'I'm okay,' she repeated, feeling her muscles relax as she got her balance.

'You sure?' Tristan asked, looking up at her.

Kate took some more deep breaths and nodded, thinking how unfit she was, and how her puny arms had struggled under the extra weight of her body. She took a final breath and stood up in the footwell with her head sticking out of the car, shuffling and twisting around so that she had her back to the drop. It meant that her heels poked out over the edge of the footwell and mud rained down off her boots. Luckily there was a roof rack on the car. She tested it with one hand, while holding on with the other. Feeling it was firm, she gripped it with one hand and was able to get a good look at the crow.

It was a little weather-beaten, and its feathers had been soaked by the rain and were ruffled. She pulled out her mobile phone and took a few pictures of it, then she reached around to her pocket and pulled out the carrier bag.

'It looks like it's a real crow, packed with something, like stuffing. I think it's a taxidermy job,' shouted Kate. The talons were fixed to the roof rack with cable ties. She looked around in the car and saw some shards of glass from the front window, which had smashed and covered the front seats. Carefully she bent down and picked up a piece, then started to work on the cable ties. It took several minutes of sawing at them before they broke apart. There were two on each of the claws, attaching them to the roof rack. The air was cold and her hands were sweating. She had to be careful not to cut herself.

110

Finally, the crow came loose. Kate put her hand inside the carrier bag and used it to pick up the crow. She reversed the bag, so the crow was now inside.

'Here, I'll catch it,' said Tristan, standing below. She aimed and dropped the bird. He caught it. Then she started the slow, awkward climb down, which was easier than going up had been.

When she reached the ground, they went to the car and sat for a few minutes, drinking cans of Coke and eating the chocolate bars they'd bought from the service station. Kate was shaking, but she couldn't tell if it was from fear, elation or the fact she had used muscles which had been dormant for years.

'It's a big bird,' said Tristan, opening the bag and peering inside. 'There was a kid at my school whose father did taxidermy. They were well off. This kind of shit is expensive. He said once his dad stuffed a Great Dane for its owner when it died. Cost eight grand. He made glass eyes to match, even fake balls . . . It was a boy dog.'

'Yeah, I got that,' said Kate.

'The stuffing is expensive and the cleaning, and then they sew everything up . . . ' Tristan was turning the bird upside down when Kate saw something.

'What's that?' she asked, pointing to the bird's backside. 'You said they sew everything up.'

Kate brushed off her hands; carefully, she moved the body of the bird around in the bag until it was facing down and its backside poked out of the bag.

'It's got something sticking out of its arse. Looks like paper,' said Tristan. Just a couple of loose stitches were tacked into place to keep it in. Kate picked at the stitches, managing to tease them open. She pulled out a long piece of paper, rolled up and encased in sandwich wrap.

'A note?' asked Tristan, trying not to get too excited. Kate put the carrier bag down and unwrapped the cling film. She knew she should call the police and hand it in, but her curiosity got the better of her.

The paper was thick and tightly rolled. It was a handwritten letter. It was all in capital letters and written with black ink.

NINE ELMS IS WHERE I BEGIN. EMMA IS THE FIRST,
BUT SHE WON'T BE THE LAST.
  UNTIL NEXT TIME.
  A FAN

'Jesus, the victim is named,' said Tristan. 'That note has been up there, I mean up on top of the car, for the past two months? This is like, actual evidence?'

Kate nodded. She had that old feeling back, the thrill of the chase, or breaking through in an investigation. But, of course, it wasn't her investigation.

'I'll hold them. I need you to take photos of the bird and the note,' said Kate.

Tristan pulled out his phone and took pictures of the note and the bird.

'Now we have to call the police,' she said.

Her hands were still shaking, but now it was with excitement.

CHAPTER 15

'They've sent local plod,' said Kate when she saw a police squad car come bumping down the muddy track towards them. Tristan and Kate were parked in a lay-by on the track, just outside the gates of the scrapyard.

'How do you know they're local?' asked Tristan.

'They always send local uniform police to check on something. Cat up a tree.'

'Bird up a car . . . Sorry, not funny,' Tristan said, but Kate smiled. The police car came to a stop a few feet from them, and its blue lights and siren activated and sounded once. 'Are we in trouble?'

'No,' said Kate. 'She just accidentally knocked the button. It's by the steering wheel.'

The driver switched them off, and she got out slowly and placed her peaked cap on her head. To Kate, she seemed so young, with creamy smooth skin and long red hair tied back. An older man got out of the passenger side and placed his hat over his buzz-cut grey hair. They made their way over.

'Wait in the car,' said Kate. She got out holding the bird in the bag.

'Morning. I was the one who called you,' she said.

The woman looked suspiciously between Kate and Tristan, still sitting in the car. Kate briefly explained what they had found, holding up the bird and the note which was now in a thin clear plastic bag they'd found in her car.

'I believe this is a piece of evidence in the murder case of a woman called Emma Newman. See, the victim is named in the note,' finished Kate. The two officers were silent. They looked at each other.

'So, you found this stuffed bird, with a note inside?' asked the woman.

'Yes,' said Kate, handing it over.

The woman took the note in the plastic bag from Kate and scanned it. Wordlessly she passed it over to her colleague. He read it with wry amusement on his face.

'Who is this Emma?' he said, holding up the note.

'Can you put gloves on? That's evidence. It refers to the body of Emma Newman, which was discovered at this wrecker's yard two months ago,' said Kate.

'And who are you?' he asked.

'I'm Kate Marshall. I was a police officer with the Met in London.'

'Is this your son?'

'No. That's Tristan Harper. He's my assistant.'

The man knocked on the car window and signalled for Tristan to get out. When Tristan came around the car to join them he looked very nervous.

'Assistant of what?' asked the woman.

'I lecture in Criminology at Ashdean University. Tristan is my research assistant,' said Kate.

'Can he speak for himself?'

'Yes,' said Tristan, clearing his throat. He seemed nervous.

'I'm PC Sara Halpin, this is PC David Bristol,' said the woman. Automatically they both flashed their warrant cards. 'What made you go looking for this?'

'Have you heard of the Peter Conway case?' said Kate. Both officers looked blank. 'The Nine Elms Cannibal case in London fifteen years ago?'

'Yes, rings a bell,' said David.

Sara raised an eyebrow, indicating that Kate should continue.

'I was the officer who solved that case.'

'Right. And?'

'And I believe that this person, the author of this letter, is copying the murders. The Peter Conway, the Nine Elms Cannibal murders . . . ' Tristan's nervousness was now rubbing off on Kate and she knew she was babbling. 'I'm aware, through a pathologist colleague, that the police found the body of Emma Newman here two months ago, and just a couple of days ago the body of a young woman called Kaisha Smith was found by the river near Hunter's Tor. It was on the news today.'

'Yes, we're aware of that,' said Sara. 'But what's the stuffed bird and the note got to do with it?'

Kate spent the next forty minutes explaining the details of the case, and how they came to find the bird. Tristan showed them the photos he'd taken on his phone. Sara took down a statement, but only because Kate insisted, and it took a long time for them to write it up for Kate to sign.

The light was fading when the officers finally left, taking their report and the bird and note with them.

'What happens now?' asked Tristan when they were back in the car.

'I hope they take it seriously, and that the bird and the note don't get shoved into some evidence storage room, or it will take days to be processed to the right department.'

They came out of the muddy track, passing under the NINE ELMS WRECKER'S YARD sign, and Kate turned left. They were back on the main road speeding towards the motorway. She checked the time and saw it was just gone 5 p.m.

'Shit!' she said. 'I said I'd Skype my son at six.' She put her foot down and sped on towards the motorway.

CHAPTER 16

Kate made it back to her house at one minute to six. She dashed inside, sloughing off her coat and leaving it in a heap in the hallway, and went to the kitchen, flicking on the lights. She had to scrabble around to find her laptop under a pile of paperwork on the breakfast bar, and then it seemed to take an age to switch on. When the screen icons finally appeared she opened Skype.

As an alcoholic, Kate had spent many years being unreliable, missing meetings and showing up late, so being three minutes late for her regular Skype call with Jake bothered her deeply. She was relieved to see that he hadn't tried to call her already. She smoothed down her hair, pulled up a chair and pressed CALL.

Jake appeared in the little box on screen. He was Skyping her from the kitchen table, and behind him Kate could see her mother at the Aga, stirring something in a large silver pan. He wore a Manchester United football shirt, and his dark hair was fashionably tousled.

'Hey, Mum.' He grinned.

'Hi, how are you?' she said, maximising the window so he filled the screen.

'I'm good,' he said, seeing himself in the camera and adjusting his hair.

'Evening, Catherine,' shouted Glenda without turning

around. She was immaculate as usual, with a pristine white apron over her pale slacks and blouse.

'Hi, Mum,' shouted Kate. 'What's she making?'

Jake shrugged.

'I'm making apricot jam!' trilled Glenda, 'for a Battenberg cake.'

Jake rolled his eyes. He leaned closer, lowering his voice.

'I've told her you can *buy* a Mr Kipling Battenberg cake for, like, less than two pounds, but she wants to waste her time.'

Kate had noticed over the past few weeks that Jake no longer worshipped Glenda in the way he had when he was little.

'I'm sure a home-made one will be much nicer,' said Kate, being diplomatic.

Jake pulled a face, making his eyes go crossed.

'If the wind changes you'll stay like that,' said Kate and he laughed.

'Did you have a good day, Mum?'

She didn't feel like she could or should talk about anything that had happened to her during the day. She was still trying to process it herself. She was just excited to see her son, and still felt guilty she'd only remembered they had a call at the last minute.

'I've been working. I went for a swim this morning as usual . . . The sea was a bit rough.'

'Did you see any weird jellyfish?'

'Not this time.'

'If you see any weird jellyfish washed up, will you send me a picture?'

'Of course.'

Jake looked down and picked at the white 'M' of his Manchester United shirt. It was coming away from the fabric.

'Cool. Have you heard of geocaching?'

'No. What is it?'

'It's really cool, people bury stuff, like a coin or a badge or some object, and it's buried with a log book and a GPS tracker,

117

and you get an app for your phone, and you join up and then you can go around and find these things and dig them up. And you, like, log it on your profile online. I've got the app on my phone, and there are loads around Ashdean, and the coast. Can we go geocaching when I come for half term?'

'Of course!' Kate's heart swelled at the thought that Jake was excited to come and stay in October.

'And it's free, which is really cool.'

'How do you spell it?' asked Kate. Jake spelled it out for her and she wrote it down. 'Have you done any in Whitstable?'

'Yeah, my friend Mike is into it. His mum likes hiking, unlike Grandma who won't stray far from a tarmac surface 'cause of mud on her shoes.'

Kate wanted to smile, but she kept her face neutral and changed the subject, asking him what he'd been doing.

'I've been to school, been to football.' He shrugged and blew out his cheeks. 'Boring stuff really ... even more so because *someone* won't let me join Facebook.'

Glenda was listening in the background, because she slammed down a spoon and turned to the camera, pointing her finger at Jake. 'I've told you what I think about Facebook, and I don't appreciate you trying to go behind my back!'

'Calm down, Glenda ... I'm just talking to Mum.'

'And don't you start that. I am your grandmother, not some friend down at the skate park.'

Jake rolled his eyes. 'I don't have any friends called *Glenda*, especially ones who'd be seen dead with a name like that at the skate park.'

Kate could see her mother go bright red, and about to burst. 'Jake, don't talk to Grandma like that,' she said. 'And don't roll your eyes at me.'

'I'm going to be fifteen next year and she's ruining my life. Everyone is on Facebook, all my friends! There's a guy in the year above who found a job working at a festival through a post on Facebook, so you could be damaging my future career!' he shouted. He got up and stormed off. They waited a moment and Kate heard a door slam.

'His future career,' said Kate. 'He knows exactly what buttons to push.'

Glenda pulled out the chair and sat down at the table. 'He's turning into an argumentative teenager.'

'When did he start calling you Glenda?'

'Last week, when we disagreed about what time he had to come home. "Calm down, Glenda" is his new favourite phrase.'

'Does he call Dad Michael?'

'No, your father still gets to be Granddad. I'm always the bad cop.'

'Where is Dad?'

'He's playing snooker with Clive Beresford. He sends his love.'

'Clive Beresford sends his love?' said Kate, unable to resist teasing.

'Catherine, don't you start.'

'Shouldn't we be happy Jake is becoming a normal moody teenager?'

'That's easy for you to say.'

Kate raised her eyebrows, but let it slide.

'Mum, we should let him join Facebook.'

'But—'

'Hear me out. If we don't, then he might set up some anonymous profile that we don't know about. Tell him he can join, but we have to know his password. We also have to be friends with him.'

'I have to join too?' said Glenda.

'Yes. And I'll join. Then we can monitor things, and we can also hoick him off it if there's anything we don't like.'

Glenda thought about it. 'What if you-know-who, or his bloody mother, gets in contact with Jake?'

'Peter and Enid are banned from all communication with him, Mum, including social media and email.'

'What if he finds something?'

'We can't ban him from looking at the internet for the rest of his life,' said Kate.

Glenda took off her glasses and rubbed her eyes.

'This scares the shit out of me too, Mum.'

'Language, Catherine . . .'

'We have to be smart. Banning things never works. It often makes things worse. We have to practise our surveillance techniques. We monitor him online.'

Glenda smiled. 'You're probably better at that than me.'

'I don't know. You did break the lock on my diary when I was twelve. Not that I was writing anything salacious.'

Glenda shook her head, conceding defeat. 'Okay, fine . . . but I need your full support on this. I'm not being the bad guy and the one who takes him away from Facebook.'

'If we want him to come off, I'll be the one who tells him,' said Kate.

'It will have to wait until tomorrow. I've got this bloody Battenberg cake to make for the WI fundraiser, and I haven't got a clue how to set up a Facebook profile.'

'You'll have to stand over him while he does it. I can get my assistant to look at Jake's profile when it's done, and I'll set up a profile tomorrow,' said Kate.

'Do you want to tell him?' asked Glenda. 'I can get him from his room.'

'No. You tell him. Be the good guy.'

'Thank you . . . oh bloody hell, my jam!' said Glenda, leaping up. 'Bye, darling!'

'Speak to you tomorrow, and give Jake a kiss from me,' said Kate, and she ended the Skype call.

It was always uplifting to speak to Jake, but there was a

horrible emptiness when she ended the call and was suddenly alone. It was silent, and she heard the wind keening around the house. She went back out to her car, retrieved the box file with all the information about Caitlyn, brought it in and made herself a sandwich and a glass of iced tea.

She'd been very abrupt with Tristan when she'd dropped him home, and she gave him a call after she'd eaten.

'Is this a good time?' she asked.

'I'm just running a bath,' he said. 'Hang on.' She heard the squeak of taps being closed and a splash of water.

'I won't keep you. I just wanted to say thank you for your help today. I didn't expect things to take such an odd turn.'

'I know. What's going to happen now? It looks like the bird has linked Emma Newman's death at the wrecker's yard to Kaisha Smith's.'

Kate thought about it, and she didn't feel so enthusiastic as Tristan. She didn't want to be part of another case so closely linked with Peter Conway.

'The police have it now, and they have my address if they want to talk to us . . . ' It was frustrating for Kate to be on the other side of policing, and to be kept in the dark. She was curious, and horrified, but she had to focus on what she could do, and that was finding out what had happened to Caitlyn.

'We're not in trouble, are we?' asked Tristan.

'With who?'

'The police.'

'Why would we be in trouble? We weren't trespassing. Admittedly, it was a little weird to explain what we did, but I was the one who climbed up the cars . . . Not my most elegant hour. And we had justification for doing it. And we handed over the evidence immediately.'

'Do you think they'll call us in for an interview, at the station?'

'No. We've given a statement. They might ask us to elaborate on it, but that would be over the phone, or they might want to visit informally. If they ever catch who it is, we might be called to the trial . . . ' Kate's voice faltered. She hadn't thought that far. She changed the subject. 'Are you in tomorrow morning? I've got two lectures in the afternoon.'

'Yeah, I'll be in. I'm interested to get cracking on the Caitlyn Murray case,' said Tristan.

He still sounded a little nervous, but Kate didn't press him on it. Malcolm and Sheila had wanted to discuss payment with Kate, but she and Tristan had agreed they would do this for free, and asked if they could use the case in the future for one of the cold case modules in the Criminology course. They didn't feel they could take a penny from the grieving pair, and they could use work hours to do the research, just as they did when they were preparing other cold case material for lectures. It was a bit of a stretch to justify using university resources, but Kate thought ultimately it would help all parties involved.

She ended the call with Tristan but she felt wide awake, so she opened the box Caitlyn's parents had given her and started to look through everything inside.

CHAPTER 17

The day at Great Barwell Psychiatric Hospital started early when the breakfast bell rang at 6.30 a.m. Peter Conway's allotted time to visit the shower and shave was 7.10.

The small bathroom at the end of his ward always made him think of the boarding houses he and Enid stayed in during his childhood holidays: scuffed wood partition walls, draughty air, the drip of water in ancient porcelain sinks and toilets, bare bulbs, the clinging smell of boiled food.

He stood naked in front of the spotted mirror, scraping at the foam on his face with the cheap plastic safety razor, and looked at his body properly for the first time in months. In his glory days he had been broad-shouldered with strong arms, a thin waist and muscular legs. Now he had run to fat. His hairy white belly protruded and hung over a thatch of pubic hair. His arms were puny and pouches of fat sagged under his armpits, and his legs were now skinny, like two Woodbine cigarettes poking out of the packet, as Enid liked to say. His penis was flaccid. Asleep. And, like the rest of his body, numbed by a cocktail of mood-dampening drugs.

He had used the gym for a few years, but since the nose-biting incident, he had lost his gym privileges. He was let out twice a day into the exercise yard, but it was a godforsaken little snatch of outdoor space.

'How you getting on there?' asked Winston, poking his head around the doorway to look through the grille. A grille with a small square hatch at waist level had been installed in this bathroom so that Peter could be watched at all times, but Winston always gave him privacy, something he was grateful for.

'The best I can with a crappy blade,' said Peter. He scraped the last of the foam off his chin. He rinsed the razor in the sink. When he turned on the tap, Winston appeared again and Peter handed him the razor, handle first.

'Thank you, Peter.'

Winston was powerfully built with big muscles, and for the first time Peter compared himself and saw how he could be easily overpowered, even without Winston's mace, baton and Taser.

As Peter pulled on his clothes, he dared to think, to *dream* about leaving, and he wondered exactly how he would be broken out, or if it was possible. He might need to run, or climb, and what a tragedy if his flabby weak body gave out on him and caused the plan to fail. He felt frustrated that he hadn't heard any more from his mother. She hadn't answered the phone the night before, which was unusual. He thought back to their last meeting. Did he say something wrong to make her angry? He shook the thought away. Prison gave you acres of time to obsess about what was going on outside the gates. Paranoia crept up on you very easily. He would give anything to have an email account. The joy of instant communication with the world. He had listened to the news reports several times about the dead girl, Kaisha, but they were frustratingly scant on details. There would be more on the internet, so much more.

He slipped the spit hood over his head and did up the buckles, then backed up to the hatch in the grille. Winston reached through and cuffed his hands together. Peter pushed his washbag through the grille, and only after Winston had searched it and was satisfied did he open the grille. They stepped out of the bathroom and briefly into the kitchenette opposite while another inmate was taken past them to the bathroom.

They carried on along the hallway where a row of windows looked out over the exercise yard. A lanky, pale man with thinning brown hair was pacing up and down, agitated and beating his chest. Peter didn't know his real name – everyone called him Bluey. He was a schizophrenic, and prone to paranoia.

'I'm not coming in. I'm not!' he was shouting, pacing the tiny yard. His T-shirt was torn.

They turned the corner into Peter's corridor, and saw that a group of eight orderlies – six big strong men and two strong women – were waiting at the door leading to the exercise yard.

'You need to come inside. You've had your fifteen minutes,' one of them was saying through a hatch in the door.

'FUCK YOU!' shrieked Bluey, his voice ragged. 'NO! NO! NO!' He carried on walking in a circle, beating at his chest and screaming. Peter's room was past the door to the exercise yard, at the other end of the corridor. Winston's radio beeped. He put out his hand in front of Peter.

'Okay to hang back there with Peter, Win?' crackled a voice through the radio. Winston took it off his belt.

'Of course. Peter, please can you stop there for a minute.'

Peter nodded, watching as Bluey paced round and round, slapping himself in the head and pulling at his hair.

He tried to remember having that energy, that feeling of rage, and he dug deep inside his chest, but it was as if he was stuffed with cotton wool. There was nothing. The tiny exercise yard was surrounded by ten-foot walls and razor wire, and it had netting above it. There was a dead pigeon caught up in the netting, its wings and feet tangled. Despite the chill, a couple of flies crawled over its eyes.

'How long has that pigeon been there?' asked Peter.

'Two days. They have to get rid of it today or it's a health hazard,' said Winston, looking between Peter and the other orderlies, keeping an eye on everyone. Bluey was still screaming, and he threw up. Next, he charged at the door, smashing his head into the reinforced glass.

The orderlies moved into formation outside the door, in two rows of three plus one at each end. The door opened as Bluey charged at them. They moved swiftly, caught him and flipped him over onto his back. Three held him on each side, gripping his legs, arms and torso. One cradled his head, keeping it locked in position, and the other held on to his feet. They carried him away, still screaming.

They would now take Bluey to his room and lay him on the bed, all eight of them crammed in and holding him down. A nurse might administer some sedative, and then, one by one, they would exit, in smooth fluid formation. The person holding his head would run out last, and the door would be slammed shut. It had happened to Peter on several occasions, back before they got his meds right. He admired Bluey's fight, even after all these years. When the hallway was clear, the radio beeped and they moved off again.

'How often do you exercise?' asked Peter.

'Two, three times a week,' said Winston.

'Weights?'

'No resistance, just using the body.'

'Do you think you could help me, give me some exercises?'

They reached Peter's door.

'Patients aren't allowed to exercise in their rooms.'

'I'm banned from the gym. That exercise yard is a health hazard, with dead pigeons and Bluey's puke. Just some tips on exercises . . . ' Peter looked up at Winston. Winston had huge brown eyes, the eyes of an old soul.

'I can get you a printout, but you need to keep it on the d-lo, Peter. You didn't get it from me.'

126

'Sure. Thank you.'

The nurse appeared with the medication trolley. There were rows of small plastic cups, each with a name written on it in marker pen.

'How are we this morning?' she trilled as if they were out shopping and had just bumped into each other. She was an unfortunate-looking woman, well and truly beaten by the ugly stick – fat, with a hooked nose, a weak chin and myopic bug eyes magnified by huge glasses. Peter wondered what she had to be so cheerful about, doling out pills to crazy people all day long. 'Let's see, Peter, Peter, here we are,' she said, handing him a tiny plastic cup filled with pills. He tipped them back into his mouth, took a small cup of water from her and took a gulp, tipping back his head to swallow.

'Open wide for me,' she said. He showed her the inside of his mouth, and she peered inside. 'That's lovely. You have a lovely day, and you too, Winston!'

She trundled off, the wheels squeaking on the trolley.

Winston opened the door to his room, and they went through the ritual of uncuffing and unbuckling the hood, then he was left alone.

He spat the pills out into his palm, dropped them into the toilet in the corner of his room and flushed.

He hoped Winston would give him those exercises, but he didn't want to wait. He dropped to the floor and started to do press-ups. His body protested, but he carried on, determined to get fighting fit.

CHAPTER 18

Kate woke at 7.30 to a beautiful sunny day. The sea was still and clear, but the sandy bed had been churned up by the storm, making the visibility low when she dived into the water. There was also a glut of seaweed that she had to swim and then wade through. When she came out of the water, she pulled on a robe she'd left on the sand and took a walk along the beach, where a long line of detritus ran close to the water.

She was determined to find something she could photograph and send to Jake. She walked past the row of houses at the top of the cliff and the small caravan park and stopped at the rock pools that had been exposed by the low tide. The black rock was like razor blades and in places a soggy blanket of vivid green seaweed clung to it. Kate was thrilled to find a strange bloated fish with short spiky fins lying beached next to a deep rock pool where the sun sparkled off the water, and below in the depths an eel swam in lazy circles. The bloated fish was the size of a dinner plate and had huge expressive eyes. She snapped a photo with her phone and sent it in a text to Jake.

He wrote back instantly:

> GROSS! I miss the beach there ☺ did Grandma tell you?
> I can join facebook!!! ☺☺☺

Kate texted back that he would have to give them his password, but she didn't get a response.

When she arrived at work an hour later, Kate still hadn't had a response. She put her phone away and made a mental note to follow it up later with her mother.

Tristan arrived ten minutes later, and excitedly handed her a printout of a LinkedIn profile.

'Who is Vicky O'Grady?' she asked. There was no photo.

'I didn't have the box file at home,' he said. 'But I remembered Malcolm and Sheila said that in 1990 Caitlyn worked at a video shop in Altrincham called Hollywood Nights. I took a punt and had a look on LinkedIn to see if anyone worked there at the same time, and this Vicky O'Grady came up.'

'Are there any contact details?'

'I messaged her last night and she got back to me straight away. She works at the BBC studios in Bristol as a make-up artist. I was upfront and said we were looking into Caitlyn's disappearance, and asked if she remembered her.'

Tristan gave Kate another piece of paper with the printout of the messages. It went to six pages. Kate scanned them.

'Blimey, you had a good chat with her. And she says they were close friends? Malcolm and Sheila didn't mention her.'

Kate went to the box file and pulled out Caitlyn's school photo. She scanned the names on the back, then she flipped it over and peered at the photograph. 'Okay. That's Vicky O'Grady.'

Tristan came over and peered at a picture of a haughty-looking young girl with long dark hair and high cheekbones. She was fixing the camera with a confident glare.

'She lives in Bristol. She said she can meet us this afternoon or this evening.'

'This afternoon is out,' said Kate.

'What about this evening?'

'Does she have more to tell you? We could drive all the

way over there when a phone call would save us time, and be enough.'

'She's got pictures from when she and Caitlyn went away on a weekend camping trip, and other photos from the youth club. She also said that Kate was hanging around with a couple of dodgy blokes – her words, not mine. She went to talk to the police at the time.'

'And what did the police say?'

'They took a statement, but nothing came of it. She never heard from them again.'

'What if we did it tomorrow? Saturday would be easier. I have something tonight.'

'Sure.'

'We also need to schedule a Skype call with Megan Hibbert, the friend from Melbourne. It would be good to do that before we meet Vicky, to see if she knew about her. Perhaps she could do nine-thirty our time, tonight. I'll email her,' said Kate.

'I thought you said you were busy tonight?'

Kate had her AA meeting at six, but it would be over by seven.

'I'll be done by then,' she said, not wanting to elaborate. She knew she would have to tell him soon. It was surprising how much the topic of alcohol came up, especially in the academic world. There were endless drinks parties and formal dinners with speeches and toasts. She'd lost count of the times she'd had to ask to switch her drink for orange juice.

'Okay, I'll try and schedule that call for tonight,' said Tristan.

'We should work through this school photo of Caitlyn's and track down each of her classmates, and the teacher, and we can hit LinkedIn and Facebook.'

'I thought you said you weren't on Facebook?'

'I am about to join,' said Kate. She quickly explained about Jake and Facebook.

'I was sixteen when I joined Facebook,' Tristan said.

'Bloody hell, now I feel old!'

They sat at their desks and logged onto their computers. Kate set up a Facebook profile, and she heard a ping from Tristan's computer a moment after she sent him a friend request.

'That's cool. I'm your first friend,' he said. '*That's* your profile picture?' he asked, laughing. She'd uploaded the picture of the dead fish she'd taken that morning.

'That's me, first thing in the morning without make-up,' she said dryly.

'I'm sure you look great when you wake up ... I mean, you don't wear make-up anyway, do you, and you look really good ...' His voice trailed off; he had blushed bright red. 'Sorry, that came out all wrong.'

She waved it away. 'I'll take it as a compliment! I'm old enough to be your mother.'

She saw Tristan had a hundred Facebook friends. She typed 'Jake Marshall' into the search field and a list of profiles came up. Three down, she found Jake.

The little monkey didn't wait, she thought. Jake had used a photo of him with Milo the Labrador, taken in the garden. And she saw he already had twenty-four friends. His wall was covered in messages from his classmates, welcoming him. She sent him a friend request before turning her mind back to the task of finding Caitlyn's classmates.

They worked for a couple of hours and managed to find ten of Caitlyn's schoolfriends. Kate also found the teacher, who was living close by in Southampton.

'Do you fancy a coffee break?' she asked Tristan. 'Who knows how long it will take people to reply.'

They went down to Starbucks, where Tristan grabbed the good comfy seats by the window and Kate ordered. When she came over with their coffees, he was on his phone.

'This is on the BBC News site,' he said.

Kate took his phone and watched the short video. It was a statement from the parents of Kaisha Smith, recorded at the front gate of their terraced house. Tammy and Wayne were both pale and thin, and looked as if they hadn't slept in days. They were dressed in black, and a small girl dressed in a grubby pink fake fur coat stood by Tammy. They were flanked by a police officer who was reading out an appeal for witnesses, and there was a hotline number and website address. They blinked at the flashing cameras. Kate could see that Wayne and Tammy were poor. Wayne wiped at a tear in his eye as the police officer read out the statement, and Kate saw that he had LOVE and HATE tattooed on his knuckles. She wondered how the newspapers would frame the story. The working class were usually built up as tragic heroes, but if the story cooled the press would go for the jugular. The school photo of Kaisha flashed up again – her hopeful smiling face in her school uniform, unrecognisable from the hideous corpse. When the report finished, Kate handed the phone back and took a long pull on her coffee.

'There's nothing on the news about what we found at the wrecker's yard, or the other girl,' said Tristan, swiping through his phone.

'The police will want to keep that information back. I would keep it back if I was working on it.'

They finished their coffee, and went back up to the office, hoping that they had some replies waiting. When they walked through the door they found a man and a woman in the office. The man was sitting on the sofa looking through the box file containing the Caitlyn photos, and the woman sat at Kate's desk looking at her computer.

'Excuse me, who the hell are you?' asked Kate.

CHAPTER 19

'I'm Detective Chief Inspector Varia Campbell,' said the woman, 'and this my colleague, Detective Inspector John Mercy.'

They got up and flashed their police warrant cards.

'Do you have a warrant to search through our private paperwork?' asked Kate.

'No. But do we need one?' Varia tilted her head and put her shoulders back, as if squaring up to Kate for a fight. She looked to be in her mid-thirties and wore a blue trouser suit with shoulder pads. Her cappuccino-coloured skin was very smooth. DI John Mercy was a big, strapping redhead with a ruddy complexion. His broad shoulders and muscular build strained against the constraints of his smart black suit.

'Yes. You do. Put that down,' said Kate to John, who was holding a photo. He put it back and closed the box file.

'Your visit to the Nine Elms wrecker's yard yesterday. I need some clarification as to how you stumbled upon the stuffed bird and found the note inside,' said Varia. 'May we sit?'

Kate indicated the small sofa in front of the bookshelf and they both sat. Kate and Tristan sat at their desks.

'Common sense,' said Kate. 'The crime scene at the Nine Elms wrecker's yard matched the crime scene at the original

Nine Elms Lane wrecker's yard in London. I'm referring to the Nine Elms Cannibal Case. The case I solved.'

'You were also involved in a relationship with Peter Conway, and you have a son together,' said Varia. 'Are you still in contact with him?'

Kate folded her arms across her chest. This Varia wasn't messing about. 'No.'

'Does he write to you?' she asked.

'You must be aware you can check Peter Conway's communications. And you'd see that since his arrest and incarceration, I have never visited him or written to him and we've never spoken on the telephone. He wrote to me once.'

'What about your son?' asked John.

'He's fourteen, and he has no contact with Peter Conway,' said Kate. The police officers knew that coming into her office would put her on the defensive. 'Was there a note at the second crime scene, where Kaisha Smith's body was found near the river by Hunter's Tor?'

Varia folded her arms and pursed her lips.

'You can drop the poker face,' said Kate. 'Alan Hexham called me in for a second opinion on Kaisha Smith's post-mortem. Both her murder and the murder of Emma Newman have the same hallmarks of Peter Conway . . .' Kate could see a flicker in Varia's eyes, and John looked over at her. 'Ah. There was a note, wasn't there?'

Varia looked back at John, and then got up, taking a notebook from her back pocket. She pulled out a photocopied sheet of paper and placed it on Kate's desk. Tristan came over to look.

'There's a parish noticeboard twenty metres down the river from where Kaisha Smith's body was found. This note had been left there. It wasn't discovered until yesterday.'

TO THE POLICE 'FORCE',
   I'M STREETS AHEAD OF YOU CLOWNS. KAISHA

WAS A SPIRITED YOUNG WOMAN. HOW MANY
MORE DEATHS WILL THERE BE UNTIL YOU TAKE
NOTICE OF <u>ME</u>? THE PARISH NOTICEBOARD SEEMS
FITTING SOMEHOW.
   A FAN

'He's annoyed that no one is taking notice of his work,' said
Kate. 'He's killed two and there's nothing yet in the news. A
copycat craves the attention. Like the first note, he's signed it 'A
Fan', which says more about him than he realises. He's caught
up in the cult of celebrity surrounding Peter Conway and the
Nine Elms case.'

'The original case still has to be officially referred to as
Operation Hemlock,' said Varia. Kate rolled her eyes. *Jeez, this
woman was pedantic.* 'At this stage, a copycat killer theory needs
to be proved,' Varia added, picking up the note and slotting it
back in her notebook.

'What else do you need? Another body? I'm sure there will be
one. Peter Conway killed four women before I caught him. Well,
four women that we know of. You need to focus this investigation
on finding a copycat killer . . . They're not as clever as the killer they
ape. They want the notoriety and fame involved with repeating
the terror. One of the things that will make him a success is if he
becomes notorious and makes the news, and you could use that.'

'Hey!' said Varia, putting up her hand. She looked really
pissed off. 'I don't need you to tell me how to do my job.'

'Well, you walk into my office and start rummaging through
my private papers without a warrant . . .'

'You left your door open,' said John.

'I remember dealing with house break-ins, where the suspect
said exactly the same thing,' said Kate.

He gave her a hard stare. 'Do you have any other information
to share?' he asked.

'No. We called the police as soon as we found the bird and the note.'

'Why were you in the area? It's a bit out of the way for both of you.'

Kate outlined their visit to Chew Magna, and details of the letter from Caitlyn's father. 'Malcolm Murray had already asked the Greater Manchester Police to re-open this case, but they declined due to lack of evidence,' she finished. There was a moment's silence, then Varia looked over at Tristan.

'And you went along on this *field trip* in your capacity as an academic assistant?' she asked.

'Yes,' said Tristan, his voice cracking a little with nerves.

'You live with your sister. She works for Barclay's Bank?'

'Yes.'

'How is this relevant?' asked Kate.

'Has he told you he's got a criminal record?'

He hadn't, but Kate didn't want to give these pushy, rude police officers the satisfaction of hearing that. She didn't say anything, and looked over at Tristan.

'I was fifteen and got drunk with some mates. Well, they weren't mates,' said Tristan, blushing. 'I broke the window of a car parked down the other end of the seafront.'

'You broke into a car,' said Varia. 'That's what the police report says.'

'No. I broke the window.'

'And one of the other people in your gang stole the radio.'

'I wasn't in a gang. He ran off when the police arrived. I stayed there and faced the music,' said Tristan, recovering his composure. 'And I wasn't charged, I was cautioned. I don't have to declare a caution.'

'Does your boss know?' asked John with a nasty grin. Kate stood up.

'Hang on, I don't like this. You don't come in here and bully a valuable and trusted member of my staff,' she said. 'We've shared all the information we have. Instead of snooping around without a warrant, why don't you get back out there and do some police work?'

Varia gave her a cold stare. 'We ask that you share any other information with us immediately, and you say nothing to the press, should they come knocking, which they will if they publicly link this with Peter Conway ... '

'Neither of us has any interest in talking to the press,' said Kate.

Varia and John turned their attention to Tristan.

'No. I won't be speaking to anyone,' he said.

'Right then, that's all for now,' said Varia. They left the office and John slammed the door.

'Shit,' said Tristan, putting his head in his hands. 'I'm sorry, Kate. I'm so sorry. I was fifteen. It was just a stupid— '

'You don't need to apologise. I've done my fair share of stupid things on booze. Listen, earlier I said I had something to do before our phone call. I'm going to an AA meeting. I was an alcoholic for, well, too many years. It's the reason Jake lives with my parents ... Do you think you have a drink problem?'

Tristan looked surprised. 'No.'

'Then that's all we need to say about it. They wanted to bully you; don't let them succeed.'

Tristan nodded. 'Thank you. And thank for telling me and for being cool. Do you think they will be back?'

'I don't know. They're rattled, I can see. She's under huge pressure to catch him, obviously, but when it hits the press it will be big, and the police never come out of it in a good light.'

Kate grabbed a piece of paper and started writing.

'What are you doing?' asked Tristan.

'Writing down what was in that second letter, before I forget.'

CHAPTER 20

Tristan came to Kate's house after her AA meeting. She made them tea, and then they settled at the breakfast bar in the kitchen and Skyped Megan Hibbert in Melbourne. She answered immediately. She had a broad smile, and was tanned with green eyes and long ash-blonde hair. She sat in her living room in front of large windows looking out onto a swimming pool and a big garden.

'Hi Kate, and Tristan, is it?' Her accent was a mix of Australian and British.

'Thanks for talking to us so early in the morning, Melbourne time,' said Kate. She quickly ran through what had happened at their meeting with Malcolm and Sheila.

'I feel so sorry for them. Malcolm looked a shadow of the man he used to be when I bumped into him at the cemetery . . . It broke my heart when he said he wished he had a grave for Caitlyn. Imagine being at the point in your life where you say that about your own child . . . ' Her sunny disposition dimmed, and she took out a tissue and wiped her eyes. 'What are the chances you think you'll find her body?'

Kate paused, and Tristan glanced across at her. 'I often think cold cases favour private investigation,' said Kate. 'The police often don't have time, and the UK police don't put a lot of funds into looking at cold cases unless there's more evidence.'

'They didn't think my conversation with Malcolm was enough to open it?'

'No.'

'I didn't hear about Caitlyn until a few months after it happened. We left the UK at the end of August 1990. My whole family emigrated – me, Mum, Dad and my kid brother who was five. We had no other relations, and letters from friends and neighbours got held up. We lived in a youth hostel for three months. Anyway, that's why I didn't hear about Caitlyn.'

'You were Caitlyn's best friend?' asked Kate.

'No. That was Wendy Sampson.'

'Were you and Caitlyn close to the girls in your class?'

'We were the only three scholarship girls at the school. Me, Caitlyn and Wendy. The rest of them were moneyed, not all bad, but a lot of stuck-up bitches, if you pardon my language. Caitlyn and Wendy's fathers were more acceptable than mine. Malcolm worked for the council and Sheila was a homemaker, or housewife as you say back home. My father was a builder, and we were working class in the UK. I was the lowest of the lows. We stuck together.'

'Were you bullied?' asked Tristan.

'No. I was a big strapping girl, Caitlyn had a quick wit and Wendy was a strong sportswoman – that can often deter the bullies. But this was a girls' school. When people bullied it was much more psychological,' said Megan.

'So as far as you knew, Caitlyn wasn't close with any other girls?' asked Kate.

'No, we didn't get invited round for tea at any other girls' houses.'

'She must have been gutted you were leaving?' asked Tristan.

Megan paused. 'It was odd. We were all close, but the school year had finished and I left at the end of August, and as that last month progressed, I saw her less. She spent more time with Wendy. I understood that.'

'In what way?'

'Well, we stopped arranging to all go out together. And to be fair, I was distracted. My mother was taking us up and down to London to the Australian Embassy to get our visas and paperwork for the move. There was no bad blood.'

'Didn't Wendy tell you about Caitlyn?' asked Kate.

'Yes, but I didn't get her letter till a few months after. It was awful, but you have to remember there was no internet then. It didn't make the news in Australia – why would it?' Megan started to tear up and she pulled out a tissue. 'Sorry.'

'Do you remember a girl called Vicky O'Grady in your class?'

'Yes.'

'Were you friends?'

'No. I hated her. She was a bit of a bitch, and she was always playing truant. She got caught drinking during a break time,' said Megan.

'So, none of you were friends with her?'

'No.'

Kate looked down at her notes. 'But Caitlyn worked at a video shop with Vicky?' she asked.

'Yes. Vicky's dad owned a franchise, I think, for the video shops, and Caitlyn worked there as a Saturday job. Vicky was supposed to work there, but she spent most of her time ordering Caitlyn around and flirting with the customers.'

'We're meeting with Vicky tomorrow,' said Kate.

'Really? What's she doing now?'

'She's a make-up artist for the BBC in Bristol.'

'Okay, well, good on her. What's she got to say about this?'

'We don't know. She does say that her and Caitlyn were good friends.'

Megan looked surprised. 'Seriously?'

'Apparently so,' said Kate.

'I don't understand, but a lot of water has gone under the bridge. It was a long time ago. Good luck to her.'

There was a pause, and for the first time Megan looked awkward.

'Okay, let's move on to the night where you saw Caitlyn outside Carter's youth club. Can you remember when it was?' asked Kate.

'Yes. It was right at the end of July. I remember the day because my mum was freaking out about our visas not arriving and we only had four weeks. It was really hot, and the youth club was nothing more than a big old hall. Mr Carter, the caretaker, couldn't open the windows because he'd lost the window pole. There was a stream that ran past the back, and most of the kids were out there paddling. Me and Caitlyn were playing table tennis, and she went off to the loo, but didn't come back. I found her out front, standing by a car belonging to this older guy, a policeman. She said she'd met him at the video shop. He came in to rent a movie, they got chatting, and he came to show her his new car. The new H-reg car had just been released.'

'What kind of car?' asked Kate.

'A Rover, blue.'

'Did you see him?'

'Yes, but he was inside the car, and it was dark out front and he was under streetlights. He had slicked-back black hair and strong features, a broad smile and very white teeth, 'cause I remember him poking his head out of the window and smiling when he kissed her.'

'And what happened?'

'Caitlyn got in the car, said goodbye and they drove off.'

'Was this out of character for Caitlyn?'

'Yes. But she was sixteen, and we were all going on dates with guys. Both me and Wendy did the older guy thing. A car was a place to make out with them ... and there was nothing in the press about any weirdos going around killing young women. We just thought she was really lucky, and she came to school the next day, no problems.'

Tristan took a printout from his notebook and gave it to Kate. It was Peter Conway's warrant card photo. Kate held it up to the screen.

'I can email this too, but do you think this could have been the guy? This was taken in 1993.'

Megan tilted her head and stared at it.

'I've seen the photo before, and it could have been him, but it was a long time ago ... His face was in shadow.'

CHAPTER 21

Enid Conway lived in a small end of terrace house in a run-down street in east London. It was a desperate place, with a row of filthy front gardens filled with rubbish, old cars and fridges, dog shit and broken glass.

It was where Peter had grown up, and he had bought it for her when he came back from Manchester to work in London in 1991.

In 2000, Enid had written a tell-all book called *No Son of Mine*. She'd been paid a considerable advance, and a ghost writer had been dispatched to the house to interview her. One of the questions he'd asked was if she was going to move house now that she could afford something better?

'I wouldn't last five minutes in middle-class suburbia,' she'd said. 'People respect me in this street. You see all sorts, day and night, but you keep out of other people's business and you never talk to the police.'

She thought of this conversation when she opened the front door to the red-haired Fan, as she called him. She didn't know his name.

'Did anyone see you?'

'No one important,' he said. She didn't fear anyone, but he made her uneasy. He looked to be in his late twenties and was a tall, broad, muscular man. His red hair was buzz-cut to a couple of inches in length and he had strange features. It was as if baking soda had been added in the womb. His skin was smooth, but his face was puffy with oversized, rubbery lips and fleshy hooded eyes, and his nose had a bulbous quality. He wasn't unattractive, though, and he dressed well in leather shoes and sharp neutral jeans shirt and jacket, and he always smelled freshly showered.

They went through to her kitchen, which was modern with glass and steel and expensive appliances.

'The photos are there,' she said, indicating an envelope on the counter. 'You want tea?'

'No.'

He didn't take off his coat, or sit. Enid lit a cigarette and watched him as he took the four passport-size photos out of the envelope. There were two of her that she'd taken earlier that day at a machine in the train station. And there were two of Peter.

'Is this a joke?' he said, holding them up.

'It's the most recent I have. They were taken a week before he was arrested. People age, don't they?' She figured that Peter didn't look vastly different, but he now had long grey hair and a craggier face.

'The passports need six to eight years left before they expire. This. Won't. Work,' he said, chucking the photos down on the counter.

'He's a prisoner. There isn't a passport photo machine in the bloody canteen!'

He turned to her and moved closer and held up a finger to her face. 'Don't speak to me like that, do you hear?'

She closed her eyes and opened them again, shaking her head. 'What should I do?'

He went to the fridge and opened it, taking out a carton of milk. He unscrewed the lid and took a long drink. The milk shone on his wet, rubbery lips and a drop or two escaped from the corners of his mouth. He took a last swallow and replaced the carton. Then he went to Enid's roll of kitchen towel and tore off a square, folding it neatly before dabbing at his lips. He gave a deep rumbling belch.

'What kind of phone have you got?' he asked.

Enid went to the Chanel bag which was perched on the end of the counter. The gassy smell of his stomach acid made her feel queasy. She took out her phone, a Nokia, and held it up.

He shook his head. 'That's no good. You need to get the newest iPhone. It has a five mega pixel camera.'

'What does that mean?' Enid asked.

'It means it will take a high-quality photo. Will they let you take a photo of Peter when you next visit?'

'Yes. I took one before on my phone last year. They made me show them the photo.'

'Good. I'll download it when I next see you,' he said. He reached into his pocket and took out two small brown envelopes, one thick and one thin. He slipped her passport photos inside the thin one, and put the thick one on the counter. 'Where is your toilet?'

He had never asked on any of his other visits.

'First door off the landing.'

When he had gone upstairs, Enid went to the thin envelope and opened it. She found her passport photo, along with one of him. She listened for a moment, hearing the floorboards creak in the bathroom upstairs. She switched on her phone and waited impatiently for it to boot up, then took a picture of his passport photo. The quality wasn't great, but she needed some insurance. Leverage if things went wrong. In his passport photo, he stared straight ahead. Eyes cold. Those oversized lips wet and glistening.

Enid heard the toilet flush and floorboards creaking above,

and replaced the photo. She heard the creak of him walking out of the bathroom and across the landing, but he didn't come back downstairs. He carried on into Peter's old room. She hurried out of the kitchen and up the stairs.

'What are you doing?' she asked.

He was lying in the darkness on Peter's single bed, with its blue-and-green-striped woollen blanket. Enid switched on the small overhead light. There was a poster of David Bowie striking a pose as Ziggy Stardust on one wall, and a small shelf of sports trophies above the bed. On a desk was a photo of Peter and Enid after his passing-out ceremony from Hendon Police College. He was in his uniform, Enid in a blue dress and matching hat. Next to it was a collage of photos from Peter's days in Manchester: a photo of him sitting on his first squad car, a Fiat Panda; another of him with Enid on the grass outside the flat he rented in Manchester; and another three taken with friends he had at that time.

'Was this Peter's bedroom?' he asked, looking up at her from where he lay.

'Yes.'

'Is this where he slept?'

'Yes.'

'Why are there bars on the windows? Did you have discipline issues when he was growing up?'

'No. It's to stop people getting in.'

'For many people this is a shrine,' he said. He sat up. 'Come to me.' He put out his hand.

'Why?' she said, her voice sharp.

'Why don't you humour the man who is paying for your son's freedom?'

In the lean years of her past, men had paid her for sex, knocking on the door late at night, all shapes and sizes. She went to him and took his hand. There was something about him that repulsed her. He buried his face in her belly. Rubbing against her. Inhaling. He smoothed a hand over her crotch. Stroking.

'You made him. He grew in here,' he said, his voice cracking.

Enid tried not to recoil. He kept smoothing and rubbing. It wasn't sexual. He was worshipping her.

'Yes. He is my flesh. I am his,' she said.

He finally pulled away, leaving a snail's trail of drool on the front of her sweater. He held eye contact with her, then abruptly got up and left the room. She followed him back downstairs. He was staring at the passport photo she'd left on the kitchen counter.

'I needed to check mine. I thought I'd signed the back,' she said quickly. 'Force of habit. If I'm going to have a new identity I can't have a photo with Enid Conway written on the back.'

He nodded and tucked them back in the envelope. He put it in his pocket and touched his fingers to the thick envelope.

'Instructions for you. And another letter from me to Peter.'

He took a roll of cash from his pocket and placed it beside the envelope.

'Do you drink?' she asked.

'Yes.'

She took down two whisky glasses from the cupboard and filled them with two fingers of Chivas. She slid one across the counter and took out a pack of cigarettes, offering him one. He shook his head. She tapped one out of the packet and lit up.

'What's in it for you? Breaking Peter out?'

'I love chaos,' he said with a grin, taking a sip, the whisky shining on his big lips.

'That's not an answer,' Enid said, tipping her head back to exhale the smoke. He watched it float up to where it spread across the yellow ceiling. 'I have a decent life here. I don't want for many things, but Peter. If I leave here, I can't come back. Now tell me, what's in it for you?'

'I'm subverting my father's expectations.' He smiled.

'Who's your father?'

He waggled a finger at her. 'No, no, no. That would give the game away.' He reached into his pocket and pulled out a sheet of paper and handed it to her.

Enid unfolded it and saw it was a printout of the Facebook profile of a young boy with dark hair.

'Who's this?'

'Can't you see the name? Jake Marshall. He's your grandson.'

'He's a handsome boy, like his father. But he's no use to me right now,' she said, handing back the piece of paper.

'Won't you miss him? When we leave?'

'You can't miss what you don't know.' She looked back at the photo, tilting her head. She could see Peter in there, amongst his features.

'Has Peter seen this?'

'No. I don't want him to,' said Enid. 'There is no chance he can find it himself. He hasn't got internet access.'

He downed the whisky and got up. 'Read what's in the envelope, and get me those photos. I'll be back next week.'

'I don't want this,' she said, giving him back the printout.

Enid walked around her house after he had left. She had been born a prisoner of her class and her circumstances. She'd taken the cards she'd been dealt at birth, and done the best that she could. Fighting. Always having to fight for everything in life.

Now there was the prospect of leaving and starting as a new person in another country. She wanted it just to be her and Peter. The world was better when it was just the two of them. She didn't want to know about the boy. She had no doubt he'd been brought up thinking Peter was a monster, but they'd probably told him worse about her. The boy could poison him. Enid never got scared, but she felt the fear now. It was a dirty emotion.

She went back to the kitchen and poured herself another whisky.

CHAPTER 22

Kate didn't sleep much that night, after the call with Megan. She kept thinking of the policeman who picked Caitlyn up from outside the youth club, his face bathed in the shadow of his car. Could it have been Peter?

Kate thought back to the two nights she'd spent with Peter, back in 1995. The first night when they came back to her place, after the night out in the pub, she'd found him so magnetic and sexy and couldn't resist him. She had tried for so many years to separate the feelings from that night. His firm muscular body, the rich smell of his hair and skin. His strength as he had scooped her up and placed her on her bed and undressed her. He had been passionate and tender, and while it made her skin crawl that she'd been so intimate with someone who did things so sick and vile, those memories were there. They couldn't be changed. It also made her feel closer to Caitlyn. Did she feel caught up in Peter Conway's facade? Did she find him desirable when she climbed into that car and it sped away? Where did they go, and what did they do?

Kate never thought of herself as a victim, but just like Caitlyn she'd been duped by his mask of normality.

The photo she'd shown Megan was lying downstairs on the breakfast bar. It was inside her notebook, but as she lay in bed her mind kept playing tricks on her. She imagined the notebook lying there in the darkness, then slowly standing up by itself, the pages flicking through and stopping at the photo of Peter. His eyes opened and he started to look around, eyes darting from within the still image of his face. Then his mouth started to twitch, and the lips peeled back to reveal his teeth, so straight and white as he shouted, 'KATE!'

Kate woke up sweating, her heart thumping against her chest. The room was dark and it was 2.11 a.m. by the clock on her bed-side table. She threw back the bedcovers and went downstairs, flicking on all the lights and making a lot of noise on the stairs. The living room was still and empty. The notebook lay closed on the breakfast bar – of course it did – but she still took out the photo of Peter and put it in her shredder, enjoying the whirring sound as the shredder did its work. Only then did she go back upstairs and fall asleep.

The next morning, Kate and Tristan drove to Bristol where they met Vicky O'Grady for lunch at The Mall at Cribbs Causeway. They were half an hour early, and found the fancy Italian restaurant Vicky had suggested.

'She chose somewhere expensive,' said Tristan, when they'd been seated in the smart restaurant next to a huge window looking down at the teeming food court below. 'It would be much cheaper down there.'

'We couldn't have a decent conversation at the food court,' said Kate. 'This is good. Quiet.'

'Jeez. Fourteen quid for a glass of red wine!' whistled Tristan. 'Do you want me to hide the wine list?'

'No. The aim of this meeting is to get information,' said Kate.

'Do you want to get her tanked up on booze, in case she talks more?' Tristan was for the most part a mature young man, but there were occasional flashes of a twenty-one-year-old.

'We need to make her feel relaxed and see what happens,' said Kate.

Just then a large lady wearing a bright floral dress was brought to their table by the waiter. She had an immaculate bob of brown hair, dramatic smoky eye make-up and designer shades on her head.

'Hello? Kate and Tristan?' she asked. 'I'm Victoria.' She was very well spoken and confident. They got up and shook hands.

'Is it Vicky or Victoria?' asked Kate when they were seated again.

'I haven't been Vicky since school,' she said, pouring olive oil onto her side plate, adding a dot of balsamic vinegar and mopping it up with one of the bread rolls the waiter had brought over in a woven basket.

They made a little small talk, and ordered. Kate could see Tristan was relieved Victoria didn't order champagne – sticking to tonic water. Tristan and Kate had the same.

'So, the mystery of Caitlyn Murray?' she said after the waiter delivered their drinks.

'You said in your messages with Tristan that you'd expected to get a call about her from a private investigator?' asked Kate.

'Well, perhaps I was being a little over-dramatic ... Only because the police at the time did so little. They didn't seem to talk to anyone. They came in a few days after she'd vanished and told us that a police officer would be in school all that day in case any of us had anything to tell them. I don't know how many girls went to talk to them.'

'Did you talk to them?'

'Yes, I told them the little that I knew, but I never heard from them again,' she said, grabbing another bread roll and tearing it in two. There was something off about the way she answered. *Was it guilt?* wondered Kate.

'You worked with Caitlyn at your father's video shop?' asked Tristan.

'One of *six* video shops, thank you very much. Daddy was the north of England's top franchisee.'

'Did Caitlyn have a boyfriend?'

'No one special,' said Victoria. 'There were a few suitors in the mix. Like any young girl of sixteen she was *quite* the little shagger.'

A look passed between Kate and Tristan.

'She had several boyfriends?' asked Kate.

'No one serious. There was a lad who delivered soft drinks to the newsagent next door . . . A delicious blond with a washboard stomach, very Abercrombie & Fitch. We were both guilty of sleeping with him . . . He looked a bit like you,' said Victoria, fixing Tristan with a beady stare. He shifted uncomfortably in his seat and poured himself more water. Victoria had the breezy confidence of someone from the upper class.

'Can I ask where Caitlyn met with this delivery lad?' asked Kate.

'He delivered drinks and popcorn to the video shop. One lunchtime, when Caitlyn went out for some food, he was all flirty. I was a thin slip of a girl back then, with tits like rocks. It was all over in ten minutes, but rather fun . . . A couple of weeks later I came back early from lunch to find Caitlyn and him at it in the same place . . . Up until then I'd thought she was a little prim and frigid, but we bonded over the sexy delivery lad.'

'Are you sure you're happy to talk about this?' asked Kate, who was surprised the conversation had taken on such a confessional tone before the first course had even arrived. Victoria waved it away with her third bread roll.

'Of course. Although I seem to be making young Tristan uncomfortable.'

'No. I'm good,' he said, trying to hide his annoyance. He

looked pleased when the food arrived. Kate and Victoria had ordered the spaghetti carbonara, and Tristan the macaroni cheese with a breadcrumb crust.

'This is scrumptious,' said Victoria as they tucked into their food. Kate was finding her difficult to read. Everything seemed so breezy and confident and jolly hockey sticks.

'There's one thing about Caitlyn's disappearance that's really troubling us,' said Kate. She went on to explain that Megan Hibbert had seen a man picking up Caitlyn from the youth club in a brand new Rover.

'Well, I never went to this Carter's youth club,' said Victoria through a large mouthful of spaghetti. 'I remember the three scholarship girls talking about it – Wendy, Megan and Caitlyn. The youth club sounded ghastly, but that was probably Paul who picked her up.'

Kate felt Tristan's knee press against hers under the table.

'I'm sorry. Paul? Paul who?' asked Kate.

'Paul Adler. He was a police officer for a couple of years, a very good one too, but he was attacked on the beat one night. Two thugs with a knife jumped him and he lost an eye . . . he had a glass eye made, a very good one. It almost exactly matches his real one.'

Kate and Tristan had expected her to describe Peter Conway, but now she had veered off in another direction.

'You knew this Paul Adler?' asked Kate, unable to hide her disbelief.

'Yes, well, I knew of him. He owned Adler's the chemist two doors down from Hollywood Nights, where myself and Caitlyn worked. He took the compensation he got from the accident and opened up the chemist, or should I say pharmacy. He bought the building, so he had that and all the shops paying him rent. He became very well off. He used to stop by and rent videos,' said Victoria.

'Do you still see him?'

'Good lord, no, me and him are all in the past.'

'Did you have a relationship with him?'

'No!'

Kate wanted to press her more on this – her reaction had been so quick and vehement – but she needed to concentrate on Paul Adler and Caitlyn.

'How long were Paul and Caitlyn an item?' she asked.

'I don't think they were an item. He was married, still is, but they used to go off for "drives",' Victoria said, indicating inverted commas with her fingers. 'He was quite eligible. He always used to get the new registration cars the day they came out each year. He was the first to have the new H-reg car in the area.'

'A friend of Caitlyn said she saw Caitlyn talking to a bloke in a new H-reg car,' said Tristan. He took out his mobile and found the picture of Peter Conway. 'Did you ever see Caitlyn with this man?' He held up the photo.

Victoria took a sip of her tonic water and almost choked. It took her a moment to compose herself. 'Sorry,' she said wiping at her chin with a napkin. 'You surprised me. That's Peter Conway, the whatsit, the cannibal killer ... Why on earth have you got that picture?' She pulled a conspiratorial face at Kate. 'Who else's photo has he got on that phone? Jack the Ripper? You are a naughty boy!'

'I'm showing you because we think Peter Conway may have been involved in Caitlyn's disappearance,' said Tristan.

'He was a police officer in Greater Manchester in 1990,' added Kate.

Victoria sat back in her chair, chastised. 'I know all this. I do read the newspapers ... And I wasn't Caitlyn's nursemaid. I rather think I gave her confidence to chat up men. That's all. She did the rest.'

'Peter Conway never came into the video shop?' asked Kate.

'I can't remember everyone who came in, and I only worked there part-time!'

'Do you think Paul Adler could have known Peter Conway?' asked Tristan.

'Absolutely not! No, no, no,' Victoria said. She saw her glass was empty and called the waiter over and ordered another.

'You said you haven't seen Paul Adler in years. How could you be so sure?' asked Kate.

'Well, we've spoken over the years, and it came up in conversation. Peter Conway worked in the area, and there's been all those rumours about if there were previous victims . . . You have to remember the police force in Manchester is big, and Paul told me that he never came into contact with Conway.'

The waiter brought over her drink. She had become flustered and fumbled in her bag. She removed a bottle of pills and had trouble with the lid. Tristan took it from her, twisted it off and handed it back.

'Thank you, blood pressure medication, forgot to take it.' She popped a pill in her mouth and swallowed it with a gulp of tonic water. 'I wish I could go back to my young svelte sixteen-year-old self and *shake her* for thinking she was fat.'

'Okay, so you think it was Paul Adler who picked Caitlyn up that night from the youth club?' asked Kate. 'This would have been late July, early August 1990. And it was definitely an H-reg Rover.'

Victoria rolled her eyes. 'I feel like we're going around in circles. It certainly sounds like Paul Adler. He's on Facebook, and I think he's got a picture of his younger self on his profile.' She had pulled a powder compact from her bag and was reapplying her lipstick. It seemed she had had enough and wanted to go.

'Do you have Paul Adler's details?' asked Kate. 'I'd like to get in contact with him.'

'Erm, I'm not really comfortable giving out other people's phone numbers without their consent,' she said, snapping the lid back on her lipstick.

But you're happy to label Caitlyn, who is missing and presumed dead, as 'quite the little shagger', thought Kate.

'We're going to look him up anyway, and I just want to ask him a few questions. He might know something useful.' Kate smiled and didn't break eye contact.

Victoria turned and unhooked her bag from the back of her chair, taking out a small silver address book. She flicked through pages and pages until she found an address. 'Here we are. Paul Adler.' She gave Kate his details. 'You know, the police spoke to him about Caitlyn going missing, and he had a cast-iron alibi. He was in France with his wife on the day Caitlyn disappeared. They have a place out there, Le Touquet. He's a nice family man.'

Kate felt her heart sinking into her boots. 'Why didn't you say so before?' she asked.

'I didn't think Paul Adler would be a suspect.'

'Can you give us a list of any other men who Caitlyn was involved with?'

'Four that I know of. The drinks lad. Another young lad who delivered the videos each week, the new releases. He was barely eighteen and, again, blond ... I don't know their names or their addresses. They were fun, silly boys.' She faltered for a moment. 'And, er, she slept with my father ... That's why myself and Caitlyn fell out in the end. Shagging around is all well and good, but you don't shit where you eat. And Caitlyn was stupid enough to think I would turn a blind eye.'

'Where was your father the day Caitlyn went missing?' asked Tristan.

Victoria turned to him, all her faux jolliness gone. 'At a wedding,' she said, her smile now thin. 'My whole family was at the wedding, in case you want to know where I was too. My cousin Harriet Farrington got married in Surrey. Leatherhead church . . . I know Sunday is an unusual day for a wedding.' She saw Tristan and Kate exchange a look. 'I have photos, if you need me to prove it.'

'Yes. If you could send them, thank you,' said Kate, matching her thin smile.

On the way home in the car Kate and Tristan were quiet until they reached the outskirts of Ashdean. It was grey and had started to rain.

'I didn't get a good vibe off Victoria,' said Kate. 'She was very nervous.'

'That pill she took wasn't for blood pressure. It was Xanax. I saw the bottle,' said Tristan.

'She could just be a person who suffers from nervous anxiety.'

'She seemed completely different in her messages,' said Tristan. 'I didn't like her in person. There was something a bit weird about her.'

'Well, being a bit weird isn't enough evidence. If it was this Paul Adler who was seen outside the youth club with Caitlyn,' said Kate, 'he has an alibi, and Victoria's father has an alibi. So who else is there?'

'The lads who delivered stuff to the video shop. We could track them down,' said Tristan. 'And we need to show Paul Adler's picture to Megan in Australia.'

'Why didn't Malcolm and Sheila know about the boyfriends, the boys?' asked Kate gloomily, taking a left turn onto the coast road.

'What parent knows everything about their teenage son or daughter?' said Tristan.

'Oh, lord, I've got all that to come with Jake.'

'Wouldn't the police have told Malcolm and Sheila, if they'd known?'

'Probably not. They might not have been assigned a family liaison officer who would give them this information.'

'What do we do now?'

'We need to do our due diligence. We need to follow up everything we've looked into. The teacher, the other girls in the school. And I want to talk to this Paul Adler, if only to confirm what Victoria said.'

Over the next four days Kate and Tristan managed to track down Caitlyn's teacher and the other girls in her class, none of whom were able to add anything new to the investigation. Kate also called in a favour from Alan Hexham, asking him to look into Paul Adler. Victoria's version of events checked out. He had been a police officer and retired with a commendation in 1988 after an attack where he lost an eye. At the time of Caitlyn's vanishing he was questioned by the police, because Caitlyn passed Adler's Chemist on her route to the cinema, but he had been out of the country the day she went missing.

Kate had a look at Paul Adler's Facebook profile and found an older photo of him and sent it to Megan Hibbert in Melbourne. She messaged back and confirmed he was the man in the H-reg Rover she'd seen picking up Caitlyn outside Carter's youth club.

On Thursday morning Malcolm sent Kate an email, asking how things were going. Kate knew their leads had gone cold.

It seemed Caitlyn had vanished into thin air.

CHAPTER 23

The Carmichael Grammar School's sports field was set back behind the school and backed onto the edge of Dartmoor. Thursday afternoon was cold, and at around 5 p.m. the light was fading enough for the coach of the school hockey team to switch on the floodlights for the first time since the spring.

Layla Gerrard was easily the best hockey player and the most popular girl on the team. She was small but wiry and strong. She had a burst of freckles across her nose and cheeks, and wore her long strawberry-blonde hair in a thick plait. After practice, the girls went back to the warm changing rooms, pulled on sweaters and tracksuits, and packed up their sports bags and hockey sticks. Most of the team made their way back to the school building, but Layla and Ginny Robinson, who both travelled home by bus, left the school fields by a small gate behind the changing rooms.

Layla usually walked part of the way home with Ginny, who was rather posh. Layla liked her though; she was a good player and their mutual love of hockey overcame their differences. Once they were out of the floodlit field, they were swallowed by the darkness, walking along a thin path bordering the train tracks, which came out onto a main road. The nights had been drawing in for some weeks, but this was the first evening that they made this journey after the sun had set. They felt secure walking in a pair, and they each carried a hockey stick. As they walked, they munched on protein bars and chatted about their coming match on Saturday.

As they reached the main road, the bell sounded and the railway barriers came down. A train rumbled out of the trees and over the crossing. The girls took advantage of the red lights and crossed the road. On the other side they parted company. Ginny carried along the main road to her bus stop, and Layla turned off on a residential street. She hunched down in her fleece, feeling the cold air stinging her bare legs.

The street was pleasant, one of the posher areas of town, and lights glowed in the windows behind curtains. Layla checked her watch and picked up the pace, seeing that her bus was due in less than five minutes. The side of the road was lined with cars where the residents parked, and a couple of cars pulled into vacant spaces as she passed. A man in a suit carrying a bunch of roses got out and hurried up the steps to a front door with big white pillars, and a woman with a small boy and girl emerged from the other car, the children whining that they weren't allowed fish and chips for their tea.

'You can have them tomorrow, now shut up!' said the woman. She followed along behind Layla, with the children whining and dragging their feet.

'I don't want to eat steamed vegetables,' the little girl was saying.

Layla smiled, remembering the protracted torture of being made to eat her greens as a little kid. She looked back as the little boy dropped the school satchel he was carrying.

'Pick that up! The ground is wet!' his mother trilled. Layla thought how much she was looking forward to Friday, when her dad always got fish and chips on the way home from work.

*

There was a railway bridge with an underpass, which cut through to another residential street close to her bus stop. It was now dark, and the underpass up ahead was poorly lit, but with the family following behind, Layla felt more comfortable taking this shortcut to her bus stop.

But just as Layla entered the underpass, the mother and her children took a right into the gate of a house and their voices dropped away. The noise from the surrounding street was muffled and Layla's feet echoed in the enclosed space. It was dank and stank of urine, and she hurried on to the other end. She emerged at the end of another residential street. Next to the arches of the underpass was an overgrown play park and a large house whose windows were in darkness. There were no streetlights, and at first she didn't see the black van parked at the kerb in the shadows.

Just as she came level with it, the side door slid open and a tall man dressed head to toe in black reached out and clamped a square of surgical cotton over her nose and mouth. His other arm encircled her shoulders in a powerful grip, and he yanked her off her feet and bundled her into the van. It happened smoothly. There was a brief moment where her hockey stick caught on the edge of the door, but he pivoted her around deftly.

The back of the van was empty apart from a small mattress. They went down soundlessly, hitting the mattress together. The man used his weight to keep Layla still for the fifteen seconds it took the drug soaked into the cotton over her nose to take effect, and for that brief moment she fought back, writhing, until the drug hit her system and she went limp.

The street was quiet, and in the dark pool of shadows by the underpass no one saw the gloved hand drop Layla's mobile phone into the drain by the van.

The door slid closed with a soft click, and a moment later the engine started and the van moved along the quiet residential street, joining the traffic at the main road and heading towards Exeter.

CHAPTER 24

On Friday, Kate woke when it was still dark and, skipping her usual morning swim, left her house very early to drive up to Altrincham on the outskirts of Manchester. For an hour the sun struggled to come up, and when the dawn finally broke, only an eerie grey light filtered through the clouds. With the light came the rain, hammering on the car roof as she crossed the hills and moors. She arrived just before lunchtime, and was starving when she drove through Altrincham.

She'd phoned Paul Adler the day before, and he'd been very helpful and amiable on the phone, answering all of her questions. He had even offered to meet her in person at the pharmacy, which he still owned, to give her some photos he had of Caitlyn. Kate was dreading having to go back to Malcolm and Sheila, but she thought she'd take one last roll of the dice and go up and have a look at where Caitlyn lived, and collect the photos. It was something. On the way back she would call in to see them in Chew Magna.

Tristan had a 'performance review meeting' with Ashdean University's HR department. He had been working as Kate's assistant for three months now, and on her recommendation, he would be made a permanent member of staff. It was a meeting he couldn't miss. Kate had promised that she would call him with any updates.

Kate grabbed a sandwich from a petrol station and wolfed it down in her car. She then drove to her first stop, the house where Malcolm and Sheila had lived when Caitlyn went missing. Altrincham was quite a smart, well-heeled little suburb of Greater Manchester. Their old house was a small, modern terrace, and was now a solicitor's office for a company called BD and Sons Ltd. It had recently been renovated and had gleaming sash windows with the name of the firm stencilled onto the glass. The black soot had been sandblasted away from the bricks to reveal their original biscuit colour. The front garden was now a small car park. Kate got out of her car and stood on the pavement for several minutes, staring at the house and willing some kind of feeling or insight. She tried to imagine Caitlyn leaving the house or returning after school, but nothing came to her, so she got back in her car and drove on.

Her next stop was the church hall where Carter's youth club had been. It was demolished in 2001, and now it was part of a vast distribution centre which ran half the length of the street. As Kate stood outside, watching huge lorries come and go, she wondered what had happened to the river that ran past the back of the youth club. The corrugated building seemed to cover acres.

It was just before 2 p.m. when she pulled up at Paul Adler's pharmacy, which was a couple of miles from Caitlyn's old house. It was at the end of a parade of shops which also housed a Costa Coffee and two estate agents. A large red fluorescent sign spelled out ADLER'S CHEMIST above the door. A long line of huge multi-coloured apothecary bottles filled a window display on one side, and they were covered in dust.

A bell on the door rang when Kate went inside, and there was a pleasant antiseptic smell and library hush that older chemists seem to have. There was a polished wood floor and countertops, and a couple of old ladies at the counter speaking in low tones to a very young girl behind the till. The rattle of a prescription being filled came through a hatch at the back.

The pharmacy also sold cosmetics, and Kate browsed the make-up and waited until the old ladies were gone. She went to the till and told the young girl wearing a white smock that she had an appointment to see Paul Adler.

'I'll just see if he's available,' replied the girl. She was doll-like, thin and blonde with huge eyes. She spoke with a small, almost squeaky voice. She went out back and returned moments later with a tall, broad, greying man. He had put on weight and was a little stooped, but Kate recognised him from his photo as Paul Adler.

'Hello, pleased to meet you,' he said, coming to shake her hand.

'Thank you for seeing me,' said Kate. He held onto her hand, clasping it in both of his. His eyes were clear and strikingly blue as he looked down at her. Kate only noticed the false eye when he glanced over at the girl behind the counter. 'Tina. We'll be in the back. Please don't disturb us.'

'Of course, Mr Adler,' she said meekly.

'Come this way,' he said, releasing Kate's hand. He led her through a door at the rear of the room and down a dimly lit wood-panelled corridor, past a closed door on the left and an open door, which was the pharmacy proper, where medication was stored in a wall lined with drawers.

Two young women were inside, and they were similar in appearance to Tina – small and pretty with long blonde hair. They were making up prescriptions, working in complete silence, and they looked away when Kate passed. At the end of the corridor was a smart little staff kitchen with a wooden table and chairs. A glass door looked out onto a small loading bay.

'Please, sit,' said Paul. He closed the door. Kate pulled up a chair next to the glass door and sat. 'Would you like coffee?'

'Thank you. Black, no sugar,' said Kate. With the door closed, the room felt even smaller. 'You've kept all the original features of the shop out front. It reminds me of the chemists I went to as a child.'

'It's all being ripped out next month. I'm having a new shop-front, new wiring and a digital security system put in. I only have cameras on the till and in the dispensary, and they still use VHS,' said Paul. 'Here are the photos,' he added, picking up a packet of prints that were next to a capsule coffee maker. He dropped them onto the table and started to fuss with the machine. Kate opened it and found six photos, all taken of Caitlyn on a bright, sunny day. She had posed for the pictures in a field of buttercups. She wore a long, white dress and had a chain of daisies on her head.

'She was beautiful,' said Kate as she flicked through. Paul didn't answer. There was a whirr as the coffee machine finished and he brought the cups over. He pulled a chair out and sat opposite.

'You kept the photos? Was she special to you?' asked Kate.

'Listen, I'm happy to answer any questions, but I don't appreciate being under suspicion,' he said. His voice was soft with a tinge of menace.

'You're not under suspicion. I told you I've been hired by Caitlyn's parents to clear up a few questions . . . and it was more of an observation, as to why you kept the photos?'

'I used to process photos here, back in the day before we all went digital. Some of my clients were actors and modelling agencies. They would pay me a fee to keep negatives on file for reprints. I kept the negatives of Caitlyn for memory's sake. I was being an old softie,' he said.

Kate thought the way he loomed over her with his unseeing eye didn't conjure the image of him as 'an old softie'.

The door suddenly opened and Tina entered with a bag of rubbish.

'Oh, sorry, Mr Adler,' she said.

'Go ahead,' he said. His chair was pulled out, and he didn't move, so she was forced to squeeze past him. She opened the glass door and went out to the loading bay. The door closed behind her. Kate watched her cross to a large rubbish bin filled with bags. She tossed the bag onto the pile and came back.

'It's a revenue stream I greatly miss, photo processing,' said Paul, turning his attention back to the photos of Caitlyn. Tina came back to the door and tapped four numbers into a security keypad. She mouthed the numbers as she punched them in: *one, three, four, six*. The door clicked open.

Paul tilted his head to look at a photo of Caitlyn leaning against a tree, smiling at the camera with her back arched.

Tina squeezed past Paul, and he waited until she was out of the room, then shifted his chair so he was sitting with his back against the door out to the pharmacy.

'I'd just got married when I had the affair with Caitlyn. She was, er, tasty, shall we say . . . ' He smiled, and it was made more unnerving because it didn't reach his right eye.

'Where did you take these photos of Caitlyn?' asked Kate.

'Out near Salford. There was a nice walk you could do, and go swimming in the lake. We used to go skinny dipping.' He raised an eyebrow suggestively. Kate felt alarm bells going off. She was shut in this room, at the end of the corridor. The door was closed, and he was sitting halfway across it.

'When was this?' she asked, forcing herself to stay calm.

He blew out his cheeks. 'June of 1990. It's all gone. There's a new housing estate there.'

Kate nodded. 'And the video shop where you met Caitlyn?'

'It was just on the other end of this row, where the Tesco is . . . ' He knocked back his coffee in one.

'You didn't see anything or anyone around Caitlyn who was odd or strange?'

'When?'

'The times you met?'

He shook his head. 'I've never lost my copper's instinct. You must have it still too?'

Kate nodded. He stared at her again.

'Are you sure I can take these photos? Caitlyn's parents will want to know where they came from.'

'Perhaps you should leave out the part about the affair.' He smiled and shook his head. 'It's best kept in the past. I have a good marriage.'

'Of course. The photos don't show you in them. I'm glad we found you through Victoria. It's cleared up a line of enquiry.'

Kate just wanted out of the tiny little room. She could smell Paul's sweat, but she knew her next question was the most important. 'Did you ever meet Peter Conway? He was a police officer in Greater Manchester at the time when Caitlyn went missing.'

'No. I never knew him. Our time didn't overlap. Terrible man. Did terrible things.' He shook his head.

'Did any of your colleagues know him?'

He blew out his cheeks and tilted his head back.

'I only ever heard people talk about him after you caught him and, like you, they'd always thought he was a great police officer. He fooled you all, by the sound of it.' He looked at her for a moment, a mocking smile twitching at his lips. 'Would you like more coffee? Although you haven't touched that one.'

'No, thank you.' She stood. 'I'd better be going.'

Paul looked surprised that she was leaving. Kate moved around the small table to the door. There was a long pause when she thought he wasn't going to move, but he then heaved himself up off his chair and, to her relief, opened the door.

As they walked along the corridor and back to the front of the shop, Kate saw the door opposite the pharmacy was now open. It was a storeroom with shelves of folders, a large photo-processing machine and a stack of old promotional branding signs for cosmetics. The sign on top said ONE HOUR PHOTO and it was written inside a stopwatch.

'Thank you,' said Kate when they were back in the front of the shop.

Paul put out his hand, and she shook it. 'Anything else, don't hesitate to call me,' he said, holding on to her hand a little too long.

It was raining when she came out onto the pavement, and as she looked back Paul was standing in the window, next to a revolving display of reading glasses, staring at her. She nodded and hurried away, shaken, but not quite able to put her finger on why. Was it the glass eye that gave her the creeps? Or did he enjoy dominating women? The three young women who worked in the pharmacy seemed so subservient and quiet. But he was in the clear. He had an alibi.

Kate left Altrincham just before three, and it was dark when she arrived in Chew Magna. The uneasy feeling hadn't left her as she drove. Almost every place from Caitlyn's past was gone, apart from that creepy pharmacy, which felt trapped in time.

As she reached the end of the dirt track to Malcolm and Sheila's cottage, flashing blue lights bounced off the surrounding houses. A siren blared and an ambulance came shooting out of the dirt track and turned off to the left at high speed, streaking away in a blare of sirens.

'Shit,' said Kate. She turned into the track and when she reached the end, she saw an old woman with white hair coming out of Malcolm and Sheila's cottage. Kate wound down her window, and the woman came over.

'I'm here to see Malcolm and Sheila. Are they okay?'

'It's Sheila. She collapsed and she's in a coma,' the woman said.

'I'm Kate Marshall . . .'

'Oh yes. You're the private investigator they hired to look into Caitlyn going missing? Have you any news?' Her lined face brightened briefly.

Kate still didn't feel comfortable calling herself a private investigator, especially when her investigation seemed to be going nowhere. 'I was due to deliver it,' she said, holding up the file she and Tristan had put together. 'I'm afraid we've drawn a blank.'

The woman shook her head sadly. 'I'm Harriet Dent, neighbour and friend. Do you want me to give Malcolm the file?' She didn't seem keen, and Kate could imagine she didn't want to be the bearer of bad news.

'No. Thank you. I'll hold onto it,' said Kate. 'Can I give you my number? I'd like to know when Sheila is better.' She scribbled it on a piece of paper and Harriet took it.

'It's not looking good for Sheila. She's been waiting for a donor for three years. We all had tests to see if we were a match.' She shook her head. She held up the piece of paper. 'I'll phone you when I know more.'

Kate watched as the old woman picked her way down the muddy lane back to her house, and then she set off on the long journey home.

CHAPTER 25

Layla Gerrard felt a throbbing pain throughout her whole body, like a hangover mixed with dehydration. It was pitch black, and she had stared into the darkness so hard it felt as if her eyes were going to fall out of her head.

She had woken several times in darkness and was trying to piece it all together. She was strong, and had always thought she could look after herself in a fight, but it had happened so quickly. The man – he smelled like a man – had been dressed in black. She'd seen a flash of a woollen balaclava, eyes glittering and a full mouth with wet red lips, but it had been so fast.

She remembered being on the road with the kids behind her, and going down that underpass thinking they were following her. The underpass always gave her the creeps, but for the past few months it had always been light on her way home.

She didn't know how much time had passed. All she wore was her underwear. Her hands and feet were bound tightly, and she could feel a cold damp concrete floor underneath her back. Her mouth was filled with some kind of rag or bundle of cloth, and taped over. She had fought her fear of the man coming back, almost as much as the fear of choking on the bundle of rags. The drug he'd used to knock her out had made her nauseous.

Her panic ran in cycles, and each time it threatened to

consume her, the blood pulsed painfully through a huge lump on the side of her head, wanting to burst out. Had he hit her? Or did she hit something when she was dragged into the van?

There was a crashing sound, far away, which seemed to echo around, giving her the first indication that the place where she lay was somewhere big, with a high ceiling. Three times she had woken to hear a soft far away click-clack of a train on tracks.

There was a rolling sound, like a large sliding door being pulled back, and a crash. Without warning, lights came on above. Her pupils contracted and she closed her eyes, wincing. Footsteps came towards her, and she felt a freezing gust of air.

'Open your eyes,' said a man's voice. It was well spoken with a ring of authority. He didn't sound angry. 'Open your eyes, please.'

She felt a kick in her ribs. The pain focused her and she managed to open her eyes. She lay in the middle of a large warehouse, with rows of strip lights above against a curved metal roof. The floor was concrete, and the walls were clean and made of old red bricks. Along one of the back walls was parked a row of six black vans, all bearing the logo 'CM Logistics'. This was different to the dank dungeon she had imagined in the long hours of darkness.

A man stood above her, tall and broad in a smart blue suit. He had short red hair, and Layla recoiled at his large wet lips and almost rubbery features. He wore a black leather glove on his right hand. His left hand was behind his back.

The man came closer and stood over her. Vapour streamed from his mouth and nose. He crouched down and took his left hand from behind his back. He held a long sharp knife. Layla winced and whimpered as he moved closer and grabbed her legs. She angled her body, scraping the backs of her legs and wrists on the floor as she tried to push away.

He tilted his head and looked at her face, then abruptly let her go and moved away into the shadows. He returned carrying a six-pack of water bottles by a plastic handle. Using the knife, he carved the plastic away and released a bottle, throwing the rest across the warehouse. He brought the bottle to her. She was moving away, edging towards the back wall.

'Stay still,' he said, putting his hand on her belly. He placed the bottle beside her head. 'If you scream, I'll cut your throat.' He tore off the tape on her mouth and pulled out the rags, keeping the knife pointed at her face. She swallowed and gulped in air. 'I'm serious. If you scream, I'll slit you open.' His voice was calm, almost like a newsreader's. Layla nodded, her eyes wide. He picked up the bottle and opened it. Cradling her chin with the knife hand, he tilted the bottle to her mouth. 'Drink.'

She didn't take her eyes off him and gulped at the water as he poured, coughing and sputtering as it went over her lips and nose. She didn't realise how thirsty she was and she drank half the bottle.

He set the bottle down, the knife still hovering beside her head. The water had given her hope. He wanted her to stay alive. He smiled at her. It was a broad, warm smile, but his eyes were malevolent. His teeth were so white. Like a Hollywood smile. He placed his foot under her side and flipped her over. She landed painfully on her front on the cold concrete, yelping.

'Sorry,' she said, hating herself for her subservience, but she knew it was hopeless to fight him.

'If you scream,' he said in a low voice.

'I won't ... I promise,' she started to say but he forced the rag back into her mouth. Her mind was racing. What was this place? It looked like it belonged to a delivery company. The parked vans meant there could be delivery drivers arriving. Maybe one would hear her, or save her?

For a moment she didn't know what he was doing as he bent over her. Then she felt his breath on the back of her left thigh, his wet rubbery lips next to her flesh and his teeth as they sank into her skin. The pain was terrible as he bit down. He grunted and twisted his head from left to right, like a dog with a piece of meat. He bit down harder. The pain almost made her black out as his head snapped back, pulling a chunk of her flesh free. He spat it out beside her and she felt the warmth of her blood running down her thigh. She screamed and writhed but he held her down and his mouth and teeth moved up to her lower back.

He knows no one is coming. He knows he has me all to himself, she thought desperately. And then the pain was so bad that she felt everything fade to black, and she passed out.

CHAPTER 26

Tristan went to a friend's wedding over the weekend, and Kate spent Saturday and half of Sunday catching up on university work she'd missed during the previous week's investigations. It was tough to refocus her mind on the day job. She had no resources, and had drawn a blank with Caitlyn. She knew she had probably made things worse for Malcolm and Sheila. She should never have agreed to help them and get their hopes up. She heard nothing from Malcolm over the weekend, which made her think the worst.

Sunday afternoon was brightened by coffee and a walk with Myra on the beach, then a Skype call with Jake. Kate didn't see Tristan until Monday afternoon, when they met in Starbucks and she brought him up to speed on everything that had happened in Altrincham.

'And Paul Adler insists he didn't know Peter Conway?' asked Tristan.

'Yes. I've already had Alan Hexham pull files on Caitlyn and Paul. He left the force before Peter Conway joined, although of course that doesn't mean he didn't know him,' said Kate.

Tristan pulled a face.

'What?'

He bit his lip. 'Would you ever consider visiting Peter Conway?'

'No. And he would have to send me a visiting order. And that won't happen.'

'Has he ever sent you one?'

'Never. Tristan, I'm the reason he's locked up.'

Tristan nodded. 'You're the badass who caught him!'

Kate smiled. Her phone rang.

'It's Alan. I'll kill him if he's cancelling his lecture on Thursday . . .' She answered the call, and listened. She checked her watch. 'Okay. We'll be there as soon as possible.'

'What?' asked Tristan when she came off the phone.

'Another body's been found, on Higher Tor near Belstone. A young woman, dumped naked with bites and a bag over her head.'

When Kate and Tristan arrived at the edge of Dartmoor forty minutes later, the light was fading. They drove through the small village of Belstone, and then they hit the moorland and the road became a gravel track lined with drystone walls. The vast moorland was eerie in the twilight. They drove for a mile or so, and then the rocky hill formation of Higher Tor came into view, just visible against the darkening sky. At its base were a group of police cars and a van.

There was a gate in the drystone wall, and Kate drove through it and parked the car on a patch of rough ground next to it. A police car was parked on the moor a little way back from the gate. Kate switched off the engine and they got out. The police officer in the squad car was in the middle of eating a Cornish pasty. He looked up when they approached, and wound down his window.

'Good evening,' said Kate. 'We've been asked to attend by the forensic pathologist, Alan Hexham.' She hoped that Alan was still in charge of the crime scene, and hadn't yet handed over control to the police. The officer swallowed and reluctantly put down the pasty, wiping his mouth.

'I'll need some ID,' he said. They scrabbled around for their driving licences and handed them through the window. He took the licences, and then closed his window.

'You're certain Alan asked me to come too?' said Tristan, as the police officer peered at their driving licences and murmured something into his radio.

'Yes.'

There was a whirr and the police officer's car window opened.

'I can't get hold of him. Have you got a warrant card, either of you? I'm just trying to work out why you're here.'

'We're not police,' said Kate. He looked over at her mud-splattered car by the gate and his face became stern.

'You're not press? Because I can have you for wasting police time.'

'We're private investigators,' said Kate. It felt odd to say it out loud. She was a university lecturer, an academic. There was a difference between advising the police and becoming a full-blown private investigator, but the latter made her independent. She wished she had a card. 'I'm a former DC,' she added. 'I worked on the Nine Elms Cannibal case. Dr Hexham asked me and my associate to attend the crime scene because we've been sharing information about the murders of Emma Newman and Kaisha Smith. Dr Hexham believes this murder is linked.'

The officer looked at their driving licences again. There was a burst of static and Kate heard Alan's voice come over the radio.

'This is Dr Hexham. I requested Kate Marshall attend with her associate, please let them through.'

'Go on then,' said the police officer, putting the radio down and picking up his half eaten Cornish pasty. 'You'll need to sign in at the crime scene.'

Kate and Tristan set off towards the police cars. On either

side of them the moors stretched out with gorse and scrub, now bathed in long shadows in the fading light.

'Do you think it will smell bad, the body?' asked Tristan, looking at the dark shape of the Tor up ahead.

Kate looked over at him. 'I don't know. You've never seen a dead body before?'

He shook his head.

'Do you want to go back to the car?'

'No. No, I'll be fine,' he said. He didn't sound too sure.

A police cordon was set up in front of the police cars, and they were met by a police officer who signed them in, and a woman from the crime scene investigation team.

'I'll need you to put on coveralls,' she said, holding a pair out to each of them.

Tristan gulped. Kate put an arm on his shoulder. 'I won't judge you if you want to go back,' she said quietly.

'No. No. I'm coming up there with you. Final answer.'

He steeled himself as they pulled on their coveralls. When they were ready, the CSI officer took them up the rocky slope to the tor. As they drew close, it towered above them and reminded Kate of a stack of pebbles left by a giant. To the right of the tor, a small square forensics canopy had been erected over a circle of rocks.

Alan was briefing a group of police officers in coveralls, which included Varia Campbell and John Mercy. Varia turned when Kate and Tristan arrived, and her face clouded over.

'Good evening. Thanks for allowing us to attend, Dr Hexham,' said Kate.

'Good evening. I've only just started,' said Alan, towering above them all in his white coveralls. Kate and Tristan moved closer and saw there was a depression in the circle of rocks. The naked body of a young woman lay on her side. She was filthy and spattered in blood. Three crime scene officers were working around her, two taking soil samples and the third assisting the crime scene photographer.

'Jesus,' said Tristan. He put a hand over his mouth and gave a loud retch.

'Is he a puker?' Alan asked Kate. 'We'll have contamination to deal with if he pukes next to the crime scene.'

'No. I'm fine, sir,' said Tristan, wincing and swallowing.

'Maybe a sick bag would be wise,' said Kate, putting her hand on his back.

One of the CSIs handed Tristan a paper bag. A couple of the male officers smirked. Kate felt protective of Tristan, but she didn't say any more. Tristan looked embarrassed enough.

Alan went on: 'Right, for the benefit of former Detective Constable Marshall, who has just joined us with her associate, I believe – but don't quote me – that the cause of death is asphyxiation. We have a plastic bag over the head, and her face and neck are covered in petechial haemorrhages. Note the *type* of plastic bag and the knot on the twine or rope. A drawstring bag, tied with a monkey's fist knot. She is posed: on her left side, right arm out, head resting on the forearm.'

The crime scene photographer punctuated this by firing off a photo. The flash lit up the body in the circle of stones and the rocky side of the huge tor.

'If we can turn her over, please,' said Alan.

The CSIs gently turned the body over, face down onto a waiting black PVC body bag. The camera flash went off again, and a gust of wind blew across the dark moor, causing the material of the forensics tent to crackle.

'Yes. And that's the last piece of the puzzle. You'll see one, two, three, four, five, *six* bites on the back; two on the left side of the spine, two on the right, and two on the upper right-hand thigh. One of the thigh bites on the right-hand side is very deep.' Alan moved closer to the body. 'Time of death is more recent than for the other victims. I can give you the exact time of death when I conduct my post-mortem, but these look fresh enough for me to have a crack at getting bite impressions back in the lab.'

Kate looked over at Tristan. He had a hand up to his mouth again. He shook his head and moved off back down the hill. The photographer fired off another couple of shots.

Alan crouched down next to the girl's feet. 'The question is, *how* did she make it up here? There's nothing to show she was dragged barefoot, nothing on the heels or toes, no grass or plant fibres. Any more information will come from the post-mortem.'

The CSIs set to work, bagging up the body and transferring her from the rocky pit into the van. Varia came over to Alan with a clipboard.

'Thank you for letting us attend,' said Kate to Alan.

'This is number three. I hope people start taking this seriously,' he replied.

'I take any murder scene seriously,' said Varia, holding out the clipboard and a pen. 'And now, Dr Hexham, if you could sign off and hand this crime scene over to me.' Alan took the clipboard and started to check through the paperwork. 'When that's done I'd like you to leave, please,' Varia added to Kate.

'Who found the body?' asked Kate.

'Two hikers,' said Alan, looking up from the paperwork.

'This is Higher Tor? It's one of the letterboxing tors, I think,' said Kate.

'Letterboxing?' asked Varia.

'Yes. Have you heard of it?'

'I can hazard a guess.'

'You haven't heard of it and Dartmoor is on your beat?'

'I was assigned here a month ago,' said Varia. She looked

181

impatiently at Alan. 'Dr Hexham, if everything is good, please sign off.'

'If he's left another note, I'd check the letterbox,' said Kate.

'There is no letterbox,' said Varia, indicating the landscape.

'No. The letterbox is usually built into the rock of the tor,' said Alan, still reading through the paperwork. Kate could see he was deliberately spinning things out. Varia couldn't get rid of her until she had Alan's signature.

Kate followed Varia as she moved around the tor, past the body which was now in the black bag and being loaded onto a stretcher. Varia took out a torch and shone it on the smooth rock at the base of the tor.

'There it is,' said Kate, pointing to a small metal door which had been sunk into the rock at the base. Varia pulled on a pair of latex gloves and Kate took the torch from her, training it on the box as she undid the latch and opened it.

'There's a postcard,' said Varia, pulling it out. On the front was an image of a famous pub on Bodmin Moor, the Jamaica Inn. Something about it rang a bell in Kate's head, but she was eager to see what was written. Varia turned the card over. Kate was pleased that Varia wasn't petty enough to shoo her away.

SO, BODY NUMBER THREE SHOWS UP, AND FINALLY YOU CLOWNS ARE CATCHING UP.
  I SAW THE NEWS REPORT. AND HOW EXCITING TO HAVE A WOMAN HEADING THE CASE. THE STAGE IS SET. THE PLAYERS ARE ALL COMING TOGETHER.
  I ALREADY HAVE MY EYE ON NO. 4.
  A FAN

'It looks like the same handwriting as the other notes,' said Kate.

'Get this finger-printed and tested for any DNA,' said Varia, placing the postcard in a plastic evidence bag and handing it to John, who had joined them.

'If we're in any doubt he's copycatting, then this confirms it,' said Kate.

'There's no "we",' snapped Varia. Her radio beeped in her pocket and she pulled it out. 'Go ahead.'

'The body is in transit. We can have officers bussed in from sunrise tomorrow to do a fingertip search,' said a voice.

'Copy that,' said Varia.

They came back around the tor. An officer handed Varia the paperwork from Alan Hexham.

'That's my paperwork signed, which means you need to leave,' said Varia. Kate could see she was trying to stay calm.

'You have my number, if you need anything,' said Kate, but Varia ignored her and went over to her team. Kate walked back down to the police cordon and handed in her coveralls.

She found Tristan close to the car. He was shivering. Kate unlocked the doors and they got in. She switched on the engine and put the heater on full. The cold and damp seemed to have got into her bones. They set off back along the track towards Belstone Village, and came up behind the forensic pathologist's van, which was moving slowly over the rough terrain. Its brake lights flashed on as it stopped suddenly, causing Kate to stamp on the brakes. Their car skidded a little, and came to a stop inches from the back of the van.

'Shit, that was close,' she said, putting the car in reverse and backing up.

'Rear-ending a pathologist's van with a body in the back wouldn't have been great,' said Tristan.

The passenger door of the van opened, and Alan Hexham got out. He waved and hurried over to Kate's window. She wound it down.

'Listen, Kate, one of my colleagues heard over the radio

that you tried to get access to the crime scene as a private investigator?'

'Sorry. I only had my driving licence. We weren't sure what to say.'

'I'm not really keen on the idea of private investigators per se. Lots of them seem to be knicker sniffers poking their noses into marital affairs.'

'Alan. I'm not that kind of—'

'Of course not. What I mean is, you're the perfect candidate to be a private investigator . . . I just wanted to say you should get some business cards printed. I know they're nothing more than paper, but they go a long way to making you legitimate. And, if there is any way I can help you, within the bounds of professional ethics of course, you can rely on me.'

'Thank you,' said Kate, surprised.

'What do you make of this DCI Campbell?'

'I don't know. She doesn't know the area, but she's smart, she'll learn,' said Kate, eager not to be seen slagging off the lead officer on the case.

'Let's hope she learns quickly,' said Alan. 'Oh, and what's your associate's name again?'

'Tristan,' he said, leaning across Kate and offering Alan his hand.

'Good to meet you,' said Alan, leaning over and shaking it. 'And well done. You didn't puke!'

'Thanks.'

Alan hurried off, throwing them a wave, and got back in the van. Kate waited until it had a head start. Her head was spinning, not only after seeing the poor dead girl and the latest note, but also having Alan approach her and give her his advice. It was a revelation. For so many years she had been the butt of jokes, painted as a corrupt police officer, mentally unsound and a bad mother. Even as a university lecturer she knew her tabloid past had played a part in her appointment, as a way of bringing in fee-paying students. Was there a chance Alan was right, and she could make a go of it as a professional private investigator?

CHAPTER 27

'Are you feeling better?' asked Kate when they pulled up outside Tristan's flat, which was right on the seafront in Ashdean. He'd kept his window open during the journey home and stuck his head out several times to gulp at the fresh air.

'Yeah, I'll be okay,' he said. He flicked on the light above the mirror. His face was grey. 'I just feel stupid.'

'On my first day as an officer on the beat, I was called out to an incident where an old lady had been hit across the face with a baseball bat. There was lots of blood and I puked my guts up,' said Kate.

'Really?'

'It was in Catford in south London, by the market. All the market traders were laughing and jeering at me, so don't beat yourself up about your reaction to seeing a mutilated dead body.'

He put a hand to his mouth again. 'I just know I'm going to see her when I close my eyes tonight.'

'Me too,' said Kate. 'Pour yourself a stiff drink, and I'm giving you that advice as a member of AA.'

He smiled. 'Thanks.'

'Do you want to come for breakfast tomorrow? We can meet before the ten o'clock lecture and discuss everything.'

He raised a thumb and grinned. 'Don't talk about food. I

have to go,' he said, opening the door and dashing out and up a set of steps to the second floor flat. Kate watched until he made it in, and hoped he wouldn't decorate the carpet in his hallway.

When Kate got home, she poured herself a large iced tea and went through to the living room. She sat on the piano stool, trying to work out how she felt. She'd had to harden her emotions over the years. She felt horrified that there was another dead young woman, but there was also a spark in her chest, an eagerness to look into the case and solve the mystery.

She tapped the glass against her teeth. There was something about that postcard they found in the box on Higher Tor.

'The Jamaica Inn. Where have I heard that before?' she said out loud. She drained her iced tea, wishing almost subconsciously that it was Jack Daniel's with ice, but the thought was fleeting, peripheral, then was gone. She put her glass on the piano and went to the bookshelf, moving past the rows of novels, the crime fiction and academic papers. Tucked in at the end of one of the shelves was a hardback with the title *No Son of Mine* by Enid Conway.

She pulled it out. The cover was filled with a split-pane photograph. On the right was a picture of a sixteen-year-old Enid Conway cradling baby Peter. The picture was blurred in a nostalgic way, and baby Peter's eyes were wide and staring at the camera, whilst Enid looked down at him adoringly. Enid was a hard-faced young woman with a shock of long dark hair. She wore a long flowing dress, and behind her was the sign AULDEARN UNMARRIED MOTHERS' HOME. Through a window was the blurred image of a nun, in full penguin habit, staring out at them.

The other half of the cover was a police mug shot of Peter Conway, which was taken on the day he gave evidence at his preliminary trial. His hands were cuffed and he was smirking at the camera. His eyes had a crazed look. 'A crazed come-hither

187

look' one tabloid journalist had written at the time. He still had stitches above his left eyebrow – even in his semi-conscious state at Kate's Deptford flat, he had violently resisted arrest.

Kate opened the book and flicked through the pages, first seeing the signature and the charming dedication from Enid.

Rot in hell, you bitch, Enid Conway

Kate remembered showing Myra the book one evening, when she first became Kate's sponsor.

'Look on the bright side. My mother-in-law never bought me a book!' Myra had quipped. It had helped Kate laugh about the awful situation.

She flicked through to the index and scanned down until she found 'The Jamaica Inn', which was on page 118. With her heart racing, she paged through until she found the paragraph.

We had so many happy holidays on Dartmoor. There is nothing better than God's free earth, and Peter – who was a sickly child growing up, always suffering from coughs and colds – loved being out in the fresh air. Our local vicar, Father Paul Johnson, had a contact with several boarding houses owned by the Christian association, and we were able to stay, often for free, during our holidays. The Brewers Inn was the first stop on our holiday. A small, cosy pub in the middle of nowhere, overlooking Higher Tor . . .

Kate almost dropped the book in shock, seeing the tor mentioned. She carried on reading.

On our first day, armed with a picnic, we climbed Higher Tor because Peter was keen to try letterboxing. Several spots on Dartmoor have postboxes where you can leave a postcard for the next person who opens the box to find. When we got to the top of the tor, it was all a bit of an anticlimax, as when we opened the box, there was nothing inside. Peter had bought a postcard from one of the pubs we'd visited, the Jamaica Inn, and he left this postcard, which was addressed to me with a lovely note. Sure enough, five weeks after we got home from our holiday, the postcard showed up with a postmark from Sydney, Australia! A woman who ran a dog shelter was on holiday in the UK and she had taken the postcard all the way home before posting it . . .

Kate flicked through to the index of photos at the back of the book, all printed on glossy paper. And three pages in, she found two images, front and back of the Jamaica Inn, and Peter's scrawled message on the back of the postcard.

Dear Mummy
    We are having a lovely time in Devon, and I don't want it to end. I love you more than everything in the world.
    Peter xxxx

Kate went to the kitchen to refill her glass of iced tea, then came back and looked through the index, searching for the other locations where the victims had been dumped – the Nine Elms wrecker's yard, and Hunter's Tor by the river.

The next morning, Kate was working her way back to the shore after her swim when she saw Tristan coming down the dunes.

'Morning!' he shouted, holding up a large white paper bag. 'I have breakfast.'

When she came out of the water, he averted his eyes and held the robe out for her, which she'd left on the sand with her towel. 'You hungry?' he asked when she had it on.

'Starving,' she said, tying the robe and rubbing at her wet hair with the towel. They came up the dunes and into the house, and she put the kettle on. Tristan had brought two huge white rolls filled with fried egg and bacon. They didn't wait for the tea, just tucked in.

'God, that's good,' said Kate through a mouthful. The roll was soft and there was melted butter, slightly soft egg yolk, not too runny, and crispy bacon. 'Where did you get them?'

'A transport cafe off the high street in town.'

They wolfed them down, then Kate poured the tea.

'Thank you. That hit the spot,' she said, putting strong steaming cups in front of them. 'You feeling better today?'

He nodded awkwardly, taking a gulp of tea.

'Good. Take a look at this.'

She slid the copy of *No Son of Mine* by Enid Conway across the breakfast bar. He looked at the cover and opened it.

'Jeez. That has to be the gnarliest dedication I've ever read,' he said.

'The note written on the Jamaica Inn postcard last night rang a bell. Enid and Peter went on holiday to Devon when he was little in the summer of 1965. And in the book she lists the places they visited. I've marked the pages with Post-Its.'

Tristan flicked to the first.

Kate went on, 'They drove from London in a very old Ford Anglia whose fan belt broke one hot day. They were stuck in the middle of nowhere, and they happened upon the Nine Elms wrecker's yard. Enid chatted up the man who was working there at the time. He gave them an old fan belt from one of the wrecks, and helped them on their way.' Kate flicked the pages. 'Next, they went for a picnic to Hunter's Tor. They sat on the riverbank nearby, and they ate potted meat sandwiches. Look.'

190

She pointed at a picture of a young Peter on a picnic rug next to the river, which sparkled in the sunlight. She turned the pages again and indicated another photo. 'Then we have Peter on Higher Tor, pushing his postcard into the letterbox.'

'Jesus. How many other places does she mention?'

'Cotehele House, which is quite a posh National Trust place. Enid went in to get Peter a drink in their tearoom and they were ignored. People refused to serve them. They visited kistvaens, which are medieval tombs, and Castle Drogo, which has huge grounds and is close to the edge of Dartmoor. They stayed the night at a B&B on a farm in Launceston. This was the day before they were due to go home. Enid overheard the farmer's wife calling them "scum" so she stole one of their chickens. She describes how they smuggled it into the back of the car just before they left.'

'If the killer is working from this book, then he's not really a copycat,' said Tristan. 'It's more of a homage or a reboot of Peter Conway's crimes. What are you going to do with this information?'

'I sent an email to Varia Campbell and shared this all with her. She got right back to me.'

'What time?'

'Four in the morning. She said it's an interesting theory, but she doesn't have the manpower to deploy officers to all of these locations. They're dotted around five hundred square miles of countryside, so I understand what she said about the manpower.'

Tristan drank the last of his tea. 'But that's crazy. You've given her a motive for the killer. A blueprint of where he could strike next.'

'And she'll pursue it, I'm sure, but who knows what else the police are doing?' said Kate.

'What about Malcolm and Sheila Murray?' asked Tristan.

'I've left another message with the neighbour, but she hasn't got back to me. Listen, what did you think of what Alan said last night, about doing this properly, as private investigators?'

'I think it's exciting. Reading through the cold case stuff I've been preparing for your lectures has been so interesting. This is a step up from that, but something we'd have to do on the side, yeah?' asked Tristan.

Kate nodded. She could see he was worried about money, and remembered him saying that he'd been unemployed for a long time before he got this job. While their investigations into Caitlyn's disappearance were stimulating and exciting, they weren't going to make them rich.

'Reading week is coming up, and we could use some time then, but there could be times when we need to work outside hours. And I'd like to make it official in that I'll pay you for any overtime you do, outside of being my assistant,' she said.

'Okay,' said Tristan. He put out his hand and they shook on it. Kate suddenly felt daunted again. By making things official, it was now more than just an interesting hobby.

'We've already been looking at what happened to Caitlyn,' she said. 'At one stage I thought Malcolm and Sheila were just clutching at straws, and that it was Peter Conway who killed her, and I know we've hit a wall, but there's still something that's bothering me. Paul Adler and Victoria O'Grady.'

'She did seem to change her tune between my messages with her and when we met. Do you think she spoke to him? I know we've no proof of that.'

'I thought the same.' Kate picked up the book again. 'This person, whoever they are, is delving into Peter Conway's past for inspiration. We're delving too, to try and find out what happened with Caitlyn. I think something is linked, and I think if we start looking into the last three victims of this copycat, it could give us answers about Caitlyn, and we could find whoever is doing all of this.' Kate paused. After saying this all out loud, her confidence was ebbing. She shook the thought away. 'I want to look into these three victims – Emma Newman, Kaisha Smith and whoever this latest victim is. We don't have access to any police files, but we can talk to people. We have the internet. We have access to the microfilm at the university. We have Alan Hexham.'

'You also have a lecture in twenty minutes,' said Tristan, noticing the time.

'Shit! I'd better get ready. Let's reconvene afterwards and talk more.'

CHAPTER 28

After the lecture, Kate and Tristan went to the office armed with coffee. Kate had managed to find an article from when Emma's body had been found earlier in the summer. It was from a local newspaper, the *Okehampton Times*.

FORMER RESIDENT OF MUNRO-DYE CHILDREN'S HOME FOUND DEAD

Emma Newman (17) who lived at the Munro-Dye Children's Home near Okehampton from the age of six, was found dead at the Nine Elms wrecker's yard, close to the edge of Dartmoor. It is believed she had been missing for two weeks before her body was discovered by a worker at the yard. Friends had been concerned for Emma in the months leading up to her disappearance. She had recently been arrested for drug possession and soliciting with intent. Janice Reed, director of the home, described Emma as 'a bright little button' during her stay, but recently they had lost touch. Police are treating her death as suspicious, but as of yet they have no suspects.

'Do you want to see what you can find out about Emma on Facebook?' said Kate. 'I'm going to track down the journalist who wrote this piece and call this Janice Reed who runs the children's home.'

Just before lunch they came back together to share what they had. Kate had spent a couple of hours on the phone and had made lots of notes.

'Okay. Emma lived at the Munro-Dye Children's Home from when she was six,' said Kate. 'She was born to a single mother, who was a drug addict and who died during childbirth. There was no other family. I spoke to Janice Reed. She seemed helpful. Emma was a happy, sporty young girl and when she left the children's home at sixteen she seemed to have a promising future. She'd done well in her GCSEs. She had friends. They found her a small flat in Okehampton, and she was able to claim benefits and get a part-time job. She was planning to do her A levels.'

'She left the home at sixteen?' asked Tristan.

'Yes. When she was legally classed as an adult.'

'Bloody hell. I can't imagine having to go it alone at sixteen.'

Kate thought about Jake. In less than two years he would be sixteen too.

'She said that Emma went on to start her A levels at the local college, but she dropped out last July after her first year. But she said things had started to fall apart as early as last February when she was picked up by the police for soliciting. Janice said that Emma wasn't identified until two weeks after her body was found, using dental records. No one had reported her missing. Janice said she last saw Emma in late July. She was in a bad way, and very depressed, after her boyfriend Keir left to go to the States for six weeks. Keir had stopped replying to her messages. That was the last time Janice saw Emma – she did try to call two weeks before her body was found, and she left a message, but got no reply. Janice arranged Emma's funeral, and it was paid for out of charitable funds from the children's home.'

'Okay. I think I might be able to fill in some gaps,' said Tristan, turning his computer screen round to face them. 'I found Emma's Facebook profile. It's completely open. There are no privacy controls activated.' He clicked back to the beginning of her photo album. 'She joined Facebook around 2007. Didn't post much – pictures of her with a cat; here are some friends from the children's home; a picture of her with Father Christmas; another of her in a running race at sports day.'

Kate watched as he clicked through the photos of Emma growing older and morphing into a young woman.

'Who's that?' asked Kate when they got to a photo of Emma at a music festival with a tall older man. In the photo they looked drunk and Emma was draped over him. He looked to be in his late twenties or early thirties, and he was a redhead. He had large features and very red, pronounced lips. He wasn't unattractive, but in some photos where he was cleanshaven his face looked strange, almost like a plastic mask.

'This was taken on the beach in June. He's tagged as Keir Castle.'

'The boyfriend, Keir,' said Kate. He appeared suddenly in the photo stream in early May, and from then on was in scores more photos taken in parks, on the beach, back at Emma's flat, and on nights out in the pub.

'Keir's Facebook profile is locked down with privacy controls,' Tristan continued. 'It does give a bit of info. He's privately educated. Went to Cambridge and he now lists his occupation as "music promoter".'

'Is that as broad as it sounds?'

'Yeah. He could be managing bands, or he could be giving out CDs in the street,' said Tristan.

'Any other friends who stick out?' asked Kate.

'No. She only started posting regularly on Facebook when she got together with this guy,' said Tristan, clicking through more photos. Kate leaned closer. As the weeks passed, Emma appeared to lose weight in the photos and dress more provocatively, and the shine went from her eyes. There were more photos taken of partying, one in particular of Emma and Keir with dilated pupils.

'They were doing drugs, don't you think?' said Kate.

'Looks like it.'

'Would you be willing to friend him? This Keir?' asked Kate.

'Why? He has an alibi; he was away in America when Emma went missing.'

'Yes, but he was close to her. He could have information.'

'Okay.'

'Are you into bands?'

'Some.'

'Could you pretend to be in a band?'

Tristan shook his head. 'He'd check. What if I said I was a booker for bands?'

'What if you worked for one of the big breweries?' said Kate. 'You could be their person who gets bands into the pubs run by the breweries.'

'That's good. New bands always book gigs in smaller venues.'

Kate nodded and smiled. 'Brilliant.'

Tristan wrote a short message and sent it with the request. Then they went downstairs to get coffee.

'Bingo,' said Tristan when they got back. 'He accepted.'

'Jesus. Do people realise what Facebook really is? I wonder how different my conviction rate would have been if I'd had Facebook profiles to snoop around,' said Kate.

They started to look through his profile. Various posts on Facebook said he was a music promoter, or a music journalist. He had links to three abandoned blogs, none had any effort put into the design. The first two had brief articles about gigs and the third had been set up to accommodate a GoFundMe page for Keir to become a Reiki healer. His goal was to raise £3,500 for the course, but it had been abandoned after only £54 was raised.

'He's set it so we can't see his friends,' said Tristan.

'He must come from money with a name like "Keir", private school and Cambridge, and his work life seems vague, yet in all these photos he's well dressed,' said Kate.

'He's creepy. That fleshy face, the hooded eyes. He's an odd-looking guy.'

'That's no measure of a serial killer. Remember, Ted Bundy was handsome. So was Peter Conway.'

'Yeah, but his eyes are so cold, even in the photos where he's smiling,' said Tristan.

Keir had only posted a couple of pictures of him with Emma, and she vanished from his newsfeed a few weeks before her death, when he went to America. Kate turned her computer round and googled him.

'Aha,' she said, scrolling through results. 'He has a criminal record. Article in the local paper in 2009. Keir Castle, charged with threatening his girlfriend with a knife. The girlfriend wasn't Emma. She's not named. He got off with a fine and a hundred hours' community service.'

'I would have thought he'd get time for that,' said Tristan, reading from her screen. 'He must have been able to afford good representation.'

'Any more info about his family?' asked Kate. They went back to Tristan's screen.

'Keir attended King's York independent school in Oxfordshire. Doesn't look like he graduated from Cambridge. He's got two sisters: Mariette Fenchurch and Poppy Anstruther. Also sound posh. The sisters' profiles are locked with maximum security settings by the look of them, but they all went to the same school,' said Tristan.

Kate sat back in her chair, deep in thought.

'He was linked closely to Emma,' said Tristan.

'And if he gets about, he could have come into contact with the other girls,' said Kate. 'What if we could arrange a meeting with him?'

'Where?'

'Locally. What if you messaged him and told him that you were looking to book bands for the south-east pubs you manage, in your capacity as a band booker, or whatever? You'd meet him in public, of course. You talk shop, and then you could get him to open up. Especially if he thinks he's going to get something from you. We might learn the names of the other people Emma hung around with.'

'Okay,' said Tristan, warming to the idea. 'I'll send him a message and get him talking.'

Kate got up and picked up her bag and coat from the back of her chair. 'I've just had an idea about something. I'll be back in an hour, and I'll get some lunch.'

CHAPTER 29

'Are you sure about this? They're not going to talk to us,' said Tristan.

They were driving towards Crediton, a small town seven miles outside Exeter. Kate wanted to speak to the parents of Kaisha Smith, the girl found beside the river at Hunter's Tor.

'These should help,' said Kate, handing Tristan an envelope. Tristan took it and pulled out two small stacks of business cards, each fastened with an elastic band. 'A set with your name on it and a set for me. I went down to reprographics and got them printed. They owe me a favour. There's twenty of each.'

'I like how my name looks in fancy silver embossed writing,' said Tristan, turning the card over. Kate had worried he might object to being 'Assistant Private Investigator' to her 'Private Investigator' and she was relieved to see all was good.

'I think the best thing is that we're honest. We say we're investigating the disappearance of another young woman, which we are, and we think there could be some crossover,' said Kate.

The house belonging to Tammy and Wayne Smith was at the top of a row of terraces that snaked up the side of a steep hill. Kate could only find a parking space at the bottom.

They arrived at the front door a little breathless after the steep climb, and Kate wanted a moment to compose herself, but the front door was pulled open and a thin woman came out carrying a black bag of rubbish.

'Yes?' she asked. 'If you're Jehovah's Witnesses you can piss off. I'm not in the mood. The last copy of *The Watchtower* I got through my letterbox was put down in the cat litter tray.' She walked past them and went to the black bin by the gate.

Kate explained who they were and they showed their business cards.

The woman looked them up and down, taking in Kate's casual jeans and sweater with a long coat and Tristan's bright red and blue jacket, jeans and green trainers.

'You're not press?'

'No,' said Kate.

'Come in,' said Tammy.

The house inside was cheaply furnished but cosy. The cluttered front room was filled with a sagging sofa, armchairs and a huge flat-screen television, which was showing an afternoon cooking programme where a bespectacled chef was carving a lattice into a leg of lamb with great enthusiasm.

A man who Kate recognised as Wayne from the news report sat in an armchair wearing a grubby dressing gown, staring listlessly at the TV. Tammy explained who they were and he looked up at them blearily. Kate instantly saw he was drunk.

'This is Ruby, our other ... our daughter,' said Tammy. A thin, sad-looking girl who looked to be seven or eight years old sat next to the television brushing the hair of a pink My Little Pony. Tristan and Kate said hello and sat down on the sofa. Tammy took the other free armchair.

Kate noted that Wayne and Tammy were heavy smokers. They both lit up cigarettes and there was an overflowing ashtray on the coffee table. Kate couldn't help judging them, though, as they puffed away in the presence of Ruby, who came to sit on the side of Tammy's armchair. She was a sweet little pale-faced girl, with shoulder-length white blonde hair parted to the left above her ear. Even though she wore a faded pink tracksuit, the way she wore her hair gave her a seriousness beyond her years.

'What do you want to know?' asked Tammy.

'When did you know Kaisha was missing?' asked Kate.

'Me and Wayne work shifts, in a garden centre warehouse,' started Tammy. 'We was both working on the day Kaisha went missing. She was due to pick up Ruby from school.' She took a drag of her cigarette. Her face was bloodless and she had huge dark circles under her eyes. Wayne, equally pale with a bulldog set to his mouth, nodded along grimly, staring at the gas fire glowing in the corner of the room.

'Kaisha was happy at school?' asked Kate.

The use of the past tense was obviously a shock to Tammy and Wayne. They both looked like they'd been punched.

'She was,' said Wayne. He rubbed at his unshaven face. He wore several gold rings, and Kate saw the LOVE tattooed on the fingers of one hand, and HATE on the other. 'She's . . . she was at Hartford School doing A levels – maths and science. We don't know where she got the brains from . . . ' he slurred, his voice trailing off, and he looked up at Kate, desperation on his face.

'She went missing on her way home from school?'

'Yeah. She had to pick up Ruby, most days,' said Tammy. 'Kaisha gets the bus to school and back, and Ruby's primary school is only down the road.'

'How long is the walk from school to the bus stop?'

'She goes from the school playing field and gets the number 64 bus, which comes to the bottom of the road.'

'She does sports on Tuesdays and Thursdays,' said Ruby, speaking for the first time.

Kate smiled down at her. 'What kind of sports?'

Ruby cuddled up to Tammy, who moved the glowing tip of her cigarette to the other hand and put her arm round her.

'Hockey. She was really good. She was on the under-eighteens team.'

'I didn't like her playing,' said Wayne, grimacing and looking down at his feet. 'It's not ladylike. I know I'm not supposed to say that, but fuck it, there's blokes who go and watch them girls practise. I seen them lining up at the fence, peering through,' he said, his voice rising an octave with emotion.

'Is it a private school?' asked Tristan.

'Yeah. She had a scholarship. Case you're confused,' said Wayne, glaring.

'Did Kaisha mention a new friend? A boyfriend from school? Or someone older?' asked Kate.

'There was no boys. I used to wish there was,' said Wayne. Tammy shot him a look.

'Oh, did Kaisha have a girlfriend?'

'No, she fucking didn't,' said Wayne. Kate could see he was becoming more alert, and angry.

'You were both on night shifts the day Kaisha went missing?'

'You think I did this to my fucking daughter?'

'Wayne, she has to ask these questions,' said Tammy, who obviously could see he was becoming agitated. She turned to Kate and Tristan. 'We was both on a night shift from six p.m. to six a.m. But we have to leave the house to get the bus at four p.m., to make two connections.'

'What time did you get back on Friday morning?'

'Just after eight,' said Tammy.

'Hang on, hang on,' said Wayne, pulling himself up to sit on the edge of the armchair. 'Who the fuck are these two? Are you police?'

'They're private investigators, Wayne, I said!' cried Tammy.

'What did you do when Kaisha didn't come home?' Kate asked Ruby, seeing their time could be coming to an end.

'I waited for her, then I rung her mobile, then I rung Mam. I went to Mrs Todd's next door,' said Ruby.

'I was proper furious with Kaisha,' started Tammy. 'I thought she'd gone off somewhere . . . I cursed her good and proper to Wayne . . .' She shook and then broke down. Ruby reached out to cuddle her, but Tammy brushed her away, dropping her cigarette onto the grubby carpet. Ruby dutifully picked it up and stubbed it out.

'Can I ask if you've seen this man?' asked Kate. She held up Keir Castle's Facebook photo. Tammy and Wayne peered at it. Tammy looked hopeful for a second but then shook her head. Wayne grabbed the printout and put it close to his face.

'Is this one of the bastards who hang around the hockey pitch?' he said.

'We just need to know if you recognise him. You see he's quite distinctive with the red hair, and the strong pronounced features . . . How about you, Ruby?' asked Kate.

Ruby shook her head.

'This is one of the dads, isn't it? One of them stuck-up fuckers . . .'

'Wayne!' cried Tammy.

'Fuck you too! Do you know him?' he said, holding up the photo. 'You didn't look at it properly. Look at him.' He pushed the photo into her face, creasing the paper against her chin.

'I did look!' she said, slapping his hand away.

He screwed up the photo and threw it in her face, then staggered about, having to grab the corner of the coffee table.

Kate looked at Tristan, who was about to get up and intervene. She shook her head. There was no placating a drunk, she knew from bitter experience. Things could escalate fast. She was relieved when the news headlines appeared on the TV, and

Wayne was distracted. They saw the familiar view of the crime scene from a couple of days ago. Tammy went to pick up the remote on the table but Wayne beat her to it.

'I run the remote,' he said, jabbing a finger in her face. He tottered on his feet, and turned up the volume.

It was a repeat of the drone footage above the crime scene, and a picture flashed up of Kaisha in her hockey gear, smiling and posing with a gold trophy.

'Police have discovered the body of another young woman. They believe it is linked to the murder of sixteen-year-old Kaisha Smith,' said the announcer. The picture cut to the base of Higher Tor, and showed police officers crouching down in a long row conducting a fingertip search in the daylight.

'The victim has just been formally identified as sixteen-year-old Layla Gerrard, a pupil at Carmichael Grammar School who was reported missing last Thursday.'

More drone footage showed a school playing field and, next to it, a path alongside train tracks.

Wayne sank down onto his haunches.

Tristan went to him. 'Mate, can I get you anything?' he said, helping Wayne up and back onto the armchair.

Wayne broke down in tears, heaving a sob. Ruby left the room and returned a moment later with a glass of water which Wayne drank, dribbling it down his chin.

Kate noticed that Tammy was rummaging around in a cupboard under the TV.

'Where did they get that picture of Kaisha in her hockey gear? I didn't give it to anyone. Did that policewoman take it?' said Tammy.

'Was it on Facebook?' asked Kate. 'They could have lifted it off.'

Tammy was now absorbed in a photo album, flicking through photos of when she was pregnant, full of hopeful smiles. It pierced Kate's heart.

'Get out, just please, get out,' said Wayne, his face in his hands. Ruby went and picked up the balled-up printout of Keir Castle's photo from the floor.

'I'll get them to look at this again when they've calmed down,' she said. Kate nodded and she and Tristan left the room with Ruby.

'Are you going to be okay?' asked Kate when they got to the front door.

Ruby nodded. 'I've been going to Mrs Todd's in the evenings and sleeping there. She's nice. She used to be our lollipop lady. Mum and Dad don't really notice. They just drink and fight.'

Kate took out another card. 'If you have any problems, or if you're scared, this is my number. I can help,' she said, giving it to her. Tristan gave her his card too.

Ruby nodded.

When they got back to the car, Tristan and Kate sat in silence for a moment.

'Jesus, that was awful,' said Kate.

'Yeah,' said Tristan.

'They identified the third girl quickly. I'll see if Alan Hexham will give us any details from his post-mortem,' she said, searching through her bag for her phone. Tristan took out his.

'Shit,' he said.

'What?' said Kate, pulling hers out from the depths of her bag.

'Keir Castle just unfriended me,' he said, holding up the screen. 'I'm locked out of his profile again.'

'You think he suspected something?' asked Kate.

'I don't have work info on my profile . . . ' He looked at Kate. 'People are weird on social media.'

'But why would he unfriend someone who could help his career? Have they put your picture on the Ashdean University website?' asked Kate.

'Not yet.'

Kate scrolled through her phone. 'I'm going to get the post-mortem info, and I'm going to see if Alan can pull some strings and look into Keir Castle.'

CHAPTER 30

They heard nothing more that afternoon, and Kate came home in the evening feeling restless. However, she was excited to talk to Jake on Skype, especially as their regular Skype call had been delayed a day to Thursday, because he had football practice.

He was bouncing around the kitchen when he called, and he held up the bag he was already packing to come and see her for half term.

'It's less than two weeks!' He grinned. 'I've got Grandma to buy me some sea shoes, 'cause of the rocks.' He held up a pair of bright green rubber shoes.

'They're snazzy,' said Kate.

'No, they're *cool*, Mum. Don't say *snazzy*. You sound like Grandma, and she's way older than you.'

'*She* is the cat's mother,' said Glenda, appearing on screen behind him with a bag of shopping, which she placed on the kitchen counter. 'Hello, Catherine.'

'Hi, Mum. What have you got for tea?' asked Kate, a pang of jealousy flaring up inside her. She wished she was there to sit around the table for dinner with them all.

'Salmon en croute,' Glenda said, holding up a box. 'Marks and Spencer do a lovely one.'

'That's posh for salmon pie,' said Jake to Kate in a low voice, making her smile.

'We're having it with asparagus and new potatoes,' Glenda added.

'Can you hire me a wetsuit when I come? The sea will be cold, won't it?'

'Yes, I can ask Myra at the surf shop. Although I swim every day with no wetsuit.'

'That's nutty,' said Jake, shaking his head. 'Nutbag.'

Glenda finished unpacking the shopping, turned and saw something on the kitchen table and came over. 'Jake. Did you eat all of these?' she said, holding up an empty packet of Haribo cola bottles. He shook his head. 'I hope not, young man . . . Look. You're jiggling your leg, Jake. I can't cope with your hyperactive behaviour, not tonight.'

Jake put his fingers in the corner of his mouth and rolled back his eyes so only the whites were showing.

'This is Grandma before she puts on her make-up,' he said.

'Jake, come on, that's not nice,' said Kate.

'Has he told you about Facebook?' asked Glenda.

'No. What?' asked Kate. Jake folded his arms and looked guilty.

'He defriended me.'

'No one else has their grandma as a friend, and have you *seen* her profile picture? She's wearing her swimming costume!' Jake cried.

Kate opened Facebook on her laptop screen, shifting the Skype screen over. She found Glenda's Facebook profile. Her mother still had a fabulous figure, and in her profile photo she was posing on a deckchair in a blood-red one-piece swimsuit. She was sitting bolt upright, her slim brown legs shining with lotion. A croupier's visor with a matching red shade sat on her perfectly coiffed blonde hair.

'That's quite a picture, Mum,' said Kate.

'Thank you. That was at the villa in Portugal, two years ago. Is Jake still friends with you?' asked Glenda.

Kate checked and was surprised to see that she had also been unfriended. She could only see his name and photo.

'No, he's not. Jake? We told you that you could only be on Facebook if we were friends with you, and we had your password,' said Kate.

'Mum, you know I love you,' he said in a pleading, silly voice. 'But I have a reputation to keep up. Please, please, please forgive me.' He put his hands together and fluttered his eyelids. Kate could see he had eaten the whole bag of sweets.

'You're fourteen. What kind of reputation do you need?'

'A cool one,' he said, still grinning. 'Doesn't mean I don't love you, just not in public.'

Kate couldn't be mad with him, but he had to understand.

'You need to friend us both now, or we'll have your profile deactivated,' she said.

'You can't do that,' he said.

'I was a policewoman, and I still know officers. They can go in and close down people's Facebook profiles and delete everything.'

'But I've got pictures and messages and loads of likes!' he cried.

'Friend us both now and nothing changes,' said Kate.

Jake did so, then stormed off out of the room. There was a thudding sound as he stomped upstairs and the distant sound of a door slamming. Glenda sat down wearily and rubbed her eyes.

'Thanks, love,' she said.

'Now he hates me,' said Kate.

'No, he doesn't.'

'It easier for you. You can follow him upstairs and talk to him.'

Glenda smiled at her. 'I know, love. Why don't you try and phone him later?'

Kate nodded. Glenda put her finger to her lips and pressed them against the camera.

It was the first occasion in a long time that Jake had got upset with Kate. She had been right, of course, but it played on her mind as she fried herself some eggs. When she put them on hot buttered toast and went through to the living room, the sun was just sinking down over the sea.

Summer sunsets always filled her with positivity, but as the nights drew in they made Kate feel gloomy and lonely. She looked down at the food she'd made, but she wasn't hungry. She went back to the kitchen and chucked it away. She looked up out of the side window and saw Myra on her way down to the beach, hunched over, her white-blonde hair blown flat by the wind, trying to light a cigarette.

Kate put her plate in the sink and hurried out of the back door.

'Myra! You got a minute?' she shouted, following her down the sandy cliff.

'Hello, stranger,' said Myra. 'I missed you at the last AA meeting.'

'Sorry.'

'Don't be sorry to me. It's your sobriety.'

'Things have got crazy. Can we talk? Can you open up the shop? I need a wetsuit,' said Kate.

'Sure, I'll grab the keys,' said Myra.

The inside of the surf shop smelled musty, and the long windows looking out over the sea had been boarded up now the season was over. Myra pressed a switch and the fluorescent strip lights flickered on, lighting up the interior. At the front, Kate saw a row of shelves stocked with tinned and dried goods, camping stoves, bottled gas and a few small tents.

Myra led Kate to the surf section at the back, where racks of wetsuits hung with flippers, snorkels and some faded cardboard adverts for surf gear – handsome muscled men standing with lithe bikini-clad babes. The wind moaned around the building.

'How tall is Jake?' asked Myra, sorting through a rack of kids' wetsuits with her glowing cigarette stuck in the corner of her mouth. 'He was below my shoulder the last time he was here at Easter.'

She pulled out a small black and blue wetsuit with a Rip Curl logo on the back.

'I saw him last month and he was up to my shoulder,' said Kate.

Myra held it up to Kate. 'Has he got fat? Some kids balloon when they hit puberty. When I hit fourteen I got very fat and bossy,' she said.

'He's not fat.'

'There are other colours if you want to take a look,' said Myra. She lit up a fresh cigarette with the dog end of the old, which she stubbed out on the grubby concrete floor.

Kate searched through the rack.

'You can't say fat any more,' Myra went on. 'One woman came in over the summer with a little girl who was a right porker. I said to her, the sea is lovely and warm and she's well insulated. Save yourself a few quid on wetsuit hire.'

'You didn't!'

'I didn't shout it out. I took the mother to one side. Still, you'd think I'd declared World War Three!'

'This one, he loves green,' said Kate, pulling out a suit with what looked like a pattern of green paint splashes.

'When is he coming?'

'Half term, in twelve days. I just wanted to send him a picture of it.'

'Take it, love,' said Myra, putting the other suit back.

'How much?'

'What do you think? Nothing.'

'Thanks.'

'Kate,' Myra said, putting her hand on her arm. 'Don't miss another meeting. Okay?'

'It's this case I'm working on.'

'Nothing is as important as your sobriety. You see this empty wetsuit? It will still be empty in twelve days if you fall off the wagon. Your mother won't let him near you if you start drinking,' said Myra.

'I know. Is it always going to be this hard? Sobriety?'

Myra nodded. 'I've got twenty-three years' sobriety on you. I still go to meetings and see my sponsor. But I'm alive.'

CHAPTER 31

Kate sent Jake a text message with a picture of the wetsuit, but she didn't hear anything back all evening. Just as she was about to go to bed she got a phone call from an unlisted number.

'Kate, hello. It's Dr Baxter at Great Barwell.'

'I was just going to bed,' said Kate.

Meredith Baxter was Peter Conway's consultant psychiatrist at Great Barwell. She was a little 'new age' for Kate's liking. She always spoke about Peter as a 'patient', not a prisoner. She'd phoned Kate two years ago wanting to connect Kate and Jake with Peter, saying it would be good for his healing process. The last time Kate had spoken to her, she'd used colourful language and told Meredith where to go.

'I'm going to be in London tomorrow. I'd like to meet you,' she said.

'Why?' asked Kate.

'It's about Peter and Jake.'

'I told you before, he is not having contact with Jake.'

'It's not about that. I can meet you at Paddington station. There's a fast train from Exeter.'

'I know there's a bloody train.'

'Please, Kate. It's important.'

*

Kate was up early the next morning. It took half an hour to get to Exeter St David's train station, and she only just made the 7 a.m. fast train to Paddington. She managed to get a seat with a table, and she'd brought work with her, but she couldn't concentrate. She kept checking her phone to see if Jake had texted back, but he hadn't. She arrived at Paddington just before 9 a.m., and she found Meredith waiting for her at a table in Starbucks at the train station.

She was a pleasant-faced woman in her early forties with long strawberry-blonde hair tied back in a ponytail. She carried a leather satchel and wore jeans, a red woollen jumper and a short denim jacket. The laminated lanyard around her neck showed her ID, and that she was a doctor.

'I took the liberty of getting you a cappuccino,' said Meredith. 'Please sit.' She had a soothing voice, and Kate wondered if it was an affectation, or if she spoke the same way when she was at home, moaning at her husband to do the dishes. The seats in Starbucks were half empty, but there was a huge queue of commuters waiting for takeaway. Kate was glad of the noise of the coffee machines and station announcements.

'You've made me very uneasy. I didn't sleep well last night,' said Kate.

'I'm sorry, but I really wanted to speak face to face, and I figured you didn't want to come to the hospital . . .'

Kate's phone pinged to say she had a text. She pulled it out, but saw it was only from Tristan.

'Do you need to deal with that?'

'No,' said Kate, putting her phone back.

'My patients' communications are kept private, but something addressed to Peter Conway was intercepted because it violates a no-contact order that you had put in place.'

Meredith pulled a small brown envelope from her bag and put it on the table. It was addressed by hand and in the top

215

right-hand corner was written in thin black handwriting, 'from a fan'.

The sight of those words made Kate feel sick.

'Have you fingerprinted this?' she asked.

'No. Why would we fingerprint it?'

'What's inside?' asked Kate. She opened it and took out a single sheet of paper. It was a printout of Jake's Facebook page with his photo, and underneath was written, in the same handwriting,

I'M THE ONLY PERSON WHO WANTS YOU TO SEE HOW WELL HE'S DOING – HE'LL SOON BE 15! WHO KNOWS, HE MIGHT BECOME A CHIP OFF THE OLD BLOCK . . .
  A FAN

'I know this is horrible and shocking, but remember that anyone can print this off and send it. Jake's Facebook page is public. It's not illegal to send it privately,' said Meredith. Her voice was irritatingly soothing.

Kate's heart thumped against her ribs and her hands shook when she saw it was signed 'a fan'. She thought of Jake and his Facebook page, of how he'd unfriended Glenda. She took out her phone and tried her mother, but it went straight to voicemail.

'Mum, call me when you get this. It's urgent,' she said. They were sitting by a huge window looking out into the station concourse. Opposite there was a luxury drinks store. A tower of Absolut vodka bottles was displayed in the window, and two good-looking young men were standing outside the shopfront with trays covered in tiny sample cups filled with the clear liquid.

'Kate? Kate?' said Meredith. Kate turned back to her. 'Are you okay?'

Am I okay? thought Kate. *You have a degree in psychology and you ask if I'm okay? You have no comprehension of how scared and angry I feel!*

Kate took out her phone again and scrolled through until she found the photo she'd taken of the note at the Nine Elms wrecker's yard. She showed it to Meredith and told her the whole story of the dead girls and the notes that had been left.

Meredith sat back when Kate was finished. 'Talk to me, Kate. You shouldn't bottle up how you feel.'

Kate resisted the urge to grab Meredith by the back of her neck and slam her face into the table.

'Is this the first note that's been sent to Peter, which is signed in this way? From a fan?' she asked, trying to keep her voice even.

'No. He gets so much mail from all over the place, and many of them profess to be his fan.'

'No, I mean, this specific way of signing "A Fan"?'

'I'm unable to discuss contents of his private mail—'

'Jesus Christ. You call me all the way here, show me this letter, and then tell me you can't discuss it!' shouted Kate, banging her fist on the table.

'Kate. I need you to calm down.'

'You're a psychiatrist. Does telling someone who is upset to calm down ever work?'

'Kate. I'm on your side. You know all Peter's communication is monitored. Everything that comes in, apart from privileged communication from his legal team, is checked. You should know this as a former police officer.'

'Detective Constable,' said Kate. She paused and took a deep breath. 'Please look at the handwriting on this paper, and on the letters left at the crime scenes. It looks like the same hand.'

Meredith glanced at them. 'I don't know. It does, but I'm not a graphologist. I will of course now share this with the police. You have to understand, Peter gets a great deal of strange mail.'

'Have the police been in contact and asked to see his mail? Just a yes or no answer?'

'Yes, but we get regular requests from them. Once or twice a year, and they don't have to share with us the reason why they want to see it.'

'So, there is a chance that this person is communicating with Peter?'

'No.'

'Does he receive many visitors?'

'Kate . . .'

'For God's sake, Meredith! My son is high risk. I have a court injunction out that Peter cannot communicate with him. And there is someone sending this fucked-up shit! You have a son, don't you? Why can't you show me as much compassion as you show all your convicted paedophiles and murderers?'

Despite her calm demeanour, Meredith gritted her teeth and smoothed down her hair. 'Peter has very few phone calls. All are monitored and recorded, and very few people visit him. He meets with a priest, who he got to know through writing letters. They meet once every six weeks, and there's glass between them when they meet. If and when his solicitor visits, it's the same, behind glass.'

'Is Peter still violent?'

'Kate, I'm telling you more than I should. I can't comment on his mental state . . . The only person he meets face to face is Enid. They meet twice a week. Visits are monitored very closely and they are both searched before and after.'

'Have they talked about this case, about the dead girls' bodies recently found?'

'No.'

'When did he last see his solicitor?' asked Kate.

'Last week, and their visit was privileged. Do you know who represents him? Terrence Lane is a respected human rights lawyer. He wouldn't risk his career. And for what? Peter has a few hundred pounds in savings . . . Now this is all confidential.'

'Look at this note again. It's like he's picking up on a conversation. He doesn't introduce himself . . . ' Kate rubbed at her face. 'I have to go.' She got up abruptly and took a photo of the note with her phone.

'Is there anything else I can do?' asked Meredith. 'I will be sending this to the police.'

'Will you search Peter Conway again, really search him? Turn his cell over. Search everyone who comes into contact with him. Staff included.'

'My patients have legal rights, and . . . ' started Meredith, her tones almost aggressively soothing.

'I just hope you never find yourself on the wrong side of a crazed psychopath,' said Kate. 'If you spent some time in my shoes, you'd feel differently about their human bloody rights!' She picked up her bag and walked out of Starbucks.

She hurried to the nearest toilets in the station, which were under the concourse. They were empty and she locked herself in a cubicle. She let herself cry, and the release felt good. After a few moments she heard the sound of a cleaner's bucket on wheels and a knock on the door.

'What are you doing in there?' said a sharp voice.

'Nothing. Go away,' said Kate, catching her breath, determined not to let her emotions show in her voice.

There was a pause, then the bucket rumbled on. Kate wiped her eyes and pulled out her phone. She had no signal. She took some deep breaths and wiped her eyes again, then came out of the cubicle and back up into the station. She tried to call her mother, Jake, her father and even her brother, but nobody was answering. She called Jake's school and was told by a rather pious-sounding secretary that Jake was busy in classes.

Kate found she'd wandered down the concourse, and she was close to the luxury wine and spirits store. The bottles stacked high in the windows glowed with a soft, welcoming light, and the two young men outside offering samples were tall, dark and beautiful.

'Care to try Absolut Elyx?' one of the young men asked, moving over to her with a tray covered in little plastic sample cups. The clear liquid shimmered. Kate took one. 'It's copper pot distilled and very smooth,' he added with a smile. He was perfect. Smooth skin and floppy dark hair. The little plastic glass felt cold in her hand. The vodka was chilled, and it was such a small amount. Just a sip. A man and woman, both smart and well dressed, took a sample each and knocked them back.

'Very good,' said the man. The woman nodded in agreement, and they placed their empty sample cups back on the tray and carried on walking down the platform.

Kate moved away from them all, towards a quiet place in the station where a van was parked next to a line of tall pillars. It was a red Royal Mail van. Kate's whole focus was on that tiny glass, still cold in her hand, and the smell, the cool sharp smell of really smooth vodka.

Everything seemed to go in slow motion as she turned back and saw the two beautiful young men, standing together with laden trays. She could easily have more.

Kate went to lift the cup to her lips, and as she did she didn't see the man with the box of parcels. He crashed into her arm and the little cup was knocked from her grip and fell on the concourse, the vodka making the smallest spatter on the tiled floor.

'Mind out!' he said, moving around her. Kate came to her senses.

She backed away from the little cup lying on its side, the

vodka spreading out over the tiled floor, and she hurried away, past the luxury wine and spirits store and onto her platform. She saw it as fate that a fast train was due to leave in one minute. She ran along the platform and hopped on board just as the doors closed.

CHAPTER 32

Kate calmed down a little on the train home. She found a quiet corner and managed to speak to Glenda, who said she would contact the police liaison they had been assigned over the years.

'He's safe, Kate. I promise. The school is secure and they know Jake's background.'

'Keep me posted, Mum, and ask Jake to text me back, tell me what he thinks of the picture I sent him of the wetsuit.'

'Of course. Are you okay, love?'

Kate looked out at the landscape rushing past. She didn't want to think that she'd come so close to drinking.

'I'm okay,' she said. When she ended the call, her phone rang again. This time it was Tristan. She quickly told him what had happened, omitting the part where she almost drank.

'I'll be back in time for my three o'clock lecture,' she said.

'Cool. Listen. I just saw online that at seven this evening there's going to be a candlelit vigil for the third victim, Layla. It's in Topsham, the village where she lived. It's only about ten miles away from Ashdean. It could be a good place to talk to people, find out more information, especially if it's a small village.'

Kate had a quick think. *I've got a lecture from 3 to 4 p.m., there's a 5 p.m. AA meeting I should go to with Myra. Afterwards I could drive to Topsham.*

'Okay, let's do that,' she said.

Keeping busy was good, she thought. It kept her mind off other things.

Later that afternoon, Peter was doing push-ups in his cell when he heard a bang on the door. Winston opened the hatch.

'Peter, we need to search your room,' he said.

'Why?'

'Routine,' said Winston, looking at him with impassive eyes.

Peter came to the hatch and was cuffed and hooded, and taken out into the corridor. Winston stayed with him as Terrell pulled on a fresh pair of latex gloves.

'Anything you want to tell me before I go in?' he asked.

'No,' said Peter.

Terrell went inside, closing the door.

Peter tried to remain calm. He was keeping the letters from Enid and his 'fan' inside capsules in the bottle of vitamin C tablets. He figured that, at a glance, the white paper packed inside looked the same as a full capsule. He hoped that the radiator knob wouldn't be discovered loose. It would be a shame to sacrifice that hiding place.

'You okay, Peter?' asked Winston. 'You're sweating.'

'I was exercising,' he said. Glad to be able to tell the truth for once. He had noticed how much better his clothes fitted.

Winston's radio bleeped and a call came through for medical backup in solitary confinement.

'Urgent. We have a patient caught up in the new razor wire . . .'

Winston reached for the knob on the radio and turned the sound down.

'New razor wire?' asked Peter. 'Did someone try to escape? I didn't hear the siren go off.'

'The yard in solitary now has razor wire on top of the walls,' said Winston.

'How did he get through the net?' asked Peter.

'The nets have been removed,' said Winston. 'Too many birds were getting caught in them and dying. It's very expensive to get them removed ...' Winston checked himself and stopped talking.

Peter was one of the few lucid patients, and Winston was a nice bloke. Peter noticed how he sometimes fell into a rhythm of talking to him like he was a normal person. The door opened and Terrell came out of Peter's room.

'We're all good,' he said. 'We just need to check you, please, Peter.'

They went back into the cell, where they conducted a strip search, and shone a small torch into all the places where he might hide something.

Peter heard them move on to search the other cells in his corridor.

There's now no net above the yard in solitary confinement, he thought. *This changes everything.*

He tore a small strip of paper, and sat down to write another note to give to Enid on her next visit.

Meredith was waiting for Winston and Terrell at the entrance to G Wing. Her meeting with Kate had rattled her, and on her way back to the hospital her concern grew that Peter could be communicating in some way.

'All rooms are clean,' said Winston. 'We found some food stashed away, but that was it. There's no correspondence. No weapons or anything prohibited.'

Meredith nodded and paced up and down. 'And you're a hundred per cent sure that you've checked every patient who comes into contact with Peter?' she asked.

'The only contact he has with other patients is during group therapy with you each week,' said Winston. 'And we watch everything.'

'What about staff members?' she asked.

'My team is straight down the line,' said Winston, his face clouding over. 'We go through security checks in and out.'

'I'd like all staff areas checked and I'd like interviews with everyone who works on G Wing or has worked on G Wing over the past three months. And I want that done now.'

'Absolutely,' said Winston. 'But I'd like to add for the record that I have a loyal, honest team, with strong players. We have to be. I can confidently say that there is no one working for a prisoner, delivering messages or contraband.'

Meredith looked at Winston. He was staking a lot, saying so.

'That's noted. Please, I want the search done now. Close down all areas. No one leaves until it's done.'

CHAPTER 33

Kate and Tristan arrived in Topsham at half six that evening and parked in a residential street on the outskirts of the village. They each had a small lantern and some tea lights and matches, and they stashed them in Tristan's rucksack and set off down towards the main street in the village. Kate had pushed the events of the morning to the back of her mind. She had attended the AA meeting and sat at the back half listening, but her mind was on the case. Kate knew she had to talk to Myra, but she didn't want to miss the opportunity to join the vigil and glean new information.

As they got closer to the main street they joined crowds of people, and the BBC and ITV regional news teams had their vans parked up in the market square. There was an energy in the air, and Kate couldn't put her finger on it. It was as if people who didn't usually have a voice suddenly had one. Topsham seemed a well-heeled area, and the village was full of traditional shops enjoying a resurgence – a cheese shop, butcher and baker sat next to the usual high street banks and post office. The high street was closed to traffic, and there was a police presence with a small police van and six uniformed officers milling around.

Kate and Tristan were glad they had worn woolly hats and

gloves. The air was sharp, and it grew colder as the sky faded from blue to black, and the streetlights flicked on.

The vigil was due to start at the bottom of the high street and go all the way to the church.

'All of these shops are supposed to close at five thirty or six,' said Tristan as they passed the butcher and the baker.

'Staying open for the crowds,' said Kate. 'I can't imagine that any friends or family will stick around afterwards, even if they do come to it.'

Now that they were here, she realised it seemed unlikely they would get the chance to talk to anyone, and if they did, it wouldn't be appropriate to start grilling people about their alibi.

At the start of the high street, a man and a woman were being interviewed by the local news crew at the centre of the gathering crowd. They were both well dressed, with a haunted, sad look, and they were flanked on either side by a young boy and girl.

Their winter coats were all open and they wore T-shirts with HAVE YOU SEEN LAYLA? CALL 0845 951 237 printed across the chest. Underneath was a photo of Layla smiling into the camera.

'We want to pay our respects to our daughter, and to keep the investigation alive,' said Layla's father. He was handsome and in control of his emotions. 'We appeal to anyone with information to contact the police on this number.'

Layla's mother clung to him, unable to speak. Layla's brother and sister too were equally mute and looked to still be in shock. Kate felt a nudge in her ribs and Tristan tilted his head. Further up the road DCI Varia Campbell and DI John Mercy stood to one side with three uniformed police officers. They stood out because they weren't lighting candles, and were scanning the crowd.

'Let's keep out of their way,' said Kate, as she retreated behind a tall man and his wife.

Tristan pulled his woolly hat over his eyebrows. The crowds were starting to gather behind Layla's parents, brother and sister and some other friends and relations, who were wearing the Layla T-shirts and had linked arms to form a line.

Kate cupped her hands around Tristan's lantern as he lit a tea light before helping her light hers. The procession started off slowly up the hill. It had swollen to several hundred people, all quiet and rugged up against the cold. As they passed Varia she noticed Kate, and looked a little surprised, but her attention was taken by one of the uniformed officers who leaned over to talk to her. It took half an hour to slowly walk back into the village. The roads were closed and everyone was silent. The candles were undeniably beautiful. Hundreds of golden lights.

When they reached the church, the vicar met the crowd at the gates of the church and led everyone in prayer, speaking over a loud hailer.

Then a girl from Layla's class at school sang 'Amazing Grace', unaccompanied. It was a haunting moment. Kate scanned the crowds. Everyone looked sombre – men and women of all ages, a group of schoolchildren, all wearing Layla T-shirts.

The red-haired man, Peter Conway's 'biggest fan', had walked the vigil very close to Layla's family. It had given him a kick to be among the crowds of mourners in the market square, and to be so close, close enough to almost smell their tears. The cold weather had given him the confidence to attend. Everyone was wearing heavy coats, woolly hats, and scarves over their mouths. It was easy to blend in.

He'd seen the police officers, scanning the crowd so intently. Their vigilance had a sense of theatricality. They didn't really believe that the killer would show up. And they had nothing to go on. He had been so careful. He'd used different vans with fake number plates to abduct the girls. He'd avoided

CCTV. No one had seen him – well, no one that mattered. If they had any kind of e-fit they would have released it to the public by now.

So, in light of all this, why were the police here? Were they hoping to identify the killer because he looked like a 'bad' man?

He'd walked right past DCI Campbell and her officers and their eyes had moved over him, past him, searching, searching.

And then he'd joined the prayers amongst the crowd outside the church, keeping his head down as the news cameras filmed everyone. He was amazed at how many people had prayed studiously outside, and then ignored the vicar's invitation to attend the evening service and surged back to the high street, where the shops and pubs had stayed open.

Perhaps it was only worth praying if people could see you on camera.

So many had gone across to the pub, including Layla's parents.

He queued for a cheeseburger at one of the takeaway vans, and was taking a large bite when he saw Kate Marshall with a tall thin young lad. She wore a hat, but was instantly recognisable, and he gulped down the mouthful of burger, a little starstruck. She was part of the history of the Nine Elms Cannibal. And here she was mingling in public.

He circled the crowd, and moved a little closer. She was older than the photos he'd found online, and a little dumpy in her red winter coat, but he still thought she was attractive. She was *edible*. He bit into his burger and tried to imagine what it would be like to bite into the soft flesh on the backs of her thighs.

No, he couldn't conjure it. The nasty flesh of the burger was now dry in his mouth . . . The young lad she was with seemed close to her. They didn't look like they were an item. But she could be a dirty bitch. They might role-play. Would he go home with her and suck on her MILF titties?

Kate looked up, still talking to the boy, and she seemed to

look right at him, but she didn't see him. She looked through him, as part of the white noise of the crowd.

He pushed the last of the burger into his mouth, pretending to enjoy it, and moved off into the crowd.

CHAPTER 34

It was freezing cold by the time Tristan and Kate arrived back at the car. The line of parked cars had cleared, and theirs was the only one left under a row of trees, set back in the shadows from the streetlights.

Kate saw the note tucked under the right windscreen wiper, a square of thick cream paper. For a moment she thought it might have been put there by a person from one of the houses on the street, but then she saw her name written in black ink. The handwriting looked the same as in the note Meredith had shown her. With a shaking hand, Kate slipped the paper out from under the wiper and unfolded it.

KATE, YOU LOOKED POSITIVELY EDIBLE TONIGHT
IN YOUR RED COAT.
    YOU WERE SO CLOSE.
    A FAN

Kate's head snapped up and she looked along the street, but it was quiet, save for a man and woman walking with a small girl, and an older lady struggling with two bulging bags of shopping. She felt exposed, like she was being watched.

Tristan came around and took the letter from her shaking

hand, reading it over. She gripped the side of the car, feeling faint, and he opened the door on the driver's side.

'Sit down a second,' he said. Kate felt all the blood drain from her head. Cars rushed past on the road, their lights dazzling them. Tristan looked up and down the road.

He's getting closer, he's writing notes about Jake, and now he's writing to me, thought Kate. She wasn't afraid for her safety; what she feared was the power of this individual to disrupt her world. The safe, sane world she had so carefully created in the aftermath of the first case. For the first time, she wished she hadn't answered that email from Caitlyn's father. She should have passed it on to the police. It had opened a door that she had stupidly stumbled through.

She looked up and saw that Tristan had flagged down a black car, and Varia Campbell was coming towards her with John Mercy. Tristan handed the note to Varia. She read it with a concerned face and passed it to John, who instinctively started to look up and down the road. Cars were now streaming past, and Tristan and the two officers huddled on the grass verge around Kate sitting in her car.

'What time did you get here?' asked Varia, having to raise her voice above the traffic.

'Five minutes ago,' said Kate.

'No. What time did you arrive for the vigil?'

'We parked here just before six thirty,' said Tristan. Kate saw that John had the note, and it was now in a clear plastic evidence bag.

'Did you see anyone suspicious, or anyone acting suspicious around you?' asked John.

'No,' said Tristan. 'We walked the vigil. It was packed, people were quiet, and just walking with candles.'

'Whoever left the note did so within the last three hours,' said Varia, looking up and down the road as more cars roared past.

She pulled out her radio. 'This is DCI Campbell. I'm still here at the vigil in Topsham. Pull all CCTV coverage available from Pulham Road, and everything in the village up to the church between four p.m. and now.'

Varia came to the driver's door and crouched down beside Kate. She took one of her shaking hands between hers. 'Are you okay? You look like you're going into shock.'

Varia's hands were warm, and she wore several beautiful silver rings on her slim fingers. Kate's own hands were freezing cold and she was shaking.

'He knows who I am. What I was wearing. He's talking about my son,' said Kate. 'He sent Peter Conway a picture of my son . . . You need to compare the writing with the letter he sent Peter, and the other letters found at the crime scenes. It looks similar, but you need to check.'

A motorbike roared past, its engine going right through them and masking the conversation.

'This is not a good place to talk. Can we take you to the police station in Exeter? It's only four miles away,' said Varia. Kate nodded. 'Do you want us to call a doctor?' Varia added, her forehead creased with concern. She was still holding Kate's freezing hand and rubbing it between hers. This was a much softer side to her than Kate had seen previously.

'She could do with a brandy. Always works for shock,' said John to Tristan.

Kate agreed with him. It would be the perfect excuse to have a drink. To just drink herself into delicious oblivion.

'No! No alcohol. Let's get her a strong hot cup of tea,' said Tristan.

They drove in convoy to Exeter police station, and Kate and Tristan were taken through to an office where Varia and John made them all a mug of tea. Kate and Tristan sat on a large sagging sofa, and Kate took a long gulp of the tea, which she was pleased had been sweetened. She took a deep breath and began to think clearly.

'Who touched the letter?' asked Varia.

'I took it out from under the windscreen,' said Kate.

'I had a look. She passed it to me,' said Tristan.

'We'll need to take both of your fingerprints so we can eliminate you when we test the note,' said Varia.

Kate nodded. 'My fingerprints will be on file from when I was in the force,' she said.

'I was fingerprinted,' said Tristan.

'When you vandalised the car?' asked John.

Varia turned to John. 'I'm sure our guests would like some biscuits. There's a packet of Hobnobs in the staff kitchen,' she said.

John scowled and left the room.

Kate explained that she'd met Dr Meredith Baxter from Great Barwell, who showed her the note addressed to Peter on the picture of Jake, which the hospital had intercepted.

'I'll check to see if this information has been shared with us yet,' said Varia.

'I think this person who signs themselves "A Fan" is communicating with Peter Conway,' said Kate.

'But you said this letter was intercepted. Peter Conway never received it?'

Kate's phone rang in her pocket. She pulled it out, fearing that it was her mother to say something had happened to Jake.

'Oh. It's Meredith Baxter calling,' she said. She answered and listened for a moment. 'Meredith, I'm here with Detective Chief Inspector Varia Campbell. Yes, the lead officer on the case.' She held out her phone to Varia. 'She wants to talk to you.'

'What did she say?' asked Tristan as Varia moved away with the phone.

'She says they searched the whole wing at Great Barwell. All the cells, including Peter's, and all staff too. There was nothing. No hidden letters.'

'That's a good thing,' said Tristan.

'I don't like it ... Something is going on. I can feel it in my gut.'

Varia came off the phone and handed it back to Kate. 'That was useful to talk to her. Dr Baxter is going to send over this letter, and anything else she intercepts. If anything else happens, you'll be the first to know.'

'I hope you can get his DNA from the letter he left on my car,' said Kate.

'It wouldn't prove conclusively that it's from him,' said Varia.

'It must be from him,' said Tristan. 'You haven't released any information about the letters to the press? Have you?'

'No, we haven't. But plenty of people sign letters from "a fan",' said Varia.

'Come on, it's more than a coincidence,' said Kate.

Varia got up, signifying their meeting was over. 'Kate. I'm going to have a patrol car stationed outside your house for the next few days, and we are going to study any CCTV we can get from Topsham. Although it's a small village.'

'They've already stationed an officer and squad car outside my mother's house where my son lives in Whitstable,' said Kate.

'I'll make sure we coordinate with them, of course.'

When Kate and Tristan left the station and headed for the car park, a local TV news reporter and camera crew were waiting. They hurried over, a bright light shining, and followed Kate and Tristan to the car.

'We've had information that a note was left on your car from the murder suspect?' said the news reporter, a woman with very short black hair. She thrust the microphone under Kate's nose. Kate ducked around them and made it to the car, while Tristan

235

pushed a man with a sound boom who was blocking the passenger side. 'Can you confirm what the note says, and if this is linked to the Nine Elms Cannibal case you solved in 1995?'

Kate pressed the central locking button and tried to open her door. The news reporter put her hand on it.

'Do you visit Peter Conway? You have a son with him. Does Jake visit him too?'

It felt like a low blow, the news reporter naming Jake.

'Why don't you fuck off?' said Kate, yanking her door open, knocking it into the news reporter, who lost her footing and fell. 'Tristan, get in.'

When they were inside, she activated the central locking and started the engine. The news reporter was being helped to her feet as Kate honked the horn and drove towards the crew, forcing them to part. As they sped out of the car park, they saw a van with 'BBC Local News' written on the side.

'How did they know about the note?' asked Tristan.

'There's always a leak in every police station,' said Kate. She was more concerned that the journalist named Jake.

'That's not going to look good if they got it on camera,' said Tristan. 'It was only local news, though.'

'It doesn't matter. They all share the footage,' said Kate. 'And now I've invited them back into my life, and they have what they wanted. Crazy Kate Marshall. Shit.'

She slammed her hand on the steering wheel. She felt paranoid and scared. She had been in control of her life, and over the past few years she had found normality again, but now this person was taking it away from her.

CHAPTER 35

The next day was a Saturday. Kate woke at seven after an erratic few hours of sleep, and pulled on her bathing costume.

She had missed her morning swim over the past few days. It was windy on the beach with huge waves, and she had to fight her way past the breakers before she swam out. The water temperature had dropped, making the scar on her belly sting. She swam out, losing herself in the roar of the surf and the cawing of seagulls. After a few minutes, she stopped and floated on her back. The water fizzed and bubbled, and the calm rhythm of the rolling water soothed her.

She'd spoken to Glenda again last night, and reluctantly told her about the note. Her mother had been concerned, and had already cast doubt on Jake coming to stay for half term. The thought of Jake's next visit always kept Kate going, something positive to focus on, and to think she might not see him until Christmas hurt. Kate floated on her back for a moment longer, then took a deep breath and dived under the water.

Strands of seaweed hung suspended like ribbons in the water, rippling lazily with the surf. She swam down deeper, feeling the pressure on her ears and her goggles pressing against her face. The way the light was hitting the water gave the seabed a green gloaming. Kate kicked hard, her lungs bursting as she went deeper and deeper. The currents in the water were now still, the sand undisturbed. She exhaled, and felt her body drop through the water.

As she sank down the water pressure was hard against her face. Her toes hit the seabed with a soft bump. It was so cold, and she felt a current of water move around her body. She looked up at the ribbons of seaweed rippling and dancing above. Her lungs were starting to ache and there were stars moving into her vision. Her head started to feel light, and she thought of how long it had been since she was drunk. If only she could 'drink responsibly' – whatever that meant. Kate wished she could enjoy the floating light-headedness a glass of whisky used to give her. The first drink after a long day was always the best, where she felt her problems recede. She longed for that feeling.

Any day now, she was going to fall down and take a drink. She had come so close yesterday, at the train station, and had only been stopped by accident.

Things were starting to spin out of control. There was a police car stationed outside her house. There was a malevolent threat towards her and Jake which would keep them apart until . . . until when? What if this man kept doing it, or worse, just vanished?

A cold current moved past, shifting the sand around her toes, and it cut across her skin and the scar on her belly. Stars had almost filled her vision and she couldn't blink them away. The pulse in her neck and arms intensified, beating against her skin.

What about Jake? Think about him. Mum won't live for ever. There will be a time in the future when you are all he's got, and in the eyes of the law he'll be an adult in less than two years. You're just going to give up? Don't be so fucking weak! Life is worth fighting for!

A jolt of sanity woke Kate up. With her feet flat on the sand she pushed upwards, kicking hard, moving up away from the sandy bottom to where the warm water moved and churned, through the ribbons of rippling seaweed, and then she broke the surface, taking a huge breath. The life flooded back into her, with the roar of the waves and the wind, and a wave hit her in the side of the head with a stinging slap.

She took deep breaths, flexing her numb fingers and toes. She felt the current pulling her back to shore.

Never give up. Never. Life is worth fighting for. Never drink again.

She kicked out with the tide at her back and swam towards the shore.

Kate took a long hot shower, ate breakfast and drove with Myra to the Saturday AA meeting at the church hall in Ashdean. She sat with Myra and listened to the people sharing. Myra got up first to share, telling the room that she had had twenty-nine years of sobriety, but every day was still a fight. She ended by saying, 'My recovery must come first, so that everything I love in life doesn't have to come last.'

When it was Kate's turn to share, she didn't hold back, telling the room how she had almost drunk, and how much she yearned to take a drink and numb everything. She knew some of the faces who stared back at her; some were new but she drew strength from the fact that they all wanted one thing. Sobriety.

When Myra and Kate arrived back at Kate's house, they saw the police car sitting outside, and the officer inside put his hand up to wave.

'Fancy a cuppa?' asked Myra.

'Thanks, but I've got work to do.'

'Just concentrate on today,' said Myra. 'You know how it works: one day at a time. All you need to concentrate on is not drinking today. Tomorrow is a way away.'

'You're full of quotes.'

'I thought you were going to say I was full of shit!' said Myra with a laugh.

'Well, that too.' Kate smiled. She leaned over and gave Myra a hug.

'Keep your chin up. If that police officer had seen some weirdo in the bushes, he wouldn't be waving,' said Myra.

'They can't afford to keep an officer out here twenty-four hours for long,' said Kate.

'I'll make him a cup of tea and give him a slice of cake, keep his energy levels up.'

When Kate got back inside the house, her phone rang. She almost didn't pick up because she didn't recognise the number, but she was glad she did. It was Malcolm Murray.

'Hello love, I'm sorry I haven't been in contact,' he said.

'How is Sheila?' asked Kate. She explained how she'd arrived at the house just as the ambulance was leaving.

'Well, it's been terrible. It was touch and go for a couple of days, but then we had a real miracle. A donor became available, and she has a new kidney. It's going to take her time to recuperate, but she's off the awful dialysis.'

'That's wonderful news,' said Kate, feeling that something was going right, and then she remembered what she'd driven to Chew Magna to tell them.

'I'm sorry, Malcolm, but we hit a dead end.' Kate outlined everything that had happened, and how the man in the car Caitlyn had met had turned out to be Paul Adler, who had an alibi. Kate didn't share her reservations about him – she thought it best to give Malcolm the facts. He was silent for a long time on the end of the phone.

'Well, thank you, love. We both appreciate everything you tried to do. I thought I'd lost them both, Caitlyn and Sheila. Maybe Caitlyn was only meant to be in our lives for a short time. The brightest stars burn out fast.'

Kate felt a deep sadness for Malcolm and Sheila, and she wished she could do more. She heard herself promise that she would keep looking into it.

She came off the phone hating that she'd promised too much.

CHAPTER 36

On Monday morning, Kate and Tristan were in their office working on the slides and notes for her lecture that afternoon when there was a knock at the door. Laurence Barnes, the dean of the university, entered. He was in his late forties with greying hair. He had replaced Professor Coombe-Davies, who had passed away the previous year, but he didn't share the same affection with his staff. He was petty and divisive, and liked to rule with fear.

'Kate, I need a word,' he said, slapping a copy of the *News of the World* down on her desk.

'I'll go down and get the projector set up,' said Tristan, making to leave.

'No. You stay. This involves you both,' he snapped, pointing at Tristan to sit. 'Have you seen this?'

He turned to a lurid double-page spread about Kate and her involvement in the Nine Elms Copycat Killer case.

'I read the *Observer* at weekends,' she said coolly.

'Did you watch the news?'

Kate's confrontation with Janelle Morrison, the BBC local news reporter, had made the news over the weekend, and journalists had made the link between the Nine Elms Cannibal and the latest copycat murders.

'Yes.'

'You know, this really doesn't reflect well on the faculty.' He reached into his pocket and pulled out a photocopy of Kate's private investigator business card. He placed it in front of her. 'And neither does this. Running a business from your office. You have your direct number and university email on this card.'

'Where did you get the card?' asked Kate.

'Detective Chief Inspector Varia Campbell, when she was put through to my office by mistake. She says she's concerned that you are getting in the way of her police investigation.'

It felt like a punch to the gut that Varia had sold her out to her boss.

'She didn't seem concerned last week when we spoke to her,' said Tristan. 'We were able to give her information about the case.'

Laurence turned his attention to Tristan for the first time.

'We?'

'Er, we . . . ' started Tristan, looking to Kate.

'Tristan is my assistant in work, and he has been assisting me privately in an unpaid role,' said Kate, scrambling to remember the terms of Tristan's employment contract, hoping that she wasn't landing him in it.

'I'm afraid I'm going to have to give you a formal warning. And Tristan, your probationary three months will be extended to six.'

Tristan opened his mouth to protest. He looked devastated.

'Tristan, would you excuse us for a moment?' Kate gave him a look and he reluctantly left the office. Kate smiled at Laurence and went to the filing cabinet and retrieved a piece of paper. 'Have you read the UCAS submissions report for the 2011 to 2012 academic year?' she asked.

'Of course. What's that—'

'Then you'll see that my Criminology and Psychology course

has five hundred applicants for eighty places. You'll also be aware that when those eighty places are filled, come August, a large percentage of those students who are rejected will be offered the courses in Forensics and Psychology, which I also lecture. That's a lot of bums on seats, thanks to me. Now, depending on who wins the next election, and it's not looking good for the Labour Party, tuition fees could increase and university places become a buyer's market,' said Kate.

'Are you threatening to leave?' asked Laurence.

'No. But I am telling you, Laurence, to get off my back and leave my staff alone. I do a good job, and so does Tristan. Almost all my colleagues have second jobs and do research projects.'

'You listen to me, Kate.'

'No. You listen to me. I'd hate to have to make an official complaint about you *harassing* me. I'm sure the newspapers would love another juicy story. I'm pretty newsworthy right now.'

Laurence had gone very pale. 'Now come on, Kate, there's no reason to be like that. I just came to have a friendly word, off the record.'

'There's always a record,' said Kate. 'Oh, and Tristan's probationary period ends today. If you could get HR to email him with the good news by the end of the day that would be great.'

Laurence threw the newspaper into the wastepaper basket, went to the door and pushed at the handle. It wouldn't budge and he got more annoyed and pushed against it.

'It opens inwards,' said Kate.

Laurence was now red in the face. He yanked the door open and slammed it behind him.

Kate hoped she hadn't overstepped the mark, but if the past few years had taught her anything, it was that you had to stick up for yourself. She'd much rather be admired than liked.

There was another knock at the door, and Tristan came in. He was holding up his phone.

'Kate, it's all over the news,' he said. 'They've just arrested a man in connection with the three copycat murders. The police have taken him into custody.'

He came to Kate's desk and showed her the footage of a man, with a coat over his head, handcuffed and being bundled up the steps into Exeter police station. He was surrounded by press and members of the public screaming abuse.

'When was this posted on BBC News?' asked Kate, frustrated that his face was hidden.

'An hour ago. If we go down to the cafe, there might be an update on the news. It's five to twelve,' said Tristan.

Kate grabbed her bag and they hurried out of the office.

CHAPTER 37

A hundred and ninety miles from Ashdean, the Bishop's Arms pub sat overlooking the Chiltern Hills. It was an ancient thatched building which had been gutted and was now a Michelin-starred gastropub. The Bishop's Arms sat in one of the wealthiest and most affluent pockets of the English countryside, and was the place to be seen.

On this Monday lunchtime, the car park out front was full, and a row of helicopters was parked on the lawn at the back, next to a custom-built helipad.

The red-haired Fan of Peter Conway looked around at the busy bar.

Braying fools, he thought.

The men, young and confident, were boorishly shouting over each other, already drunk and flushed in the face. The women were huddled in groups, better behaved, and all well turned out and beady-eyed.

He'd been coming to the Bishop's Arms for several years, first with his parents before they had retired to live in Spain, and now with his brother.

His brother was fickle and lovable, and had tried for years to pursue a career in the music industry, but he was constantly sidetracked by the drugs and partying.

He thought of Emma Newman, and a memory came back to him of her lying naked on her front, her hands tied behind her back, feet bound and pulled up to meet them, and masking tape over her mouth. Her skin had been soft and creamy to the touch, but the taste had been spoiled by the drugs that leaked through her pores.

The television mounted on the wall caught his eye, and he watched in fascination as the news report played out. A man had been arrested for the three murders. *His* three murders. He felt panic. The man hadn't been identified. He'd been led into the station with his face covered.

What if this idiot was charged, and took the credit before his work was done – before the big reveal?

He looked over at the woman he'd brought as his lunchtime date, India Dalton. She was pretty enough. They'd been introduced, via email, by his sister. India's father owned a luxury travel agency and was a little too nouveau riche for this crowd, but her good looks more than made up for it.

India was talking animatedly with Fizzy Martlesham, a severe-looking woman with her hair scraped back from her large forehead. The Martlesham family owned vast amounts of farmland around Oxfordshire and were a major supplier of the strawberries consumed at Wimbledon.

He looked back at the screen, downed the rest of his pint, and picked up his jacket.

'I'm terribly sorry to interrupt you, ladies.' He smiled, taking India by the arm. 'But something urgent has come up. You'll have to excuse us.'

'What about lunch?' asked India. 'I *so* want to try the turmeric and raspberry sorbet.'

'Another time. I can drop you back at the heliport, and we'll reschedule.'

'Shame you have to fly off, quite literally,' said Fizzy, leaning in for an air kiss.

'Please relay my apologies to my brother, he seems to have vanished.'

'Yes. Of course. I saw him heading to the bathroom a little while ago ... Oh, and India would love a selfie in front of your helicopter for her social media account,' said Fizzy with spiteful glee.

They left the pub, crossing the wet grass to the helipad.

'Could I get a photo before we take off?' asked India, picking her way carefully in her sandals. She had his leather jacket draped over her thin shoulders.

'No,' he said, opening the door of a petrol-blue helicopter. The glass bubble of the cockpit was glistening in the sun. India pouted, petulant, but still took her phone from her bag. He leaned over and put his hand over her phone.

'I said, no. No photo.'

'Oh, come on, you own this magnificent machine. It's just crying out to be photographed.' She grinned and pulled her hand away, and went to snap a picture. He grabbed her wrist and twisted. She yelped and dropped the phone.

'I said no fucking photo. When I say no, I mean it!'

He leaned down and picked up her phone, then opened the door for her. India had tears in her eyes as she clambered inside. He slammed the door.

At the back of the pub he could see Fizzy smoking. She raised her cigarette, smiling. He waved back, muttering *Nosy bitch* under his breath.

He climbed into the cockpit, pulled on his headset and got clearance for take-off. It took a minute for the blades to start spinning, then with a roar they took off, the grass below them flattening and then seeming to drop away. India refused to put on her headset, so he was unable to talk to her over the roar of the engine.

It was a ten-minute journey back to the Oxfordshire heliport where they'd met up. He left the engine running when they touched down, and turned to her with a smile and a wave. 'Bye, bye, India.'

She motioned to him that she couldn't hear, but he carried on smiling and waving as she jumped out and was met by one of the stewards from the heliport. He watched them move away, their hair flattened by the wind from the whirring blades.

An image of India flashed into his mind, naked and pleading. That perfect hair plastered to her face with sweat and tears.

He took off again, and the helicopter sheared up and off into the sky, heading west.

It worried him the police had made an arrest. They had the wrong man. *He* was their man, and he would reveal himself. Soon, but not yet.

CHAPTER 38

When Kate got home, the police car had vanished from outside her house, and Glenda called to say the police car watching Jake was also gone.

Kate tried to call Varia to ask what was happening, but was told to expect a callback. Kate didn't want to wait so she drove over to Exeter, went into the police station and asked to see her. She waited for an hour, and finally Varia appeared.

'What's going on?' asked Kate. 'You've arrested someone and you take away police surveillance on me and my son. Have you got him?'

'Come to my office,' said Varia. Kate followed her along a corridor, past offices with support staff. Phones rang, officers walked and talked. It felt odd to be back in a large police station – odd, but at the same time it felt like home.

'Would you like tea?' asked Varia, taking her into a small office overlooking the car park.

'No, thank you,' said Kate, taking a seat as Varia closed her office door.

'Okay. We arrested a teacher from Layla Gerrard's school. His DNA was matched to a burglary in 1993 in Manchester. At the time blood was taken from the point of entry. He broke a window and cut himself. He then beat an elderly couple badly and took off with their valuables.'

'Is he a suspect?'

'No. He has an alibi. He was in France when Layla went missing. His wife is French and they were visiting relatives. I have passport records and CCTV. His arrest should not have been publicised. I have the news cameras to thank for that.'

'Are you going to release him?' said Kate.

'We are going to charge him for the 1993 assault and burglary. He won't be released, but I will still face the wrath of the press. I have twenty officers assigned to this case who are all working harder than you can imagine, going without family time,' she said.

'I'm not questioning that. Are you looking into all the schools that those girls went to? That was Peter Conway's way in.'

'Yes. We've looked at the schools that the three victims attended. Teachers, support staff, caretakers, casual workers. We've taken voluntary DNA samples from almost every male teacher and support worker who came into contact or who was associated with the girls. Hence the arrest. We've also taken DNA samples from males in the families, and in the case of the first victim, Emma Newman, we have looked at the children's home she went to and everyone who works there has been cross-checked.'

'And nothing?'

'The DNA samples gave us the arrest today, and also we had a hit on the caretaker at Layla's school. He was involved in a sexual assault in 1991. He picked up a girl on her way home from school and raped her. We interviewed him. His wife is his alibi, but he now has limited movement; he's registered as partially blind and he can't drive. With the logistics of how these girls are being grabbed and abducted, he would have had to take the bus to do it. He'll be charged for the historical

251

crime, but there is no way he was able to kill these three young women.'

'Did you get anything from the CCTV at the candle-light vigil?'

'Kate, I got a crowd of people surging through the village. The point where your car was parked isn't covered by CCTV, nor is the first half mile of the route the vigil took, then we've got fields and trees in the other direction.'

'What about satellites, Google Earth?'

Varia raised an eyebrow. 'I work for the Devon and Cornwall police, not MI5. If this were a matter of national security then I might be able to request still images from Google Earth data, but for a note left on a car windscreen by a potential suspect we're not there yet. Besides, I already thought of that and pulled up Google Earth to check the location ...'

She typed on her computer, clicked the mouse a few times and swivelled round the screen. 'You can see that the road where you parked is covered by a tunnel of trees. Even without leaves we'd have trouble getting a clear image. The CCTV we have got from the vigil is difficult to view because of the limited visibility with it being dark, and the hundreds of candles screw with the image. And almost everyone there wore woolly hats and had their heads down out of respect. The few cameras we have footage from are set at a high angle looking down and we can't see faces.'

'Okay.'

'I'm also in contact with Dr Baxter. She is sending me all of the correspondence coming in and out of Great Barwell to Peter Conway: letters from members of the public, transcripts of phone conversations with his mother ... ' She rubbed her face. 'I'm trying my best to stay positive, but there are no witnesses to any of the abductions. It's as if he took them and vanished into thin air. I've had all the male police officers and support workers in the borough submit to a DNA test. That's not a decision I've taken lightly.'

'I know how horrible that must have been,' said Kate.

'So, when you come to my station and act like I'm slacking off—'

'You're not,' finished Kate.

'Handwriting analysis shows all the notes match: the three left at the crime scene, the picture of Jake sent to Peter Conway, and the note left on your car. I was about to call you and say that we'll be continuing with a police presence for you and Jake, reviewed every few days depending on the progress of the case.'

'What about Enid Conway's autobiography?'

'I've already told you I don't have the resources to police the tourist hotspots of Devon and Cornwall. I've asked officers to be vigilant on their beat patrols, I've flagged the areas. Now, I've been candid with you. I ask that you share any information with me, if and when you have it.'

'Yes,' said Kate.

'Now, if you'll excuse me, I have a killer to catch.'

CHAPTER 39

The red-haired Fan sat in the darkness on the terrace of his London apartment. The air was crisp and the sky clear. He could see out across Regent's Park to where the city twinkled and shimmered against the dark sky. All the lights were out, and he sat in the shadows.

His family's wealth was huge. His father was a retired barrister and his mother came from money. She was the heir to a European haulage company. Thanks to his parents, he had the use of vehicles and warehouse space. He also had an apartment in central London and a house in the country.

He loved London. It was a vast melting pot. It was loud and vibrant and people didn't watch you too closely; they were too busy and absorbed in their own lives and problems. It was the perfect location to hide out and make his plans.

His apartment was on the top floor of a grand pillared terrace. His family owned the building, and he and his three siblings had been 'gifted' an apartment each for their twenty-first birthdays. His two sisters were married with lives of their own – both now lived in New York and let out their apartments. His brother in a fit of independence had borrowed against his apartment, and then, unable to pay the mortgage, had lost it to the bank.

It was late, and the planes had stopped flying. There was just the sound of a far-off police siren, and very faint classical music. It was peaceful. He would miss it.

He came back inside and went to his office. It was a wood-panelled room with heavy leather furniture, but the wood panels were obscured and every spare inch of wall was covered in a collage of newspaper clippings, photos and printouts.

He took a moment to walk the room, something he never tired of. Every article that had ever been written about the Nine Elms Cannibal case was pasted to the walls, from the first few headlines about the corpses of the dead girls, through to the articles about the hunt for the Nine Elms Cannibal, and then the stories about Peter Conway, star cop, unmasked as a killer, and his beautiful sidekick, Kate Marshall.

He reached out and touched the photos of Peter and Kate and the photos of the dead girls – Peter Conway's four victims – and then the photos of Kate's flat, when she almost became his fifth victim. He had known about the case since he was a young boy, and had seen the stuff in the press. For many years it had been a hot topic of conversation in the family.

His mother and father and his siblings were united in one thing: that Peter Conway was an evil killer who deserved to be locked up. But he'd always felt he was different – he had violent urges and dark thoughts, and he felt that he would never be able to live a normal life. For many years he'd sympathised in secret with Conway, felt kinship with him. It was only in his adult years, when his parents had retired to Spain and his siblings scattered to the wind, that he was able to think for himself. His obsession started to develop. He became a true Fan.

He went to his desk where he'd put a copy of the *News of the World*. He cut out the latest article, a piece about his copycat murders. The photo they'd used thrilled him. It was three circular images connected by arrows: at the top was Peter Conway, next was Kate Marshall and the third circle was empty with a huge question mark. It contained the words WHO IS THE COPYCAT?

'Me, me, me, me!' he chanted as he carefully cut out the article and applied glue to the back, before moving to the wood panelling where he pasted it on, smoothing it down so it stuck like wallpaper.

He stood back and admired his handiwork. The room was an assault on the senses. Wall to wall pictures, articles, photos of death. He imagined the moment when the police broke down the door to his apartment and burst in. They would find this room, this shrine, and it would be photographed and those photos would be published in print and online – and one day, very soon, a book would be written about him too.

There was a soft tone as an email came through on his computer. He went to it and guided the mouse to open the email. It was a message from an eBay seller. He had won his bid on a vintage bedspread. He smiled a gummy smile. He printed off the image of the bedspread and took it over to the article glued to his wall, where there were photos from the inside of Kate Marshall's flat in Deptford. He held it up against the photo taken of her bedroom in the aftermath of Peter Conway's attack on her, and the image of her bedspread.

'Yes,' he said, comparing the two. 'It's a perfect match.'

CHAPTER 40

Ten miles away, Enid Conway sat at her kitchen table preparing to take the latest messages from The Fan to Peter. It was a messy job, slicing open the sweet toffees to scrape out the soft centres. Her clothes were covered in stains, and her kitchen table was strewn with lumps of melted toffee and chocolate. She worked with a surgical scalpel, which made the neatest, cleanest cut, and she wore latex surgical gloves. The toffee couldn't be handled for long, it quickly melted in her hands, so she had to work with frozen toffees. She also made sure the heating was switched off and all the kitchen windows were open. Cold air circulated and with it the smell of takeaway food and exhaust fumes.

It was often noisy at night, and it was something she was used to after so many years, but tonight it made her jittery. A couple of kids were roaring up and down the street on a motorbike and the high-pitched drone of the engine was going right through her.

She took another toffee and carefully removed the wrapper. Her hands were sweaty under the latex gloves, and she had trouble keeping the toffee still as she carefully pressed the tip of the surgical blade into the centre, working her way around it. She needed to slice it clean in half, so when it was put back together the join looked neat.

There was a shout from next door, and it made her jump. The toffee she was holding slipped and the tip of the blade went into the ball of her thumb. The sweaty latex glove began to quickly fill with blood and she hurried to the sink.

'Shit,' she cried, pulling off the glove and holding her thumb under the cold tap. It hurt like hell. She looked at the wound, squeezing it. It was deep. 'Fucking hell!'

She held it under the tap for a few minutes until the bleeding stopped. Then she took out her first aid kit, applying antiseptic cream and a tight gauze and plaster. When her hands were dry, she took a bottle of Teacher's whisky from the cupboard, poured herself a glass, and downed it with a couple of painkillers.

She surveyed the mess on the kitchen table: the melted lumps of toffee, the balled-up latex gloves and the heat-sealing machine that sat on the edge. The whisky warmed her insides. She went to the two passports sitting on the counter next to the microwave. Enid checked for any blood spotting through the bandage on her thumb, and seeing the bandage was clean, she opened the passports.

The first had her photo, but the name was June Munro. June was born in the same year as Enid, but on a different day. She was astonished at the quality of the fake. The paper felt right to the touch, and there was the thick plastic last page with the biometric data. The passport would expire in nine years. There were a few stamps in the back for authenticity – a two-week trip to Croatia the year before, and another to Iceland, and another to the US. There was also an America B-1/B-2 traveller's visa. She picked up the second. It had the same stamp for Croatia and America. The photo of Peter that she'd taken in the visitors' room at Great Barwell looked good. His name in the passport was Walter King, which she thought was odd, but he looked almost distinguished with his grey hair. His birthday made him one year younger.

Inside the microwave was a four-inch-thick packet of euros:

four hundred and fifty 500-euro notes, totalling 225,000 euros. She also had another packet of smaller-denomination notes totalling 7,000 euros, and some fifty- and twenty-pound notes coming to £5,000.

The sight of it all made her shake with excitement and fear. She had taken three of the 500-euro notes to the bank, choosing them at random from the pile. It had been a risk, but she had to know. She'd successfully changed them for pounds. They were genuine. The passports looked kosher. He'd told her that they'd cost fifteen grand apiece from a very reliable source. None of this had come for free. On delivery of this all, she'd signed her house over to a blind trust. The house had been valued at just under £240,000. It was worth more, especially for the ghoul factor, as the childhood home of a serial killer.

Enid poured herself another whisky. It made her nervous having all this money in the house. She was due to visit Peter the next day, and she needed to stash it all somewhere safe.

It would be worth it, she told herself. They would cross the Channel by boat and slip into a Spanish port unnoticed. The passports were set up for the Schengen Area, covering the whole of Europe. As far as the authorities were concerned June Munro and Walter King were both in Spain. After Peter's escape every port, train station and airport would be on high alert, but once they were in Spain they would be able to lie low for months or even years and move around Europe without having to go through extensive passport checks.

She worried about money. She would have to leave all her bank accounts, and give up her pension, but she hoped they could buy a small place outright and save some money. There were always ways to earn money.

For so many years she had longed to hold her son, to talk to him endlessly for hours, like they used to. She didn't want to think about anything else, about what Peter would need to do

259

to secure their freedom. Like always, she pushed it to the back of her mind.

Enid downed the last of her whisky and took another packet of chocolate eclairs from the freezer. This time her hand was steady. The toffee yielded, splitting into two even halves. She scraped out the chocolate with the corner of the scalpel and replaced it with a large vitamin capsule. This had been emptied and now contained a note to Peter, detailing the latest developments. She placed the two halves back together, using the heat of her fingers to mould the toffee back into shape. She prepared the second toffee, placing inside it the note from Peter's 'Fan', then she repacked the toffees and put them into an opened bag.

She was relieved to reseal the bag, using the plastic heat sealer, and place the bag of toffees in the freezer overnight.

They were so close, so close. This would be the last time she smuggled notes in and out of Great Barwell. It would also be her last visit.

She poured herself another whisky and even though she wasn't a religious woman, she prayed for it all to be a success.

CHAPTER 41

Tristan was celebrating being made a full-time member of the university staff, and he came over to Kate's for dinner that evening. She wasn't much of a cook, so treated him to takeaway pizza. They spent the whole evening discussing the case, which was now all over the media.

'There's a few things I've thought we should follow up,' said Kate, pouring them each a second cup of coffee to go with a second slice of the raspberry cheesecake Tristan had brought with him. 'It all comes down to Enid Conway's book.'

There was a copy of it on the breakfast bar, and Tristan picked it up. 'How are we going to work out where he'll dump the next body? There are so many places Enid and Peter went on this holiday,' he said, flicking through to the index.

'Think bigger,' said Kate. 'We know he's going to do this again.'

'What if he gets knocked over by a bus? There must be serial killers out there who suddenly come a cropper themselves, and that's why the killings stop,' said Tristan.

'Maybe that's why they never caught Jack the Ripper, because he crossed the road one day and got hit by a cart.'

They both laughed.

'We shouldn't be laughing,' said Tristan, sawing off another chunk of cheesecake and putting it on a plate. He offered it to Kate.

'No. Not that big. I've already eaten an enormous piece ... Sometimes you need to laugh or you'll go mad.'

'Speaking of which, how are you coping with the police being out there?'

'It's comforting, but I remember back when I used to do stakeouts and watch houses. The more time that goes past and nothing happens, the more complacent you get. And Myra keeps going out with cups of tea and cake for them.'

'We should give them some of this cheesecake. It's huge.'

'You should take it home.'

'My sister doesn't like sweet stuff. Wouldn't you have liked people to give you nice stuff to eat when you were doing surveillance?' asked Tristan.

'Good point. Anyway, I'm sure Varia will move them onto something else once the threat dies down,' said Kate.

She went to the back window of the kitchen and looked out. The police car was parked out front and a bored-looking officer was drinking tea and scratching at his chin. She wondered if Glenda was taking out tea for the officer watching Jake, and how spooked she was getting by it all. It was now less than a week until Jake was due to come and stay for half term.

'She's never written another book?' asked Tristan, picking up *No Son of Mine* again and looking at the back cover.

Kate was suddenly struck by something so obvious she couldn't believe she'd missed it. 'How could I be so stupid?' she said. 'Enid didn't write this book. She had a ghost writer who came over and interviewed her and made her words into prose. Well, I say prose in the loosest sense ...' She took the book from Tristan and scanned the inside, remembering at the time it was published that she'd seen the name of a ghost writer. 'That's it, Gary Dolman. He was the ghost writer. I remember back whenever it was I had a message from him, asking me to contribute to the interviews he was doing to write the book. We should talk to him. There could be stuff that he heard, that was never published, stuff that Enid talked about . . .'

'He might have information about Peter Conway's time spent in Manchester. It could lead to something on Caitlyn Murray's disappearance,' said Tristan.

'Maybe, but I'm interested in the sequence of events on this holiday they took. There were four victims in the original case; our copycat has killed three. We should also be asking the question: what happens after number five?'

'What do you mean?' asked Tristan.

'Peter Conway only stopped because I caught him. This guy is copying Peter. And presumably he wants to be caught, that's why copycat killers happen. Is he just going to go to four murders and then stop?'

'Carry on living his life, and risk getting hit by a bus before anyone catches him,' said Tristan.

Kate sat down. 'That's depressing. I want us to look at everything again, all the people involved. There must be a link. How is this guy finding the girls? Why has he chosen to copy all these killings around this area and not in London like Peter did?'

'CCTV? Back in 1995 there wasn't as much CCTV coverage in London. He could move around a lot more easily without the risk. I've never been to London, but I read there's CCTV everywhere, and a system of cameras that run the London congestion charge.'

Kate nodded. 'You're right. Every car coming in and out of London is photographed and its number plate logged. In comparison Devon and Cornwall are still very rugged and it's easier to get lost on the moors and in the surrounding towns. I told you that Varia wasn't able to pull any CCTV the other night from Topsham.'

'Don't you think it's weird that he's hitting the part of the country you moved to?' said Tristan. 'Have you thought of that?'

'Yes. I have, and it terrifies me.'

They were both quiet for a moment.

'I can get in contact with the ghost writer,' said Tristan. 'If he's willing to talk do you want to do it over the phone or face to face?'

'I'd like to meet him face to face,' said Kate.

She took a sip of her coffee and looked out of the window. Tristan's words went through her head again: *Don't you think it's weird that he's hitting the part of the country you moved to?*

CHAPTER 42

Peter paced his room, impatient. He was desperate to get the next note from Enid. When the knock on the door came, he hurried to the hatch.

'Morning, Peter, I'm here to take you to visit with your mother,' said Winston. He said the same thing every time, in a slightly monotone voice. 'I'll pass through your hood, if you could place it on your head, buckle it up, then back up to the hatch ...'

'Yes, yes. Just get on with it,' said Peter.

Winston pushed the spit hood through the hatch, and Peter grabbed it and slipped it over his head. The mesh felt cold against his skin, and he could smell his sweat and the acidic tang of his dry saliva. When the straps were done up, Peter backed up to the hatch, put his hands through and Winston fastened the cuffs on his wrists.

Winston's radio beeped, and he was given the go-ahead to open the door and take Peter to the lift.

Enid waited for Peter in the usual meeting room with the green walls and the screwed-down furniture, the bag of sweets at her feet. She drummed her fingers on the bare table and checked her watch. Peter was two minutes late. She shifted in her seat, uneasy. Things at Great Barwell ran with an almost military precision, to the minute. Where was he? She looked up at the security cameras in the four corners of the room.

What's your game? she thought. *Are you on to us?*

Enid sat back and crossed her arms, feigning relaxation. But inside her stomach was churning.

The surveillance room at Great Barwell Psychiatric Hospital could rival the CCTV control centre in any of the London Underground stations. The back wall was covered in a vast screen where the view from every camera, of which there were 167, was displayed in a checker-board of images; every corridor, doorway, therapy room and interview room was monitored, along with the exercise yards, the visitors' centre and every major entrance and exit. Six officers were on duty at any one time, and they each worked in front of a smaller screen and were assigned to a different sector of the hospital. They could communicate with every member of staff on duty via a radio link, and from the CCTV centre they could remotely open and close doors the second there was any kind of trouble.

Ken Werner was the duty manager that day. He sat at the desk nearest the door. He was a veteran of the hospital, and had been a member of staff since the early days when there was no CCTV and you kept your wits about you. He was surprised when the intercom rang on the entrance door. He switched to the camera outside and saw Dr Meredith Baxter peer up and wave.

'Morning, Doctor,' he said, buzzing her in.

'Hello, Ken. Have you got a minute?' she asked, coming to stand by his desk.

She was always fragrant, and softly dressed in pastel colours and woollen jumpers. Her hair smelled good too. Whenever he saw her it made him think how much Great Barwell had changed from his early days as an orderly. Back then it was a brutal asylum, where the staff all wore starched whites. The patients were called prisoners and you could give them a good kicking if they got out of line, which, Ken thought privately, often worked better than hours of expensive therapy.

'What can I do you for?' he asked.

Meredith flashed him a professional smile. 'Can you pull up the video feed for visitors' room one in G Wing? On the big screen if possible, please?'

'No problemo ...' Ken tapped at his keyboard and an image of Enid waiting for her visit with Peter appeared on the huge screen.

'Thank you,' said Meredith. She went close to the screen and peered at the image for a moment, tilting her head.

On the screen, Enid crossed her legs and shifted in her chair, checking her watch.

Ken looked down at the row of images in front of him. He could see two patients on their way to a group therapy session, another emerging from the bathroom on his corridor, flanked by an orderly.

Peter Conway was being led down the corridor towards the lift at the end with Winston. Meredith turned.

'Could you delay Peter at the lift please, Ken?'

Her tone told him that it wasn't a question.

When Winston reached the lift with Peter, the orderly pressed the call button and the doors pinged and slid open. The lift was empty.

'Can you hold it there please, Winston?' said a voice crackling through his radio. Winston took a step back and pulled the radio from his belt.

'Okay. Holding position,' he said. The lift pinged and the doors closed. Winston turned to Peter. 'We've been asked to stop here for a—'

'I know. I heard. I'm right beside you,' snapped Peter.

There was another ping and the doors opened to the empty lift. A moment passed, and with a further ping they closed. Peter looked up and saw that the lift remained on their floor. He saw Winston check his watch. It was now 11.04. He took out his radio again.

'Waiting for clearance. I have Peter Conway for visiting at eleven a.m. . . . .'

'If you could hold there, Winston, thank you,' came the voice.

Peter heard a voice in the background say, 'I'm going to initiate a strip search.' It was a woman's voice and Peter recognised it as Dr Baxter.

Peter could feel sweat starting to form under the hood. What was the delay? They were only ever delayed when there was an incident, and the different kinds of incidents had numbered codes. A fight was signalled by 101, 102 was a suicide attempt, 381 was if a staff member had been attacked. He'd only ever heard 904, a riot, used once, a few years back. Winston had been told to halt, but there had been no numbered code given. *Something was going on.*

Back in the control room, there was another buzz at the door. Ken saw it was Dr Rajdai, Dr Baxter's deputy in the psychology department.

'Please let him in,' said Meredith, keeping her eyes on the big screen. He came in and went straight to join her.

'How are we doing?' he asked, looking up at the screen.

'Enid Conway's been through security checks, full patdown at the main gate. All her belongings and the sweets she's brought him have gone through X-ray. They are all sealed,' said Meredith. She looked at Dr Rajdai and he nodded.

'I'm happy to sign off with you, but she could complain,' he said.

Meredith nodded and pulled out her radio. 'This is Dr Baxter. Please can you take Enid Conway out of visitors' room 1 and give her a full strip and cavity search.'

'Copy that,' came the voice on the other end.

Ken watched as Enid was taken out of the visitors' room by two female orderlies. He shook his head. Dr Baxter liked to think of herself as modern and sympathetic, but she was just as brutal as the old-school doctors.

Peter was held in the corridor for another ten minutes, which felt like it stretched to hours. There was no explanation. Finally, Winston was given the go-ahead and Peter was taken to visitors' room 1.

When he saw his mother, her eyes looked red from crying, and this shocked and terrified him. He rarely, if ever, saw her cry. He waited until Winston and Terrell had gone and then gave her a hug.

'What's going on?' he said, sitting opposite her.

'Those bastards. They gave me a full search, latex gloves, and they were rough and all ... They said if I didn't submit to it I couldn't see you.' She took a balled-up tissue out of her sleeve and dabbed at her eyes.

Peter looked up at the security camera and fixed it with a glare.

That fucking bitch, Dr Baxter, he thought. *Just you wait.*

'Come here, Mum,' he said. She got up and they embraced; he held her close, burying his face in the top of her head and smelling her hair. She pressed her face against his chest.

'You've lost weight,' she said, stroking his pectorals with red nail-varnished fingers.

'Yeah, getting fit for, well, the future,' he said. She pulled away and looked up at him. 'And I was getting to be a porker.' She smiled and laughed. 'There, that's my girl,' he said. 'You look years younger when you smile.'

The orderly outside leaned forward and knocked on the glass, indicating they should separate.

Back in the control room, Meredith stood with Dr Rajdai. She watched their embrace on the screen.

'Jesus, we've got our own private showing of *Oedipus Rex*,' said Ken from behind her. 'If you ask me, it's not drugs he wants to slip her . . . '

A couple of the other orderlies manning the computer monitors chuckled.

Meredith turned and gave him a withering look. 'Unless you have a clinical opinion, which I doubt, keep things to yourself,' she said. She turned to Dr Rajdai who was standing in front of the screen with her. 'I want Enid Conway stopped on her way out at the front gate for another full strip search and cavity search. If she objects, tell her we'll withdraw all visiting rights. And I want Peter searched too,' she said.

When the visit came to an end, Enid held onto Peter for a long time. She ran her hands down his back and squeezed his buttocks, feeling his new, trimmer body. She felt him stiffen as he pushed himself against her.

'Not long now, Mum,' he whispered in her ear.

'I love you,' she whispered back.

There was a knock on the window and the orderly signalled she had to leave. She reluctantly pulled away and broke their embrace.

'Don't forget to take your sweets,' she said, placing the bag on the table.

'Thanks, Mum. Next time you hear from me it'll be by phone.' She nodded.

Almost home free, she thought to herself. *If they knew about the sweets they'd have taken them off me.*

Enid was stopped at the body scanners on her way out and taken off into a side office for another body search.

Afterwards, when she was dressed, she was taken towards the exit by the big female officer who had examined her.

She was still anxious. What was happening to Peter? Had they found her note and the note from his fan? The notes had the final details of their plan.

'If you could join the queue. I'll leave you here,' said the woman, indicating the line of people waiting at the X-ray machines.

'After all that, you still need me to go through?' said Enid.

'Yes please, madam,' said the woman.

'You call me "madam" after shining your torch up my arse? Fuck you,' she snapped.

'I need you to moderate your language.'

'And why don't you sit on this and spin?' said Enid, giving her the middle finger.

The woman gave her a hard stare and walked off.

The line of staff and visitors already waiting gave Enid a wide berth as she went through the X-ray machines. The young lad with the thin hair and odd-shaped head checked her through the X-ray machines.

'Your hearing aid, it's in a different ear,' he said.

'What?'

He tapped the right side of his head.

'Wasn't it in the other ear the last time you visited?'

'You must be mistaken,' she said. She took her coat and her phone from the tray and hurried out of the entrance. She was breathless with fear and excitement. She hoped that Peter was able to retrieve the note without being rumbled by the guards.

Peter knew something was up when four orderlies were waiting at the door of his cell. The plastic bag of sweets felt slick in his sweating hands.

'We need to conduct a body search please, Peter,' said Terrell. 'Is there anything you would like to tell us about before we do this?'

Peter shook his head.

One of the orderlies held out his hand and Peter gave him the plastic bag. The strip search, conducted by all four officers, took twenty minutes, but the whole time the plastic bag of sweets lay discarded on the bed, and they left without touching it again.

Peter waited twenty minutes until the corridor outside was empty; only then did he open the bag and find the two notes written to him.

His heart started to thump, this time with excitement. It was time to put his part of the plan in action.

CHAPTER 43

The van bearing the logo of the Southwestern Electrical Company was parked up against the kerb. It was a quiet street, lined on one side with several run-down terraces, three of which were boarded up, and on the other side there was an expanse of fenced-off scrubland with a low brick windowless building which housed an electrical substation. A streetlight was flickering on and off in the twilight.

The Fan sat watching the empty street through a small mirrored window in the back of the van. His preparations had been meticulous, and his method of tracking down his victims was taken directly from the Nine Elms Cannibal himself. Find a girl who has a routine. It's the routine that leads her to you. After-school sports clubs attended by young women were a fertile ground. Sure, many of them had loving parents to pick them up, but he had found success by zeroing in on the poorer girls, the ones with the scholarships. They often had working parents and were forced to take the bus.

This was now the fourth victim, and even though he loved it all – the stalking, abduction and killing – he was eager to get this one over and done with. He needed it out of the way for the final, most exciting part of his plan.

The van was borrowed from the family company.

Southwestern Electrical was one of many companies that leased vans from CM Logistics. He'd stocked it with everything he needed: a drawstring bag with a thin cord, a baton, duct tape, a fresh medical kit with hypodermic syringes and surgical gauze, a black balaclava and leather gloves. He also had a fresh set of clothes: the uniform of a delivery man working for the Southwestern Electrical Company. The number plates were fakes, registered to a stolen van. He hadn't done the stealing, but the plates had been put up for sale on the black market. If the van was caught and identified on CCTV, it wouldn't come back to him.

The final piece of kit he'd placed in the van were two glass vials of isoflurane. It was commonly used to anaesthetise animals, and deliveries to veterinarians were not so closely monitored as controlled drugs delivered to the NHS and private health clinics.

He saw movement outside, and an old man entered the road, walking his dog.

'Fuck,' he said under his breath.

The old man saw the van and stopped at the electrical substation. The Fan had forced the gate open to make it look as if the substation was being serviced. The old man looked inside, then back at the van. His dog started to sniff around, and he called it to heel. Then he came right up to the van and peered through the front window.

'Go on, fuck off,' The Fan growled. He craned his head to see the other end of the street. If she was coming now, he would have to call it off. Weeks of work would be fucked up and down the drain.

The old man dawdled for another moment, staring at the van and back at the open gate. His dog went back to the gate and stepped through to sniff some weeds before cocking his leg and urinating. Finally, the old man whistled and carried on up the street, the dog trotting after him. The Fan watched him through the tinted glass. He seemed doddery and wasn't wearing any glasses. Hopefully this meant he wouldn't remember too much detail.

Five minutes later, his heart leaped when she appeared in his vision, walking along the pavement opposite. Her name was Abigail Clarke, and she was *perfect* – tall and athletic enough to present a challenge. He loved the girls to have a bit of fight about them, which made it all the more thrilling when he overpowered them. Abigail's hair was long and tied back, and she wore a baseball cap. In the weeks leading up to this he had watched her walk home in daylight. Her hair had shone like gold in the sunlight, and her face had been flushed from training.

As she walked towards the van, she had her head down, engrossed in her phone. She didn't hear the sliding door as he popped the lock open, and as she came level he slid the door open in one smooth motion and put out his hands to grab her.

CHAPTER 44

Abigail didn't notice the van until the hands emerged to grab her. The man was dressed all in black and he was wearing a black balaclava. She yelled and fought hard as she was lifted off her feet and pulled into the van. She was thrown forward onto a mattress in the back.

Just before she landed, she reached for the small canister she kept in the front pocket of her hoodie. She thrashed and fought, feeling him on her back, and when he turned her over, she aimed for the eyes of the balaclava and sprayed him. It wasn't mace or pepper spray but the legal alternative her mother had bought her; a bright red gel that temporarily blinds your attacker – and stains their skin red for days.

He screamed out and put his hands to his face, scraping at the red gunge and pulling off the balaclava. His hair was almost as red as the gel. Abigail crawled and kicked and fought her way up to a standing position, then made for the sliding door which was still open. He managed to grab hold of the hockey stick tucked in her backpack, but it came loose from her bag as she fell out of the van, landing painfully on the pavement.

She got to her feet, but he was right behind her, spitting red and gagging, sounding like a wild animal. Abigail made the fatal mistake of running through the open gate to the electrical substation. If she had run right or left she would have quickly emerged onto busier streets and might have got away.

She ran around the small square brick building and saw there was a small door in the back. She tried the handle, but it was locked. He appeared around the building and was on her. She felt her hockey stick around her ankles as he tripped her up and she went down, landing in the grass.

He screamed something unintelligible and hit her hard across the back of the head. Stars and pain exploded in her vision. Abigail felt her baseball cap being pulled off and she was dragged along the concrete path behind the small brick building. It was littered with the shards of a broken wine bottle, and she cried out as the pieces of glass sliced through the skin on her bare legs.

It happened so fast, but she turned and tried to get up. His face, teeth and the whites of his eyes were slick with the red gel, and it was foaming up with drool against his rubbery lips.

He lifted the hockey stick, and before she could get her arms up he smashed it into her throat, crushing her windpipe. She gagged and flailed, and he began to beat her with the hockey stick. Over and over again. Each blow made her body numb, and as she lost consciousness she heard the crack of her bones breaking.

Later that evening, a genuine Southwestern Electrical Company van pulled up at the substation. The run-down street was deserted, and not the kind of place the engineer wanted to be after dark. An old man had called in to head office, asking when the work would be completed on the substation, and if his house would be without power. The message had been passed along, and it had been flagged up that the substation wasn't due to be visited by an engineer. A break-in had to be taken seriously.

He parked, grabbed his torch and toolkit and went to the

gate. It was closed, but he saw the lock was broken. He had an odd feeling as he opened it and went through. Shining his torch on the scrappy grass, he made his way around to the back of the substation. He thought the young girl lying on the path was wearing red trousers, until he saw that it was blood caked on her bare legs. Her long hair was a tangle of red and her face a battered pulp. Congealed blood had seeped out into a circle on the concrete around the body. A bloody, broken hockey stick lay discarded on the grass.

Flies often hung around the heat of the substation, and he could see they were already swarming over the face. It was then that he dropped his tool bag and he only made it to the gate before he threw up.

CHAPTER 45

Kate stopped at the petrol station on her way home from work. She had filled up her car and was looking through the limited selection of frozen food when she saw the evening news on the TV mounted above the till.

Varia Campbell was holding a press conference in front of Exeter police station. She was flanked by DI Mercy, who looked exhausted and solemn.

'Can you put the sound up, please?' she asked the bored-looking man sitting behind the till. He grabbed the remote and unmuted it.

'The young woman in question has been identified as Abigail Clarke. Her badly beaten body was found behind an electrical substation in Tranmere Street, on the outskirts of Crediton,' Varia was saying.

A man came up to the till to pay for his petrol, and Kate stepped out of his way, her attention glued to the screen.

'A witness describes seeing a black van with tinted windows in Tranmere Street opposite the electrical substation with Southwestern Electrical branding. However, Southwestern was unaware of a call-out or anyone from the company working at this substation. We are putting out an appeal for anyone else who saw this van in the area around five to six p.m. yesterday evening.

We believe this murder may be linked to the abduction and murder of Emma Newman, Kaisha Smith and Layla Gerrard.' Pictures of the three young women flashed up on screen, followed by a photo of a young girl with strawberry-blonde hair. 'We believe that this individual intended to abduct Abigail on her way home from school, but instead she was murdered at the scene.'

The news report cut back to the studio, and the presenter repeated the appeal for witnesses. 'Police are eager to speak to the driver or any witnesses of this van caught on CCTV two hundred yards from the scene of the crime.'

A blurred CCTV image of a black Southwestern Electrical van flashed up on screen, then the news report went on to show a map of the sports ground where Abigail had been training that evening, and the bus stop they believed she was heading to.

Kate paid for her petrol, and as she went back to her car her phone rang. It was Tristan.

'Did you see the news?' she asked.

'Yes,' he said. 'They must be really desperate if they're releasing so much information to the public.'

'I'm home in five minutes. Come over and let's talk it through.'

Tristan arrived at Kate's just as she was putting a frozen lasagne in the oven.

'Do you always eat ready meals?' he asked.

'Yes. I don't have a wife to cook for me,' she said, setting the timer. 'Do you?'

'Have a wife? No. I do like to cook though, when I have time.'

'There's enough for two if you're hungry,' she said.

Tristan sat at the breakfast bar in the kitchen, and they started to talk through the case so far.

'This is a huge breakthrough,' said Tristan. 'They have a witness to a vehicle, and he was obviously surprised at the scene.'

'They also have a definite point where he wanted to abduct her,' said Kate. She went to the countertop and picked up her computer. 'They've put down the location as Tranmere Road, Crediton—'

'Tranmere Street,' said Tristan.

'Tranmere Street, near Crediton . . .'

'Crediton is a bit rough. What the hell was she doing walking through it on her own?'

Kate opened up Google Maps and typed in the address. She pulled up the map and zoomed out. 'This is the playing field they mentioned on the news,' she said, pointing at the map, 'and this is the bus stop where she was due to catch her bus home.' She traced her finger along the map and found Tranmere Street.

'Bloody hell. She got so close to catching that bus,' said Tristan. 'Look at the scale. She was four hundred metres away.'

Kate zoomed out of the map.

Tristan went on, 'We don't know where Emma Newman went missing because she was the only one who didn't have a fixed routine. The other girls were on their way home from somewhere . . .'

'I've got the location of where Kaisha Smith went missing,' said Kate, going to her bag and pulling out her notebook. 'She took the number four bus from the stop closest to the school training ground.'

'We just need to find out where Layla Gerrard went to catch the bus,' said Tristan.

'I can phone Alan Hexham and see if he can get it from the police report,' said Kate. 'Let's look at the routes taken by the other victims, and let's start thinking like a serial killer. Where would be the best spot to lie in wait and abduct someone?'

They spent the next few hours working painstakingly through the routes on Google Maps, cross-checking where the victims lived with the bus routes they would take, and in each instance they found a shortcut.

'I want to go and look at these locations,' said Kate. 'These shortcuts the girls took or could have taken. Someone in the area might have seen something, or someone, without realising the significance.'

CHAPTER 46

The next morning, it took an hour to drive to the point where they believed that Kaisha Smith, the second victim, had been abducted. When they searched the route they found a point where two residential streets, Halstead Road and Marham Street, connected through a small alleyway.

Halstead Road was fairly busy, but where the alleyway emerged onto Marham Street it was a quiet cul-de-sac, shrouded by bushes and only overlooked by one house, which happened to be empty and up for sale.

'It would be the perfect spot,' said Tristan. 'He could have parked the van and lain in wait for her here.'

Kate spied a woman coming out of a car in front of the house diagonally opposite. She opened the boot and took out a small box of cleaning supplies.

'Looks like a cleaner,' said Kate, seizing the moment. 'Let's see if she'll talk.'

Tristan followed her and they caught up with the woman as she was about to go through the front gate of a large white house. Kate introduced herself and offered her business card.

'We're trying to find out about a young girl who went missing. We think she passed through this road.'

The woman looked suspiciously between them, trying

to work out their relationship. She was very pale with short dyed black hair and her huge eyes were rimmed with thick black mascara.

'We're not police,' Kate added. 'We work privately, and we need help.'

The woman seemed to soften a little at this. 'I clean six houses on this street. I'm here a lot.'

'Do you clean Thursdays? That's the day she went missing,' said Kate.

Tristan took out a photo of Kaisha Smith they'd printed off, and showed it to her.

The woman tutted. 'I saw about her on the news! You think she was abducted here?'

'It's a theory we're working on,' said Kate.

'I saw the news last night. Bloke in a black van – well, they think it was a bloke – killed that girl,' she said, shaking her head.

'Can you remember if you were working . . .' Kate pulled out her phone and scrolled through ' . . . on Thursday sixteenth September? That was the day Kaisha vanished.'

The woman thought for a moment. 'When was the August bank holiday?' she asked.

'That was thirtieth August,' said Tristan.

'Yes, I was working. It was the week before I was away.'

'Do you work until late?' asked Kate.

'Four, five o'clock.'

'Can you remember if there was a van parked up here at the end of the cul-de-sac late afternoon on that day?' Tristan took out his mobile phone. 'It could have been a van like this, from the Southwestern Electrical Company?'

The woman looked at the photo on the screen. 'Not that I remember. The house there has been up for sale for a few months. The old lady who owned it died in there, and they

284

didn't find her for a couple of weeks. Saying that . . . there was one of them security vans parked up here around that time. I remember noticing it there because it was one of those armoured vans, you know the ones that pick up cash from banks.'

'Do you remember the date?' asked Kate.

The woman chewed it over, quite literally, moving her mouth while weighing it up. 'I can't be sure. It was around that time. All the days tend to blur into one after a while.'

'Can you remember if the van had a company name on it?'

'It wasn't Securicor, 'cause those vans always make me laugh when they reverse and that posh woman's voice asks you to get out the way . . . three letters, I think. It was written in gold. It had tinted windows, and I remember thinking what the hell is that doing there? There's been nothing going on there, what with the house being empty for so long. Apart from when the bin men reverse their lorry.'

'Did you see anyone inside? Did anyone get out?' asked Kate.

'No.'

'Have the police talked to you?'

At this point the woman narrowed her eyes. 'The police? No. I don't talk to the police unless I have to. They might have talked to the people who lived here, but I don't know. Lots of them commute to Bristol or even London, with Exeter being close by. Now if you'll excuse me, I have to go.'

After she'd gone, Kate and Tristan walked back through the alleyway. It was a stinking, dingy little passage with litter and broken glass.

'There's not a lot of dog shit,' said Tristan. 'So, not a route for dog walkers.'

'It seems like the kind of street where people don't walk much,' agreed Kate. 'What do you think about the van she saw?'

'She was too vague. She can't remember the exact date or what was written on the side of it.'

285

'But it would be weird for one of those security vans to stop here. We're a long way from a bank.'

They arrived at the car.

'Where to next?' asked Tristan.

'Butterworth Avenue,' said Kate. 'Where we think Layla Gerrard was abducted.'

CHAPTER 47

The Fan woke in the darkness, pain throbbing in his left eye. He scrabbled around next to his bed and pulled open the curtains. He was staying in his country house, tucked away near the North Wessex Downs. The light came flooding through the window, and he winced at the sudden brightness. He got up and went to the bathroom and stared at his reflection in the mirror.

The skin on his face and hands was stained a deep red. The colour was more pronounced around his left eye, which was also bruised and swollen from where the bitch had kicked out at him. The gel had seeped through the balaclava and covered his face and the side of his neck.

He'd felt so enraged and surprised when Abigail fought back. He'd never dreamed any of them would retaliate, and he didn't know how much time had passed when he found himself standing over her lifeless body, her blood flooding out in a widening slick on the concrete.

He was aware that it was dark, and the streetlamp above was flickering. The road was deserted. He'd gone back to the van and locked himself inside, trying to clean himself up, but the red dye was everywhere. He picked up her baseball cap. It was dark blue, with a red Nike tick on the front. He'd pulled the peak down low, and hoped it would be enough to disguise his dye-covered face.

This had destroyed his plan for victim number four.

He'd taken several baths and showers, scrubbing at his skin, but still the stain remained, like a port wine birthmark. He did a little research and found out that the colour would fade in a few days, but it put him out of action at a crucial time of planning.

He'd driven a vast circuitous route back to the distribution centre in the Southwestern Electrical van, and had switched the plates as soon as he'd returned, but he now had to clean the red stains from the van, and he couldn't let anyone else do it. The police would know about the red dye. This detail hadn't been mentioned on the news yet, but that old man was a worry. He had seen the van.

The Fan had planned to dump Abigail's body the following Tuesday, with a note, but now he wouldn't be able to do that, and it was no longer the perfect crime that he had planned so carefully. If the old man spoke to the police, and they knew that he was using vans, how long would it take them to trace things back to him? The fake plates would only buy him so much time.

He took off his underwear and stepped into the shower. The red stain from the gel had seeped down his neck and onto his chest. He took a tub of industrial cleaner and shook the acrid-smelling powder into his palm. He mixed it with a little water and started to rub it over the stain on his chest, up the side of his neck and over his face. It burned and stung. He ran the water, as hot as he could bear, and was pleased to see faint pink water running off.

The chemical smell, that swimming pool stench of bleach and detergent, was pricking his nose and waking him up. This was a setback, but not everything was lost. He smiled as he scrubbed at his teeth, which had also been stained pink. The industrial cleaner made him retch, but he kept on scrubbing.

As the stain began to fade, he felt back in control again. For his plan to work, he had to be in control of his emotions.

CHAPTER 48

It took forty-five minutes for Kate and Tristan to drive to the next location. It was a leafy avenue of posh houses, which became an unmade road with an arched railway bridge, and an underpass. On one side of the bridge was a patch of scrubland which had once been a children's play area but was now overgrown, and on the other side was a high brick wall, connected to the railway bridge.

Kate and Tristan walked through the underpass, a long dark, dirty passage which stank of urine. It opened out onto a busy road with houses and a few shops.

'Would you walk down this?' asked Tristan. 'Even if there was a shortcut?'

'Not if I stumbled on it, but this looks like a very posh area. The houses are smart. I don't know. It's a shortcut that would make the journey to the bus stop a lot shorter,' said Kate.

They came back through the underpass, and as they emerged on the other side, a train rumbled and clattered on the tracks above.

'This would be a quiet place to wait,' said Tristan, when they got to the overgrown playground.

The last house on the road, just before the tarmac ended, was a grand old building in decay. Kate imagined that it had once been the only house in the area, and surrounded by fields.

They walked back up the road a little way to get a better look at it. Ivy grew up the walls and around the large bay windows at the front. A lamp was on inside the front room downstairs, which looked very cosy. An old man wearing thick-rimmed glasses was sitting under the lamp in a high-backed chair reading a newspaper. A set of steps led up to a pillared front door with a brass knocker. Kate moved closer to the house and saw something tucked up under the eaves. The man noticed them, put down his newspaper, and took off his reading glasses.

'Look. Up there, under the roof eaves, there's a small mounted security camera,' said Kate, pointing. 'You can't really see it until you're up close.'

The man was now standing at the window, and he waved a hand to shoo them away.

'He doesn't look happy,' said Tristan.

'Let's see if he'll talk to us,' said Kate. She waved at the older man, and they climbed the steps to the front door and rang the bell. It chimed deep inside. No one answered.

'What if he's a ghost?' said Tristan with a grin.

Kate rang the bell again. A moment later the door opened. The old man stood in the doorway holding on to a walking frame. His right leg was encased in plaster.

'Are you blind, woman? Can't you see I'm walking wounded?' he said waspishly. There was a smell of baking and tea brewing, and warmth flooded out into the chilly autumn air. The old man looked past Kate to Tristan, and smiled. 'What can I do for you, young man?'

Kate nudged Tristan in the ribs and he stepped forward and offered their card.

'Hello. We're private detectives. I'm Tristan Harper and this is Kate Marshall.'

'I'm Frederick Walters.'

'Hello, Mr Walters. We're investigating the abduction of a

young girl, and we believe that she could have been abducted on the road outside your house.'

'Oh my lord! When?'

'A couple of weeks ago.' Tristan went on to explain about the abduction and murder of Layla Gerrard.

'How terrible,' said Frederick, clutching a hand to his chest. 'You look very young to be a private detective. How old are you?'

'Twenty-one, sir,' said Tristan.

'You don't think it was me who abducted her? I've only just got back from a few weeks in hospital.'

'Sorry to hear that. The reason we're calling is that we see you have a security camera on top of your house, looking at the road,' said Kate. 'Have the police been in touch? In case it captured anything of the abduction?'

'No. They haven't . . . ' He peered up and down the road and turned back to Tristan. He smiled. 'I was just about to make a pot of tea. Would you like a cup?'

'Yes, thank you,' said Tristan.

'That would be lovely,' added Kate. The invitation seemed to be directed only at Tristan.

'Do come in.' Frederick stood back to let them into the hallway. 'Perhaps you could give me a hand, with the tea?' he asked Tristan.

'Sure.'

'Karen. You make yourself comfortable in the living room,' he added to Kate.

'It's Kate,' she said, but he had already taken Tristan off down the hallway. She went into the living room. It reminded her of a house from the 1930s, with heavy wooden furniture and a bar in the corner with a soda siphon. There was a gramophone on a sideboard with an old-style horn, and the front windows were inlaid with lead, with stained glass in the corners. The light cast soft colours over the edge of an oyster-shell-patterned sofa with matching chairs. A modern flatscreen television had been plonked on a low credenza, and she peered behind it and saw an internet modem flashing.

A few minutes later, Frederick returned with Tristan, and he was asking him about his tattoos.

'Are they only on your forearms?' he asked.

'I've got an eagle with his wings spread on my back and shoulders,' said Tristan, placing the tray on the small table in front of the sofa.

'My goodness, may I see it?'

Kate gave Tristan a look, but he obliged Frederick and lifted his T-shirt, showing a washboard stomach and muscular pectorals. He turned around to show the spread wings across his back and shoulders. Kate had thought it sounded tacky, but when she saw it, it was beautifully done.

'My, my ... I think I'll have to have a lie down when you leave,' joked Frederick. Kate was grateful to Tristan for playing along, but thought he shouldn't have to start pulling up his clothes.

'Would you like me to pour the tea?' she asked.

'Yes, you be mother,' said Frederick. Tristan pulled his T-shirt down and sat on the sofa. Kate poured the tea and waited until Frederick had eased himself into the armchair opposite, then passed him a cup. She passed one to Tristan, then sat beside him and took a sip from her cup.

'When was the security camera put on the front of your house?' she asked.

'Four months ago. It was put in for insurance purposes,' said Frederick, sitting back in his chair and adjusting his glasses. He blew on his tea and took a sip.

'Would you mind if we took a look at the footage for the day the girl went missing?' asked Tristan.

'What girl?'

Kate briefly explained again.

'I don't know how it works. My niece had it put in and she comes to check it.'

'Where do you keep the system?' asked Tristan.

'The cistern?'

'No. The computer system for the security cameras. Is it in a box?'

'Oh. Yes. It's in the cupboard under the stairs. Feel free to have a look.'

Kate and Tristan went into the hallway. They had to move a small table and lamp from in front of the door to the downstairs cupboard, and inside, amongst the dust and old boots and shoes, they found a small box with several green LED lights winking and flashing.

'It looks like it records the video from the camera onto a hard drive,' said Tristan. 'It has an app-based security system, which we can log on to remotely.'

He pulled a piece of paper off the top of the box and held it up to Kate. It had the login details and the password. He pulled out his phone, took a photo of it and put it back.

They went back and finished their tea, and Tristan asked if they could have a look at the footage. Frederick didn't understand how it worked, but said Tristan was welcome to look through it.

'I hope you find the person who abducted this young woman,' said Frederick, accompanying them to the front door. He seemed sad that his impromptu visitors were leaving.

'Thank you, this could be hugely helpful,' said Tristan.

They walked back to the car, and Tristan downloaded the security camera app for his phone.

'I feel bad. He didn't know I took a photo of the password,' he said.

'We're just looking for the footage from one date, and it could help find Layla's killer,' said Kate. 'And you flashed him your abs – I'm sure that's a mental picture he'll be dining out on for a long time.'

Tristan laughed. They set off back to Ashdean and he logged into the app and started to scroll through the video files.

'Okay. I have the footage from the day Layla Gerrard was abducted. The video files are in hourly increments. I'm just downloading the files from three p.m. to nine p.m.'

When the footage was downloaded, he clicked on it and started to scroll through it at high speed. Kate glanced over from driving. The view from the camera stayed the same: the stretch of road with the overgrown play park and the edge of the underpass. He paused it when a dog walker went past and a postman on his bike. As the light began to fade, a black van appeared in the shot and drove slowly past the camera towards the underpass, and out of shot.

'Shit,' said Tristan, slowing it down and then winding it back. He played it again and paused the video when the van appeared. On the side was written 'OMV Security'. It was a black van with tinted windows. Kate had that feeling, a tingling in her belly, which had long been dormant: it was the thrill of a breakthrough.

'What time is that?' she asked, trying to look at the tiny timestamp in the corner and keep her eyes on the road at the same time. She could barely contain her excitement.

'Timestamp is 5.25 p.m. when the van pulls past . . . ' He scrolled through the footage. 'He must have been waiting there out of shot for almost an hour. It's a dead end at the underpass. He turns the van around and passes the camera in the other direction at 6.23 p.m.'

He ran the footage back and paused it. The letters OMV showed on the reverse side of the van.

'He must have been waiting at the underpass, grabbed Layla and had her inside when he drove away,' said Kate.

Tristan quickly googled the company. 'OMV are a company who deliver cash to ATMs,' he said.

'We need to share this with Varia,' said Kate. The realisation that all they could do now was pass on the information dampened her excitement a little. Tristan took screenshots from both videos of the van, and loaded them up into a new email.

Just as he sent off the email, Kate had a call. It was from Gary Dolman, the ghost writer who'd worked on *No Son of Mine*.

'He's based in Brighton,' said Kate when she came off the phone. 'He says we can meet him tomorrow at his house. He can answer any questions we have and talk about writing the book with Enid.'

'I'd be up for that, something to focus our minds whilst we wait to hear back about this security video. Looks like things are moving,' said Tristan.

Kate nodded and tapped her phone against her teeth, nervous about the prospect of meeting him.

'What? You don't want to go?' asked Tristan.

'I do,' said Kate. 'He wanted to talk to me when he was writing the book. I kept saying no, and things got nasty . . . I think I told him to go fuck himself. I was drinking at the time.'

'How did he sound on the phone?'

'Fine. Normal.'

'He was a tabloid journalist, so maybe he's lost track of how many people told him to eff off,' said Tristan.

Kate laughed, but as a member of AA she knew she now had to apologise to Gary and make amends.

CHAPTER 49

Gary Dolman lived on Brighton seafront in a small end of terrace house. When he opened the door he was all smiles as he welcomed Kate and Tristan. He was in his early fifties, with a pierced nose and eyebrow, and his silver hair was topped with pink. He showed them through to an office crammed with bookshelves, which had a large bay window looking out to sea.

'I can't believe after all these years I finally get to meet you,' he said, indicating they should sit on a large sofa.

'Thank you,' said Kate. 'I owe you an apology for the last time we spoke, when you asked me to contribute to the book. I was very rude. I'm sorry.'

He waved it away. 'It's all good. I know how the press hounded you. If it's any consolation, I wasn't happy with how the book turned out.'

'Why?'

'Before we get settled, would you like tea or coffee?' he asked.

They both asked for tea, and Gary left the room.

Kate looked around the office. There were several framed front pages of the *News of the World*. The first headline concerned a well-known actor who'd been caught snorting cocaine, and the second a supermodel who was photographed taking drugs with a rock singer. The third framed front page had the headline, NO SON OF MINE and underneath it was the now-famous look on Enid Conway's face as she left the High Court in London after Peter had been found guilty and jailed for life. She wore a smart navy-blue two-piece jacket and skirt, her short dark hair was perfectly coiffed, but her face was streaked with mascara-smudged tears and she pressed a small white square of a hanky to her mouth. The *News of the World* had been the only newspaper to use a photo of Enid instead of Peter to announce the guilty verdict, and for this reason it had been all the more powerful. Kate went up to look more closely.

'I didn't know he wrote this headline,' she said, peering at the small print. 'I wonder why he gave it up? He was obviously good at his job.' She heard how the last sentence came out of her mouth with a tinge of bitterness in her voice.

'Let's be careful. Once a journalist, always a journalist,' Tristan said.

'Good point,' said Kate.

She looked out of the window at the sea, and the twisted burned-out remains of the pier, which seemed to perch on the calm waters like a deformed spider. She felt mixed emotions about Gary Dolman. She had apologised and done her duty as a good member of Alcoholics Anonymous, but she thought back to the time of Peter's arrest and the court case, and how he had hounded her for comments, quotes and a story. He had accepted her apology, but didn't he owe her one?

A moment later, Gary came back to the office, smiling, with a tray of tea and biscuits.

'Right,' he said, sitting at the chair by his desk. 'Fire away.'

Kate elaborated on their phone conversation, and their theory that the copycat killer was using *No Son of Mine* to inspire where he disposed of the bodies. 'Have the police been in contact with you?' finished Kate.

'No. Not yet,' he said, and dunked another biscuit in his tea.

'I'd expect a call,' said Kate. 'I've notified them about my suspicions, and how the crime scenes link to Enid's book – or should I say your book?'

'If you solve the case, *No Son of Mine* could get a new print run,' he said with a grin.

'Teenage girls are being murdered,' said Kate coldly.

He put his hands up. 'Sorry. I'm just being realistic. Nothing sells a book like death . . . I've seen the news, ugh, horrible stuff.' He shook his head and shuddered, making a big deal of being horrified.

'What made you want to be a ghost writer, and not a writer in your own right?' asked Tristan.

Kate looked across at Tristan. She felt the same hostility towards Gary, but showing it could make him clam up.

'I was fed up with the grind of working on a newspaper,' he said. 'I got the offer off the back of the reporting I did on the Nine Elms case, and my famous headline. They paid me a hundred grand. I paid off my mortgage. I think that makes me a proper writer.'

'Did Enid ever say, "no son of mine" during the trial, when she was talking about Peter?' asked Tristan.

'No . . . Did you ever hear her say it, Kate?'

'I didn't attend the whole trial. I just gave evidence,' said Kate. She thought back to her four days on the stand, where she was ripped apart and humiliated by Peter Conway's defence team.

'Of course, and you'd had his baby by the time the trial kicked off? Yes?'

'Yes.'

There was an awkward pause, and Kate fixed him with a glare.

'But you use quotation marks around that headline,' said Tristan.

Gary shrugged. 'That's journalism. It reflected the mood

of the public, and that's what good tabloid journalism is all about.'

Yeah, and journalists like you fuck everyone who gets in their way, thought Kate. With a huge effort, she pushed her feelings to one side.

'So how did the idea for the book come about?' she asked, steering the conversation back to her line of questioning.

'I got to know Enid Conway a little during the trial,' said Gary. 'She'd cadge a ciggy now and again on breaks outside the court house. She'd chat about this and that, nothing too revealing, but enough to have a rapport. I'd heard her asking another journalist how much he thought her story might be worth, and it was then that I knew there could be a big market for her story. I went to the publisher with the idea a couple of weeks before the guilty verdict, and they put the book deal together soon after.'

'How many times did you meet with Enid for the book?'

Gary sat back and rested his empty tea cup on his leg. 'Six or seven.'

'Where did you meet?'

'Here. Usually the ghost writer goes to the author, but Enid wanted to visit Brighton and stay in the Grand Hotel. The publisher put her up in the hotel for a week. She wanted to stay in the same room as Margaret Thatcher had when they bombed the hotel! But it was already booked, so they gave her the suite next door. We met there a couple of times, and here at my house. It was an interesting gig.'

'In what way?' asked Tristan.

Gary rolled his eyes. 'She's the mother of a notorious serial killer, and because, as our conversations went on, it seemed like a different book was emerging,' he said. 'The publisher had conceived it from my headline, *No Son of Mine*, and it was agreed that it would be a sort of redemption piece. Enid would renounce her son. But as our talks unfolded, I got the impression that she had a powerful love for him, and she was in denial.'

'She didn't believe Peter killed those young women?' asked Kate.

'Oh, no, Enid knew Peter did it. She believed he couldn't help himself. She said that she was raped by an evil man, that Peter's father was evil. And it gave him a dark side he constantly fought against. She said the good side far outweighed the bad. It wasn't his fault he killed those young women. It was his genes which made him do it.'

Kate closed her eyes and felt sick at the thought. Most of the time she could mentally separate Jake from Peter, and even though she knew Enid's words came from a place of denial, they made her deeply troubled for Jake's future. She dropped her cup and it shattered on the floor.

'Oh, I'm sorry,' she said weakly, and got up to pick up the pieces.

'No worries,' said Gary. He went to Kate, putting a hand on her shoulder. 'Are you okay?'

'She's fine. Can you give us a minute?' asked Tristan, shooting him a look.

'Sure. I'll go and get a cloth,' Gary said and left the room.

'You okay to carry on?' asked Tristan, seeing the tears in Kate's eyes. He made her sit down and started to gather up the pieces of broken cup.

'I don't know,' she said, wiping her face with the back of her hand. 'I always try to look at this objectively, but . . . ' She started to cry. 'Peter is Jake's father, and all this fucked-up stuff, it's part of Jake. I get so scared when I think about it. Jake is just a kid who wants a normal life, but is he going to get that?'

Tristan stacked up the pieces of broken cup and placed them on Gary's desk, then took Kate's hand. 'I was looking online, at serial killers in particular. Do you know how many of them have children who have turned out to be normal? Charles Manson apparently has a son who lives a very quiet life with his girlfriend and child. The daughter of the Happy Face Killer is now a motivational speaker who helps the children of serial murderers. I wouldn't be surprised if Enid Conway spouted a load of bollocks that she thought would sell books.'

'No one knows how their kid is going to turn out, do they?' said Kate.

'Exactly,' said Tristan. 'When I got done by the police for breaking that car window, my mum freaked out and thought I was destined for a life of crime, and look at me now. I'm working at Ashdean University, and I'm not cleaning the toilets. I work for you, and that's something to be really proud of.'

Kate looked into Tristan's kind brown eyes and felt so pleased she had taken a chance on him at the job interview. He was fast becoming like a second son to her.

'Thank you,' she said, smiling and squeezing his hand.

Gary came back with a cloth. He stopped in the doorway. 'I'm sorry if I've upset you,' he said.

'No, no, I asked the question,' said Kate, wiping her face and composing herself.

Gary grabbed a box of tissues and Kate took one and blew her nose. He cleared up the mess and sat back down

'Do you want to carry on?' Tristan asked Kate.

'Yes, this is about more than just me,' said Kate. She wiped her nose then looked up at Gary. 'Did you know that Peter told most of his colleagues in the police that his mother was mentally ill, and sectioned in hospital?'

'I'd heard that. Enid said it was lies.'

'Peter told me and my colleagues on three occasions.'

'Enid never mentioned that. She loved Peter fiercely, and I think it went beyond a mother's love,' said Gary. 'She talked about dressing for him during the trial. To keep his spirits up.

You must remember some of the stuff she wore to court: short skirts and stockings, suspenders. She would sit there showing him a bit of leg. A flash of lace . . . I remember we used to joke about it in the press gallery.'

Kate felt sick but was determined to continue. 'Did she talk about her relationship with Peter when he was growing up?'

'She talked about the holiday they took to Devon, but it seemed pretty normal, apart from the run-in with the farmer's wife when Enid stole a chicken. She did talk a lot about the two years Peter spent living and working in Manchester as a police officer, when Enid was back in London. She said she missed him like crazy. At the time she was working at a bookie's in Whitechapel and she only got every other weekend off. They would alternate visits to each other. One weekend, when she came to Manchester and they'd been drinking in the pub, they went back to Peter's flat and he showed her a new camera he'd bought. He started to take photos of her. She said things got a bit silly, and she started posing for him, for a laugh, but then he asked her to change into another outfit, and he carried on taking photos of her as she got changed, and it turned into him taking photos of her naked.'

'Bloody hell, his own mother?' said Tristan.

Gary nodded. 'Enid framed it that they were having a laugh and then he got naked so she could take photos of him, and then she said, "one thing led to another" – those are the words she used – but then she back-tracked very quickly and told me I couldn't put it in the book.'

'She said this in an interview with you, for the book?' asked Kate.

'Yes. It was after she'd had a couple of drinks in the lounge at the Grand.'

'Why didn't you put it in the book?' asked Tristan.

'She had the final say, and when I told my editor, she was

disgusted. She said the publisher didn't want that kind of speculation about the relationship between Enid and Peter. It wasn't that kind of book.'

Kate and Tristan sat back for a moment and took it in. Kate wasn't shocked, just horrified.

'Have you got any other material you could share, any other photos from Enid that didn't make it into the book?' she asked.

'Yes. There were a lot, ones of Peter as a baby, his early years in the force in Manchester.'

'Could we take a look?'

'Sure. Let me see,' said Gary, getting up and scanning the crammed bookshelves. He found a shoebox and pulled it down. He took off the lid and put the box on the coffee table. 'I had all the photos copied.'

Kate started to sift through the old holiday photos and pictures of Peter as a baby.

'I take it she didn't give you any of her dodgy photos? If what she said was even true?' asked Tristan, picking up the blurred photo of sixteen-year-old Enid cradling baby Peter outside the unmarried mothers' home.

'No. She told an odd story about that,' said Gary. 'Peter had a friend in Manchester, Altrincham I think she said, near where he lived. He owned a chemist's, but he was one of those people who would process dodgy photos, on the side, under the table like, for a fee.'

Kate and Tristan exchanged a glance.

'Did she say what this friend was called?' asked Kate.

'No, but apparently he was an ex-copper. That's how Peter got to know him.'

'Bloody hell,' said Kate. 'That's Paul Adler, the guy who owns the chemist in Altrincham.'

CHAPTER 50

Since his visit from Enid, Peter had put the next part of the plan in motion. The orderlies and doctors who worked in the hospital were observant, and rules were strictly enforced. Sharp objects were forbidden, and anything that could be fashioned into a weapon was banned or strictly monitored. Toothbrushes, combs and razors were only given out for use in the bathroom, and then collected up and disposed of. All cutlery was plastic and given to patients just to eat their meals, and collected back up and accounted for when plates were returned. If anything went missing the patient and their room would be searched thoroughly until it was found. Any foods or snacks that were wrapped in silver foil were also banned, and even toothpaste, after one patient had sharpened the flat edge of a tube of Colgate and slashed one of the orderlies.

As the years and months of his incarceration passed, Peter had been granted little perks here and there, for pockets of good behaviour – books (soft paperbacks with no staples) and a radio (housed in thick form-moulded plastic and checked regularly). The previous year, his collection of books had become so large that he put in a request to have a bookcase in his room. After lots of paperwork had passed back and forth, it was agreed that he would be allowed to choose a small bookcase and pay for it through his hospital account. It had to be a model that would be glued together, and he wasn't allowed to assemble it himself. When it arrived flat-packed, a request had been put in for one of the maintenance staff to come and assemble it. It was around this time that Great Barwell had outsourced maintenance work.

On the morning of the bookcase being assembled, Peter was taken out of his room to give the maintenance worker access. He never met whoever did it, and when he returned, the bookcase was waiting for him. It was about waist height and had been fitted beside his sink. The orderly had checked it over and searched the room again to make sure no tools had been left, and then Peter was locked in for the night.

It wasn't until Peter tried to move the bookcase to beside his bed that he saw the maintenance worker had fixed it to the wall with a small metal bracket.

Peter had stacked his books in the case and used the top to store more books and paperwork. The bracket had gone unnoticed and unseen, even throughout the past four or five routine room searches.

Peter had taken up smoking again. Matches were cheaper than buying a lighter, so he bought cigarettes and a box of matches from the hospital shop, and the next time he went for a cigarette he was doled out a few matches. He used two and tucked one behind his ear, managing to get it back to his room without it being detected.

Every morning, toothbrushes were given out with breakfast. They were used when patients went for a shower, and orderlies collected them up again the moment they were finished. Three days previously, when his toothbrush came through the hatch with his breakfast, Peter took it out of the cellophane and cleared off the top of the bookcase. He opened his window and struck the match on the sill. Then he held the end of the toothbrush to the flame for a few seconds. He extinguished the match and threw it out of the window. He then went to the bracket on the back of the bookcase and pushed the melted plastic end of the toothbrush into the head of the screw fixing the bracket to the wall. He held it there for a few minutes, and when he pulled it away the plastic had set hard. He now had an improvised screwdriver.

He kept the window open to clear the smell of burning plastic, and quickly unscrewed the metal bracket from the back of the bookcase and stashed it inside the plastic housing of the radiator knob. He lit his second match, held the flame against the end of the toothbrush, then flattened out the impression of the screw on the sill of the window.

After this he went about his morning as normal – showered, shaved and brushed his teeth. Winston collected up the toothbrush when he was done and it was thrown in the recycling bin. Over the next three days and nights, Peter worked at filing down the keen edge of the bracket on the bars outside his window until it was razor sharp.

On Sunday afternoon, Peter had his regular group therapy session with Meredith Baxter. The sessions were held in a small room next to her office. Peter's group comprised the five long-term prisoners on his corridor – Peter, Ned, the blind paedophile who delivered the mail, Henry, a morbidly obese child killer, an arsonist called Derek whose meds rendered him a drooling zombie, and Martin, a schizophrenic.

Martin was seen as the riskiest of all the patients, and despite his size – he was tiny and weighed only 45 kilos – his strength was remarkable. Peter had once witnessed one of his meltdowns outside the bathroom, where Martin had hooked his fingers under the waistband of his jeans and torn them off his body in one movement. Peter had tried this back in his own cell when he was wearing an old pair of Levis, and he just couldn't do it.

They filed into the room just after 2 p.m., and they were checked over by three orderlies, their clothes patted down. Peter had the bracket tucked behind his left ear, under the spit hood, where it was kept in place with the stem of his glasses, matching the curve. He could feel it cold and sharp against his skin.

Winston patted him down for the third time that morning, then removed Peter's spit hood. He gave Peter's hair a quick check, ignoring the glasses, and told him to take his seat in the semicircle around Meredith.

Today she wore faded blue jeans and a pink woollen jumper. The only thing that set her apart from the patients was that she was female and she wore a lanyard around her neck. The orderlies had warned her about wearing this in sessions due to the risk of strangulation, but Meredith liked to act like they were all equal and friends, so she had ignored the warning.

On a couple of occasions, Peter had overheard Winston and Terrell talking about Meredith's group sessions, and how wary they were of what could happen. It was one of the only times that the Category A patients were all in one place and allowed to mix without restraints. The orderlies made sure to carry mace, Tasers and their batons, and were hyper-alert during these sessions. This didn't matter to Peter. He knew he was going to get caught and punished for what he was about to do. He wanted them to punish him; he just needed a few seconds in which to make it happen.

The room was small and tight, and the three orderlies were so close that Peter was unsure if he could do it. He made sure he was the first to share, saying how much he worried about his mother being out in the world on her own as she got older. Meredith smiled, her shiny face creasing around her mouth, and a dimple appeared in her cheek.

'Yes, Peter. We all worry about our loved ones. That's a very human emotion to have,' she said. 'We're lucky to live in a predominantly socialist country that looks after its elderly. Would you like me to request that you are given an extra phone card, to contact the social security office to explore options for your mother?'

'Yes. Thank you,' said Peter, nodding enthusiastically.

She smiled back. It was a smug smile, which gave her the hint of a double chin.

Meredith then moved on to Ned, who was sitting next to Peter. He told the group that he was worried about the wheel on his mail trolley. It was wobbly and about to come loose.

He spoke in an agitated staccato. 'What if the trolley goes tits up and all the post I've sorted goes everywhere? I have it all nicely arranged, so that as I go down all the corridors, I have everyone's mail ready. If it breaks, then I won't be able to deliver the mail!'

Peter looked over at Henry who was chewing on the sleeve of his pullover, attempting to get some flavour out of it. His vast buttocks spilled over the edges of his chair. Derek was asleep and drooling and Martin was jittery, his leg jogging up and down.

Peter was trying to work out the exact moment when he could make his move, when there was a sudden commotion in the corridor outside. One of the catering trolleys rounded the corner from the next corridor and collided with the door, cracking the small pane of safety glass and emptying a tray of stew down the window. It was accompanied by a scream from a patient who was in the corridor. Winston and Terrell leaped up and went to the door to check everything was okay.

At this moment of distraction, Peter slipped the sharpened wall bracket out from under the stem of his glasses and gripped it between the thumb and index finger of his right hand. He got up and moved calmly to Meredith. She looked up at him, curiously, and barely had the chance to say his name when he grabbed her by the back of her head and slashed at her throat twice with the sharpened bracket, left to right in quick succession. He hit the bullseye and her jugular vein ruptured, bathing him and the screaming patients in red.

Meredith's eyes and mouth opened wide and her hands clawed at him as she gurgled, thrashed and flailed, and made an anguished wet sound as blood poured from the gash in her throat, saturating her clothes. She twitched and slid sideways off her chair. Peter ignored the screams and climbed on top of her, pressing his knee into her stomach.

As he bit down on her left cheek, aiming for that dimple, he felt a jolt of pain as Terrell shot him with the Taser. The electric current made his teeth clamp down, and by the time they pulled him off her, he had a chunk of Meredith's smooth dimpled cheek in his mouth.

CHAPTER 51

Kate and Tristan had stopped at a coffee shop further down the seafront to talk over the revelation that Peter Conway knew Paul Adler.

'I thought you said Paul Adler had an alibi for when Caitlyn went missing?' asked Tristan.

'He does, but he denied having any knowledge of or friendship with Peter Conway, and here we have a direct link, as told by Enid,' said Kate.

'What do you want to do? Take this to Varia Campbell?'

'No. This isn't Varia's case. The Caitlyn Murray case has been closed by the police. They didn't think they had enough evidence to investigate it any further. I want more proof before we go to the police. I told you about my visit to Paul Adler's pharmacy. There was something creepy about the harem of submissive young women who worked for him. And he'd kept those photos of Caitlyn. They weren't in an album. They were still in the original processing sleeve, and it was marked with a number and a date ... He said he used to do film processing at the chemist. He also said that he would store negatives for modelling agencies and businesses, and I saw the storeroom when I was there. There were shelves and shelves of folders.'

'Do you want to confront him again?' asked Tristan.

Kate looked at her watch. It was coming up to 2.30 p.m. She thought back to her visit to Paul Adler's chemist in Altrincham. When they were sitting in the small staff kitchen next to the loading bay, Tina had gone out to chuck away a rubbish bag. When she'd come back in she'd keyed in the door code and mouthed the numbers at the same time: *one, three, four, six.*

'Do you want to?' he repeated.

'I've had a crazy idea,' said Kate, lowering her voice.

'What?'

'Crazy, and risky too, but we'd be doing it for the greater good.' Kate leaned closer and told Tristan about the staff kitchen and the door code. 'If we set out soon, we could be in Altrincham in about five hours.'

'Break in? Are you nuts?' he hissed, glancing around at the other patrons dotted around at tables drinking coffee.

'Tristan. This is the kind of thing I used to do as a copper, but back then I had a badge and I could get a search warrant. Look, if we go to the police he could get tipped off, and if there are any photos kept hidden there he could get rid of them.'

'What kind of photos do you think are there?' asked Tristan. 'Not snuff photos of girls being murdered?'

Kate shook her head. 'No. If Paul Adler was the go-to for printing pornographic photos, then he could have got to know Peter Conway . . . well, we think he *did* know him, because Enid told Gary he processed their racy photos. What if Conway took photos of other girls? And he used Adler to process them? There could also be more photos of Caitlyn. Paul said there was a place he and Caitlyn used to go for walks, and a lake where they swam. He could have taken photos of other places they went, other people. It could lead back to Caitlyn's disappearance. He was worried enough to lie to me about knowing Peter Conway.'

'It's a pharmacy. Won't there be alarms? People break in to steal drugs,' said Tristan.

'He said he only had cameras in the dispensary and looking at the till. This storeroom was at the end of the corridor away from where the drugs were kept.'

'It's still breaking and entering,' said Tristan.

'We could find important evidence about Caitlyn's disappearance. It could lead to evidence for the copycat killer case. If we're serious about being private investigators we have to take risks. I wouldn't do this unless I'd seen that code and I thought we had a chance,' said Kate.

'Kate. I watch crime dramas,' he said. 'If we . . .'

He stopped to let an elderly couple squeeze past with their cups of coffee, and waited until they were out of earshot before continuing. 'If we steal photos that then need to be used as evidence, is that evidence admissible in court?'

'Not admissible in court if the police break in without a warrant. But what if we find photos with people and locations that we recognise? It could be a potential location where Caitlyn's body was dumped . . . Tristan. Sheila and Malcolm asked us to find her, and we said we would try. Imagine if walking in through an unlocked door is the way we find her body? They could give her a proper burial.'

Tristan paused and rubbed his face, looking out of the window to sea.

'Okay. Let's do it.'

CHAPTER 52

Peter regained consciousness moments after being Tasered. He was cuffed and lying on his front in the corner of the small therapy room. Winston was sitting on his back, his large weight pressing him into the floor. He had one hand holding the back of Peter's head and with the other he was radioing for backup.

Peter rolled the piece of flesh around in his mouth, sucked on it and then swallowed it down. He was grateful his head wasn't facing the wall, as he got to watch the chaos erupting around him. The white walls were covered in a fine spray of blood, as were the patients. Ned, Derek and Martin were each being restrained by an orderly. Martin was twitching and writhing. Derek was a drooling zombie so wasn't putting up any resistance. Ned was too frail and small to resist, but he was shouting, 'Tell me what's going on! I can taste blood! Whose blood is it?' as his milky eyes blindly rolled in their sockets.

Obese Henry had fallen off his chair, and two orderlies were vainly trying to get him up, but were slipping on the thick pool of blood spreading out from Meredith's body.

The orderlies fought vainly to revive her, but Peter could see that she was dead.

'The weapon? Where is it?' shouted Winston.

'It's on the floor by her chair, you bloody idiots!' shouted

Martin as he continued to fight against being restrained. The bent piece of metal lay in the congealing blood.

'I need backup urgently to meeting room six on G Wing. We have a code three-eighty-one. I repeat, code three-eighty-one,' said Winston into his radio.

Peter could see that there was no one with a free hand to pick the weapon up.

A moment later eight orderlies arrived in the already crowded room with a first aider carrying a medical box. Derek, Ned and Martin were taken out of the room, followed by Henry who was heaved up by three orderlies into his wheelchair. Its wheels ran tracks of blood across the white tiled floor as he was pushed out of the room.

Peter was surrounded by four of the orderlies, with Winston still on his back, and he felt the prick of a syringe as he was given a sedative. The chaos in the room dissolved away to white.

When he came round he could feel the cold wind through the spit hood. He was outside the hospital, strapped to a rolling cart, being wheeled out of the large main building of Great Barwell, past the tall razor-wire-topped fence. He couldn't move his body. He wore a straitjacket and the spit hood, and his legs were bound to the trolley. He tilted his head back and saw Winston pushing the trolley, his face blank and stony.

As the path curved around the main building, he saw a red air ambulance helicopter. Two paramedics were loading an empty gurney into the back before going around to the door. As they climbed inside, the engine started to roar. Meredith Baxter had no need for a hospital, thought Peter. She would be heading straight for the morgue.

The solitary confinement block was set apart from the rest of the hospital, against the back wall of the perimeter fence. They had to wait at the heavily fortified main entrance as they were buzzed in and the doors were unlocked. Peter heard the roar of the helicopter take off, and saw it circle in the sky above.

Winston came with him into solitary, and his face remained passive as Peter was checked in by the head orderly, a large bald man with an angry rash on his face and arms. Peter was taken to a small room where he was untied from the trolley and left to strip off his clothes. He submitted to a full body search by the surly bald orderly. He was then given a block of soap and taken to a shower.

Peter stood for a long time under the water, watching it flow red, then pink and finally clear. He soaped his body down and felt every nerve ending jangling.

His last visit to the solitary confinement block had been over a year ago, after the fight with Larry, when he had bitten off the tip of his nose. Peter knew he would now be kept in solitary confinement with no access to the phone, and his visits would be stopped. Someone from Great Barwell would call Enid and tell her what had happened. She would be informed of any legal recourse, and they would tell her that Peter would be kept in solitary confinement twenty-four hours a day with two fifteen-minute visits to the exercise yard. By law they had to inform her what time his fifteen-minute exercise would be scheduled.

After his shower he was given a blue overall and placed in a cell devoid of anything but a small bench and a stainless-steel toilet bowl. A tray of food was put through the hatch a short time later, a gelatinous mess of grey on a plastic plate, and he ate it all. He needed to keep his energy and strength up. After the plate had been taken away, the hatch in the door opened again.

'Exercise yard,' said Winston. A mesh spit hood was thrown in through the hatch and it closed again. Peter pulled it on and did up the buckles at the back. The hatch opened again.

'Stand by the door with your hands behind your back. Do not turn around.'

Peter could detect anger in Winston's voice, that he was disappointed in him. He got up and stood patiently at the hatch, and his hands were cuffed tightly.

'Step away.'

He did as he was asked. The hatch closed and the door opened. Winston stood with a young orderly with blond hair. They led Peter out of the cell and along a windowless corridor, past the other cell doors. There were six cells in the block, arranged in a hexagonal shape. A corridor ran around them and in the centre of the hexagon was the exercise yard. The door leading out into the yard had a small murky window of thick safety glass. Peter could see it was dark outside.

'What time is it?' he asked. There was silence. 'Can you please tell me the time?'

'It's nine p.m. Stand to one side,' said Winston. The blond orderly set to work with a bunch of keys. Three locks had to be turned before the door opened. 'You have fifteen minutes.'

Peter stepped through the open door and into the cold fresh air. The exercise yard was cramped and small, just bare concrete with a tiny drain in the centre. The walls were fifteen feet high, with an additional ten feet of razor-wire-topped mesh fencing. A small hexagon of sky glowed orange. As he had heard from Winston, the net had been removed.

Peter tipped his head back and looked up at it, breathing in the cold air. He smiled. 9 p.m. and 9 a.m. By now his mother should know about the murder of Dr Baxter, his move to solitary confinement and what time he was allowed out into the exercise yard.

She would now pass the information on to his greatest fan.

CHAPTER 53

It was dark at 7 p.m. when Kate and Tristan drove into Altrincham town centre. The shops were all closed, but the pubs and clubs were open, shining bright colours onto the pavements, which were busy with teenagers on their way out for the night.

'There's not a pub near this chemist?' asked Tristan as they stopped at a traffic light.

A stream of lads in smart shirts and trousers and young women wearing skimpy outfits weaved across the road. A large hen party tottered past, all wearing plastic tiaras and matching pink T-shirts. One of the girls spied Tristan in the passenger seat and stumbled over to the car. Without warning she lifted her T-shirt and pressed her bare breasts to his window. Tristan sat there for a moment, and his mouth dropped open.

Kate was stunned and a little jealous to see how pert the young woman's breasts were. 'For God's sake, don't just stare at her,' she said, leaning over Tristan to bang on the window.

The girl staggered back. The traffic light had turned green, but the hen party was congregating around the car. They were all completely drunk and, egged on by the first girl, they lifted their T-shirts and flashed Tristan. Kate was surprised how few of them were wearing bras. She honked the horn. There was a thump as a girl with dark hair and smudged mascara climbed up on the car bonnet and pressed her face against the windscreen.

'Hi, sexy,' she said to Tristan. 'Is that your mother?'

'This is ridiculous,' said Kate.

Technically, she could be Tristan's mother, but the scorn in the young girl's voice burned at her. Kate activated the windscreen wipers and screenwash, dousing the girl. She squealed as she was squirted with water and leapt off the bonnet, swearing. Kate honked the horn again and slowly advanced on the hen party, who parted and started to jeer and heckle.

'You okay?' asked Kate.

'Fine,' said Tristan, blushing.

'We need to concentrate.'

They drove towards Adler's Chemist. The crowds thinned out as they left the pubs behind. The dark roads were deserted. A silence fell over the car.

'It's not too late to bail,' said Kate, realising that what they were doing was crazy.

'No. If there is a chance we can find something that leads us to Caitlyn, we should take it,' said Tristan. He rubbed his sweaty hands nervously on his trousers.

A few minutes later they reached the parade of shops with Adler's Chemist. The shops were all closed. The two estate agents had lights on in their display windows, but the windows in Costa Coffee and Adler's Chemist were both dark.

Kate circled around the block twice until they saw the entrance to a narrow road which ran behind the parade of shops, leading to the delivery bay at the back of the building. She carried on past and they parked two streets away, outside a row of houses in darkness. Kate turned off the engine and headlights. They sat for a moment in the dark, listening to the engine ticking over as it cooled down.

The last time she'd been on an active investigation as a police officer was the night of the crime scene at Crystal Palace, when

Peter Conway dropped her back at her flat. It seemed like a lifetime ago. She remembered her hunch when she'd found Peter's keys and flask, and how scared she'd been to act on it. She now had a similar feeling about Paul Adler.

Tristan was rummaging around in his backpack. He pulled out some running gear and two battered-looking baseball caps, and handed her one.

'Must be fate. I had these in my bag,' he said.

They pulled them on and Kate checked her reflection in the mirror. The baseball cap looked a bit stupid with her jeans and black leather jacket, but its bill cast a shadow over her face.

'Pull it down further and keep your head down,' said Tristan, adjusting her cap and then his.

'Okay. If there's any hint of trouble, we run for it,' said Kate.

It didn't seem like the best pep talk, but Tristan nodded. They got out of the car and walked back to the road leading behind the parade of shops. It was dark and empty. The side walls of two terraced rows ran alongside the parade. They were windowless and loomed high, cutting out the glow from the surrounding streetlights.

When they reached the gate leading to Adler's loading bay, they saw it was unlocked. It creaked loudly in the silence as Kate opened it.

The loading bay was dark and Tristan tripped over a pile of plastic rubbish bags.

'Shit,' he hissed as he went down.

'You okay?' Kate asked, fumbling to help him up.

'Yeah,' he said. She could hear the fear in his voice.

They moved slowly to the back door.

'It's here,' said Kate, feeling for and finding the electronic keypad.

'What if there's an alarm?'

'Then get ready to run.'

Kate took out her phone and activated the light. She keyed in the number on the keypad. There was a horrible pause. It beeped loudly, then it gave a buzz and a click and the door popped open.

'It worked,' said Tristan, shock in his voice.

'I'll switch my light off,' said Kate.

They were plunged back into darkness. She poked her head through the door. She couldn't see much, but she could see that there was no small red light by the ceiling for an alarm box. She could smell stale coffee and cleaning fluid, and a minty antiseptic smell, and the memory of the last time she was in this kitchen came flooding back to her.

They went inside and Kate closed the door.

Tristan crashed into a chair and Kate nearly cried out. 'Sorry,' he said.

Kate moved around the small table to the other door. She tried the handle and it opened. They could see down the long corridor, past the two closed doors, the dispensary door on the left and storeroom on the right, and down to the shopfront. The glow from the streetlights out front penetrated the gloom. As they crept along the corridor to the door on the right, Tristan's trainers squeaked on the floor. Kate checked, but there weren't any cameras mounted on the ceiling.

'This is the door,' whispered Kate when they reached the storeroom. She tried the handle. It was locked. Using the dim light from the screen of her phone, she saw there was a padlock on the outside. 'Shit.'

'What do we do? Look for a key?' whispered Tristan.

'If he's padlocking it, he won't leave a key lying around.'

Kate thought how ridiculous it was of Paul Adler to padlock the room. It might look more severe than a lock, but a padlock was actually easy to open.

'I need a hairgrip,' she said.

'Why are you asking me? I've got a buzz cut,' Tristan said,

panic sounding in his voice. 'I thought we were just going through unlocked doors.'

'We will be, if we can find a hairgrip or a paperclip,' said Kate. The chemist sold hair accessories, but there were security cameras in the front. She thought back to the girls who worked for Paul Adler. They all had long hair. 'There must be a staffroom or toilet,' she added.

They crept around and found a small toilet next to the kitchen. There was a mirrored cabinet above the sink, and inside was a packet of tampons and a hairbrush thick with blonde hair. Underneath the hairbrush was a hairband wrapped around a stack of hairgrips.

'Brilliant,' said Kate. When she closed the cabinet she caught sight of their reflections, their faces in the shadow of her phone light. Scared. They returned to the door with the padlock.

'Does this really work?' whispered Tristan, as Kate knelt down and straightened out one of the hairgrips.

'Yes. When I was a PC, or WPC as they called us back then, we had training with a locksmith and lock picker – an ex-con. They used a padlock made of clear plastic for training. It showed how the lock works inside. There's a row of pins inside the padlock which all need to be lined up level. That's what the key does when you push it in, and when you turn it, it opens the lock mechanism . . . '

There was a bang, which made them both jump, followed by the drone of a car engine.

'Shit,' said Tristan.

'Just a car backfiring,' said Kate. She could feel sweat starting to trickle down her back. 'Here, hold the light on the lock.'

Tristan trained her mobile phone screen onto the padlock. She put the first hairgrip in the padlock, pushing it to the bottom of the lock. Then she opened another hairgrip, straightened it out and bent the tip of one end. She slipped it into the lock above the other pin and started to push it in and jiggle it up and down.

'I wish I could see if the pins were lifting up.' She kept jiggling and pushed it all the way in. 'Okay. Here we go.' She turned the pins and the padlock sprang open.

'Nice one!' said Tristan, a little too loudly. 'Sorry.'

Kate unhooked the padlock, pocketed it, and opened the door.

The room inside was bathed in shadow. They closed the door behind them and switched on the lights on their phones. On one side the room was filled with junk; there were old branding signs for sun cream and make-up, and a stack of chairs against a wall. In the corner sat the huge old photo-processing machine. The walls were all lined with floor to ceiling shelves, and on each shelf were scores of box files. On the back wall there was a thick velvet curtain which was grubby and dusty.

'Bloody hell,' said Tristan. 'Look at all this.'

The box files were all labelled: tax, invoices, conference work, staff, payroll.

'What about those right up there?' said Kate, pointing to a row of ancient-looking files right up by the ceiling. They looked around. There were no ladders.

'The printing machine, it's on wheels,' said Tristan.

They managed to pull it out and push it to the opposite corner. Tristan climbed up and starting pulling down the old box files. He handed them to Kate and she piled them on the floor. She opened each one, dust billowing up around the room. The first two were filled with old paperwork and bank statements, but the next contained packets of photos. There were actors' headshots, and corporate modelling shots. Kate could see dates written on the packets.

She took some more box files from Tristan and, hurriedly looking through, found photo packets from 1989 to 1991. The first couple of packets were actors' headshots, but then there were photos of two young girls in school uniform, posing in a sunny bedroom. As the photos progressed, the girls took their clothes off, and then they were naked.

'How are you getting on? Oh Jesus,' said Tristan, climbing down and joining her. There were six or seven box files left to look through, and he opened them.

'I've got photo packs dated 1990 and 1991,' he said. 'Mostly teenage girls ... And there's more.'

'What was that?' said Kate.

They froze at the sound of a car pulling up outside. There was silence and then they heard a door slam.

'People live here. There are those houses opposite,' said Kate. 'Bag these up. I saw a pile of old promotional tote bags over there.'

She went to the velvet curtain and pulled it back a little. Behind it was a small window, and she could see Paul Adler dressed in jeans and a jacket. He was with Tina, the young girl who worked for him. She had on a short dress, and was tottering on high heels, holding onto his arm. She was laughing and they were making their way along to the front of the shop.

'Shit. We need to move, now,' said Kate, her heart hammering in her chest. She saw Tristan had tipped out the photo packets into an Oil of Olay-branded giveaway tote bag, and he was on top of the photo machine with the box files.

'Pass the rest up!' he said.

Kate handed them up to him, then went to the door and opened it a crack. There was a slow whirring sound and she could see the metal security grille covering the shopfront windows rising. Tina and Paul's feet were visible and then their legs as it slowly rose up.

Tristan jumped down from the printing machine and together they rolled it back in place.

'Run for it! Take the bag!' she hissed. She pushed him through the door and followed him out. She took the padlock from her pocket just as the security grille cleared the door. Kate knelt down and went to hook the padlock back onto the door, but she dropped it.

'Hurry! He's coming in!' said Tristan.

'Go, just go,' said Kate.

She scrabbled around on the floor in the dark. She could hear a key being pushed into the lock in the front door. Her hand closed over the padlock. She picked it up, hooked it back in the door and clicked the lock shut. They heard the second lock turn in the front door, and as it opened Kate and Tristan ran for it, down the corridor and into the kitchen. Kate closed the door as softly as she could. Tristan got the back door open and when they were through Kate closed it. They ran out into the loading bay, Kate closing the gate behind them, and they didn't stop until they emerged onto a side street.

'Oh my God!' said Tristan, as they slowed.

'That was so close,' said Kate.

They kept checking behind them as they speed-walked back to the car, but no one was following.

Kate yanked the car door open and got in, starting the engine. Tristan barely had his door closed as the car pulled away. They were silent for a few minutes as they sped through the dark streets. Kate looked over at Tristan, clutching the bag containing the photos.

'What do you think they were doing there so late?' he said.

Kate raised an eyebrow. 'I'm sure they weren't there to count aspirin.'

'Have we crossed a line here, stealing?' he said, looking visibly shaken.

'No, no. Those photos don't look innocent.'

'What if Caitlyn's not in any of them?'

'Let's just breathe and take a moment,' said Kate, her nerves still jangling.

It had been a risky move, and they had almost been caught. Kate waited until they were on the motorway home before she took off her baseball cap.

She hoped they would glean something from the photos.

CHAPTER 54

Tristan fell asleep when they were on the motorway, and Kate drank in the peace and silence as she drove. It felt like this was the first time she was able to process everything that had happened over the past few days: Jake's photo addressed to Peter Conway sent by 'The Fan', the note left on her car after the vigil, then meeting Gary Dolman again, and him making the link between Peter Conway and Paul Adler. And amongst all this, she had almost fallen off the wagon.

She didn't know if she should feel fear or triumph, having survived the past few days. She felt so much guilt – guilt that she wasn't able to protect Jake, guilt that she would now have to rush around and ready the house for his stay at the last minute, guilt that she had put Tristan in a dangerous situation.

Kate wondered if men felt guilt so acutely. They never seemed to feel guilty as absent fathers. Paul Adler had his photo collection, and it seemed he was sleeping with at least one of the young girls in his employ. Didn't he feel guilt that he had a wife at home? She looked over at Tristan, sleeping slumped with his head over the bag of photos. How was he able to just switch off and sleep after everything that had happened? Her nerves were still jangling and her head was crowded with thoughts, all wanting to be heard.

The road stretched out ahead, dark and empty. The only spot of light on the horizon was Jake. He was coming to visit for four days. Four days without Skype calls and having to make the time count. They would have so much time to talk and catch up and have fun.

They arrived back in Ashdean after midnight. The adrenalin had left Kate's body and she was very tired. It was a relief to finally see the twinkling lights along the seafront.

Tristan was still asleep when they arrived outside his flat.

She leaned over and gently shook his shoulder. 'Hey, we're here.'

He opened his eyes and looked around blearily, and then down at the bag of photos. 'I didn't dream it, then?' he said.

'No. And thank you.'

He nodded and smiled, rubbing his eyes. 'Okay, so what time tomorrow?'

'It's reading week,' said Kate.

'That's so cool. A lie-in.'

'I've got Jake coming on Tuesday ... well, it's now Monday so I should say tomorrow. I have a million things to sort, but do you want to come over in the afternoon and we can look through these photos and plot our next move?'

He nodded and got out of the car. 'Get a good night's sleep,' he said.

Kate watched until he was through his front door. He waved at her and she drove home. The police car had gone from outside her house, and she made a note to call Varia in the morning. When she got indoors, she made herself a cup of tea and went to sit in the armchair by the window.

Despite her exhaustion, she took out the packets of photos and fanned them out on the carpet. As well as the prints, each packet contained a little pocket of negatives in the front. Kneeling down, Kate started to go through each packet. They were dated between 1989 and 1991, matching the years that Peter Conway had lived in Manchester. The photos were all of young women, and looked like impromptu amateur modelling shoots. The girls were in their late teens, and each was small and petite with long hair. All the photos were taken in the spring and summer months, and outdoors in the sunny countryside. The girls slowly disrobed until they were naked, posing with their arms across their bare chests at first, and then fully nude; some lying back in the sunlight on a blanket, others leaning against a tree, backs arched with their eyes closed, a performance of fake desire.

At first glance they didn't look to be in distress, although it was impossible to tell what they were thinking from a photograph. Did Paul Adler promise them something? Did he pay them? Or were they just caught up in his charm and their wish to please him?

She searched through and found another set of photos, and she thought she recognised the girl as Caitlyn. She went to get the ones Paul had given her to check. They matched – it was Caitlyn. The photos she and Tristan had taken looked to be from another day. Her hair was shorter and this time she was in a wooded area. Caitlyn lay naked on a rug and posed, resting on her arm.

The next photo was taken from far away. A naked man with dark hair sat with his back to the camera and Caitlyn straddled him, her legs wrapped around his waist. There were several photos like this, taken in quick succession.

Another photo was a close-up of Caitlyn with a man's penis in her mouth. She knelt on the same rug. There was something about the two naked legs in the photo that made Kate stop and stare. They were both covered in dark hair, but the legs were of slightly different proportions, and belonged to two different men, sitting close together. The second man was photographing Caitlyn with the first man.

They were both naked.

Kate looked through the rest of the photos, and found there were two more women who went to the woods for sex. Again, there were two men involved, and neither had their face showing.

Then a photo of a dark-haired woman made Kate stop in her tracks. She held it close and peered at the woman's face.

'Jesus,' she said. 'I know who you are.'

CHAPTER 55

Just before nine the next morning, Kate and Tristan knocked on the door of a smart terraced house on the outskirts of Bristol.

They'd only had a few hours' sleep, but they'd left at 6 a.m. to beat the Monday morning traffic.

'What if she's not in?' asked Tristan.

Kate didn't want to think about it. Nothing was ready for Jake's visit. She would somehow have to fit in shopping, cleaning and changing beds. She pushed it to the back of her mind as they saw through the stained-glass window in the front door a figure moving down the hallway towards the door.

Victoria O'Grady opened the door wearing leggings and a long pink jumper. Her face was devoid of make-up and it made her look younger, more vulnerable.

'Hello?' she said, confusion and annoyance on her face. 'What are you doing here?'

'Can we talk to you?' asked Kate. 'It's important.'

'No. I'm getting ready for work, and how did you get my address?' she said.

'We googled you,' said Kate. 'Please, this is important. It's about Caitlyn's disappearance.'

'I've told you all I know. Now really, you must leave.' Victoria tried to close the door, but Kate put her foot in the jamb. 'Take your foot away.'

Kate took a photo out of her bag and held it through the gap. It wasn't the most explicit photo. It was of Victoria kneeling on a rug, next to the two men's naked legs. Her face was turned up to them and lit up by the sun. Her arms were crossed protectively across her chest, and she looked to be steeling herself for what was about to happen.

Victoria stared at the photo for a moment, then started to shake. She went to close the front door again, but slumped against the wall. 'Oh, oh, no,' she said, her face crumpling. She put a hand to her mouth and bolted away down the hallway and through a door, slamming it shut. They heard her throwing up. The front door swung inwards and hit the wall.

'Do you mind waiting in the car?' asked Kate. 'I don't think she'll want to talk in front of a man.'

Tristan sighed, then nodded. 'Okay,' he said, taking the keys. 'But keep your phone on.'

Kate stepped into the hallway and closed the front door. She followed Victoria to the bathroom and knocked softly.

'Victoria?' she said.

'Go away,' came a muffled voice. 'Please.'

'I have more photos. Paul Adler doesn't have them any more. And if you talk to me, I think I can help you.'

There was a long pause and then the door opened. Victoria's eyes were puffed up and she was shaking.

Kate reached through the gap and took her hand. 'It's okay.'

Victoria nodded.

Kate made them tea and they went to sit in Victoria's cosy living room. It took a few minutes to get her talking.

'I was always made to feel plain at school, by the other girls. You've seen the school photo. It was a high-achieving girls' school. And you know what teenage girls can be like. Paul Adler

331

started to come in to the video shop, and he was flirty with me and Caitlyn. One day he came in at the end of the day, just as I was closing up, and asked if I wanted to go for a drink. He was handsome and had this magnetism. He was dangerous and exciting, and he said he thought I was beautiful. I started seeing him. We'd go for drives in his car, and then one day he arranged this amazing picnic, and took me out to this lake. He was the perfect gentleman, and it was me who made the first move and we kissed ... A couple of weeks later he asked if I wanted to go again, and this time he told me he had a new camera and he wanted to try it out. We'd been drinking wine, and I was feeling a little bit tipsy, and it gave me confidence. He took pictures of me, he asked me to pose. I had all my clothes on and it was another lovely day. He even gave me the prints afterwards ...'

She wiped a tear from her eye. 'He just seemed like such a nice guy, when I now realise he was ...'

'Grooming you,' said Kate.

Victoria rolled her eyes and grabbed a tissue. 'It's so obvious when you say it like that. I was so stupid and naïve ...' She blew her nose.

'Did you tell anyone about your picnics?' asked Kate.

'No. He told me not to. He said that he would lose his licence, and that he had a sick mother to look after. He said that we should wait until I was sixteen and then we could get married ... Looking back, I thought it was a relationship. How screwed up is that?'

'What about Caitlyn?'

'I found out that she'd been seeing him as well. I thought I was the only one. I had a huge fight with Caitlyn, and I got my father fire her. Then I confronted Paul about it. I think he was shocked at how angry I was ... He invited me for another picnic the next day, and he said he wanted to make it up to me. This time we went out to the country, to Jepson's Wood, which was different to where we'd been before. He said it was this magical place, his favourite place, and that he wanted to ask me something.'

'A proposal?' asked Kate.

'That's what he hinted at . . . ' Victoria shook her head again. She took a deep breath. 'He'd packed a beautiful picnic, and he'd brought wine . . . But I don't remember him having much. He kept topping up my glass, and then I started to feel really strange, disconnected . . . Like I was floating out of my body. The rest of the afternoon is like a blur. Another man was suddenly there and I just remember them talking to me, and I couldn't hear, and then they were naked . . . and I remember putting my hand down to my legs and feeling that my shorts and my underwear had been taken off . . . ' She broke down, her head in her hands, sobbing.

Kate went to her and took her in her arms.

'I don't remember much else. The next time I was lucid I was at home in the bath and I was bleeding, you know, down there,' she said.

'Where were your parents?' asked Kate.

'They were out that day, and they didn't get home until late that night, when I had cleaned myself up . . . The next morning, Paul rang me and said he wanted to talk. He wanted to meet at the chemist's, and that's when he showed me the photos. All the things they had done to me and photographed. He said if I ever spoke about it he would send these photos to my parents, and he would send them to the readers' wives section in all the top-shelf magazines. This was before the internet and so many blokes would look at the readers' wives, even my dad did. If he'd seen me there . . . '

'Oh, Victoria, I'm sorry.'

'Just knowing all these years he's kept these photos.'

'Do you want to see the photos?' asked Kate.

'No. I saw them once. They are disgusting and explicit . . . I've never been able to enjoy sex since.'

'Did you know when Caitlyn met them? I have a similar set of photos where Caitlyn is with the same two men.'

'I don't know. After we rowed and she left the video shop, I never saw her again.'

'You must have thought about her, going missing?'

'You don't think I feel *guilty*? You don't think this has hung over me? The fear of what he might do one day with those photos? And then, as the years pass, you just start to think in terms of survival. I've survived this long, everyone has forgotten, I'll just bury it away and it will never be talked about again.'

'Was the other man in the photos Peter Conway?' asked Kate.

'I don't know. Over the years, I've had memories come back, but I see them from where I lay on the ground, and they have the sun behind their heads, blurring their faces . . . I do have something, though.'

Victoria wiped her eyes and got up from the chair. She turned her back to Kate and started to lift her long jumper and the corner of a T-shirt underneath. 'It's stretched over the years as I've got bigger, but this is where one of them bit me.'

There was a scar in the shape of a bite mark. The skin was puckered around a clear impression of teeth.

'Peter Conway,' said Kate.

Victoria turned and sat again. 'But I never saw his face . . . I had bruising around my neck afterwards – I think they tried to strangle me.'

'Yes, the photos show that,' said Kate softly.

'What happens now?' asked Victoria, suddenly starting to panic. 'Does he know you have the photos?'

Kate explained how she'd got the photos, and told Victoria that she would call the police, and they would need to take a full statement, with the photos as evidence.

'We have the originals, and the negatives,' said Kate. 'Please talk to the police about this. Put it on record.'

It was late afternoon when Kate and Tristan left Victoria's house. Kate had contacted Varia, who had a team of officers come and talk to Victoria and take a statement. Victoria's story was another shocking revelation for Kate.

'What happens now?' asked Tristan.

'I hope they talk to Paul Adler. It makes me wish we were police officers. I'd love to be the one to knock on his door and haul him in for questioning.'

As they drove, Kate felt torn, and the guilt came back. She wanted to continue with their investigations, but then she thought about Jake coming, and wanted nothing more than to spend time with him.

Kate dropped Tristan at his flat.

'I'll let you know as soon as I hear anything,' she said. 'I've got to go and clean my house and get ready for Jake.'

'Okay, keep in touch,' he said.

Kate went shopping at the supermarket, loading up on food for Jake's stay. As she drove back to her house, she glanced in her rear-view mirror a few times. There was a car, two cars back, she was sure had been behind her on the way to the supermarket. But, then again, she hadn't been watching closely. Was this a manifestation of her anxiety? Or was she being watched?

Just as she thought this, the car turned off before she could get a good look at the driver. Kate shook the thought away, but still felt an unease in her stomach.

CHAPTER 56

Kate was excited to see Glenda and Jake when they arrived at 3 p.m. the following day. It had been a long car journey, so she took them straight down to the beach for a walk.

It was a sunny day, a little windy, but pleasant enough to take off their shoes and paddle. Jake ran ahead and was poking around in the rock pools with a stick.

'He's been very excited about seeing you,' said Glenda as they walked along the sand.

Kate smiled and watched Jake as he leaned in close to look into a wide rock pool and then jumped back.

'There's a bloody enormous jellyfish in here with blue stripes!' he shouted.

'Jake. Language!' trilled Glenda. He ignored her and started poking around, wading into the rock pool. 'You will keep an eye on him?'

'Mum. I'm not stupid,' she said. Jake was peering into the water, taking pictures with his phone. 'What have you told him about the police car?'

Kate had been in touch with the local police in Whitstable to tell them Jake was coming to stay, and they had coordinated with Devon and Cornwall police. A police car was stationed again outside Kate's house. They seemed to think that Kate and Jake together were more of a target.

'I told him that there's a bad man involved with Peter Conway who the police are looking for, and they are here just as a precaution,' said Glenda.

'And Jake bought that? Didn't ask any more questions?'

'He did, but I was very vague. If I'm honest, I wanted to cancel him coming here, with all that has been going on. At least if the police are here I feel a little better about it,' said Glenda.

'I'm going to look after him, Mum,' said Kate, annoyed that her mother still didn't trust her with Jake.

'I know you are, darling. And keep an eye on the police. Make sure they're not nodding off on the job.'

'Surveillance police don't "nod off on the job",' said Kate. She remembered all the times she did surveillance, and felt protective of her former career.

Jake was now in the middle of the rock pool where the sandy bottom dropped away a little and he went in up to his waist.

'Ahh! Cold water!' He grimaced.

'Jake! Those trousers are clean on. They are your only smart pair!' shouted Glenda.

Kate suppressed a smile as Jake ignored her.

'Mum,' she said, putting her hand on Glenda's arm. 'It's just sea water, and I'm not planning on us going to any ritzy restaurants, or church. We're going to have fun, and you can have a rest until Saturday.'

When it was time for Glenda to leave, Jake wasn't sad to see her go; he was more concerned with getting back to the beach to make a huge sandcastle. They came out to the car, and Glenda insisted on going to meet the police officer stationed in the car outside. He was only in his twenties, and was in the middle of eating a sandwich when she knocked on his window. He swallowed quickly and wound it down.

'Hello. I'm Glenda Marshall. What's your name?' asked Glenda, fixing him with a beady stare.

'I'm PC Rob Morton,' he said, wiping his hands on a tissue. He took out his warrant card and showed it to Glenda, who gave it the once-over.

'I want you to take good care of my grandson, Jake. And this is my daughter, Kate. She was a police officer too!'

'Hello,' he said.

Jake fidgeted next to them in his wet trousers. He didn't seem interested in the fact he had police protection. Kate didn't know if this was a good or bad thing. *Was he used to this craziness?* she wondered.

Glenda handed back the warrant card. 'I just wanted to say hello, and to tell you that we really appreciate what you do. I've asked Kate to make you a cup of coffee every now and again, which should keep you sharp and alert.'

'It's been quiet. There's the caravan park up the road, but that's pretty empty. Just a few hardcore caravanners braving the wind,' said Rob. He took his card and smiled, wound up his window and picked up the rest of his sandwich.

Kate and Jake went with Glenda to her car.

'Now, Jake. You do as Mum says, okay?' said Glenda.

'Yes. We're cool. It's going to be fine,' he said. Glenda leaned over and kissed him on the cheek. 'Ugh!' he cried, wiping at his face with a sandy hand.

'Thanks, Mum,' said Kate. 'Drive safely. Any problems, I'll call you.'

'It won't be much longer till he'll be able to stay wherever he wants,' said Glenda. Kate detected a trace of bitterness in her mother's voice. 'Keep an eye on him. He's precious.'

Kate had spent so long thinking about not living with Jake that she'd never stopped to think how attached Glenda was to him, and how hard it must be for her, him growing up.

'I'll guard him with my life,' said Kate.

She watched as Glenda drove away. She reached the curve in the road and vanished.

'I thought she'd never go,' said Jake. 'Can we go back on the beach?'

'Yeah, let's build a sandcastle,' said Kate.

The red-haired Fan sat in his car on the edge of the caravan park, amongst the parked cars of a couple of campers and dog walkers. Today he was driving an old battered Ford Fiesta, the runaround car he liked to use to help him blend in. He wore walking gear, and if anyone took too much notice of him he was ready to get out of the car and head off up the hill with a map and backpack.

He pretended to be engrossed in a large map when Glenda drove past. He had seen her arrive with Jake a few hours earlier. This was too good to be true. Kate and the kid, alone in the house. He had been watching Kate for a couple of days, and he had a couple of problems – the old woman from the surf shop next door and now a police car stationed outside.

It would involve a few changes to his plan, but he would enjoy getting creative. He waited a few minutes, then started the engine and drove away. His preparations were almost complete. The stage was about to be set, and he would be back.

Kate went back to the beach with Jake and sat on a deckchair watching him build his sandcastle. The sky was clear and the sun shone down, warming them. Her phone rang in her pocket and she took it out, seeing it was Tristan.

'Kate, there have been some developments with Victoria O'Grady,' he said, sounding excited. 'The police took her statement – she told them the same as she told you – and they've been studying the photographs we took from Paul Adler's chemist. Varia says there's enough evidence to reopen the Caitlyn Murray case, and a team want to go and look at Jepson's Wood tomorrow . . . I take it that's out for you?'

'Yes. You know I've got Jake here,' said Kate, watching as he was digging, up to his waist in a hole.

'Okay. I can go, if that's cool with you?'

'Of course. You'll let me know what happens?'

'As soon as I know anything, I'll call you.'

She came off the phone and felt far away from the investigation. A little part of her, she was ashamed to admit, wished Jake had come to visit at another time. She pushed those thoughts firmly away and joined in building the sandcastle. They managed an impressive one, with four turrets and a moat, before a huge wave obliterated it and soaked them both.

They came back to the house and Kate got them towels so they could dry off and get warm. The sun was now behind some clouds and it had grown colder.

'Mum. That was the best sandcastle ever. I can't ever build big ones like that at home 'cause the beach is all stones.'

Seeing him in her living room for the first time in a few months, Kate realised how tall he was.

'Stand by the doorframe there,' she said. She grabbed a pen and marked where the top of his head touched. He stepped away and they both looked at all the marks on the doorframe, showing how much he had grown over his visits.

'Blimey, you'll be taller than me soon,' said Kate.

He ran his finger down the markings. The time had passed so quickly, and very soon his childhood would be over. She felt the urge to apologise to him, for making his life complicated. For . . .

'Mum, I'm soaking wet, and the wet sand is rubbing on my bum,' he said, grimacing. Kate swooped in and gave him a huge hug.

'What's that for?' he asked. 'By rights, I should be in trouble 'cause I went in the sea in all my good clothes.'

'It's fine,' said Kate. 'I just needed a hug.'

'Women,' he said, rolling his eyes.

'Come on, let's get you upstairs and into some dry clothes,' she said.

She showed him up to the front bedroom, which was next to hers. It was the one he always had when he came to stay. It had a colourful striped blanket on the bed, a bookshelf loaded with kids' books, which she realised he'd grown out of, and the window looked down at the beach.

He ran his finger over the headboard to check for dust. 'Catherine, you've not been slack with the furniture polish,' he said, doing an uncanny impression of Glenda.

'Do you need a hand unpacking?' asked Kate, laughing.

He put his bag down on the end of the bed. 'I've got it covered,' he said, shooing her out.

'Okay. I'm doing Cumberland sausages with chips and beans for tea, and I'll take the skins off the sausages.'

'Cool!'

'And I've got Phish Food ice cream for pudding.'

'Best Mum award goes to you,' he said, and he closed the door.

She came downstairs to start the food, feeling all warm and happy that he was with her. The only thing that spoiled her thoughts was seeing the police car stationed outside. It made her think about the case, and that Tristan would be going to Jepson's Wood without her.

Again, the eternal struggle between being a mother and wanting to have a career reared its ugly head. She put it to the back of her mind and started to cook.

CHAPTER 57

The next morning, Tristan met a team of police officers and Victoria O'Grady at Jepson's Wood. He'd borrowed his sister's car for the day, promising her, on pain of death, that he would bring it back in one piece. The wood had shrunk in size over the past few years, and was now a couple of acres of trees surrounded by new-build homes.

The section where the police were due to search sat on the edge of the housing estate, where a long line of fences backed onto the trees. A police support van was parked next to the fence with a couple of squad cars. A man with two cadaver dogs had arrived, and he was talking to an officer. Tristan grabbed a cup of tea from the support van and went over to Victoria. Her eyes were puffy and red from crying and she wore a huge orange fur coat.

'Thanks for coming,' she said. 'I can't believe we're doing this.'

'I was expecting two huge ferocious Alsatians,' said Tristan as they watched the dog handler open the van, and two fluffy Cavalier King Charles spaniels jumped out and started to bark and scamper. Their white furry heads contrasted with their long floppy brown ears.

Victoria laughed. The dogs came galloping up to them and rolled over to have their bellies scratched.

The dog handler followed and introduced himself. 'I'm Harry Grant,' he said. He was in his late fifties, a cheery man with thin grey hair. 'This is Kim and Khloe.'

'They're so cute,' said Tristan as Kim, the slightly bigger of the two, playfully chewed on the collar of his jacket.

'Don't underestimate their cute fluffy faces. They're incredible. They are both trained to smell decomposing flesh.'

'But Caitlyn went missing twenty years ago. Even if she was buried here, what would be left of her after all this time?' asked Tristan.

'I've tested them with so many variables. Kim was able to detect the presence of rotting flesh in a cold case going back eighteen years. The police believed that a man had killed his daughter, buried her in the garden and then moved the body shortly afterwards. They were able to detect where the body had been buried, even though it had been moved eighteen years earlier and buried somewhere else. When the police dug, they found small fragments of tooth and skull belonging to the young girl.'

'How deep can they pick up on a scent?' asked Victoria.

'Up to eight or ten feet,' said Harry, as Khloe lay on her back and let Victoria scratch her pink belly.

After they'd finished their tea, the police and Tristan walked with Victoria back to the area where she remembered having the picnic with Paul Adler. They moved in silence to the edge of the trees, Victoria in her huge orange coat, flanked by four police officers and Tristan. Harry stayed back with the dogs in his van, waiting until she had identified the area where they would start to search.

Victoria walked unsteadily on the rough ground, and they were silent apart from the faint sound of far-off traffic on the motorway. They reached the edge of the trees and stepped into a clearing covered with pine needles. The weak sun shone through the branches and dappled the ground.

'It's changed so much,' she said. Despite her thick coat and the weak sunshine, Tristan could see she was shivering. 'This used to be fields for miles.'

'Where was the lake?' he asked.

'There was a lake about a quarter of a mile over there,' said one of the police officers, who was holding a map. He was pointing towards what were now rows and rows of roofs.

Victoria looked around and nodded. 'It was somewhere here, near this clearing. We went deeper into the woods, but not too far as the trees were very dense.'

A police officer with a neatly trimmed black goatee looked around. 'What makes you sure?' he asked. It was a question without hostility or doubt.

'I remember the turn-off from the main road. There's that really old King George phone box a little way before the dead end and it turns into fields. The trees are bigger, but I'll always remember what bit they brought me to,' she said.

'Roughly how wide is the area that you think we should search, from what you remember?'

'This whole clearing, and a little way into the trees there,' she said. Her eyes welled up again and she scrabbled for a tissue in her coat.

'Okay,' said the officer. He reached for his radio. 'Harry, we're ready for Kim and Khloe.'

Despite the seriousness of the situation, Tristan had to suppress a smile. *It's all down to cute fluffy Kim and Khloe. Let's hope no one drives past in a burger van to distract them.* He just couldn't imagine that the dogs would be able to smell anything other than moss and rotting leaves.

Kim was brought over first by Harry. Everyone stood back as he let her off her lead and she ran about sniffing around the area Victoria had indicated. Harry worked methodically with her, making sure that she moved up and down in straight lines, like mowing a lawn, working her way across the clearing. After about ten minutes, she reached a tall oak tree and stopped, circling round and sniffing intently, her long furry ears disturbing the piles of leaves and pine needles. She sat down, tipped her head back and started to bark.

A police officer marked the spot and she carried on sniffing around for the next fifteen minutes, then came back and barked again. Tristan and Victoria had been watching in silence, and when the dog barked for the second time, he could feel the tension in the air.

'What if she's smelling a dead bird, or a fox?' asked Victoria, her voice cracking with emotion.

'Harry said she's only trained to detect human remains,' said Tristan, feeling tension and excitement in his stomach.

Harry gave Kim some treats and took her back over to the car. The police officers remained at the edge of the clearing.

'What happens now?' said Victoria to the police officer with the goatee.

'He's going to bring the second dog back to check, just as a precaution . . . But I think we've hit the bullseye. She's detected human remains.'

CHAPTER 58

Kate had woken up at her normal time of 7.30 a.m., but Jake slept through until ten. This was another change reminding her that he was now a teenager. He always used to wake up at six in the morning, bright and chatty.

By the time he woke up she'd pottered around the house, made herself and the police officer who was stationed outside a cup of tea, and spoken to Tristan who was on his way to Jepson's Wood and promised to call her the minute he heard anything. When Jake finally stirred, they went for a swim in the sea. The weather was beautifully clear and the water calm. He had been excited to use his wetsuit and sea shoes, and they swam out together and spent a happy hour splashing in the surf and diving down under the water wearing their goggles.

They then went into Ashdean and had lunch, and when they came home Myra joined them for a walk on the beach. Kate loved how good Myra was with Jake. When they reached the rock pools she was able to name all the sea creatures hiding in the gloomy depths, and tell him all about them. He was fascinated.

PC Rob Morton was now on his third day shift outside Kate's house, and it was proving to be a long, boring grind. His shift started at 7 a.m. and would go through to 7 p.m. He was grateful for the cups of tea and coffee from Kate and her neighbour Myra, but the shitty food he had ended up eating for the past few days was doing his guts in. Since his girlfriend Danni had left him, he was forced to fend for himself when it came to catering.

He missed Danni's packed lunches, and the home-cooked meals, more than he missed her. He looked over at today's lunch on the passenger seat beside him, a sweaty cheese and onion sandwich from the petrol station. Pricey and shit, that's what his lunch would be for the third day.

As he sat with the radio playing, his mind drifted to what he would have for his dinner that night. This kind of long surveillance work wore you down, and all he wanted to do was drive home, have a bath and crash out on the sofa. He was going to treat himself and order in sushi from the new place in Ashdean. He took out his wallet and saw that he only had a tenner. There was a cash machine outside the surf shop and, wanting to stretch his legs, he got out of the car and walked over to it.

The road was a dead end after Kate's house, and on the other side of the road were fields. It was the kind of road where not much happened, but he had to keep his eyes peeled, as it was a quiet spot and not overlooked by anybody.

The screen on the cash machine was misty with a layer of salt, and he had to rub it with the sleeve of his uniform. He put his card in and withdrew fifty quid, seeing that it would charge him five pounds for the privilege. He would have words with the old woman later and ask where that five pounds went to.

As he was tucking the cash into his wallet, he noticed a small white van had pulled up a little way along the road. A tall, red-haired man wearing walking gear had climbed out and was changing into walking boots.

Rob got back in his car and watched as the man pulled on a big rucksack and picked up a map. He then started towards him.

The red-haired Fan glanced around as he approached the police car. He had already walked the length of the beach under Kate's house and seen her on the sand with Jake and the old woman from the surf shop.

As he reached the police car, he could see the thin, pasty-faced officer looked miserable sitting inside. He smiled amiably and knocked on the car window. The police officer scowled and wound down the window.

'Hi, sorry to bother you, officer,' said The Fan. 'Is this the entrance to the coastal walk to Ashdean?' In his hand was a folded map of the area, which he held up to the window. His hand moved to the pocket of his shorts, where he felt the outline of a flick knife and a little clump of cotton wool balls.

The officer ignored the map and turned his head to look behind him. 'Yeah. That's the footpath, I think,' he said, and went to wind up the window.

The Fan put the map on the edge of the window.

'Officer, I'm crap with maps. Is that the footpath where there's been a lot of erosion? I'd hate to end up going over the edge of the cliff.' He pushed the map through the window, forcing the officer to take it in both hands.

The officer peered at it. 'Listen, mate, I'm on duty—'

The Fan reached inside the pocket of his shorts and with a quick smooth movement he took out the flick knife, pushed it into the officer's right ear and pressed the button. The eight-inch blade shot out and embedded itself in his brain.

It all happened so quickly. The officer looked up at The Fan in shock, then writhed around and grappled at the hand holding the knife against his head. The Fan twisted the blade in a circular motion, pulling it through his brain tissue. The officer started to fit, gurgle and foam at the mouth. Less than a minute later, he was still.

The Fan removed the knife and plugged the officer's ear with cotton wool, propping him up so that from a distance it would look like he was still sitting up in the car.

He took out a tissue, wiped the officer's chin and the knife, then retracted the blade, putting the knife back inside the pocket of his shorts. He looked around. The road was still and quiet.

Now it was time to break into Kate's house and wait.

CHAPTER 59

Tristan stood with Victoria in Jepson's Wood as the second cadaver dog, Khloe, worked her way across the clearing, her nose hovering across the ground. She stopped in the same place as Kim, sat on her haunches and barked.

Forensics officers had arrived within the hour. Tristan and Victoria moved closer and watched as three forensics officers cleared away leaves and pine needles before beginning to dig. A few minutes later it started to rain, and a tarpaulin was hastily put up so they could continue. Tristan and Victoria were given an umbrella, and he held it for them both as they listened to the rhythmic sound of spades in soil and the rain clattering on the tarpaulin.

'I've never been back here,' said Victoria, breaking the silence. 'Not since it happened. Do you mind if I hold your hand? I'm shaking so much.'

'Of course,' he said. He took her hand, which was freezing cold.

An hour passed as the team dug deeper, the pile of soil beside the hole growing larger. The rain continued to hammer down and the clouds grew thick, casting the clearing of the wood in a heavy gloom.

The smell of the rain on the soil and plants was fresh. They were digging ever deeper but it didn't seem like they were going to find a body. Tristan was just thinking they would soon give up when a yell went up from one of the forensics officers.

'We have something! We need a torch!'

Tristan moved with Victoria to the edge. He could see the hole was around two metres deep, and roots from surrounding trees poked through the edges.

'I can't look,' said Victoria, putting her head on his shoulder.

The forensics officers were red in the face, their blue coveralls caked in the peaty soil. Tristan watched as they started to dig more carefully, scraping away the soil. Then they started to use large coarse brushes.

A police officer brought over a light on a stand and shone it into the hole. The muddy shape of a skull with teeth was looking up at them from the dark soil. They worked down with the brushes, pulling away the muddy clods of earth, and uncovered a small skeleton, intact.

'Oh my God,' said Tristan, his heart beating fast in his chest.

Victoria turned and looked into the hole. She gave a sharp intake of breath and began to shake violently. 'I've never seen a dead person before,' she said.

'It's okay,' said Tristan. Victoria slumped back and sat down on the wet earth.

Tristan moved closer as the forensics officers started to clean the bones with a finer brush. He could see there were still wisps of hair stuck to the dome of the skull, and a ragged piece of material. As they reached the feet, a pair of leather sandals was revealed, and what looked like a slim square handbag and strap.

The sandals and the bag were the first things lifted out of the soil and placed in clear plastic evidence bags. Tristan asked to see them, and he took out a photo that Malcolm Murray's neighbour had sent. It showed a picture of Caitlyn in the clothes she had worn the day she went missing: a thin blue summer dress, with a row of white flowers printed on the hem. Her sandals and bag were both made of blue leather, and had a matching pattern of white flowers.

'I remember her wearing that outfit one day to work,' said Victoria, peering at the photo.

'Caitlyn's mother said she was wearing this the day she went missing,' said Tristan.

Tristan compared the photo with the leather handbag and sandals in the plastic evidence bags. They were covered in soil and stained a dark brown, but the front flap of the handbag was still intact, and he rubbed at a pattern of flowers indented into the leather.

This has to be her. It has to be Caitlyn, thought Tristan. He handed the evidence bags back to the officer.

'We'll have to look at dental records and DNA, but there is a high chance that these are the remains of Caitlyn Murray,' said the officer.

'Oh my God,' said Victoria. 'I never thought it could be true . . . I never really thought they did it and dumped her here.'

Yes! thought Tristan, feeling triumph mixed with sadness. *Yes, we found her.* He just wished Kate was there with him to see it.

CHAPTER 60

Kate was on the beach with Myra and Jake, trying to coax a huge crab out from a rock pool, when her phone rang. She took it from the pocket of her jeans, expecting it to be Tristan with news, but saw it was Alan Hexham.

'Hello, Kate,' he said.

The wind had got up, and was roaring across the beach and whipping up the tops of the waves to white. Kate came away from the rock pools and up the beach.

'Hi, I wondered where you'd got to. Is everything okay?' she asked.

'Sorry. I had to go and work up north for a week. Listen, I've got the post mortem files which I can share with you on Abigail Clarke. I also got something back which I thought would be of interest.'

'Hang on, Alan,' she said. She signalled to Myra and Jake. 'I need to take this. I'm going to go up the beach out of the wind.'

Myra nodded and turned back to Jake who was concentrating on the rock pool. Kate moved closer to the dunes, where the wind was quieter.

'Sorry, go on, Alan,' she said.

'I was looking over the files of all the victims. Because of the nature of Abigail Clarke's attack, I can't find anything to link it to the other young women, even though the police suspect it was the same person. I also noticed a few discrepancies with Emma Newman – nothing major, but I thought I'd tell you before I send it all over. She was eighteen, not seventeen as was first reported. She *was* reported missing – a woman where she worked made the call – and Emma's boyfriend at the time was given the wrong name in the police file.'

'The wrong name?'

'Yes. The report has him down as Keir Castle, but his legal name is Keir Castle-Meads. He styles himself as Keir Castle on his social media, and the *Okehampton Times* wrongly reported his name as Keir Castle, when he was charged for threatening his girlfriend, and given a fine and community service, but when I looked back over the magistrates' records I discovered he is Keir Castle-Meads. I don't know if the police made the same error. Although he has no other criminal record . . . '

Kate looked over at Myra and Jake. They had their trousers rolled up and were wading out into a rock pool, leaving a rippling wake across the smooth surface. Something clicked in the back of Kate's mind and she didn't hear what Alan said next.

'Kate are you still there? I said I'm going to email this all over to you, but you know the drill. Mum's the word that I'm sharing this with you. Keep it somewhere safe.'

'Yes . . . Thank you.'

Alan hung up. It hit Kate like a truck, the realisation where she'd heard that name before.

'Myra! Jake!' she shouted. They turned to her, Jake with a handful of seaweed. 'I just have to run up to the house. Are you okay for a bit?'

'Fine!' shouted Myra, waving her away, and they turned back to look in the water.

Kate ran back through the dunes and up to the house. It was so close, the thought, and she had to keep hold of it. *Keir*

Castle-Meads, Castle-Meads. Castle-Meads... In the living room she scanned the bookshelves and found it, a true crime book, one of the better ones which had been written about the history of the Nine Elms Cannibal case.

She flicked through, finding the photos at the back. *Where was it? Castle-Meads... Castle-Meads.* There were twelve pages of photos at the back, and she found it halfway through. A photo of the lead barrister who tried the Nine Elms Cannibal case: Tarquin Castle-Meads QC. He was a huge man, imposing and pompous with bright red thinning hair in a combover. His jowly mouth and large hooded eyes gave him the serious stare of a bulldog.

Next to it was a picture, taken on the day of the verdict on the steps of the high court. A triumphant Tarquin Castle-Meads smiling with crooked yellow teeth with his wife, Cordelia, a dark-haired, handsome woman with a high forehead and a grim gaze. Their four children were lined up beside them, all dressed up as if for a day out at church. The children had all inherited their father's flaming red hair and hooded eyes, which made their faces look odd and almost rubbery. Kate peered at the picture of the four children: Poppy, Mariette, Keir and Joseph.

Jesus, thought Kate, as she peered at the photo. *Keir had an alibi, he was away in the States when Emma Newman went missing, but what about the other son? What if that is the link, and the way in?*

She remembered something else about the family. She flicked through to the index and found a passage about Tarquin Castle-Meads QC. He was educated at Queen's College, Oxford and he took the bar exam at an early age. His wife Cordelia had helped elevate him into the British establishment. She was the heir to the shipping firm CM Logistics Ltd.

CM Logistics, thought Kate, holding the book. *I see their bloody lorries and vans everywhere. They own warehouses all over the country.* She googled the company on her phone and its slick website came up, dominated by a picture showing a fleet of vans and lorries streaking across a vast highway.

Tarquin Castle-Meads had retired to Spain with his wife, and the kids had been fighting over the running of this multi-billion-pound company, Kate remembered this from snippets she'd heard in the press over the years.

How can I not have seen this?

Kate was shaking with excitement as she rang Tristan. His phone went straight to voicemail.

'Tristan, call me the moment you get this message. I've found the link, the person who is doing these copycat murders. It's the son of the barrister who put Peter Conway in prison. Tarquin Castle-Meads was the QC who tried the case and won. His sons are Keir Castle-Meads and Joseph Castle-Meads. Keir has an alibi, but I think it's the other son, Joseph, who is copycatting, and the reason he's been able to get around so easily is that he has access to huge amounts of money and his family own CM Logistics, the haulage and delivery company . . . They deliver goods and services and they may well have a contract to deliver money to ATMs. It was an ATM van that we saw in the CCTV from the camera on the front of Frederick Walters' house—'

'What a clever girl you are,' said a voice. Kate jumped and dropped her phone.

A tall, red-haired man was standing at the end of the book-shelves. He had the same bright red hair and hooded eyes as in the photo. Keeping his eyes on her, he leaned down and picked up her phone. He put it to his ear, then pressed a number on the screen. Kate heard the computerised voice say 'message deleted'. He ended the call.

'Joseph Castle-Meads,' she said. The sight of him standing in her living room was overpowering. He was so tall and he pro-jected so much angry energy that the air around him seemed to crackle. He dropped her phone on the carpet, and ground his foot into the screen.

'Yes, that's me,' he said. 'Photos don't do you justice. You look much better in the flesh.' He advanced on her, and Kate took a step back and felt the bookshelves against her back. His pale skin shone with sweat. Despite his good bone structure and height, he looked feral. He smiled and then punched her hard in the face. Kate felt her nose break and an explosion of pain. She went down with a crash onto the coffee table and rolled onto the floor.

CHAPTER 61

Jake enjoyed looking through the rock pools with Myra. Even though she was really old – her hair was white and her face covered in deep wrinkles – she was cool, and funny, and she knew a lot about sea creatures.

They'd found a long eel floating in the depths of the deepest rock pool, lazily pumping water through its gills, and she'd managed to catch it. She held it up for him while he took a photo and peered at its large eyes and teeth. The only thing he thought gross was when she'd pulled the shell of a mussel off the side of the rock and asked if he would like to try it.

'What? Eat it?' he'd said.

'Yes! You won't get fresher. When I was a girl this was the highlight of a trip to the seaside.'

'Eating that thing that looks like snot and earwax rolled together?'

'Yup.'

Myra put the shell to her mouth, and with a slurp she'd eaten it.

'Yuck!' he cried.

She smiled. 'Are you sure I can't tempt you?' She pulled another huge mussel from a seaweed-covered rock. It twitched in her grip and he grinned and shook his head.

'I dare you to eat it,' she said.

'How much do you dare me?'

'I'm not a gambling woman, but for you I'll bet a couple of Mr Kipling's fondant fancies?'

'If I eat that, I'll be barfing up fondant fancies all night!'

He screamed when she ate it, and Myra laughed and rinsed her hands in the water. The wind was getting up now and Jake could see grey clouds rolling towards them from the horizon.

'Where's your mother got to?' asked Myra. Jake looked back up at the house. He shrugged. 'Why don't you go and see where she is, and I'll go back to the shop and see if I can find you a body board to practise your surfing?'

'Okay!' he said.

Jake hurried off up the beach, through the dunes and up the sandy cliff to the back door. The house was eerily quiet when he came inside. There were books all over the living room floor and the big china bowl on the coffee table was broken. Then he heard a funny noise by the front door. Like thick tape being undone.

He moved through the living room and into the hall. Kate lay limp on her back in the hallway, and she had a bloodied nose. Her wrists were bound together with masking tape. A huge red-haired man was bending over her, fastening her feet together with the tape. Jake put his hand over his mouth to suppress a scream. The man stopped and fixed his eyes on him. Jake couldn't move.

'The boy,' the man said in a raspy whisper. He smiled, his lips were large and wet and he had huge teeth. He looked like a creepy clown. He stood up and he towered over Jake. He took a flick knife from his back pocket. 'If you scream, I'll slice your mother's tits off and feed them to you,' he said, his voice low and even. 'I killed the policeman outside. Pushed this knife into his ear and BAM!' The huge blade popped out. It was long, sharp and silver. Jake felt his legs start to tremble uncontrollably. 'So stay quiet and do what I say, okay, Jake?'

Jake's top lip wobbled, and he nodded. He started to cry.

'Don't cry,' said the man, reaching over. Jake flinched as he stroked his hair with the edge of the blade. 'You are the golden child. Do you know how much I wish I could be you? And you look like your father, and your mother.' He ran the edge of the blade down Jake's cheek. The cold metal brushed Jake's skin.

Fear and terror suddenly overtook Jake and he yelled out.

The man clamped his free hand over Jake's mouth and pushed him up against the wall, holding the blade against his throat.

'You are making this difficult, you little cunt ... If you scream, I'll do what I said to your mother. I mean it, do you hear me?' he said. His voice was soft and menacing, and seemed to curl around his ears like smoke. 'Where's that old woman? Answer me, quietly.'

'She, she ... she went to her house,' Jake whispered. He saw out of the corner of his eye Kate stirring a little, her eyes fluttering.

'You have the same eyes,' said the man, studying his face. 'The sunburst in your left eye.'

Jake flinched as the man took the knife away from his throat. The man then put his hand in his back pocket and took out a neat square of cotton. He leaned close. Jake could smell his breath, horrible and acidic. His body shook uncontrollably and he felt his shorts and legs warm with urine.

'Jake. You wouldn't believe how long I've planned for this. I've got such a surprise for you,' he said softly.

He clamped the cloth over Jake's mouth and nose, pushing his head back against the wall. Jake smelt sharp, strong chemicals and his vision flooded with red and black, and then he was unconscious.

*

Joseph Castle-Meads had parked the van directly outside Kate's front door. He loaded Kate and Jake into the back. He lingered a moment, crouching beside them. He put his hand to Kate's face and felt her breathing, then touched Jake's face. Mother and son together. He'd seen them on the beach, and he envied their close bond.

His own mother had been a chilly, distant presence when he was growing up. His parents had always been more concerned about their position in society and his father's legal career than their children. He was packed off to a brutal boarding school at an early age, and forgotten. When he did see his parents he had to fight for their attention.

'Mother, Father. You will both have to sit up and pay attention to me now,' he said. He gently covered Kate and Jake with a blanket and then closed the van door. Checking that no one had seen him, he set off on the long journey, waving at the dead policeman, still propped up in the driver's seat of his squad car.

CHAPTER 62

In the three days since he had murdered Meredith Baxter, Peter Conway had been kept in solitary confinement. The routine had been the same: food, medication, shower, exercise.

It had been difficult to keep track of time with no watch or window during the day, but it crawled by, and paranoia had crept in. He was now cut off from updates from Enid. What if the plan fell through? He faced a long stretch in solitary, and then what? A slow slide into a life as a geriatric serial killer.

He had asked the time at each meal, and when he was let out in the small yard for exercise. *Like a dog,* he thought, *a dog being let out to do his business in the morning and evening.*

On the previous day he had been visited by Terrence Lane, his solicitor, and for twenty minutes he had been taken into the small glass-partitioned visitors' room in solitary. Terrence had explained that he would be charged with murder, but he may not stand trial as they would push for a plea of diminished responsibility. When their meeting had finished, Terrence got up and gathered his papers.

'I spoke to Enid. She was devastated to hear what you'd done ... You were on the way to being sent to a category B prison, Peter, better conditions. What are you playing at? This doctor. She was on your side. She was working on getting you a better place to live out your final years ... She had a small son ... ' He shook his head, seemingly reminding himself that Peter was his client, and it wasn't his place to pass moral judgement.

'Thank you for everything, Terrence,' said Peter, standing. 'I wish I could shake your hand and thank you for everything over the years.'

'Going somewhere, are you?' asked Terrence, pushing the last of the papers back into his bag.

'Course not.'

'I'll see you next week then,' said Terrence, and he left the visiting room.

Peter smiled to himself. 'A better place to live out my final years ... Just you wait and see,' he muttered.

Enid Conway sat on the end of her bed and looked at the small suitcase which was open and neatly packed. The small plastic carry-on suitcase was blue and unremarkable to look at. Inside she had carefully packed several casual outfits, a couple of smart suits and shoes, and a new swimming costume. There was also a home bleaching kit and some sharp scissors. She planned to go blonde and change her hair. This was one of the things she was so excited about. She had the opportunity to become someone different. She would be June Munro and Peter would be Walter King.

On the bed beside the suitcase was a tan-coloured money belt. She took the eight-inch packet of 500-euro notes and slipped them into the pocket of the money belt. It was a tight squeeze and the quarter of a million euros only just fit. She checked their passports for the umpteenth time: June Munro and Walter King. There was a little space on top of the notes inside the money belt where she put the passports, then she zipped it up. She tried it on around her waist. It was tight, and dug painfully into her skin. She rearranged her clothes and checked her reflection in the mirror. The belt only protruded slightly under her blouse, like a little extra belly.

The phone rang and she went downstairs to take the call. It was Peter's solicitor. Terrence sounded despondent, and gave her an update on Peter's upcoming assessment to see if he would be fit to stand trial for the murder of Dr Baxter. He also told her that Peter was looking well, and that Great Barwell would be keeping him in solitary confinement for the next few weeks.

Enid came off the phone elated. They had no clue about the plan. She just wished she could tell Peter that everything was on course. She came through to the kitchen and poured herself a large whisky. Enid Conway didn't have any friends. She had acquaintances on the street where she lived, but she lived a simple life. She was either at home or visiting Peter.

Enid couldn't quite believe that shortly she would walk out of her house and her life for ever. She downed the tumbler of whisky and poured herself another. For courage.

CHAPTER 63

Tristan left Jepson's Wood just after dark, when the skeleton had finally been lifted from the soil and placed in a black body bag to go off to the forensic labs.

He had seen the missed call from Kate, but she hadn't left him a message. He had tried to call her back repeatedly but there was no answer. He felt guilty running away and leaving Victoria O'Grady, but Kate's lack of contact, when she was desperate to know the outcome of the police search, worried him, so he drove home as fast as the speed limit would allow.

When he arrived back in Ashdean and turned into Kate's road, he was shocked to see blue flashing lights and the outside of her house swarming with police cars.

Myra was standing in front of the surf shack with Varia Campbell. The car park was filled with police cars. Tristan's shock turned to alarm when he saw a pathologist's van. Police tape surrounded Kate's house. He parked as close as he could get and ran over to Varia and Myra.

'What's happened? I've been trying to call Kate,' he said. His question was answered as the body of the police officer guarding the house was lifted from the car and placed onto a trolley in a body bag.

Varia explained what had happened. 'Kate and her son Jake

are missing. We think someone broke into the house. The glass in the front door is smashed and we can see signs of a struggle.'

Tristan hadn't met Myra before, but recognised her from Kat's description of her. Myra's eyes were red from crying.

'I was down on the beach. First Kate went up and then Jake,' she said. 'I thought they were coming back. We were on the beach paddling . . . Then I came up, and found that poor police officer had been stabbed in the side of his head . . . I was only making him a cup of tea this morning.'

'You didn't see anybody?' asked Tristan.

Myra shook her head.

Tristan looked around at the police cars and the body bag which was now closed and being wheeled to the pathologist's van. He saw a receipt poking out of the cash machine outside the surf shack. He went over to it and pulled it out.

'The time stamp on this is twenty minutes before Kate called me,' said Tristan, handing the receipt to Varia.

'So?'

'Kate joked that she was the only person who used the cash machine in the winter. Do you use it, Myra?'

'No. It charges you five quid a time,' she said. 'Kate or the police officer might have used it. There's hardly anyone up at the caravan park.'

'There's a camera mounted on the front of the cash machine that activates when someone makes a withdrawal. It might have caught something?' said Tristan.

Varia's eyes lit up. She took the cash machine receipt from him and pulled out her phone to make a call.

CHAPTER 64

When Kate woke, she felt a hard surface under her back, and her mouth was wet where she had drooled. She put her hand gingerly to her face. Her nose hurt to the touch, and it was badly swollen. A light burned brightly above, and she was shocked to see that her hands weren't bound.

She sat up. She was still wearing the jeans, T-shirt and jumper from the beach, and beside her lay Jake. He was very still and pale. He wasn't wearing any shoes and his feet were still covered in sand.

'Oh my God,' she said, feeling him all over. He felt warm, and she put her hand to his neck. There was a pulse. A moment later he coughed and his eyes opened. It took him a moment to remember what had happened. He went to scream and Kate quickly put her hand over his mouth.

'Jake. No,' she said. 'Please don't scream.'

She felt his hot tears on her hand. He gulped and nodded, and she took her hand away. He huddled against her.

'Mum, what's happening?' he said, his chest heaving with silent sobs. 'Who was that man? Where are we?'

'His name's Joseph Castle-Meads, erm . . .' She didn't know what else to say. Her mind was still reeling from the revelation that the son of the barrister who tried the Peter Conway case was the copycat killer. She tried to remember what had happened. He'd got into her house. He'd attacked her in the living room. After that was a blank. She felt around in her pockets, then remembered that Joseph had smashed her phone. 'Do you know how we got here? What can you remember?'

Through tears, Jake told her that he came back up to the house and found Joseph tying her up in the hallway.

'Did he hurt you?' said Kate, checking him over.

'No. But he scared me and ... and I ... I ... I wet myself,' he said, starting to cry again. 'He put something on my face. It smelt of chemicals, and that's all I can remember.'

'It's okay,' said Kate, squeezing him tight. She had to keep it together and stay calm.

Kate looked around. They were in a windowless room with a stone floor. It was small, about ten feet square. A bare bulb burned above them. The walls were white. In one corner was a small Perspex dome containing a CCTV camera. They each lay on a thin sleeping bag, which smelt new and clean. In the corner was a two-litre bottle of mineral water and a bucket with a roll of toilet paper beside it.

Kate got to her feet. Jake stood with her, still holding onto her hand. Her head was throbbing and her arms and ankles were still dead from where they'd been bound. She felt around the walls and found the outline of a door. They were in a storage room or walk-in freezer. If it was the latter, it was switched off. Why weren't they bound and tied up? Why were they under surveillance? Did walk-in freezers these days come equipped with CCTV cameras?

They went to the door and Kate hit it with the flat of her hand but it made little sound. It must have been thick metal. She put her ear to it, but again, nothing.

Now her senses were coming back, she could smell the metallic, gamey scent of dead meat. She looked around again and wondered if there was an air supply. There were no vents. There were three drains at intervals in the concrete floor. Drains meant sewage, which meant pipes. It was an air supply. Her throat was dry and she could taste the chemicals with which she had been sedated. She looked back to Jake who still held onto her hand and was following her gaze as she looked around. His eyes were wide and he looked so scared.

'Are you thirsty?' she asked. He nodded.

'Mum. This room, it feels like it's getting smaller,' he said.

'It's not. I promise. It's okay.'

She went to the water bottle sitting by the bucket. It was still sealed. She twisted off the cap and sniffed it, then poured a tiny amount in her mouth to taste. It was fresh. She took four long gulps and wiped her mouth.

'Here, drink this and you'll feel a little better,' she said. She tilted the bottle for him and he took a few gulps. Jake was shivering now, and Kate wrapped him up in one of the sleeping bags.

Why had Joseph brought them here? Why not just her?

She searched through her memory for anything that might give her a clue to where they were, or how far they had travelled, but she couldn't remember anything. For a moment her heart leapt when she thought of the call she'd made to Tristan, but Joseph had deleted the message. And what about Myra? She hoped that Myra hadn't run into Joseph.

She held Jake close to her and looked around the room for anything she could use as a weapon. She had to be ready to defend them when he opened the door.

Joseph had checked the camera before he left, and seen that Kate and Jake were awake. He had been worried the dosage he'd given them was too strong, and that they would die on the long journey, but he was pleased to see they looked okay.

He left the warehouse shortly afterwards and drove along

Nine Elms Lane and the River Thames. The landscape had changed since 1995, and the area was under a huge amount of construction and development. He kept an eye on the cars around him as he drove past construction sites where tall cranes reached into the night sky, and on to Battersea Heliport, where he was keeping three helicopters. They were registered to a shell company which the authorities would have difficulty in tracing back to him. They would trace the vehicles, but it would take a little time, and that was all he needed.

The heliport was private, and at this late hour it was empty. His heart began to race as he buzzed in at the gate using his keycard, and he was waved through to the loading area by the river, where he parked his car.

He had used two of the helicopters for legitimate business and for pleasure, and he had registered many flight plans in the past twelve months. The laws governing airspace around London and the M25 were strictly enforced because of the flight paths of commercial jets and other aircraft coming in and out of the city airports. In other parts of the country, the rules were looser, and a small deviation from a flight plan was permitted. Great Barwell Psychiatric Hospital sat ninety miles outside London.

Joseph had already logged a flight plan that would take him out of London and up towards Cambridge and Great Barwell. He had only one chance at this, but with careful planning he was sure he could pull it off.

He wiped down the steering wheel and door handles before he left the car. He always wore driving gloves, but this would buy him more time if needed.

He grabbed a small backpack and locked the car. He went to a red air ambulance helicopter waiting for him on its helipad. He checked it had been fuelled and that everything was in place. Then he climbed aboard. CM Logistics had a vast array of contracts for commercial and private vehicles. They also had a contract for the storage and maintenance of two air ambulance helicopters used by UK hospitals. This helicopter had just been through its yearly maintenance check and would be returning to active service in two days' time. It had been difficult to juggle the paperwork, but he now had the key element of his plan.

After checking with the control tower that he had radio clearance, Joseph started the engine, the blades began to turn and the air ambulance was cleared for take-off, rising quickly into the dark sky.

CHAPTER 65

Winston had been reassigned to solitary so that he could continue dealing with Peter. They had been together on the ward for many years, and Peter knew that at Great Barwell continuity was an important factor in keeping a prisoner calm.

When Winston delivered Peter's evening meal, he stayed at the hatch for a moment longer than usual. His eyes were solemn and wise. Peter went to the hatch to take the tray from Winston.

'What are you up to?' said Winston, holding the tray back.

'I'm about to eat this slop,' said Peter.

'No. I know you better than you think. You've attacked patients and doctors in the past, but out of anger. You weren't angry this morning. You planned it.'

Peter leaned closer to the hatch.

'You're a clever man, Winston. How did you end up stuck in this shithole on a zero hours contract?'

'From one clever man to another, Peter. Why did you do it?'

'I finally found Meredith Baxter too irritating to bear. I never bought all that happy-clappy eagerness to make a difference. If I hadn't killed her, one of the other patients would have had a crack at it.'

'You want to be in solitary for a reason,' said Winston, his wise eyes seeming to reach into his head. 'What's that reason?' For a moment Peter wondered if Winston could read his mind.

'Never trust us, Winston. Never trust any of us. We're beyond help. The murderers and the rapists and the kiddy fiddlers in this place are all the same. We get off on the pain of others.'

Winston hesitated, then dumped the tray through the hatch. The gloopy food spattered down the inside of the cell door.

'You're gonna rot in hell.'

'Hell isn't real, Winston,' shouted Peter, 'but zero hours contracts are. Think about it.'

The hatch slammed shut.

Peter wasn't able to eat anything. His heart was pounding and he was sweating. Was this really going to happen? Everything seemed so quiet and small in Great Barwell. A trip to the lavatory seemed far. He'd spent so long in this place – was he really about to leave for ever?

When Winston returned for his tray, his face was an impassive mask again. The spit hood was pushed through the hatch and Peter pulled it on, his hands shaking.

Then he put his hands in front of him whilst they were cuffed. His solicitor Terrence had argued for Peter to be cuffed with his hands in front of him, due to an injury to his shoulder when he'd been Tasered and restrained. When the cuffs were secure, Winston unbolted the door and led Peter down the short corridor to the exercise yard. Winston unlocked the door slowly and methodically.

'Okay, Peter, you've got fifteen minutes,' he said.

He stood back and Peter stepped through into the small yard and smelled the fresh evening air.

He watched through the small window as Winston locked the door again, taking his time over the three locks. He removed the keys and clipped them back onto his belt and disappeared from view back down the corridor.

Peter moved around the small space. He looked up, just seeing the patch of dark sky, stained orange from light pollution. It was so quiet. Too quiet. He frowned, feeling the material of the spit hood cold against his face.

Joseph had been in contact with air traffic control as he flew over London, but as soon as he flew over the outskirts of the M25 the constant updates faded out. He'd given his final position and flown onwards. He waited until he was close, and the perimeter fence of Great Barwell and the long low buildings came into view ahead, then he put in a call to the observation tower, announcing that an air ambulance was asking for clearance to land.

'We're responding to an emergency call, a doctor working at the hospital has been stabbed, request permission to land,' said Joseph over his radio. There was silence. He knew that they would be making some checks, but hoped after the recent death of Dr Baxter that they would give him clearance, which would buy valuable time.

'You have clearance to land,' said the voice on the radio.

Joseph fist-bumped the air, grinning wildly. He checked the radio was muted and then shouted with excitement: 'Yes! Yes! Here we go, you fuckers!'

Peter waited a few more minutes, pacing and trying to look as if he was taking the air. The silence seemed to stretch out, and he wondered if his mother was on the move, heading to the place where they would meet later. So much time seemed to have passed already from his fifteen minutes. He was scared. Winston would be coming back soon.

His heart began to beat faster as he heard the far-off drone of the helicopter engine. Was it just a plane going past, or was this for him?

Then very quickly the sound of the engine grew louder, until it was deafening. The helicopter appeared suddenly in the square of sky, high above, rotor blades spinning. He felt the air pressure as it bore down. A bright light shone down into the yard, lighting up every corner of the tiny square, and Peter saw the outstretched arm of the helicopter pilot waving at him. He waved back with his cuffed hands.

A rope ladder was held out of the window, and it dropped and unfurled, the edge narrowly missing the side of Peter's head. It went taut, and he put his foot on the first rung and looped his cuffed hands through the steps of the ladder.

Winston appeared at the window in the door. At first he was confused, but he reacted quickly, fumbling with the keys in the lock.

Peter was barely able to hold on with his cuffed hands when the rope ladder creaked and he started to rise up out of the exercise yard. Winston finally got the last lock open. He burst through the door and ran over, his fingers grazing Peter's ankle before he was carried up out of his reach.

'Goodbye, Winston!' cried Peter over the roar of the helicopter. He was shocked to feel a tinge of sadness at leaving him behind. Winston gaped in shock. His eyes were wide with surprise.

The exercise yard below Peter became smaller, and he saw two other orderlies rushing in beside Winston, but they watched helplessly as he rose up, clearing the razor-wire fences, and on into the cold night sky. The helicopter stopped and hovered for a second, then flew over the hospital buildings as Peter clung on to the rope ladder for dear life.

The freezing cold wind against his face was real. The sweeping motion of the helicopter carrying him away was real. Peter couldn't believe this was really happening. As he flew over the main entrance, staff and orderlies poured out of the big glass doors and could only watch as Peter Conway, the Nine Elms Cannibal, flew past, clearing the razor-wire perimeter fence.

And then he was gone, flying off into the night sky.

CHAPTER 66

Kate didn't know how much time had passed when she heard the sound of a door opening. Jake had fallen asleep on her lap, and she gently moved him onto his sleeping bag. Then she got up and went to the door and listened.

There was a crash. Jake opened his eyes and quickly began to panic.

Kate went to him. 'Shush, it's okay, stay calm,' she said, speaking to herself just as much as to Jake.

She picked up the bottle of water, which was now half empty. She held it in her hand and moved closer to the door.

'What are you doing?' asked Jake.

'I'm going to throw this bottle right in his face. As soon as I do, you duck round him and run for it. Get ready.'

Mindful of the camera, she held the bottle at her side.

'Mum?'

'What?'

'Aim for his bollocks – swing it back and then slam him right up in the nuts,' said Jake.

'Good idea,' she said. She braced herself as they heard bolts shoot home behind the door, and then the huge door began to open. She started to swing the bottle back and forth. When the door slid open she stopped dead and almost lost balance. The water bottle fell from her grip.

Peter Conway stood in the doorway.

His eyes played over her, unblinking. He wore blue trousers, a red woollen pullover and trainers. The clothes looked brand new. The trousers had a crisp crease down the front of each leg, and one of the trainers still had its price tag. Kate saw that Peter's hair was now long and grey and he wore it tucked behind his ears. He smiled to reveal a row of browning teeth.

'Hello, Kate,' he said. 'It's been a while.'

Kate shook her head and took a step back. For a moment she wondered if she was dreaming. It wasn't possible that he could be here in front of them, out of prison.

'How? How?'

Peter smiled. 'How? What, Kate? How do I keep looking so young?' He looked to Joseph, who had come in behind him and stood beside him grinning wildly, as if he'd just met Tom Cruise.

'How are you here? Where are we?' she said, pulling Jake close to her.

'Joseph here hatched the most *genius* plan. The best plans are always the simple ones. He used a helicopter air ambulance,' said Peter.

'The police will know he stole a helicopter,' said Kate, looking between them.

'No, they won't,' said Joseph, still grinning and starstruck. 'My family's company owns and leases the helicopter, and we flew under the radar to the outskirts of London where we landed on farmland. They'll find it, but not for some time.'

'Is this my son?' asked Peter, suddenly taking an interest in Jake.

Kate was unable to speak as he moved closer. His eyes were the same brown colour she remembered. His voice sounded the same.

'Don't you have anything you want to say to me after all these years?'

Peter's presence seemed to fill the tiny room. Kate looked at Joseph. He was smiling and his eyes were bright. He was drinking this in, loving it. Peter came closer, towards Jake. Joseph lunged at Kate, grabbed her by the hair and pulled her out of the storeroom, holding a knife to her neck.

'You don't touch him!' she cried, craning her neck to keep her eyes on Jake.

Peter went to him and put out his hand. 'You're a good-looking boy. You have the same eye as your mother,' he said, indicating the starburst of orange in Jake's eye. 'I'm your dad.'

Jake looked bewildered, hesitated, then shook his hand.

'No! Jake! No!' cried Kate.

Jake and Peter looked at each other and Jake seemed fascinated. This was what she had always feared, that they would meet and have this father–son connection. She fought against Joseph, but he held her tight, one hand on her hair and the other wrapped over her chest.

'Let me see your teeth,' said Peter, crouching down. He pulled Jake's gums back. Jake stared back in shock as his straight white teeth were exposed. 'Have you been brushing twice a day?' Jake nodded. 'Good lad.'

Peter let Jake go and straightened up. He turned back to Kate, stepping out of the storeroom. Kate hoped he would close the door, shutting Jake safely away, but he didn't. 'Kate. You probably know that Joseph here is a fan of my work. He's been paying homage to me. He's quite the Peter Conway aficionado. He was *most* creative, don't you think? Although, bad luck with victim number four.'

'I'm sorry that happened,' said Joseph, his voice hoarse against Kate's cheek.

'How have you been communicating?' asked Kate.

'Toffees,' said Peter with a smile. 'My dear mother hid notes in toffees she brought in during visiting. I, in turn, placed my replies in empty pill casings, which I stashed far up in my mouth between my teeth and gums. When she visits, I'm allowed to give her a peck on the cheek. And when I did, I spat my reply in the empty pill casing out in her ear. Devilishly simple.'

'How did Enid manage to get the pill casings with your replies out of the hospital?'

'She wore a fake hearing aid. She'd switch it between her ears, pushing the pill up inside it. They always used to give my poor mother the once-over, checking every orifice with a torch, but they never thought to check that hearing aid.'

Peter smiled and came up to her. He ran his hands over her body, squeezing her breasts and smoothing his hand between her legs.

'Are you checking me for weapons?' asked Kate.

'No. I just wanted to cop a feel.' He grinned.

Joseph laughed, his mouth close to her head. She wanted to close her eyes and turn away, but she was trying to catch Jake's eye as he stood inside the open freezer. She flinched as Peter lifted her sweater and found the scar on her stomach.

'That's healed up nicely,' he said, tracing the tip of his finger along the puckered hard line of the scar tissue. He smiled and then smoothed her sweater back down. 'Right. Time is marching on. Joseph, you know I have places to be, so shall we start?'

'Yes,' said Joseph, his mouth still close to Kate's ear.

Peter turned and went to Jake, grabbed him by the hair and pulled him out of the storeroom kicking and shouting.

'You don't touch him,' cried Kate, panicking. 'You don't deserve to touch a hair on his head!'

Peter came up close to Kate.

'You don't shout at me,' he said. He slapped her hard around the face. Jake cried out. It was so hard that she almost passed out with the pain. 'You're hardly mother of the fucking year.'

There was a large van parked a few feet from the storeroom. Peter and Joseph pulled them around it, and Kate saw they were in a large warehouse. In the centre was a bedroom, but not a real bedroom. It was constructed like a film set. It had three panels making up the walls, and each panel had a bracket behind it, keeping it upright.

'Recognise it, Kate?' asked Peter.

Joseph dragged her towards it, and Peter pulled Jake by the arm.

Kate was stunned into silence. It was a perfect replica of her old bedroom in the flat in Deptford all those years ago. It had the same wallpaper, and there was a fake window with the same view overlooking the street and the row of shops.

'I re-created it all from the crime scene photos, sourced everything I could online,' said Joseph. 'I also got access to the flat, to take that photo outside the window. That's the actual view.'

Kate looked between them, petrified by the craziness of it all. There was even an identical bedspread to the one she'd had back then, the blue one with yellow cornflowers. The lava lamp was on the bedside table, the orange wax lazily blooming out from the bottom and breaking away in a circle to float to the top. The small TV was there with the lamp on top – the terrible Laura Ashley lamp Glenda had bought her the birthday before.

Kate's blood ran cold as everything fell into place.

'You've been copycatting Peter's murders,' she said. 'I wondered what you were going to do after victim number four . . . I was victim number five, wasn't I?'

'Yes,' hissed Joseph in her ear.

'She's very clever, isn't she, Joseph?' said Peter. 'Yes. You *would* have been my fifth victim. Or should I say, after tonight, you *will* be my fifth victim.'

There was something so sure in his voice, something almost religious about his declaration, and it chilled Kate.

'Why are you doing this, Joseph?' asked Kate.

'For years I've grown up living in the shadow of a so-called brilliant barrister. My brother Keir is the first-born, the heir, and I am the spare. My whole life I was told I'd never be memorable, that I would never do anything great like my father, but no. Tonight, I'm showing them what I'm capable of. My father thought he'd put Peter away for life, and now the son he never thought would amount to anything has set him free!'

Kate felt Joseph shaking. His body trembled and he gripped her more tightly.

'And what's in this for you, Peter?' she asked. 'You know they'll catch you again.'

Peter grinned and shrugged. 'My life in prison is all black and white. Yes and no. The Inside and the Outside. Wrong and right. It's regimented. There's never a grey area. Either way it's a risk, but I get to step out and experience life in the grey areas. Joseph here is setting me and Mother up with a new life on the Continent. In return, I help him complete his work. He paid homage to my first four victims, and now you are my fifth. Think of it as a cameo. A reboot.'

'What about Jake?' said Kate, thinking fast and seeing an opportunity. 'You don't need him. He wasn't even born when all this happened. It has nothing to do with him. Let him go.'

'We need a witness to tell everyone what happened. To pass on the legend. You, Kate will be dead, and myself and Joseph will be long gone. We can't just rely on the police to piece it all together.' Peter laughed, showing his brown teeth.

Kate suddenly felt reality tipping away. It was all so surreal. She heard a strange laugh erupt from her throat.

'What's so fucking funny?' said Peter, his face clouding over. 'You're not supposed to be laughing!'

A look passed between the two men, a look of panic.

'You two,' said Kate, laughing.

'You think I'm funny, BITCH?' shouted Joseph, pulling back and spinning her round to face him. 'Do you think this is funny?'

He let her go and went to Jake. In one movement he took out his knife and sliced a piece off the top of Jake's ear. It was only small, but Jake cried out and put his hand to it, blood pouring between his fingers.

'No! Please!' cried Kate, running to Jake, regretting that her stupidity was being taken out on him.

'I'm sorry. I don't think you're funny,' said Kate, holding Jake and checking the wound.

'YOU DON'T LAUGH AT ME!' cried Joseph. 'I can buy anything I want. I have so much money, and these days you can buy anything. You can buy passports and safe passage. You can bribe and fight, and you can make your dreams and fantasies come true. I pity people like you. You're nothing. And you don't FUCKING LAUGH AT ME!'

'Okay, okay,' said Peter, holding up his hands to Joseph. 'Jesus. We need to get on with this.'

Kate looked at the replica bedroom, the lamp glowing and the bed neatly made. Amongst all of the craziness and the fear, that bed looked so inviting and comfy. For the first time she wished she'd arrived home that night, after working the Crystal Palace murder scene, and she'd left the bag in Peter's car, and he'd driven home. She could have sunk into that cosy mattress and lived the rest of her life uneventfully.

Kate came out of her reverie and saw them both staring at her.

'Where are we?' she asked, a thought coming to her. 'Where is this place?'

Peter began to laugh, and Joseph joined in.

'Where we are, I think, is the most brilliant part of it all.'

Joseph pulled Jake away from her and Peter grabbed her arm. He dragged her over to the sliding door and pressed a button. He held onto her as the door slowly whirred back. The wind blew inside, whipping Kate's hair around her head. Her mouth dropped open as she saw they were looking over the River Thames, and at the London skyline twinkling in the night. The chimneys of Battersea Power Station rose up out of the water.

'Nine Elms Lane,' she said.

'Not just Nine Elms Lane,' said Peter into her ear. 'This is the location of the Nine Elms car scrapyard, now owned and redeveloped by CM Logistics. Your sad little bedroom back there sits on the exact spot where I dumped Shelley Norris's body back in 1993.'

Kate fought his grip and tried to break free. 'You're fucking crazy,' she said.

'Yes,' he said, turning her around to face him. 'That's what I always thought attracted you to me.'

The cold wind screamed through the door, and she saw that Joseph was coming towards her.

'Where's Jake?' she started to say. There was a clicking sound and she saw Joseph holding a Taser. She looked down and saw two wires hooked into the front of her sweater. A terrible pain jolted through her body, making her rigid, and blackness overcame her again.

When Kate came to, she smelled the strong scent of ammonia and her eyes shot open. Joseph stepped back with the smelling salts he'd used to revive her. She was lying on the bed, in her old bedroom, wearing a white towelling robe. Peter was kneeling on top of her, trapping her arms down by her side, just as he had all those years ago. He held a long thin knife.

In place of the fourth wall, Joseph was behind a video camera, filming. To the side of him, Jake was trussed up in a chair, his arms and legs bound with tape.

Despite his loss of muscle and age, Peter was still strong and he leaned his weight into her, making her cry out. This had escalated fast; she had no time to think. Peter had stabbed her all those years ago, and he was going to do it again. On the floor by the video camera was a bottle of water, a roll of tape and the Taser.

'Are we rolling?' asked Peter.

Joseph gave him a thumbs-up. Jake's eyes were wide and he writhed in the chair. Kate looked at him, desperate to see if he could reach the Taser, but he was too far away and his feet were taped to the chair.

'Something's not right,' said Peter. He put the knife between his brown teeth and untied Kate's robe. When he opened it, she was naked underneath. Kate yelled out and tears filled her eyes at the humiliation.

'No, no!' she cried.

Peter traced the tip of the knife across her nipples and down to the scar. 'They *did* do a good job sewing it up, didn't they?' he said.

Joseph laughed from where he was watching.

Peter turned to the camera and noticed Jake had closed his eyes. 'You open those eyes, boy! Open those fucking eyes or Joseph will peel them open with his knife!'

Jake writhed and cried under the restraints, but he opened his eyes. Peter lifted up the blade and placed the tip at the end of Kate's scar.

'Do you remember the pain?' he said. 'I've heard that the body forgets.' He went to push the knife in.

'Peter! Wait!' she cried, trying to stall him.

'What?' he said.

'You forgot to do something. If Joseph wants this to be authentic.'

'No, I didn't forget anything,' he said.

An idea came to her, and she hoped she would have the strength to see it through.

'No! It's not right! Stop! It's all wrong,' she said.

'Hang on, hang on,' said Joseph, moving around the camera and towards them. 'What is it?'

Peter sat back, digging his knees and legs into her wrists and stomach. The pain was hot and fierce, but she kept her face neutral.

'It's, er, well, embarrassing.'

'What?' asked Joseph.

'Peter knows,' she said.

'I do?' he said, confusion in his eyes.

'I said something to you on the night, just before you stabbed me. I . . . pleaded with you, for my life.'

The pain was now unbearable where Peter leant on her wrists.

'Okay, okay, let's start again,' said Joseph, moving back behind the camera. 'Go.'

Kate tilted her head up in preparation to whisper, and Peter leaned down towards her, putting even more pressure on her wrists. She felt like they were going to break. As he leaned close, Kate saw the skin on his neck, how it had changed in the years from being taut and youthful to crinkled like crepe paper. The tendons were sticking out, and she could see the pulse beating under the skin of his throat.

'You're going to die,' he said. He came closer, grinning.

Kate put her mouth to his ear. 'You're going to rot in that mental hospital, you evil bastard,' she whispered.

Then she opened her mouth wide and sank her teeth into his throat, biting down as hard as she could. She felt his skin tear and the blood from his jugular pour out. He dropped the knife and it clattered onto the floor. Jake screamed as she bit down harder and kept hold, shaking her head from side to side, biting down like a dog. Peter screamed and pulled back.

'Let go! Help me!' he cried. He was screaming and crying out, and finally broke free, holding his neck where the blood was gushing. Kate's face and eyes were covered in blood.

Joseph held his camera in shock, and he instinctively went to help Peter. Kate leapt off the bed and skidded across the floor, grabbing the Taser. She twisted on her feet, took aim and fired it at Joseph's neck. He screamed and fell forward, writhing and clutching at the wires.

Kate didn't wait a moment longer. She gathered up her robe, picked up the scissors and started to cut Jake free.

Tristan's knuckles were white as he gripped the door in the back of the police squad car. The sirens and lights were blaring, and they were flanked by four other squad cars and two ambulances. Varia Campbell sat in the passenger seat with John Mercy driving. Tristan had never been to London before, and this mad dash to the warehouse on Nine Elms Lane was the weirdest, most terrifying introduction. The River Thames flew by on their left-hand side, the dark water reflecting the lights from the cranes above.

'The turning is on the next right,' said Varia, shouting above the sound of the sirens.

Two things had alerted them to the location where they thought Kate and Jake had been taken. The cash machine outside the surf shop had caught an image of a tall, red-haired man arriving in a white van whose number plates had been reported stolen. Varia had also received a message from Alan Hexham about Keir Castle-Meads being incorrectly named.

The white van was caught on a CCTV camera heading into London. The rest had been Tristan. He found the open book Kate had dropped on the floor in her living room, containing the photo of the Castle-Meads family. Once they'd identified Joseph Castle-Meads, reports had come in that Peter had been broken out of Great Barwell, and it had all fallen into place. Tristan had asked Varia to check out the London locations of each murder committed by Peter Conway, and they discovered that the location of the first murder was now occupied by a warehouse owned by CM Logistics.

They turned off Nine Elms Lane with a screech of tyres and into the empty car park of the huge warehouse. As they pulled up to the loading bay, a large door started to roll back and a woman came running out, barefoot and covered in blood, carrying a teenage boy with his arms and legs tied.

'That's Kate and Jake!' shouted Tristan as the squad car came to a stop, flanked by the other cars and the ambulances. Tristan didn't wait. He jumped out of the car and ran towards them.

'Oh my God, where are you injured?' he shouted.

'It's not me. I'm fine,' said Kate, wiping the blood from her face. She was crying and so was Jake as he clung to her robe. The paramedics from one of the ambulances rushed over to Kate, Tristan and Jake.

'Peter Conway and Joseph Castle-Meads,' said Kate breathlessly. 'They're inside. Peter is injured . . . I bit him.'

Tristan ran with the paramedics and police officers into the warehouse. He saw the crazy tableau of the bedroom set, with a camera on a tripod.

Beside the bed, Peter Conway lay on the concrete, holding his hand to his neck, which was pouring blood. In his free hand he had a knife. On the floor beside him was Joseph, barely conscious and tangled up in Taser wires.

'You come any closer and I'll kill him. I'll slit him open!' Peter cried, holding the knife at Joseph's throat.

'Throw the knife away from your body, or we shoot you,' came a voice through a loud hailer. Four officers from the armed response team had entered behind Tristan, wearing protective gear and helmets and holding guns. Varia appeared with DI Mercy and they pulled Tristan away and back to the doorway.

'I'll kill him! I'll fucking end him!' Peter cried. He pressed the blade against Joseph's throat. 'And then I'll bleed to death!'

The line of armed officers moved closer and circled Peter and Joseph, their guns trained on him. The blood was now slick down Peter's right side, pouring through the fingers of his right hand, still clamped to his neck. The knife began to shake in his left hand. 'I'm ... I'm bleeding to death!' he said, his voice faltering.

'Drop the knife, or we'll shoot you,' came the voice from the loudhailer again.

Peter looked up at the armed response team, and the police cars and ambulances waiting outside the warehouse.

'Fuck it! Fuck you all,' he said. He pulled the knife away from Joseph's face and threw it away from him. It landed on the concrete floor with a clatter.

Joseph started to come round, and attempted to get up, but slipped in the growing pool of blood and landed on his backside with a strangled cry.

Two of the armed officers broke away from the circle and grabbed Joseph.

'I need help! I'm bleeding!' cried Peter, collapsing back onto the floor. The third armed officer quickly checked Peter for weapons and picked up the knife.

When they were satisfied, they called in the paramedics who started to work on Peter, applying a pressure bandage to his neck.

Varia and DI Mercy went over to Joseph, who was now conscious. 'Joseph Castle-Meads, I'm arresting you for the murders of Emma Newman, Kaisha Smith, Layla Gerrard, Abigail Clarke, and PC Rob Morton ... '

'Turn the camera off!' Joseph screamed, wild-eyed, as DI Mercy handcuffed his hands behind his back.

'. . . I'm also arresting you for the abduction of Kate Marshall and Jake Marshall, and for aiding the escape of a known criminal. You don't have to say anything, but it may harm your defence if you do not mention when questioned something which you later rely on in court. Anything you do say may be given in evidence,' finished Varia.

'Turn the camera off.' Joseph was crying. 'This wasn't what was meant to happen!'

He was dragged away by DI Mercy and two uniformed officers. Peter had gone still and quiet, just staring bleakly ahead. The paramedics working on him had a large pressure bandage over his neck, and an IV line in his blood-caked arm, and they were loading him onto a stretcher.

Tristan went to the camera on the tripod, and was joined by Varia. They stared at the replica of Kate's bedroom for a moment.

'Oh my lord. I've never seen anything like it,' said Varia. 'It looks exactly like Kate's bedroom in the crime scene photos from 1995.'

Tristan was intrigued to see what was on the camera and put his hand out.

'No, don't touch it,' said Varia. 'I need forensics in here.'

'Sorry, rookie mistake,' he said, pulling his hand back.

Varia smiled. 'Well done. We wouldn't have found them without your help.'

Tristan felt his chest swell with pride and relief. He hurried back out of the warehouse and into the car park.

Kate and Jake stood, wrapped in a blanket, in the car park outside the warehouse. They had been checked over by the paramedics; they were in shock, but they would be fine. Kate felt Jake shivering and she pulled the blanket closer around them.

They watched as Joseph Castle-Meads was taken past them in cuffs and loaded into the back of a police car. He was shouting and screaming at the police, and didn't see Kate and Jake.

Moments later, two paramedics rushed out of the warehouse pushing the stretcher containing Peter Conway. Peter was lying on his left side. As the stretcher went past, he shouted, 'Wait! Stop!'

The stretcher came to a stop beside Kate and Jake. Peter looked up at them with one eye and a bloody face. He held out his free hand, his arm bloodied with its IV line.

'Jake, you should come and visit me. I'm your dad, we're blood,' he said. His voice was weak, but his one eye sparkled malevolently. Kate froze, and looked down at Jake who was staring at Peter. A look passed between them, a look of recognition that they were father and son.

'We have to get you to hospital,' said one of the paramedics.

'Love you, son,' said Peter, and then he was whisked away to a waiting ambulance. It was only when the ambulance doors closed and it started to drive away that Kate began to breathe again. She looked down at Jake.

'I'm sorry. Are you okay?'

'Yeah, I'm fine,' he said, looking up at her. 'I don't want to see him again.'

Kate kissed the top of his head and hugged him close. She wasn't convinced by what Jake said. However small and tentative, he'd make a connection with Peter, and in a few years she would be powerless if Jake wanted to see his father.

Seventy-five miles away, Enid Conway sat waiting on a wooden bench at a small pier in the shadow of Portsmouth harbour. It had been a hard place for her to find, accessed down a narrow, unmade road and next to the muddy reed-covered bank.

At her feet was the small carry-on suitcase. She had to sit bolt upright on the bench, or the money belt containing the passports and a quarter of a million euros dug painfully into her skin. She wore cork-heeled wedge sandals. Again, they weren't the most practical, but they wouldn't fit in the case. Beside her on the bench was a small sunhat. The weather in Spain would be hot, even though it was October, and the hat was made of blonde straw, chosen to match her soon-to-be blonde hair.

She shivered – she'd also dressed for warmer weather, and the cold was creeping up the back of the thin cardigan. She'd been told to expect a small fishing boat at 2.30 a.m., manned by a portly bloke called Carlos with a grey beard, but looking out across the still water of the port, she could see nothing but a large tanker belching out smoke.

She got up and paced, swearing as the money belt pinched at her skin. She checked her watch. They were an hour late. She'd been told there might be a hold-up, but this was starting to make her sweat, despite the cold.

Just then she saw a small light appear around the side of the port and start towards her across the water. It was moving quickly for a fishing boat, but she felt immediate relief and excitement. Peter wouldn't be on the boat – they would rendez-vous on a larger boat a couple of miles out to sea. Enid grabbed her case and hat, and checked her money belt was secure. Then she stepped down onto the small wooden pier, making her way carefully along the rotting wood to the end in her cork-bottomed wedges.

It wasn't until the boat was almost on her that she realised it was a speedboat, and had POLICE written on the side.

Enid panicked. She grabbed the handle of her suitcase and made a run for it, back along the pier to the bank where she thought she might be able to lose them amongst the acres of tall reeds, but the edge of one of her shoes caught on the uneven wood. She tottered on the edge of the jetty, her arms wheeling at her side, then lost her balance and fell into the murky water with a splash.

'You bastards!' she screamed, as she thought of the money and passports now under the water. She attempted to swim away, swallowing a mouthful of foul-tasting water. A bright light was trained on her, a long pole flopped onto the surface of the water and she was encircled by a large plastic loop.

She was fished out of the water and dumped into the boat, where she was greeted by two police officers.

'Enid Conway, I'm arresting you for conspiracy to commit fraud and murder . . .' said one of the officers. As the other attempted to take the plastic loop off her shoulders, she slapped him across the face. 'And for resisting arrest and assaulting a police officer.'

Enid leaned back, soaking wet, as she was read her rights and handcuffed. Even though she knew it was all over, she refused to let them see her cry.

TWO WEEKS LATER

CHAPTER 67

The churchyard in Chew Magna was beautiful on the crisp November morning. Kate, Tristan and Jake arrived just as the service began and slipped into a pew at the back of the church. It was filled with mourners, and a few journalists and photographers lurked, standing at the back.

Kate could see Sheila and Malcolm in the front row, flanked by their neighbours and friends. Despite the horror, Sheila looked better than she had at their last meeting when she was hooked up to the dialysis machines. Her skin was pale with a flush of pink, and she held Malcolm's hand in both of hers.

Caitlyn's coffin sat on a plinth by the altar, surrounded by a riot of flowers – roses, lilies and carnations.

'I can see our bunch of flowers,' whispered Jake in Kate's ear, and he pointed to the lilies they had sent to the family.

Caitlyn's remains had been identified from dental records and DNA taken from Sheila and Malcolm. Kate hadn't been the one to break the news to Sheila and Malcolm, but she imagined how they must have felt, hearing their daughter had finally been found after twenty years. After all that time, they would finally be able to grieve.

The service was moving. The final piece of music to be played was 'Ave Maria'. Kate wasn't religious, but as she sat and listened to the beautiful, haunting melody she understood how important it was for Malcolm and Sheila to have Caitlyn's remains blessed, and for her to be buried under the watchful eye of a higher power.

As the final notes were played, Caitlyn's coffin was slowly carried back down the aisle and out to the graveyard. Kate wiped a tear away, and saw Tristan do the same.

Sheila and Malcolm had asked that they be left for a final private moment with Caitlyn when the coffin was laid to rest, and as the congregation filed out, Kate overheard many of the mourners say the wake would be in the local pub.

They chose to wait for Sheila and Malcolm at the front of the graveyard.

'What happens to Peter now?' asked Jake, breaking the silence.

'He's in the hospital wing at Great Barwell, but he's going to make a full recovery,' said Kate. 'And he'll be assessed to see if he's fit to stand trial for the murder of Dr Baxter.'

'And hopefully Caitlyn,' said Tristan.

Paul Adler had been taken into custody shortly after Caitlyn's remains were identified. The police had raided both his home and the chemist, and they had found more evidence of his connection with Peter Conway, and photos of other young women. The discovery of Caitlyn's body, and the subsequent reporting of the case on TV, had led to other women coming forward with stories of abuse. It was a positive development, but only the beginning.

'Is Joseph going to be put in the same mental hospital as . . . Peter?' asked Jake.

'No. There were originally plans to,' said Kate, 'but the police thought it better that they separate them.'

Had Jake been about to say 'Dad' and then stopped himself? No – when they had to talk about him, they referred to him as 'Peter'. She wondered if Joseph Castle-Meads would ever be declared fit enough to stand trial. His family had swooped in with the best lawyers and used their connections. The press wouldn't get the field day they were hoping for, on an establishment figure like Tarquin Castle-Meads and his son.

As they waited by the gate of the churchyard, a man and a woman approached them. They were well dressed and appeared to be in their fifties. The camera slung around the man's neck alerted Kate that they were local press.

'Kate Marshall, can we have a moment?' the woman asked, a tiny Dictaphone poised in her hand.

'Sorry, no,' said Kate.

'I'm after a comment, that's all,' the woman went on. 'As you may have seen, Tarquin Castle-Meads QC and his wife are coming back to the UK to deal with the news that their son is the serial killer of four young women and had hatched this bizarre plot to recreate the Nine Elms Cannibal killings. Several news outlets have recalled that Tarquin Castle-Meads criticised your relationship with Peter Conway during the original Nine Elms Cannibal trial. Does it feel like justice for you, that he is now forced to face up to his son being a serial killer?' She held her Dictaphone under Kate's nose, eyes wide and eager.

Kate thought back to all the times people had spoken out against her. She *could* give this journalist a juicy quote and get even. But she didn't want to. She wanted to move on.

'No comment,' she said.

'How about Enid Conway? The police are struggling to find evidence to charge her with. Do you know how she communicated with Peter in Great Barwell? And how do you feel now that your de facto mother-in-law will probably remain a free woman?'

Kate resisted the urge to change the subject and relive the story of how Enid was fished out of Portsmouth harbour like a drowned rat. The story had given her great satisfaction, and a good laugh, but she chose to take the high road again.

'Sorry. No comment.'

'And finally, how do you feel now that Peter Conway, the Nine Elms Cannibal, lives to fight another day? He'll soon be discharged from hospital, back into the care of Great Barwell.'

Kate had so many feelings: of guilt, of dread and fear. She would never wish death on anyone, but it would have been a huge release if Peter Conway had died.

'No comment,' said Kate. She didn't see Sheila and Malcolm walk up to their group, still tearful after saying goodbye to Caitlyn.

'Go on, shoo,' said Malcolm to the journalists, and they reluctantly moved off and left them alone.

'I know we've said it so many times, but thank you, Kate, and you too, Tristan,' said Sheila, embracing them both. 'Just for me to know that she's been laid to rest, and I can come and sit by her grave and talk to her . . . ' She began to tear up.

'If we can ever do anything for you,' said Malcolm. 'Was that journalist from the local rag bothering you?'

'No. I've had worse,' said Kate.

'You must be pleased with that article in the *Guardian*? It was difficult for us to read, but it showed you for what you are, a great private detective. And you too, lad,' he added to Tristan.

Sheila opened her handbag. 'We wanted to give you both this,' she said, handing Kate an envelope.

Kate opened it. It contained a cheque for £5,000.

'We can't take this,' she said.

'It's from the Victims of Crime Fund, from the government . . . for Caitlyn's death,' said Sheila. 'We would like you and Tristan to have it, for your expenses, and also in the hope that you'll carry on doing what you're doing. You were our last hope, and your detective work found our little girl.'

'Please, take it, and put it to good use,' said Malcolm.

They all hugged again, and Malcolm and Sheila left.

Kate, Tristan and Jake hung back for a moment. As they made their way to the car, the sun broke through the clouds.

Jake held Kate's hand. 'No one knows me here,' he said.

'I'll take what I can get. You'll soon be a grown man and won't want to hold my hand.' Kate smiled.

'Who fancies fish and chips?' asked Tristan.

'Me, me, me!' cried Jake. 'I love that chip shop in Ashdean.'

'We're miles from Ashdean,' said Kate.

'Let's find one close by,' said Jake. 'But can we go to the one in Ashdean when I come back to stay in two weeks?' Jake had asked if he could stay with Kate more often, and Glenda had agreed.

'Of course,' said Kate as they got in the car.

'Right, let's find the nearest fish and chip shop. We also need to celebrate officially being professional private investigators,' said Tristan.

Kate nodded and smiled. She was scared about the future, and how in the coming years Jake would deal with being the son of Peter Conway, and the trauma of what he'd been through. But for now, she had all she wanted. Jake was by her side, he was safe and happy, and they were going to get fish and chips.

Kate promised herself she would hold onto this feeling of happiness, and remember that the light always triumphed over darkness.

A LETTER FROM ROB

I want to say a huge thank you for choosing to read the first book in my new crime series. If you did enjoy *Nine Elms*, I would be very grateful if you could tell your friends and family. A word-of-mouth recommendation is incredibly powerful, and it helps me reach out to new readers. Your endorsement makes a big difference! You could also write a product review. It needn't be long, just a few words, but this also helps new readers find one of my books for the first time.

The UK seaside town of Ashdean, its University, and its inhabitants are fictitious, as is Thurlow Bay, where Kate Marshall lives on the clifftop. If you would like to look up the location on a UK map, I imagine Ashdean occupying a place on the south coast of England, next to a beautiful town called Budleigh Salterton. Great Barwell psychiatric hospital is also fictitious. The other locations used are real, but as with all fiction, I'll hope you forgive me for using a little dramatic licence.

To find out more about me, or to send me a message, you can check out my website www.robertbryndza.com.

Kate Marshall will return shortly, for another gripping murder investigation in *Shadow Sands*. Until then . . .

Robert Bryndza

ACKNOWLEDGEMENTS

I'm extremely lucky to work with my fantastic UK publishers at Sphere. Thank you to Cath Burke, Thalia Proctor, Sarah Shrubb and all the team for your enthusiasm for this new series, and here's to many more books.

Thank you to my editor, Charlotte Herscher. Working with you is a real joy and I learnt so much from you. Thank you for pushing me to make Nine Elms the best it could be.

Thank you also to all my readers and publishers around the world. I've had the good fortune to travel to so many new places to meet my readers, and the foreign publishers who publish my books with so much care and passion. I hope I get to visit many more of you in the future!

Thank you to my brilliant agent, Amy Tannenbaum Gottlieb, and the equally brilliant team at the Jane Rotrosen Agency.

Thank you to Maminko Vierka. I wouldn't be a successful writer without your help, love and support.

And a huge thank you to my husband, Ján, the love of my life, best friend and truth canyon ☺ You believed in me every step of the way, even when I didn't believe in myself. I'm so happy to be able to share our success together.

And lastly, thank you to the readers and book bloggers. When I started out, it was you who were there reading and championing my books. Word of mouth is the most powerful form of advertising, and I will never forget that readers and so many wonderful book bloggers are the most important people. I hope you enjoyed Nine Elms. There are lots more books to come, and I hope you stay with me for the ride!

Don't miss the next heartstopping
book in the blockbuster
Kate Marshall series

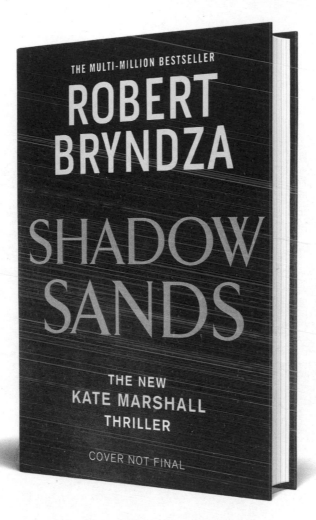

Coming 2020
PRE-ORDER NOW